A Touch of Poison

Dust jacket, paperback, and ebook cover designs by Maria Spada.

Under dust jacket cover illustration by Nate Medeiros.

Opening character illustration 'Wicked Lady & the Night Queen's Shadow' by @BookishAveril.

Opening character illustration 'You Can't Hurt Me' by @MageonDuty.

Closing character illustration by Wictoria Nordgård.

Map created using brushes from the Map Effects Fantasy Map Builder.

A Touch of Poison

CONTENT WARNINGS

Please read safely—this book contains adult themes and scenes of a sexual nature as well as the following content that some readers may find distressing:

- Death, including suicide
- Violence and torture, including domestic violence
- The threat of sexual violence
- Characters who have grown up in abusive homes
- Flashbacks to war, including the killing of civilians
- Misogyny and fat shaming
- Mention of sexual assault/r*pe
- Medical content (operation/treatment)
- Animal death

Please check my website for some key chapters that you may with to skip, skim, or have a trusted friend check over to help you decide whether to read them.

For the women turning their rage into power.
Let's burn it all down.

When the moon is dim,
    The veil is thin.

When the Wild Hunt ride
    Run, hide. Run, hide!

—ALBIONIC FOLKLORE

TENEBRI

LUMINIS

In red paint, not quite blood-coloured, but close, foot high letters read:

HYDRA ASCENDANT!

A couple of drips spattered from the dot of the exclamation mark, adding to the gory impression. It looked like it had been painted on the side of the sculptor's house by an over eager teenager.

Below, a crude serpentine form with three heads watched me, its eyes left blank so they shone with the pale gleam of Luminis's moonstone.

Hydra fucking Ascendant. In *my* city. Marking what would normally be a busy street if we hadn't cordoned it off.

In my pockets, my hands fisted.

At my side, Faolán tilted his head like this was an art gallery and he was trying to work out what this masterpiece *meant*. "What're you thinking?"

I made a soft, dismissive sound. "That someone needs to go back to art school."

He shot me a look, the full weight of his brow crashing down. "But—"

"I know. I know." I lifted one side of my mouth to tell him it was a joke. Better a joke than stating outright just how much those two painted words made my bones itch. "I thought you said they'd been quiet while I was away."

"They have... *had*." He turned his frown to the graffiti as though he could stare down the painted hydra and make it disappear.

I couldn't blame him.

Over the past few years there had been reports. Supplies stolen from a guard outpost, a hydra daubed on the wall the only clue to the perpetrators. Caravans raided by folk wearing an insignia of the three-headed creature over their hearts. Not quite the Wicked Lady, but...

Deep red hair across a crisp white pillow. Brow furrowed in a sleep that went on too long. Fingers that—

"Bastian?" Faolán ducked into my eye line, and I flinched. Not at his giant size but at the fact I'd drifted off while I was meant to be working and, even worse, he'd noticed.

I folded my arms like that could protect me from my friend's long, long look, but he knew me too well. At that moment I hated him for it—just a little.

He cleared his throat and leant in, arm butting mine. "Is she still—?"

"Yes." The word cut through the street. "Still unconscious." After a week. I went every day to the Hall of Healing, spent as long there as I could around work. If she woke alone...

I squeezed my biceps in an attempt to hold back the thought.

2

An entire week. The healer, Elthea, didn't seem worried, but I couldn't shake the feeling that each day her eyes remained closed increased the chance they would stay that way forever. Bile licked the back of my throat.

"You should bring her to dinner when she wakes up."

My head snapped around. "What? Why?"

The corner of his mouth twitched. "Because... you need to eat? And I'd like to get to know her." He shrugged casually.

Too casually.

"*You'd* like to? Or Rose would like to?"

"My wife's desires are mine."

I sighed. I might've known Faolán would be like this once he found his person. Insufferably smitten. With his hulking size and fierce glower, it was amusing, at least.

The problem was, I now found myself understanding how he felt.

"No need to grimace about it." That fierce glower furrowed his brow. "Thought you liked Rose's cooking?"

I raised my hands to ward him off. "I wouldn't dare criticise *that*. She's a sorceress of the stove. It was more... Not sure I'll have time. Especially not if these arseholes have infiltrated the city." Perfect excuse.

He huffed out through his nose like a wolf clearing an unwanted scent. "There's more to life than work, Bastian. No rush. You can let her acclimatise first. But"—his beard parted and his teeth gleamed—"you *will* bring her to dinner."

Kat. Me. Rose and Faolán. Sat together around their cosy table, eating and laughing. Resting my arm on the back of Kat's chair, fingertips trailing the lengths of her hair.

It was a seductive image... and an impossible one.

I had betrayed her, and when she woke up she was going to wring my neck. I might even let her.

3

I cleared my throat and attempted to clear my head of Kat, even though it was a doomed mission. Still, I nodded at the graffiti as much to keep myself focused as to return Faolán's attention to it rather than me. "Who's seen it?"

"Just a couple of locals. One who reported it. Dusk, so they came straight to us."

"Good." Though nothing about this was good.

All those other reports of Hydra Ascendant had been distant—none in the city of Tenebris-Luminis. And yet here I stood, not long after dawn, this red paint shoving them in my face.

Whoever the hells *they* were.

As best we could tell, they were some sort of rebel group with a taste for mythological creatures and small-scale raids and a dislike for the twin thrones. Who they were and what they wanted was anyone's guess, but it prickled me with the same sense of dread I'd had the night of Princess Sura's ill conceived coup. If this was heading in the same direction...

Not this time. It wouldn't come to bloodshed.

I was in the Queensguard back then—little more than a cocky boy with more arrogance than power. Now I had my network of whispering shadows and the Queen's ear. I had Faolán and all sorts of useful people to dig up all sorts of useful secrets.

Whatever the Ascendants thought they had planned, it wasn't happening. Not while I still stood.

"Get it cleaned up." I glanced along the road, which the guards had done a good job of keeping clear, despite the folk heading to and from work. "Make sure those witnesses understand they didn't see what they think they saw. Then see what you can sniff out about all this."

He crossed his huge arms and inclined his head. "Hmm."

Faolán had a number of *Hmm*s in his vocabulary. I'd never known a man say so much with so little.

"What else?"

His hazel eyes slid from the marred wall to me. "Rose is back from visiting her parents." He scratched his bearded chin, a study in nonchalance.

"And I owe her an apology, don't I?" I pressed my lips together, like that could keep out the sour taste at how I'd treated her on my return from Albion. My fingers twitched at the memory of Kat's still form in my arms, the desperation surging through me, the raw and awful need.

"You do." His nostrils flared as he exhaled through them. "I don't care how you talk to me. But—"

"I know." I clapped him on the shoulder. "I was an arse. I owe her an apology and I'll see she gets it."

"Hmm." This was an approving version of his signature sound, accompanied by a dip of his chin.

Maybe it was the talk of apologies or the memory of our return, but my traitorous gaze skipped up the hill to the Hall of Healing sitting atop it, gleaming and golden in the morning light.

She might've woken.

Of course, I wanted her to wake. To be safe and healthy and whole.

And yet...

I winced.

Because once she did, I would have to tell her the news.

2

KAT

Distant voices—soft, almost musical, echoing like they were in a large space. Not familiar.

I fought my heavy eyelids. The idea of lying here in some unknown place with unknown people prickled me—far too vulnerable. And the lack of footsteps punctuating the sound felt *off*.

Unsafe.

I managed to pry my eyes open, letting in bright, bright light.

Was I dead? I'd heard stories like that. King Arthur when he began his adventures in the Underworld had first seen a pure white light.

I squinted and tried to keep quiet—whoever was nearby, I didn't want them to know I was awake—but my body wasn't entirely under my command and its stiffness made me groan.

Nearby, a gasp. The rustle of movement. The sudden silence of a held breath.

So much for secrecy. I tried to rub my eyes but maybe my body was taking a while to catch up with my mind and awaken, because my arms wouldn't move. Instead I had to blink away the weight of sleep and this blinding light.

A white ceiling vaulted overhead—marble, judging by the veins creeping across it and down the walls. The veins led to a large cabinet divided into little drawers, with two large glass doors. Inside glinted jars and bottles in a hundred sizes and a hundred colours.

And *there.*

To one side, shadows churning, sitting forward in his chair, silver eyes wide—Bastian.

I smiled. I couldn't help it. Not with the way his eyebrows inched up in the very image of hope. Not with the way his familiarity soothed that uncomfortable sense of vulnerability that came with waking somewhere so *un*familiar.

His chest and shoulders sank as he let out a long breath, relief palpable in the still air. "Katherine." He said it softly, like I was a forest animal he didn't want to scare away.

Something warm kindled in my chest, and like a fool, I nodded.

In a single smooth movement, he stood.

He made it a step closer before something came crashing down inside him. His chin dipped and his eyebrows thundered together as his gaze slid from mine. For a second, his eyes screwed shut.

Was that regret? And... something else? Something dark like the shadows pooling around his feet. His hands fisted, and the shadows snapped close, like a hound whose leash had been yanked.

In silence, he pivoted and strode for the door.

He crushed my heart under the ball of his foot with that turn.

But then I remembered.

The poison. The changeling.

The truth.

I let my head sink back onto the pillow as he called into the echoing hall for someone.

He'd betrayed me and I'd betrayed him. Of course he wouldn't come to me, and I didn't want him to, either. It was only that moment when I'd woken—the instant before I remembered everything.

There were snatches of other moments, too. Asher treating me. Talk of blood. Snow. A deer's antlers. Strange fever dreams.

Eyes shut, I shook my head, like that would toss it all into some semblance of order. I could sort through the past later—I still didn't know about *now*. "Where am—?"

But when I tried again to lift my hands, I couldn't. And not because they wouldn't move. No. Because leather straps bit into my wrists, binding me to the bed.

Heart leaping, I yanked. "Bastian?" This had to be why he'd worn that momentary look of regret. What had he done? What was he going to do? Was this retribution for my plan to poison him? My throat clenched. "What's going on?"

From the doorway, he winced at my wide-eyed stare.

Was this how he'd looked at his father before he'd killed him? He was a bad ally. Not someone to be relied on. I had to remember all those hard-learned lessons.

Sitting up, I held my breath for the count of three in an attempt to control it. "What are you going to do to me?"

He flinched. "What? No, I'm not..." He shook his head, jerky rather than smooth as he returned, giving the bed a wide berth. "It's nothing like that." But another wince creased around his eyes. "You've been thrashing around in your sleep. We didn't want you hurting anyone."

He couldn't lie—not directly. Still, I tugged on the bindings. I was trapped and the sweeping arch of the vaulted ceiling and *something* in the air told me this wasn't Lunden. "Where are we?"

"Elfhame." Arms folded, he leant against the cabinet and watched me like I might still run despite the straps. He didn't come and unfasten them, either.

Alba. The fae realm. "How? Why?" But I knew and that knowledge unfolded, revealing more memories. "The poison. Asher said the healers here—"

Through the door swept a tall woman, her long, cream braids adding to the impression of height. "Awake at last." The briefest smile flashed over her lips as she pulled on a pair of gloves made of some sort of fine material that sheened in the light.

"This is Elthea. She's been looking after you." There was no warmth in Bastian's tone, just something stiff and almost formal.

"That's right." She stood over me, peering down. "You almost died." She said it as though it was my fault for doing something foolish.

Which, I supposed was right. After all, I'd known what was in the glass when I'd gulped down the aconite-laced mead. Then again, I'd been fully aware of the consequences of *not* drinking it.

Bastian may have hurt me. He might even have manipulated the simmering competition for the queen's hand. But I held with my decision: he didn't deserve to die, and if I'd let him take the poison, it would've been a diplomatic disaster.

I gave Elthea a faint shrug as if to say, "Humans, eh?"

9

She checked me over, peering into my eyes, placing a piece of carved crystal over my heart, then pausing, head tilted as though listening. As she noted the results in a book, she asked questions: whether I felt dizzy, if I could feel and move my legs. Next, she made me track a little ball of fae light that moved slowly at first, then darted across the ceiling.

All the while, Bastian watched in silence.

Eventually Elthea nodded as if satisfied. She unbuckled the straps around my wrists and took a step back before glancing at him. "Have you told her?"

Another wince. He shook his head, and unease slithered through me.

Dread. That was the other feeling I'd seen warring its way across his face, and now I felt it too.

"Told me what?" Goosebumps crept over my bare arms as I swung my legs over the side of the bed. "What is it? What's wrong?"

Elthea lifted her chin, closing her notebook. "I haven't been able to fully remove the poison from your system. Its power seems to reset with nightfall." Her lips pressed together. "Your condition is stable, but you need"—her pale eyes flicked back to Bastian who appeared frozen—"*the antidote* every day before sunset, or the poison will resume its effects as though you've just taken it."

"Is there enough antidote? Asher said it took a week to—"

"There's plenty."

"That's fine then."

But Bastian remained propped against the cabinet, still and stiff and silent. Anyone would think he was the one who'd just discovered he was poisoned.

There was more to this.

I swallowed and looked from him to her and back again. "Isn't it?"

His arms tightened over his chest, but it was Elthea who spoke. "You'll have to stay in Elfhame while I work on a permanent cure for you, but I'm confident I'll find one." And she *looked* it. Not arrogant and foolish, just confident and competent.

That was what had me exhaling my relief. I would get cured then return to my estate—*Robin's* estate—and hide from the entire world. Especially Bastian. Home, away from him and reminders of intrigue and deceit and the horrible foolishness of what I'd believed I'd almost had. Then I could figure out what to do next.

I'd have to check on Ella—but with unCavendish dead, at least she was safe. It wasn't clear whether I'd be welcome back at court or if I was banned for my behaviour at the wedding, so checking on her might require some manoeuvring. Fingers crossed I wasn't in trouble with the queen—maybe she knew I'd helped prevent war with the fae. Maybe she'd want to reward me and I would get a divorce at last.

The silence rang on and Bastian remained clenched tight.

It prickled through me like the threat of a dagger's point scraping over my skin. "What aren't you telling me?"

Elthea sucked in a breath and opened her mouth.

"I'll do it." Bastian clenched his jaw and straightened from his lean. "You're right. There is more—a side-effect of the poison and so many different magics coming together."

Different magics? I frowned from him to Elthea, but her cool expression gave away nothing.

Slowly, he stalked across the room as though I was not a wild animal who might run, but one that might attack. "Your body has been the confluence for a lot of magic in a very short space of time. There's whatever the changeling put in the poison." He raised a finger. "Asher's attempts to heal you. My..." His eyebrows flickered together. "I'm not sure what you remember from Lunden."

"You gave me your blood."

His throat bobbed. "I did. So my magic is inside you." Three fingers now. "And then Elthea used her gifts to save you."

Quiet. Four fingers. Like I was supposed to put those things together and come up with an answer. But this was a nonsense riddle. Four plus silence didn't reveal some new perspective, some surprising solution. It was just something they weren't telling me—something wrong.

"It's unprecedented." Elthea spread her hands, the gloves gone, notebook in one hand. "I've known few fae subject to so much concentrated magic, never mind a human." She watched me like I might sprout an extra head and she was merely curious about the idea. She'd probably note it in her book.

"Would you two just—"

I went to scrub my face and that was when I saw.

Deep reddish purple stains covered my fingertips and nails, like I'd been picking blackberries. No sign of my normal tan skin tone up the the first knuckle. I'd heard of gangrene turning fingers black, but there was no smell of rot and when I scraped my thumbnail over the tip of my forefinger, I could feel it, so my flesh wasn't dead.

"This?" I held my hands up. "Is this it?" I huffed a laugh. "I can deal with having purple fingers." As long as I could eventually leave Elfhame and avoid Bastian in the meantime, I could deal with anything.

Bastian's mouth twisted, and a faint ripple ran through his

shadows. Elthea watched, so obviously taking mental note of my every move, it made my nerves itch.

I swallowed. "It isn't just this, is it? *Tell me.*"

"You aren't merely a meeting point for all that power," Elthea said at last. "You now have power of your own. A gift."

"You mean, *magic*?" Scoffing, I turned to Bastian, as though he might crack a smile that said he thought Elthea was as insane as I did.

But his gaze was fixed on the floor next to my bed. His shoulders rose and fell in a breath that looked like it was a lot of effort before he glanced at Elthea and jerked his chin towards the door.

She stiffened, a frown creasing her smooth face. "But—"

"*Elthea.*" He held her gaze a long while and the air hummed with the clash of their wills.

Finally, she huffed and strode out, knuckles white around her notebook.

My throat grew thicker and thicker with each moment as Bastian took his time bringing the chair right to the side of my bed.

What was so bad he didn't want to tell me in front of her?

He sat, placed his elbows on the arms of the chair, interlaced his fingers, and watched me over them, his calmness belied by the shadows churning around his shoulders and thighs. "You aren't just poisoned, Katherine. You're poisonous."

I blinked. "What?" Theoretically I understood the words he'd just said, but in this order they made no sense.

"The poison and the magic have... fused in your system. You will poison anyone you touch."

A chill chased through me. I shook my head, but...

Elthea's gloves. The leather straps. Of course. "My wrists

were bound to stop me touching anyone while I slept." My voice started far, far away but came closer with each word as the truth bored through my skull and into my brain.

Bastian nodded.

My touch was poisonous. Deadly like aconite. I thrust my hands with their telltale purple stains into my lap. "But... but the antidote will clear that. When I take it each day, I'll stop being poisonous, right?"

His silence made my heart sputter.

"*Right?*"

His gaze dropped away. "No."

I shook my head. "You're wrong. It must. It'll stop the poison in my system, so it will stop me being poisonous. I don't believe you." He couldn't lie, but he could be wrong. "Bring me the antidote, and I'll take it and I'll show you." My words came like my breaths—too fast, too shallow.

A hug from Ella. A dance at a ball. Morag's occasional touch on my shoulder. These things couldn't all suddenly become forbidden—*deadly*.

Elthea had called it a gift. What Bastian described was no gift.

"Bring me the antidote."

He watched my fingers knotting together as I tried to hide their trembling. "It's already here."

There was no vial of liquid or jar of tablets on the side table, just Elthea's discarded gloves. No sign of an enchanted necklace like the one unCavendish had given me or any other magical jewellery, either.

Behind him, jagged reflections played on the cabinet's glass doors. "In there?" I leant forward, halfway to rising.

He swallowed and shook his head.

"Then *where?*"

His gaze drifted up from my lap and met mine. A slow, sorry smile claimed his scarred lips as he spread his hands, indicating himself.

That meant...

Bastian was my antidote.

3

KAT

Bastian was a *person* not an antidote.

And yet as I stood, he was still talking about it like it was true.

"The antidote was already in my system, fixed by Asher." He watched me take a few experimental steps. I wasn't as wobbly as I'd expected, but he looked as though he might swoop in if I fell. "With the points of connection between us—blood, Asher's magic, and Elthea's magic—she was able to use that to make it so I was... your opposite. Your touch poisons; mine remedies."

As my brain glitched on Bastian's explanation like a mechanism with a broken part, I ducked behind a dressing screen and removed my nightgown. "Why can't I just take a potion—the normal antidote?"

A long pause followed, and I yanked on the dusky grey dress that hung waiting for me

"The changeling did something to the poison to make the normal antidote ineffective. This is the only way."

"Fucking unCavendish," I muttered, fastening tiny crystal buttons down my front. After another pause, I stepped out from behind the screen, buttoning up the cuffs of the close-fitting sleeves.

I wanted it to be a joke. Or a lie. Or anything.

Anything but the truth.

But Bastian looked at me with the same dread I'd seen earlier. He rose from the chair as I emerged, all tight with anticipation of what I was going to make of all this.

What the fuck was I *supposed* to make of it? There was no guide in any etiquette book. This wasn't amongst my father's lessons. It wasn't something society had hammered into me about how I had to behave.

I was like my sister: in uncharted waters.

I shook my head and retreated into practicality. "So, what? I have to touch you every day in order to stay alive?" My words dissolved into laughter, because it was the most epically fucking ridiculous sentence I'd said in my entire life.

But Bastian didn't laugh. He pressed his lips together, sucked them in for a second, then nodded.

That sobered me. He was serious. So serious. "And if I touch anyone else, I will poison them?"

Eyebrows tight together, he bowed his head again.

More laughter caught in my throat, somewhere between hysteria and sobbing. I had to gulp in a breath and hold it to seize control of myself.

He frowned at the cabinet like he was as happy to be stuck with me as I was to be stuck with him.

Great. Just bloody great.

WE EMERGED from the quiet of the Hall of Healing and I had to pause at the top of the steps as light and bustle and chatter and scent hit me. This city was just as alive as Lunden with fae laughing and talking as they strode past. Children played in the small square at the base of the steps, swatting fae lights between them.

Beyond them, pale and gleaming buildings pierced the sky with spires and pillowed it with domes. Pink-veined marble and moonstone that shone blue then gold then green as the light hit it in different ways. I couldn't fathom how anyone had carved such huge blocks of stone—there were no joins in the Hall of Healing's walls, and there was no keystone at the centre of the graceful arcing bridge that spanned between the towers overhead. It was as if each building had been shaped from a single piece of rock... or perhaps grown from it.

Greenery softened the stone architecture—soaring trees and billowing shrubs, climbing plants that ambled up walls and around window frames, and small flowers that seemed to grow from the rock itself. Perhaps it was their sweetly spiced scent that drifted through the air, thick and heady like good brandy.

"Are you all right?" Bastian hovered at my side, looking out over the square. He asked the question and yet there was no sign he cared much about the answer. It was as though we'd left the building and a door had slammed inside him.

I gripped the sweeping marble handrail and straightened my back. "I'm fine. Wait"—I snatched my hand away—"does my... does it linger on things when I touch them?"

He shook his head, expression flat, but I knew him well enough to catch a hint of regret lingering in his eyes.

Or at least I *thought* I knew him. The man who'd looked

after me in his rooms and begged me not to give up—he hadn't seemed like someone who'd use me to uncover an enemy.

The hurt threatened to break me, but beneath that was hot anger. I broke out that layer and used it to cauterise the wound, gritting my teeth as I wobbled down the steps.

Anger was so much better than hurt. Or easier, anyway.

We walked along a tree-lined street in silence. There was enough noise around us and, with aspens hushing in the breeze, enough above us too. The flickering undersides of their silvery leaves and the iridescent moonstone homes behind were almost enough to make me forget my anger.

Almost.

But I didn't want that. So, arms folded to keep my hands away from anyone passing too close, I shot Bastian a sharp smile. "Doesn't stealing me away count as coming between me and that man I'm married to?"

Nothing marred his smooth expression, but his chin jerked up. "Your husband gave me permission to bring you here in order to save your life."

The surprise quenched my anger. "Robin?" I blinked up at Bastian. "He said you could bring me here?"

A single nod confirmed it.

I huffed. "The one good thing he's ever done for me." Maybe some part of him did care about me as a person rather than just as his property. *Maybe* he wasn't a total arsehole. Just ninety-five percent.

A tingling sensation brushed my skin, growing as we walked. In the past, when I'd been overcome with anxiety and struggled to breathe, my cheeks had felt this way, bordering on numbness, but this wasn't as intense and didn't only affect my face. It had to be some symptom of shock at being here and taking in so much—or maybe of the poison lingering in my system.

Poisoned and poisonous. I shuddered away the thought and focused on this place that was both strange and familiar.

Like Lunden, the streets were busy but not choked. Still, folk gave us a wide berth. Some threw wide-eyed glances our way before hurrying down another road. Seemed the Night Queen's Shadow had a frightening reputation even in the daylight.

When I peered along the busier intersections, I spotted fae riding, but instead of sabrecats, they sat astride deer. For all this was like any other city, there was no doubt: I wasn't in Albion anymore.

"What kind of city is this you've brought me to?" I eyed him sidelong.

"For now, it's Luminis. The moment the sun touches the horizon, it will be Tenebris." He kept his tone cool and matter-of-fact like he had to explain his nation's capital city to humans every day.

Perhaps I was just another mortal to him now he had what he wanted and unCavendish was dead. He'd said pretty things as the poison had pulled me under, but there was no hint of those now. Maybe the idea was to give me hope so I'd cling on to life. Maybe it had all been a fever dream and he hadn't said a word.

Whatever the truth, walking at his side now felt wrong. A pit in my stomach that I couldn't close.

"From sunrise, Dawn rules the city," he went on. "The Day King's word is law. My political power is... diminished." His jaw twitched. "When they are ascendant, you must be careful. You can't rely on my position to keep you safe."

Rely on him? I couldn't help scoffing, but the way his gaze flicked to me, just for a second, stilled my tongue.

I was hurt and angry, yes, but what was new? I didn't need to lash him with those things and make us both miserable. He had saved my life by bringing me here when he could've left me in Albion to die.

Instead, I cleared my throat and watched a woman who inclined her head at Bastian as she passed. At her throat, on a silver ribbon, she wore the Dusk Court insignia: a crescent moon on its side with a nine-pointed star rising from it. It was only when I saw her sleek, dark suit that I realised most of the other folk on the streets were clearly of Dawn Court with their sun insignias, lighter clothes, and hair in shades of blond, brown, and the soft colours of a brightening sunrise. She moved swiftly amongst them as though she needed to pass through without causing any disturbance.

I watched over my shoulder until she was out of sight. "So Dusk folk still walk the streets by day, but... they're conscious that they're 'diminished' at this time?"

Bastian surveyed me with a blank expression. It was the longest he'd looked at me since leaving the Hall of Healing, and I wondered if he was seeing me afresh. "The Day King is still their ruler while the sun is overhead. They will obey him, just as you would obey your queen, but their loyalties lie elsewhere."

"And how does this all work with your job?"

"From dusk until dawn, my queen rules. I brief her on what happened while she slept, take my chance to sleep, then meet with her again before the sun rises."

"So she... sleeps all day?"

He gave a low hum of amusement. "Not if she had her way. But enchanted Sleep gives her no option. It's part of the

21

bargain made with the land. The king Sleeps all night in the same way."

I was about to ask about this bargain when we turned onto a broad thoroughfare that led uphill. At its end rose a glittering mass of towers. Golden roofs and balconies marked the highest point of the city. Bridges spanned the gaps between impossible turrets, and white banners rippled in the breeze, a gilded symbol upon them catching the light. Pointed aspens and pines peeked over the lower buildings, but the towers dwarfed them, reaching for the deep blue sky.

"The palace." It wasn't a question—there was no need to ask, not with the size and grandeur and its position on the highest hill in the city. This main road pointed towards it, converging lines and leafy oaks framing it to perfection.

"Wait." I blinked at the trees. "How long was I asleep for? It was autumn when..." I threw him a glance instead of referencing my attempted poisoning. As I'd dripped aconite into his glass, the trees in the grove had been shedding their leaves, but these oaks were full and green.

"A week." He followed my gaze up. "The concentration of magic in the city affects the climate. Right now, summer is still clinging on, but soon enough autumn will come hard and fast."

Magic. That tingling sensation. It wasn't in me—it was *in the air*. It didn't feel unpleasant, just strange. New. I touched my cheeks, soothing the odd sensation.

And a week? What might've happened in that time? "Have you heard from Lunden? Or my estate? Is Ella all right?"

"I don't currently have a secure line of communication south of the border," he said, voice clipped, formal. "But Asher stayed behind to smooth things over with your queen. He'll do his best to ensure Ella is safe from any fallout."

22

It felt more like I was receiving a report than speaking to... Well, I wasn't entirely sure what Bastian was to me anymore. Not a friend, certainly. Former lover seemed most accurate, albeit a grossly simplified label for the complicated mess that stood between us.

"As for your estate"—he nodded at a pair of Dusk fae passing—"there was a large amount of cash on the changeling. What did you call it—unCavendish?" He shrugged. "The debt against your estate has been paid off."

I missed a step.

Just like that. Debt cleared. While I was asleep, no less.

The estate was safe. At least until that ninety-five percent arsehole racked up more debts. But I could breathe for now.

I hadn't let down Morag and Horwich. They still had their home and their jobs.

My eyes burned. All the fear and manoeuvring, the lies, unCavendish's cruelty, and what I'd done with and to Bastian —it had enabled me to help them. It had been worthwhile after all.

"Also..." Bastian raised one eyebrow when I caught up to him. "Every town in Albion has mysteriously received a message not to extend credit to Lord Fanshawe. A similar message may well be making its way across the continent as we speak."

My mouth dropped open. I didn't know whether to laugh or hug him. But things were different, now, making that second option impossible, so I squeezed my folded arms tighter around myself and chuckled softly. "How *mysterious*."

"Isn't it?" He flashed me a grin, then, canines showing.

Ah. There it was. The thing I'd missed through all of this conversation.

The sight of those sharp teeth that I'd glimpsed so often

before. The man who'd flirted with me and helped me break a hundred rules.

But those canines were gone as quickly as they'd appeared, smoothed away behind a flat expression like the bored one he'd worn the first time we danced.

We were in public—in his city, no less. Of course he had to maintain a certain façade: he was the Night Queen's Shadow, after all.

All of this is real.

I pushed the echo of his voice away and focused on the road ahead. The palace grew as we approached, spearing the sky. It dwarfed everything else in Tenebris-Luminis and the palace back in Lunden.

I raised my eyebrows at the gates. Tall and elegant rather than thick and sturdy like those in Riverton Palace's stone walls.

But that wasn't what surprised me the most—carved in the form of branches and flowers with dragonflies and butter-flies nestled amongst the leaves, these gates were made of *crystal.* Or glass or diamond, perhaps. Whatever the exact material, they were clear and refracted the sunlight into a thousand rainbow fragments.

Aside from the impossibility of their creation, I'd have said making gates from such a material was foolish—they'd be beautiful but brittle. Yet this was Elfhame, and I doubted they were as fragile as they appeared.

Magic was truly a marvel... when it wasn't responsible for making you poisonous.

Either side of the gates stood a dozen guards, half of them in black armour with Dusk's insignia across the chest in gold, the other half in white emblazoned with Dawn's rising sun. The six from Dusk turned and bowed their heads as we approached. Their armour caught the light as they moved, gleaming not black, I realised, but the darkest possible shade of midnight blue.

Across from them, the guards from Dawn studied us with narrowed eyes. It was only as we drew close that I realised they didn't wear white, but a pale, pale grey like shadow on a cloud.

Beyond the guards, the graceful arc of a bridge spanned a gorge and the rushing river at its base, but before we reached it, one of the Dawn guards stepped forward, hammering her spear into the ground. "Marwood." She cocked her head at him before surveying me. "And who is this?"

4

KAT

I could feel the calculation in her stare. She didn't only want to know *who* I was but why I might matter. I returned her look, keeping my face neutral. Dawn and Dusk cohabited this city and the palace, but I didn't understand the intricacies of their arrangement. And hadn't all the stories warned against offending the fae?

(Fairly sure almost poisoning one was considered offensive, though.)

"Amandine. A delight to see you as always." With the flat line of his lips, Bastian looked anything but delighted. "Katherine is a guest of Dusk and will be staying in the palace until she's ready to return home."

"A long way for a human to come." There was the briefest hesitation before the word "human" like she found it distasteful to say.

Behind her, the other Dawn guards stood at attention, but I caught their gazes snapping this way. To our left, I could feel the scrutiny of the Dusk guards and when I glanced over, I found one had stepped forward, both hands on her spear.

Clearly, it wasn't standard procedure to stop the Night Queen's Shadow from entering the palace.

Tension twisted through the air. Not only didn't I fully understand the undercurrents here, but I had no power to do anything to diffuse the situation or get Amandine to back down and let us inside.

Either she didn't notice the Dusk guard's approach or didn't care as she went on, "Has His Majesty authorised her entry to Elfhame?"

Bastian's mouth curved in what might've been a pleasant smile, but the way it made his eyes glitter reminded me of the murderous look he'd given me when I'd stolen his orrery. "*Her* Majesty has. We arrived by moonlight."

Amandine gave a soft grunt. "Of course you did."

It sounded as though that meant all was well and I should be allowed to pass, but she remained there, spear blocking our path. The hair on my forearms prickled against the silk of my sleeves.

The Dusk guard took a step closer and opened her mouth.

But with the slightest twitch of his fingers, Bastian silenced her before he met Amandine's sharp gaze. "Was there something else?"

The guard's jaw shifted from side to side before she exhaled and took a step back. "Not at this time. I trust you'll warn your human to follow our rules, Marwood."

"Of course." He smiled blandly as we continued on our way. "And when she awakens, I'll ensure Her Majesty understands just how helpful you were."

I caught Amandine flinching as we passed. I didn't know whether to revel in the small victory or reassess Bastian—even with his "diminished" power, he had more than I'd ever known in my life.

The bridge's gentle arch made it *look* safe. It was perhaps wide enough for four people or two sabrecats to walk abreast, but it had no guard rails. A moment's carelessness and *splash*— I peered over the edge—make that *crash*. Unless you fell from the very centre, you'd be lucky to avoid the dark, jagged rocks on the way down.

Swallowing, I shifted to the middle of the walkway. On the other side, a shimmering waterfall emerged from below the palace, feeding the river at the bottom of the gorge, and I fixed my attention on that.

When the tingle on my skin grew, I assumed it was my fear of falling over the edge, but as we approached the midpoint, the feeling peaked. It buzzed, like a whole swarm of bees, making me sway with the intensity, my brain foggy.

"Kat?" Bastian closed the distance between us like he might grab my arm.

Stopping, I warded him off and took a deep breath. With each second I acclimatised to the heavy feeling, less over-whelmed by it. "I'm fine, it's just..." I managed to pull my back straight and continue on the path. "Is that magic I can feel?"

He gave me another long look, sticking close. "The river is enchanted to protect the palace. It feels... thick and humming."

"Like bees."

He gave a low grunt. "Something like that, but... angrier. Wasps."

Frowning, I glanced back along the bridge as we stepped off its stone surface. The hum was intense but not angry.

But as we entered the palace grounds, surrounded by formal gardens, with a huge entrance ahead and a stable block to the right, I found myself walking alongside a stone-faced

version of Bastian. One who didn't invite argument. My mind
was still swimming from the magic, so I kept my head down,
ignoring the questioning looks that followed us as he led me to
a side entrance.

So many questioning looks. They crawled over my skin, and
I hugged myself tighter. This much attention wasn't safe.
Especially not in a place where I didn't understand the rules.

My body was still recovering, as a wave of vertigo swept
through me at one point. I waved off Bastian's help and
pushed myself on.

At last, we reached a set of double doors that Bastian
unlocked with magic. When we entered, the bergamot and
cedar scent told me they were his rooms before I even lifted my
head and took in the formal antechamber.

As the doors closed, the stone in his expression softened
the barest touch, becoming sandstone rather than granite. He
took off his jacket and hung it, then half turned to me. "Are
you...?" He finished the question by sweeping his gaze
over me.

I lifted my chin. I was fine. I didn't need looking after like a
child, and I didn't need him hovering this close like he was
going to take my arm. "I'm not about to keel over."

Nodding to himself, he stalked ahead into a grand sitting
room. It made the space he'd been given in Riverton Palace
seem not just small but *gaudy* in comparison.

Decorated in grey, black, and a dark teal like the deep sea
on a summer's day, the large space somehow managed to feel
enclosed—safe, even. Add a few gilded accents, like the
shooting star design of the fireplace and the celestial map
covering the ceiling, and it was both tasteful and luxurious.

Voice clipped, he explained where the main bathroom was
and his bedroom. A locked door led to his workroom, but he

said his offices were elsewhere in the palace, so I wasn't sure exactly what kind of work it was for.

Maybe for torturing humans who spied on him.

He herded me to the door opposite his bedroom. "And this is yours."

I raised my eyebrows at the fact I was staying in his suite, but realised before I asked—if he was my antidote, I needed to stay close.

When he leant past me and opened the door, it unleashed a waft of fresh paint smell. The walls were a pale, silvery grey, a little lighter than his eyes, covered with two huge paintings, one of the night sky with a crescent moon and one showing the sunset with a single bright star glinting. The large bed was draped with violet silk the same colour as one of my favourite gowns. On a round table before the fireplace sat a vase of white roses.

"And your bathroom is through there."

"My own—?"

When I turned, the intensity of his attention stole my words. For a second, it was as though he hadn't spent most of the time looking everywhere but at me. It was as though I was the only thing he'd ever seen.

Then it was over as he glanced around the room. "Does it meet with your approval?"

He had to know it did. From the thick carpet underfoot to the rich wood of the furniture and the clustered fae lights over-head—this was one of the most exquisite spaces I'd ever set foot in. And somehow it was mine, for a while at least. "It's beautiful."

With a curt nod, he backed away to the door. "Well. I'm sure you must be hungry. I'll have someone bring you lunch— a *late* lunch." As he paused in the doorway, the faintest smile flickered over his lips. "They make some excellent cake in the kitchens."

I think I smiled back. Because it felt like a private joke. Like old times. Like we could pick and choose what had and hadn't happened in the past, and for this short while we were choosing only the best moments and none of the bad.

The seconds drew on, marked by the ticking clock on the mantlepiece.

Then the spell broke.

He cleared his throat and turned, already halfway out the door as he said, "I need to get back to work. I have meetings and—"

"How long will you be gone?"

He frowned over his shoulder at me, shaking his head like he wasn't sure how to answer. "I don't know. However long it takes." The creases between his eyebrows deepened, edging towards annoyed rather than confused. "I don't normally have to answer to—"

"I don't want you to answer to me, Bastian. But"—I gave the clock a pointed look—"I'm on a deadline. If you're not going to be back until after sunset..." I spread my hands, attention catching on the shocking darkness of my fingertips.

"Ah." He nodded slowly. "Deadline. Dead being the operative. Of course." He stalked closer, not cracking so much as a smirk at his own joke. The man who'd taken every opportunity to tease me or make me laugh would've grinned, even if it was sardonically.

That was when I realised.

This stone face wasn't a mask—this was the real Bastian.

Aloof. All business. There was no one else around and he wore his shirt sleeves rolled up, yet he was still distant. The cool formality hadn't been an act in front of the people of his city and the guards.

The person I'd met in Albion had been the act. He'd used it to gain my trust in the hopes I'd open up to him about being a spy.

The knowledge gripped my heart.

In the library, the first time we'd kissed, I'd noticed how he'd held back—how he'd kept control. It had felt dangerous at the time, and I'd been right. Our relationship was a danger because it had edged into reality for me but hadn't for him. He'd only wanted me as a means to his own ends.

Hands folded, I held still as he approached. I had to ignore the burning of my eyes. There wasn't space for that—not when we were stuck living in such close quarters. Not when I was the foolish one for believing in a lie.

He stopped, toes at the hem of my dress. I stared ahead, noting how the light grey of his shirt was the same colour as his eyes, taking in the pearlescent gleam of its buttons and the steady rise and fall of his broad chest. He stood there a long time, as though trying to decide how to do this.

At last, I swallowed down the salt coating the back of my throat and gathered myself enough to hold out my hand. A handshake. If he was going to be all business, then so would I.

But at that same moment his chest rose and fell deeply and he reached out—not for my hand, but for my cheek.

Even before he touched me, I sucked in a breath and lifted my head. As our gazes collided, his thumb brushed over my cheekbone.

It was so light I might've questioned whether he'd made contact with my skin or just the fine hairs there. Might've, if not for the fact it reverberated through me in a more intense version of the hum I'd felt on the bridge.

It vibrated along every nerve like I stood at the centre of an orchestra as its music rose in deafening crescendo. Every part of me trembled with it like I might tear apart on the next tick of the clock.

My lips parted but I didn't have breath to make a sound.

It affected Bastian, too, because the hairs on his forearms rose and the skin around his eyes tightened. A shudder ran through his entire body and his pupils contracted in—was that pain? But even if I'd been able to speak, I didn't have time to ask because an instant later his pupils blew wide and the momentary tension vanished.

The stony faced stranger vanished at the same moment, leaving the man I knew.

This was Bastian, gaze flicking between my eyes and my mouth, leaning closer, fingertips hooking under my jaw. This was Bastian, wanting and hungry, seeing me—truly seeing, a softness in the crease between his brows that said he cared.

I shouldn't want him to care and yet it sent my heart soaring. Maybe it hadn't all been a lie. Maybe I hadn't been entirely wrong. Maybe he—

But then there was a gulf where he had stood only an instant ago. The magic, gone. My cheek, cold.

And Bastian, striding out the door.

5
BASTIAN

I'd never walked so quickly from my own rooms. It was easier to blame my thundering heart on the swift walk than on... whatever that had been. Or almost been.

I didn't want to kiss Katherine Ferrers.

And whoever said otherwise was a damn liar.

Courtiers and servants scattered from my path. Good. I hadn't softened into a pathetic mess, then—at least not outwardly.

How did that damn woman make me so weak?

When I swept into my offices, Brynan widened his eyes at me. His throat bobbed and he opened his mouth.

"Don't." I dragged in a breath, halfway to my own office door. "Not right now. Have Rose come. Thanks."

Before I could slam the door and sink against it, I caught the other scent in the room.

"Orpha is here for you," Brynan called through, an apologetic tone in his voice.

That's what he'd been trying to tell me. Of course. I'd asked her to report on her return.

Saddle bags lay heaped on the floor, and my gaze skipped past the chair in front of my desk—a symptom of Orpha's half wraith blood. She wasn't so much invisible as... hard to look at. Literally. Wraith magic made your eye skip right past her as though there was no one there.

It made her a useful operative, but it meant I had to stand still and draw a long breath before I could force my eyes in her direction. The fact I could do that much was only thanks to years of practice.

Grinning up at me, sharp teeth on display, Orpha sat back in the armchair and tossed a hazelnut in her mouth. Her pale eyes were a few shades lighter than my own, though not as light as her white hair. She might've been beautiful, but looking at her directly made my eyeballs itch.

"Brynan said you were waylaid." She shrugged and scooped up a handful of berries and nuts from the bowl on my desk.

"I see he ensured you were looked after, though." Thank the gods for Brynan. I'd completely lost track of time with Kat. I needed to watch out for that. Gaze skipping away from Orpha, I sank into the wingback chair behind my desk. Another deep breath and I shoved my attention back to her. "Well?"

"I swept the area. No sign of..." She shrugged and wriggled her fingers through the air. "Well, the power coalescing or anything like that. In fact, it seems to have dissipated almost entirely."

Exhaling, I nodded. "Good." The last thing we needed on top of Hydra Ascendant was a repeat of that situation.

"But—"

I stiffened.

"—there was one significant change. The time disturbance around the house has faded, so I was able to get into the ruins without being gone for months."

Rather than craning forward, like I wanted to, I forced my elbow onto the arm of my chair and leant my chin on my fist. Orpha would ask for an astronomical bonus if she got a whiff of my interest in what she found. "And?"

"Dust and rubble, mostly. It was like centuries had passed rather than just a couple of years. No fabric or wood remains, only crumbled stone."

I nodded, encouraging her to hurry along while I buried my disappointment. With the age of the place, I'd hoped it might contain lost relics, but it sounded as though it and its contents were utterly destroyed.

"But Rose said there was a library, right?"

I raised one eyebrow. "She did."

"I found it. I had to move some hunks of rock and wade through dust up to my knees." She rolled her shoulders as if remembering the weight. I didn't doubt they were large hunks of rock—her wraith blood also made her stronger than her slight frame appeared. "With the state of the place, I wasn't hoping for much, but beneath it all, I found some books that..." She shook her head. "They were pristine. And chained up."

Pulse speeding, I gave up fighting and sat forward. "And you brought them back. Show me."

She grinned and popped a berry in her mouth before standing and rummaging through the bags. If these books were what I suspected, she was welcome to the bonus.

A couple of years ago Faolán and Rose had found themselves trapped in an ancient mansion hosted by a woman who only called herself Granny. If anyone else had given me the report of what happened there, I'd have called them mad, but Faolán wasn't the type for flights of fancy. He was as solid as the stone beneath this palace and almost as talkative. For him to spout that story—it had to be true. And Rose backed up every word. She'd even offered to take *arianmêl* to prove it was true.

Dark things had happened in that house. Sacrifice and blood drinking. The kinds of things people accused the unseelie of doing. Through that forbidden magic, the place had gathered immense power over the span of centuries, and when it fell, thanks to Faolán and Rose, we ran the risk of that power falling into the wrong hands.

Hence the regular visits from my operatives and obscuring the location from all maps. Thank the Stars, the magic had dissipated harmlessly over time.

Where I'd hoped for artefacts, perhaps the house was going to give me secrets instead.

And weren't secrets power?

With a thud, Orpha hefted a stack of books on my desk.

There was no shift in the air as often came with powerful magic—just as Kat had felt on the bridge—but I caught the scent of scorched earth and woodsmoke. Ash and blood. Dust and age.

Old magic.

Yet the books looked as though they'd been bound yesterday—fresh leather and crisp gold leaf. The top one was a deep forest green with gold lettering across the front. Orpha explained how she'd snapped her favourite crowbar breaking through the chains, while I fingered the debossed design.

My heart thudded heavily in my chest as, my mind skipped to Kat's book and the way she'd touched it so reverently. Then to the sight of her earlier as she'd taken in her bedroom. The curve of her lips and the point of her chin. The unselfconscious gesture as she'd touched the glossy finish on the purpleheart wood furniture I'd chosen for her. I wasn't sure she realised she'd grazed her fingertips across its surface, as though the richness of its colour called to her and she just *had* to experience it.

But most of all, the sun hitting her hair, turning it aflame, so she looked like a phoenix rising from the dull ashes of the world.

I wasn't meant to want her. I wasn't meant to be this wrapped up in her, in the sight of her, the springtime scent of her, or the way she made me think of the crisp cleanness of fresh sheets or a new page.

But I was.

Good fucking gods, I was.

Whoever had made her marry that man, I wanted to disembowel them. Slowly.

Not that I was a better man. And not a more deserving one, either. Not after what I did in Lunden.

Yet I'd never have failed her as he had. I'd never have mistreated her in the dark as he had. Any destruction I turned upon her, I made into the little deaths that she made such sweet sounds for.

But I was a decade too late. Her husband was too fucking alive. And her country had marriage laws too barbaric to contemplate.

We'd taken a different path that had led here.

She'd spent ten years stuck in a crumbling estate. Ten years bound to a husband she hated. I didn't want her to resent me in the same way.

Of course she resents you. You betrayed her. You used her.

The hurt had rolled off her before she'd let the poison in

her system coat her tongue and unleash its sharpness on me. Just once. Just briefly. But it was enough.

She didn't just resent me—she hated me.

Maybe it was for the best.

"Bastian?"

I blinked and found Orpha watching me, one eyebrow raised.

Completely fucking distracted. Stars above, what was wrong with me?

I cleared my throat. "The book." Lifting it as if that was an explanation. Not a lie, since it had made me think of Kat. "What were you saying?"

"There's another stack of books in here, but I don't want to cover your desk. Where do you want me to leave them?"

I glanced at the next one on the pile, its blood red leather hard to tear my eyes from. *The Lore of the Land*, it said in High Valens, one of our ancient languages.

It sounded like a useless collection of old tales rather than old secrets. I tossed the green book on top, glad to get it out of my hands. "Leave them with Brynan. He'll find a home for them." I dusted my palms together. "Was there anything else?" *Please say no.* I needed a moment alone.

"Nothing as exciting as the books." She slipped a hazelnut in her mouth. "There was—"

"Put the rest in your written report." My voice came out more clipped than I intended.

"Of course." She stood, scooped the rest of the bowl's contents into her hand, and hauled the bags over her shoulder. "I'll send it later."

I struggled to follow her progress out of the room, but knew she was nearly out by the door clicking open. "Orpha?"

From the corner of my eye, I saw her pause in the doorway.

"Thanks." For the risks she'd taken and her hard work, but also for getting my none-too-subtle hint to leave.

I caught a flash of sharp teeth. "Just how grateful are you?"

"Brynan will see to your bonus—your *generous* bonus." More money meant fewer questions. And she had brought back perhaps two dozen ancient books—chances are, they were texts we didn't already have in the archives. Lysander would be pleased.

"That's what I like to hear." Another flash of teeth, then the door closed on her and the rest of the world.

6
BASTIAN

At last, I sank into the chair before the fireplace, bones weary like I'd been in a battle. My shadows spilled from me to the floor as though they were also tired. I scrubbed my face and drew deep breaths, feeling the air inch through my lungs and the way it brushed over my lips on the way out.

The coral pink flames flickered, and I let my shadows snake towards them. If I left them to their own devices, they were often drawn to fire, like their darkness craved the burning brightness. Perhaps I did, too. Perhaps that was why I was drawn to Katherine. Not just for her fiery hair, but to what I saw inside her that had been kept small and smothered for too long.

"Fuck." I wasn't meant to be thinking about her. On my next inhale, I gripped the arms of the chair and pushed the thoughts away.

The fire and my shadows. That was all that existed. Light and darkness. Completion. Everything in the universe

contained within those two ideas and the midpoint between them where a thousand shades danced together.

By the time a knock came at my door, I was in control once more, my thoughts my own, my shadows obeying when I gathered them close and called, "Enter."

Strawberry blond hair appeared, framing a face that today was shuttered in a way that made me wince inwardly. "You asked to see me?"

I stood and gestured to the chair beside mine. "Please, join me."

She gave the faintest frown as she crossed the room. I didn't normally rise when she entered. But, then again, I didn't normally owe her an apology.

Slowly, she sat as though she thought this might be a trap. "I don't have long. I've been visiting my parents, and Faolán's left the house a mess."

I raised an eyebrow at her. That was a lie. Faolán, for all his hulking size and hairiness, was no beast. He was the most fastidiously clean and tidy person I knew, and he'd told me more than once about how *he* was the one who had to clean up after his wife. Still, calling her out on it wasn't the best way to start this conversation.

"I'll get straight to it, then." I pulled my chair to face hers before I sat. "I'm sorry, Rose. I was a prize arsehole the last time I saw you."

Her eyebrows shot up, the shutters falling away.

I leant forward and went on, "I was angry and aggressive, and I let my shadows get completely out of hand. I snapped at you, and you deserved none of that. I didn't mean to frighten you, and although I..." I bit my tongue. "I was feeling a lot of things, I shouldn't have taken that out on you. I'm sorry I almost lost control, I was..." I shook my head, unable to voice everything that had been going on inside me when I'd stepped through the shadow door.

She took a long breath. "It's all right. I understand." The way she tilted her head and smiled softly, I believed her.

Except she couldn't understand everything I wasn't saying. She couldn't know what was in my heart.

"I've seen the way you look at her."

My shadows fell still.

Shit. She *did* understand.

I swallowed. "Does Faolán know?"

"I mean"—she gave an exaggerated shrug—"he has eyeballs, so I dare say he does."

With a groan I sank back in my chair. Was I so obvious? I was meant to be hiding my feelings for Kat. Not just from strangers—from everyone.

It was only a matter of time before people found out she was married, then Faolán would join the rest of them in judging me for... for whatever it was I felt for a married woman. For breaking a contract.

I raked my fingers through my hair and pressed the heels of my hands into my eyes.

More importantly, if people knew, it would paint a target on her back. Anyone who wanted to settle a score with me could do it through her.

Rose had spent less than a minute with us and already knew.

When I dropped my hands, I found her wearing a cheerful smile like this was all terribly amusing. "And, after what you said about human brides, I doubt he's going to let you live this down for at least a couple of centuries."

And this is what you get for taking a human bride. I'd said those words, mocking both Lysander and Faolán. I refused to acknowledge any relevance to my situation.

Instead, I gave Rose my worst glower—the one that sent courtiers scattering from my path. "Well, he needs to."

She didn't flinch at my expression, but when I spoke, her smile crumpled into a soft frown. That was the tough thing about Rose—her softness.

It got me every time and now it had me opening my mouth again. "I betrayed Kat," I whispered. "She betrayed me. And if —*if* we somehow managed to get past that, she's married. Nothing more can happen between us."

"Oh." Her eyebrows rose slowly and her gaze fluttered away. I could see the cogs turning in her mind as she worked through what that meant to fae. She'd lived in Elfhame long enough to know how seriously we took contracts and the breaking of them. "And who knows about that?"

"No one. Yet. The particulars of what happened in Lunden are a state secret, and her husband isn't exactly... present." I clenched my hands as shadows surged around my feet, rough like a stormy sea but under control.

"Oh dear, Bastian." She squeezed my knee, unconcerned by my shadows or glower. "It's quite a pickle you've got yourself into."

I grunted and turned to the fire.

"Good grief, you're almost as grumpy as Faolán. Have you two swapped personalities?"

I couldn't help the low growl in my throat. She was teasing me, like something about this was funny.

"You know," she went on, "you could apologise."

It didn't feel like enough, though, and I didn't know where to even start.

"And then," Rose went on, "once that's fixed, you could

just... not give a shit that she's married? It doesn't sound like she cares."

"It doesn't work like that. Contracts are—"

"Sacred for a reason. I know. I know. Though I don't think you'd lose your magic if you broke one." I could feel her gaze on me as she paused. "And I suspect you already have, yet look, your shadows are as dark as ever."

"That's not..." I huffed. It wasn't the point. I didn't fear losing my magic. I'd never taken that part of our laws literally —it sounded more like a threat than a promise. Rather, when I thought of the fact Kat was married, it was a wrongness in my bones—in my veins.

Contracts had bound our blood to the land, had given us magic. They were responsible for everything fae were.

To break one was like breaking the earth itself.

"I know," she said, voice sober. "It's complicated. I can't pretend to understand. I don't think anyone who isn't fae can."

I managed to give her a small smile, grateful for her acknowledgement.

"And for the record, I accept your apology, Bastian. I appreciate you giving it. Now"—she stood—"if there wasn't anything else, I have some dinner to prepare. I can make it for three, if you're going to join us?" She raised an eyebrow. "Or four?"

I winced. "Not tonight. I have a ton of paperwork to do and reports to read through."

"Still playing catch-up?"

I sighed and went to rise, but she waved off my attempt to escort her out. "I'm gone for a few months and everything goes to shit."

Spreading her hands, she backed away to the door. "You know, if you trusted someone else to help you with the bigger things, it wouldn't have backed up so much. And you were gone for more than a few months—it was over half a year."

I grumbled, but couldn't get angry in the face of her bright grin or the fact she might be right. "You sound like Faolán."

"Sometimes he's right. Just don't tell him I said that."

I couldn't help returning her grin and winking. "Your secret's safe with me."

"As is yours." Holding the door handle, she paused and her expression softened. "If you want someone to talk—someone who hasn't got the weight of old-fashioned fae ideas of contractual obligation... Well, I'm here."

Then, with a nod she was gone.

7

KAT

The summons arrived after lunch the next day, when a servant informed me that Bastian would like to see me.

I was shut in his rooms, so he could've seen me at any point over the past twenty-four hours, yet here I was, being escorted through star-ceilinged corridors to his offices. The few fae we passed watched with undisguised curiosity. At least in Albion folk usually pretended not to stare.

After Bastian had gone, I'd spent the rest of yesterday alone with only books for company.

And my thoughts.

They were the worst companions of all, reminding me of how my body had twitched and trembled out of control as I'd approached death. Reminding me that safety was impossible —this poison meant I was permanently *un*safe.

To escape it, I'd buried myself in books and stayed up until I couldn't keep my eyes open but still didn't hear Bastian return. This morning, he'd gone by the time I got up.

Now, I felt a little queasy after eating lunch, like the poison was already making its presence known.

I fingered the necklace I'd found wrapped and placed on my bed with a brief note. It hung between my breasts, cool and solid. An inch long potion bottle made of some sort of dark crystal. It flashed green-gold-blue as it caught the light, like a dark counterpart of the moonstone buildings I'd seen yesterday.

Inside was the antidote.

With it had been a large bottle of the stuff and a tiny funnel, as well as a jar of the preventative. According to the note, a sip of this concoction was enough to save anyone I accidentally touched. Thankfully, the poison that seeped from my skin was regular aconite, easily cured by the normal antidote. Not that I fancied testing that out.

Was this gift thoughtful or practical? I couldn't decide.

The Bastian who'd touched me yesterday—I'd have said he was being thoughtful. But the one who'd left me locked in his rooms?

Perhaps he was the one who'd not only left gowns in the armoire but two drawers full of gloves in varying designs to coordinate with different outfits.

Today I'd chosen a plain pair made of black silk so fine I could feel the coolness of the crystal pendant and count by touch the five pearls that formed each flower on my pearlwort necklace.

I clasped my hands against the urge to rip it from my throat as my skin crawled at the thought of the changeling. It was bad enough the poison he'd made lived in me, never mind wearing his jewellery.

I lost track of the route by the time we arrived at a large set of double doors where my escort handed me over to a smiling young man who introduced himself as Brynan. Surveying me, he stepped out from behind his desk and ushered me into a large office dominated by a dark yew desk and the man who sat behind it.

"Thank you, Brynan." Bastian didn't even look at me as I entered, his attention focused on his assistant instead. "Ensure we aren't disturbed."

Once the door was shut, he nodded to a chair in front of his desk.

My pulse pounded in my throat. Why did I feel the same as I had when the queen summoned me to the throne room?

His formality was all wrong. This distance between us was all wrong. And yet it was the only way to be in our impossible situation.

He had hurt me. I had hurt him. Perhaps I'd paid for my wrongs by taking poison. Perhaps it didn't change anything.

Surviving had changed things though—for me, in me. I had made the decision to take it and I'd been sure of it—still was—but I hadn't expected to live to deal with the aftermath.

Yet here I was.

Alive and unsure what to do with myself, unsure what my decision meant, unsure of... anything.

And across from me sat Bastian, looking like a stranger.

So I sat like this was a formal meeting, hands clasped in my lap. "You wanted to see me?"

He blinked as though realising he'd been staring at me. "I trust you're well rested, because we have a number of matters to discuss."

Were *we* one of those matters? My stomach was so tight with nerves I couldn't tell if I wanted that or dreaded it.

He opened a notebook and took a silver pen. "I need you to

tell me about every interaction you had with the changeling. From the beginning."

My throat clenched around any words I might've tried to say. That was it. He still just wanted me in order to catch his enemy. I swallowed down my anger and hurt and began at that first summons to the changeling's office.

Bastian listened, making notes in his book, asking a string of questions when I got to the end of each encounter. So many questions.

But he didn't invade my space as unCavendish had. He didn't touch me or leer at me. He was the consummate professional.

How unCavendish should've behaved.

Good gods, I should've known he wasn't the real spymaster. The realisation crumpled inside me as I described the time he'd shoved me against a wall.

I could feel his fingers on my chest and shoulders. Every hair on my body strained to attention like it wanted to escape the mere memory of his touch.

My hands squeezed together until my knuckles ached.

I should've known.

Shifting in my chair, I tried to erase the ghost of his thigh pressing between mine. I swallowed back the bile in my throat, focusing on the words, on the simplicity of forming sentences, relaying every detail like I was watching it all from the outside.

It was only when I reached the end of that encounter and Bastian asked no questions that I pulled my gaze up from the surface of his desk.

His pen had fallen still in his white-knuckled hold, and a terrible stillness gripped him. His chest barely moved with his breath. Above his collar, the pulse leapt in his throat. Otherwise, he might've been a statue.

But his shadows?

They surged from his shoulders and thrashed over the desk, reaching for me.

I didn't pull away. Maybe with how violently they moved, I should've.

Before they got halfway across the desk, Bastian's jaw twitched, and the shadows crashed to a stop like waves hitting a cliff face. He sucked in a deep breath and they retreated, spilling into his lap and out of sight. His voice grated as he continued his questions.

I had no idea how long we sat there for. I spoke myself hoarse, and Bastian brought chilled water from a cabinet and offered me tea and coffee, but his questioning didn't relent.

At last, I reached the wedding and the realisation that unCavendish was not who I thought and his death at Bastian's double's hands. I sank back in my chair when his questions stopped.

My head pounded and my heart weighed in me, but there was also a kind of relief, like in voicing it, I'd handed it all over to someone else.

I still felt foolish for not realising sooner. I still felt foolish for trusting Bastian.

But I had spilled all those horrible moments I'd kept secret and festering inside me. That poison, at least, was gone.

Bastian flicked back through his notes, a thoughtful frown between his eyebrows.

The moments after unCavendish's last breaths continued in my mind. He hadn't asked about those, since he'd been there, but it was like my brain had been set on a course and couldn't stop.

"You're not allowed to die yet. That thing is dead, but it was working for someone else."

The movement. The pain. The strange wheeling of the world round and round and round.

"*I still need you.*"

At the time it had felt true, like he needed *me*. But now I knew better. This was what he needed—my information to help him trace unCavendish's plot back to its source.

This was what I got for letting my feelings run away with me.

The worst thing was, I couldn't blame him for wanting to uncover the truth. It endangered his court, his queen, his country, and mine.

So I swallowed down my foolish feelings and asked, "Who do you think he was working for?"

Bastian exhaled, brow furrowing more deeply. "That's not for you to concern yourself with. You've dealt with that world enough."

"Have I?" I gritted my teeth. "I feel like I barely scraped the surface while so much more was going on underneath and that's how I ended up here."

After a pause, Bastian closed the notebook and placed it on the desk, hand spread over it. He watched me for a moment as if weighing me. "It's my job to work all that out. I just need you to stay safe. All you need to know is that someone didn't want us forming an alliance with Albion through marriage."

Even though this person was responsible for unCavendish upending my life, he wasn't going to tell me. State secrets. Or just that he didn't trust me. It amounted to the same outcome.

He grunted, mouth twisting in a sardonic smile. "And they got their wish."

When I'd told Bastian about the wedding, he'd explained how Queen Elizabeth had called off her marriage to Asher. Thanks to the return of Excalibur, she had magic of her own now and didn't require a husband—human or fae—to shore up her rule.

Must be nice to have a choice in such things.

His fingers tapped on the notebook's leather cover as his gaze turned distant, thoughtful.

"You don't know, do you?" The realisation burst out of me. "All that time in Albion and the week back here, and you still haven't uncovered them."

His gaze shuttered. "I'm still gathering information."

"But we could have more information, by now, couldn't we? If you'd told me you were trying to lure out the person spying on you, I could've helped. If you'd told me you'd taken the antidote—"

"You mean, like you told me about your spying? And about the poison?"

His words were a punch in the gut.

And for a moment—the blink of an eye, really—I caught a glimpse of something wounded and bloody behind the Business Bastian exterior.

The hurt cut both ways, didn't it?

On a different day, I might've found that funny in a bleak kind of way.

Instead, today, I cleared my throat and looked away. "I'm sorry, Bastian. I wanted to stop, but then he threatened Ella, and I couldn't find a way out. I never wanted—"

"Tenebris is not like Lunden, Katherine."

I jerked, back straight like I'd been rapped across the knuckles. I'd overstepped the lines of formality he'd drawn between us.

"Different rules apply here. Rules you'd do well to learn."

He wasn't wrong. Didn't rules keep you safe, after all?

His jaw turned solid. "Especially with Dawn so close."

"Close?" I glanced at the door. "I didn't see anyone from Dawn on the way here." None of the corridors had been decorated in a way that marked them as Dawn rather than Dusk—at least not as far as I could tell.

"You wouldn't. You remained in our territory."

I squinted at him. "So... they have one side of the palace. The east or—?"

"Not like that. Not so mundane."

Of course not. This was faerie.

"Two versions of the palace overlay each other." He gestured as if that explained everything.

I cocked my head.

He blasted a sigh. "You need to understand this, Katherine. As a guest of Dusk, you have some protection, but if you inadvertently walked into Dawn..." Head shaking, he scanned the desk. "Take this piece of paper." A wisp of shadow pulled one from a pile with a soft rustle. "It has two sides, both identical, divided only by the thinnest barrier, right?" The shadow passed the paper to him and he showed me its edge.

"Thin enough to cut." I scoffed.

"Many things in Elfhame cut." His smile was humourless. "Two palaces almost identical in layout." In pencil, he drew a square on one side of the paper, then turned it over and drew another. He held it up to the light and I could see through the paper—the squares overlaid each other. "But they're on different planes of existence, separated by the thinnest membrane. You could be in the library in our version of the palace"—he drew an X inside the square—"at the same time someone else is in Dawn's library"—he turned the sheet and added a small circle in the same location—"and you'd never know the other person was there. You're in the same space but on different planes." He held up the paper again.

I frowned at the circle and cross, which were together and not. "They're close... but also separated."

He nodded. "Like the veil that lies between us and the Underworld."

"Can people hear across this veil?" My stomach turned at the idea of someone from Dawn sitting in an office like this one and being able to hear all the details of what unCavendish had done to me.

"No. The only way for anything to cross is at one of the fixed points between the two. We call those lodestones." He pushed the pencil through the paper. "You experienced one yesterday when we arrived. There's a tipping sensation as you enter, but you get used to it. There are several throughout the palace. Guarded, of course. The royal suite, the library, the ballroom—there are two of each, one on either side. But the throne room, the grand hall, the royal balcony, for example— these are lodestones. There is only one throne room, accessible by Dusk and Dawn." He removed the pencil and showed me the hole.

I rubbed my head at the impossibility of it. But was it really more impossible than a city that shifted from one state to another as the sun rose and sank?

Looking at that sheet of paper, I could picture an ant walking along one side, reaching the hole, and passing through that to the other side. And weren't we just ants to the gods?

"If the lodestones are guarded, there's no danger of me accidentally crossing over, is there?"

His mouth flattened, the scar standing out pale in the light. "*You* might not mean to pass across, but someone from Dawn might try to lure or trick you through the wrong door back into their side."

"But... why?"

The muscle in his jaw flickered again. "Because I'd be powerless to follow."

I fought the urge to rub my hands over my arms as goosebumps chased across my skin. The word "powerless" on Bastian's tongue seemed as impossible as a tree growing underwater.

"You see why you need to understand my city and its rules?" The low line of his eyebrows didn't invite me to answer.

"It's imperative." He swept to his feet and circled the desk, going to one of the high windows that looked out over the city. "Never ask someone their name—it's considered taboo. Offer yours, then they should offer theirs in return."

I frowned at his back as he leant his forearm on the window frame and looked out. First contracts, then names— fae were full of strange rules.

"Tell no one about your condition. The poison or your need for... me." His hand clenched into a fist and pressed into the window. "Use the fact you can lie to your advantage. Most fae don't deal with humans often, and although they know you can lie, theoretically, they won't be used to watching out for it."

As if I didn't already use lies to my advantage.

Softly, he added, "They don't have experience of dealing with humans and their pretty, lying mouths."

I shivered at his intimate tone, at the way I wasn't sure he intended to say it out loud, and at the memory of how he'd dealt with my lying mouth so thoroughly on plenty of occasions.

I had to stand to dispel some of the sudden energy skipping along my nerves and pooling in my belly.

Turned out, it was a lot harder than I'd expected to hate

someone who'd opened up part of me I hadn't even known were there.

Or at least it was hard to *only* hate them. I could hate Bastian alongside lusting after him very easily indeed.

He straightened as though he'd spotted something interesting outside, and I approached, drawn by the strange beauty of the fae city.

"Most importantly, never—*never* reveal your heart." He bowed his head and for a moment, the desire to reach out to him was so intense, I had to grip my hands together. "Who you are. What you want. What you feel. What you love." His voice lowered, a hoarse, raw quality to it. "You must keep these things close or they *will* be used against you."

I laughed. "I thought I didn't know what I was. Guttered so low, I don't even know I'm a flame anymore. That's what you said."

He spun, then stiffened as though he hadn't realised I'd drawn so close. "I'm serious, Kat. Deathly serious." The look he gave me as he closed the distance between us was a physical thing that killed the laughter in my throat. He towered over me, frown so deep it shadowed his eyes and revealed their glow. "If they know your heart, they will tear you apart to feast upon it."

Mine thudded harder, perhaps at the threat, perhaps at his intensity up this close. But I raised one eyebrow like I was brave enough to face both. "Fae eat hearts?"

"Not literally. But still cruelly." He leant in like he wanted to take another step.

His warnings were kind. Protective, even. But it wasn't as if I didn't already know fae were dangerous. Hadn't my internal alarm bells clamoured the instant I'd realised what he was? I'd known I was in danger from that moment.

"Don't worry." I shrugged and managed a reassuring smile. "I don't know what I want anymore. How could I possibly tell anyone else?" I tried to laugh, brash and bold like the Wicked Lady on the road at night, pistol in hand. But saying it...

Saying it made it real. And the reality of it was the opposite of funny.

His gaze skipped between my eyes. "What do you mean?"

"For so long, I've been clinging to survival. For *years*." Oh, gods, the thoughts I'd tried to escape yesterday were spilling out and I couldn't stop them—as inexorable as a river bursting its banks. "And yet, I let go of that in the grove. I *chose* to take that poison. I *chose* to not survive."

He might've paled then. It was hard to say with the window behind him and his face cast in shadow. "Why *did* you choose that?"

"Because I realised there was something more important than survival." I found myself studying my poison stained hands as they wrung together. "But... I don't even know what that means. I don't know who that makes me now." It had been at the core of who I was and what I did for so long. Who was I without it? "What do I want, if not to survive? What else *is* there?"

The terror of that gripped my throat.

There was a long silence before he spoke softly, "Perhaps..." His hands closed over my shoulders, warmth seeping through my gown. "Perhaps there is living."

Before I could shake my head and tell him that I didn't know what *that* meant either, the door opened.

Brynan stood there, mouth open as he eyed the two of us. He blinked at the floor and cleared his throat. "I—uh—sorry. It's just... your next appointment is here."

Bastian's arms snapped to his sides as he backed off. Shadows bubbled at his feet.

I folded my hands and straightened my spine, poised, my feelings shut safely away.

The rules for Elfhame were clear: bargains were currency, lies were weapons, and your heart was your greatest weakness.

8

BASTIAN

"You didn't tell me your little friend had woken up."

Midway through asking Queen Braea a question, I clamped my mouth shut. Her dark, dark eyes stayed on me, level, a glint of amusement in them.

I loved her as my queen. But I also hated how she saw right through me so easily... and raised her findings in the middle of a morning report before removing her earrings like nothing had happened.

Exhaustion dragged on me. I hadn't slept well after Kat's debriefing. Any moment of quiet I found, her words gnawed on me, becoming dreams where I cut the changeling down again and again. But each time, he rose, slashed and bloody, and came after Kat, dogging her every step, sinking his fingers into her, ripping her apart while I could do nothing but wade through his blood.

My day had been filled with re-interviewing witnesses to the previous Hydra Ascendant encounters. I'd read and re-read every report from the time and summoned everyone involved to interview them personally. If I'd missed any detail the first time, I'd find it now.

So far, though, nothing.

The frustration of that had made sleep difficult last night. And when I did manage to drift off, instead of nightmares about unCavendish, frustration of a different kind found me, tightening down my spine and low in my belly as I played out how that moment in my office might've gone differently.

Except it never would've ended with fucking her on my desk until I couldn't think straight. Not in reality. I'd destroyed any hope I had with Kat when I'd used her.

Listening to her apologise to me had only added fuel to my own guilt.

Especially when I couldn't even bring myself to say it back.

It was too big. There were too many words. An explanation I didn't know how to give.

Now, I stood before my queen, fresh from those impossible dreams, groggy and grumpy and attempting to put a professional face on it all.

"Didn't I mention it?" I raised my eyebrows. "It must've slipped my mind."

Sitting at her dressing table, she pulled pins from her elaborate hairstyle, depositing them in a dish. The tight curls eased over her shoulders as they were released. "You ran a stag to death to bring her here. She must be important. Too important to slip your mind."

"She uncovered the changeling. I would've felt bad if she'd died on my account." Not untrue. Just not the *entire* truth.

Clicking her tongue, she shook her head. "Really, Bastian. First you don't report to me as soon as you return, then this? You've got me wondering what other secrets you're keeping."

I bit my tongue on the reminder that Dawn was Ascendant

by the time I reached the city. It wouldn't help. "What could I possibly be hiding from you, Your Majesty?"

In the mirror, she arched an eyebrow at me. "Isn't that the question?"

I held still, used to these games, and returned her penetrating look with a bored one. She was the person who'd taught me how beneficial it was to put others off balance, and it was from my *baba* I'd learned a mask of boredom could hide a multitude of sins.

"I want to meet her."

"That won't be—"

"Ennet," she called, voice taking on a commanding quality that would pierce the doors to her chamber.

At once, her assistant's face appeared at the door, notebook and pen in hand. "Your Majesty?"

"Arrange a ball for next week."

Ennet pulled a slim diary from her pocket. The pages flicked themselves. "Your Majesty's calendar is full all week. There's nothing until next month."

"Fine." Braea flicked her hand, impatience huffing through the solitary word. "Arrange it for then. Just don't bore me with the details."

"Very good, Your Majesty." Ennet scribbled in the diary before tucking it away. "Any particular theme or should I take care of it?"

"I want to reward this human of Bastian's for services to my court."

"She isn't mine," I said a little too quickly for my bored exterior.

Ennet shot me a glance but nodded. "Bastian is right. We don't steal humans anymore, if you'll recall. You agreed—"

"Oh, I know very well what I agreed, Ennet!" Braea

62

slammed another hair pin into the dish. "Stars above, must you be so literal? All I mean is for you to organise something in the girl's honour."

My blood ran cold. I wanted to lurch forward and stop this, but I needed to remember myself and what it meant to be calm.

Oblivious, Braea went on. "Show her the Night Queen rewards loyalty." She snorted. "Maybe even blow her little human mind with all the wonder of fae hospitality."

"That won't be necessary." I chuckled and waved my hand, proud of how at ease I seemed.

"Nonsense!" She shook her head before disappearing behind her dressing screen, which showed the night sky lightening ready for dawn.

Not long before Sleep would claim her and I still had questions—questions that related to work rather than to a ball that would draw far too much attention to Kat. "We need to—"

"The girl saved your life, and I want to meet her," her voice cut from the other side of the screen. "She will have a ball. Ennet, you will arrange it. That is that."

"Consider it done, Your Majesty." Even though the queen couldn't see us, Ennet bowed her head before starting for the door.

Braea emerged wearing a dressing robe. "Oh, and have it in the lodestone ballroom. Invite Dawn." She gave a narrow smile that made her black eyes glint. "I want them reminded that a mere human girl foiled their attempt to poison my Shadow."

I bit back a groan. Great. So Dawn would also be reminded of Kat's importance.

Not missing a step, Ennet scribbled in her notebook. "Goodnight, Your Majesty." With a bow, she exited.

"My dear Bastian." Braea sighed as she approached.

"There's no need for that scowl. I'll ensure everyone knows Kate—"

"Kat."

She flicked her fingers dismissively before cupping my cheek. "—*Kat* is not only under your protection but *mine*. She'll have a lovely time, I'm sure of it. Happy?"

"Ecstatic."

Hand sinking, she huffed out through her nose. "Fine, sarcasm will do." She swept over to the bed with a yawn. "You're lucky. Most queens wouldn't indulge you as I do, you know."

"I know. And I'm eternally grateful."

That also wasn't a lie. She alone was responsible for putting me in this position. Not just living in the palace with all the benefits that came with it, but in a role where I could hold so many strings—strings that held our two courts in balance and kept everything under control.

"I'm the one who should be grateful to you." A sadness flickered at the edges of her smile, and I wondered if she thought of the daughter I'd killed for her.

If I dwelled on it, I could feel her blood on my hands—*royal* blood—mingling with my father's. I could hear the thud of her head landing on the throne room floor and rolling, the collective gasp in response. I could smell her fear before I'd taken that head—so overwhelming it had blotted out every other scent.

That was why I didn't dwell on it.

Instead, I watched the queen I'd given so much to as she smoothed a lightly scented oil into her bronze skin. "Have you made any progress with your investigations into the changeling?" she asked, not looking up from the floating hand-mirror.

"I have a few threads I'm pulling at, but the Hydra Ascendant business is taking up most of my time. Kat was able to give me some useful information about unCavendish, though, and—"

"Un-what?"

"UnCavendish. That's her name for the changeling."

Braea's eyebrow rose, sharp as a blade. "Is it, now?"

Even in small ways like this, Kat's influence had crept under my skin. As sweet and sharp and insidious as her poison.

Despite the sting when I gave her that first touch of the day, I would gladly lick the stuff from her fingers and beg her for more. Fuck antidotes. Fuck everything else. Fuck—

Good gods, Bastian. Control yourself.

I swallowed down the rising madness and cleared my throat. "She's been very helpful. It's just a shame she burned the note I recovered from their spies." Decoding it would've given us information about what Dawn had really been up to in Lunden. It wasn't as though Caelus had made any real attempts to woo the human queen.

"Hmm." Braea's expression soured. "I suppose there's nothing we can do about that. Now—"

She yawned, wide and uncontrolled. The dressing screen showed the brightest point of night, moments from the sun breaking the horizon.

"It's time."

She grumbled and hunkered down in the bed, her mirror landing on the side table. "Of course it is. I've only been doing this for centuries." Another yawn smothered the end of her sentence. "Good morning." She waved me away.

"Good morning, Your Majesty."

When I reached the door, seconds from dawn, her voice

drifted over. "Thank you, Bastian. For all you sacrifice for my court. It doesn't go unnoticed."

I paused in the doorway, a tightness in my chest, but she didn't say anything more.

On the dressing screen, day had broken.

9

KAT

It had started off as all my evenings in Elfhame had: reading and drinking. But I'd run out of books, so now I was just drinking.

It didn't dull the pain of my loneliness though.

I'd spent years on my estate with just two other people, and much of that time working alone. It had never bothered me. But Ella's friendship and whatever I'd believed was happening between me and Bastian had left a hole.

The books had gone halfway towards filling it, and normally drink would top up the rest, helping me sleep.

But it turned out I couldn't get drunk anymore, as the half empty decanter attested to. This magic was stopping the alcohol. Had to be. I didn't feel the slightest bit fuzzy. It certainly hadn't silenced the memories that came now I was alone.

Losing control of my body as I shook and stumbled through Riverton Palace, poison creeping along my veins. The pain. The numbness in my fingers. The world turning grey and fading in and out of existence.

And underlining it all—the knowledge that the same poison lingered in my system, ready to claim my life if Bastian forgot to come and give me the antidote.

It was a week since the debriefing and I'd barely seen him. Every day I left a note to remind him about the antidote. Dutifully, he would appear while I was in the middle of eating lunch (invariably while my mouth was full), touch my wrist, then disappear before I had a chance to say a word.

Aside from the servants, that was the only time I saw another soul. I tried to speak to them. One of the women who brought me meals had caramel-coloured hair like Ella's. I'd hoped she might have something of her personality. I'd been disappointed.

There was only one Ella.

This woman was polite and answered some questions but deflected most. The other servants were the same.

The only other face I saw was in the mirror, and I didn't recognise that woman anymore. She hadn't even summoned much of a smile when a message had arrived from Elthea telling me to come for an appointment tomorrow.

Instead, I'd found people in the books on his shelves—or their facsimiles, at least. Good enough to quiet my mind. They carried me on their adventures, a silent observer sitting on their shoulder, sifting through their thoughts, seeing patterns and experiences I recognised, even though I'd never been in the same situations. They saved me from my loneliness. For a while.

Many of the stories were in Albionic, thankfully. But I finished those too quickly. One was in Frankish—the first chapter was a struggle, like pushing a wheelbarrow with a rusted axle. With perseverance, it wore off, though, and I found myself enjoying the tale of a girl who dressed as a boy in order to join the ranks of the king's famous guard. But it was over too soon.

A handful of the books were in a script I couldn't make head nor tail of—it used a slashing alphabet I'd never seen before. Several were in a language that wasn't quite Latium. The verb declensions were completely different—much simpler, thankfully—but most vocabulary seemed the same. Perhaps a precursor? Still, it was close enough for me to understand, and I read those books falteringly.

I'd finished the last one just after dinner.

And now I was alone.

For a while I'd paced, trying to distract my mind with movement, but I found myself picking at the seams of my gloves.

So, here I sat, a useless sack of bones.

A fucking gloomy sack of bones.

I downed the rest of my drink, barely tasting it, and poured another.

He couldn't mean to keep me locked in here forever, could he? I tried to ask when he appeared at lunchtime, but I'd barely managed two words before he disappeared again.

Of course. He had work to do.

Maybe he'd been in such a rush, he'd forgotten to lock the door.

I lurched to my feet, not even swaying despite how much I'd drunk. Once I reached the antechamber, I held my breath and tried the door.

Still locked. And magically, so my rudimentary lock picking skills were a waste of time. (I'd broken a few hairpins finding that out.)

I needed...

I needed *something*. Wringing my hands, I returned to the settee and threw myself onto it.

Answers. Something to do. A conversation, even. Anything but sitting here waiting to die from that changeling's poison.

If I stayed up late enough, I would catch Bastian.

So, I commanded the fae lights to dim and sat in the gathering darkness with his brandy and waited.

I WAS DRIFTING off when the door opened hours later. Head bowed, eyes aglow, Bastian slipped inside without calling for the lights, but I could see him in the odd pinkish glow of the banked fire. I found my tongue stuck to the roof of my mouth.

It had worked. He hadn't seen me—hadn't bothered to look because he didn't expect me to be awake.

And because he was so used to his rooms being his sanctuary.

I grimaced as all the words I'd planned fled.

He was almost at the door when I looked up from my drink and found him peeling off his shirt. Across his flesh, the sinuous curves of an inked snake carved their way across his shoulders and down his back. The firelight picked out flecks of light in its darkness. Were they stars?

I wasn't meant to be ogling his body. This was an ambush.

"You missed out a rule in your list." My voice cut through the quiet. "The one where I'm not allowed to leave your rooms."

He straightened and turned, eyebrows tight together as he called for the fae lights to brighten in their sconces. "What are you doing up?" His gaze landed on the empty decanter. The look he shot me pierced, not even remotely softened by the alcohol. "Drinking?"

I snorted at the accusation in his tone. "You locked me in your rooms. The guards at the door won't let me leave. What did you expect me to do?"

He stiffened, a wince adding to the darkness around his eyes. "There are plenty of books—"

"I've read them all." I waved my hand. "Except for the ones in that strange alphabet that looks like knife slashes."

His eyebrows rose. "How did you read them so quickly? And the—"

"It's been a week, Bastian."

Blinking, he raked a hand through his hair, gaze skipping across the thick carpet as though reckoning the days. "Shit. I... I wasn't fully prepared for you to wake when you did, and I hadn't considered that you'd be left here without entertainment. That being said, drinking is not the answer."

The breath left me in a loud huff of disbelief. Not quite a laugh, but close. "Business Bastian is lecturing me." Because that was how he sounded—all formal and judgemental. I stood, hands on hips. "The man who dropped me in the middle of a palace and fucked off for a week is lecturing me. That's bloody rich."

His jaw rippled, and I could see the effort it took to lower his squared shoulders. "Go to bed, Kat. You're drunk."

"No. I'm not. That's the problem—I can't get drunk, but I can still get a lecture from Business Bastian, it seems." I smiled and spread my hands. "Please continue. Tell me what it is I'm supposed to do while locked in your rooms. If drink isn't the answer, what is?"

His eyelids fluttered and he drew a breath, but no words came.

Part of me ached at the sight of the dark rings around his eyes and the way his shadows barely summoned more than a ripple around his feet. He was exhausted.

But so was I.

Exhausted and alone and lost.

So fucking lost.

My eyes burned as I squeezed my hands into useless fists. "What do you want me to do, Bastian? I have no purpose here. Nothing to do. No one to speak to. You've clearly ordered the servants not to talk to me."

He bristled. "I did no such—"

"Even if you didn't—they won't. I tried. But..." I held my breath as the pressure behind my eyes grew. But it was no use. I couldn't hold either thing back. "You left me here with nothing but my own mind. And I can't stop thinking about... about everything." I tugged at the pearlwort necklace. "The only time I'm not alone is when you appear for thirty seconds, touch my wrist, and disappear because... because..." I held up my hands, the purple stains covering my fingers and bleeding onto my palms—the poison as uncontrolled as my garbled words. "You put your blood in me and now I'm this *thing*."

"I saved your life," he growled.

"It wasn't worth saving."

Stillness rushed into the room, sucking out every sound.

Bastian stared at me, eyes wide. He couldn't have looked more shocked if I'd slapped him.

My stomach condensed, tight and roiling around the brandy. If I could've pulled the words out of the air and stuffed them back into my mouth, I would've.

"You don't mean that," he murmured so softly I almost didn't hear. "It's just the drink talking."

Maybe he was right. Maybe the brandy had affected me

and I hadn't realised. Did that make it wrong, though? Or was it a truth the drink had allowed me to say?

If the poison had killed me, my death (and thus my life) would've had meaning. Now...

I shook my head.

I needed direction. I needed something to do. I needed to not feel like unCavendish was ruling my fucking life from beyond the grave. The poison was his. The fact healing hadn't removed it was down to him. I was here *because of him*. And this necklace—this fucking necklace was his constant touch upon me.

I didn't even know *why*. Who was he working for? Were they here in Tenebris? In the palace? Were they still after Bastian? Or me?

What—or *who* had put him on my path? On Ella's... on Lara's?

"Kat, I..." Bastian started closer, stopped, let his hands fall to his sides. The broad expanse of his chest heaved a few times before he spoke again.

Shoving away the questions chasing through my mind, I watched the glint of his piercing—better that than meeting his gaze.

"I'm sorry." His shoulders sank. "I didn't realise how cruel it was to lock you in here." He looked around the room as if seeing it afresh.

I was only too happy to pretend I hadn't said what I'd just said. This argument was just about being locked up. The dark turn of my thoughts—let him believe that was down to alcohol.

"I've been so absorbed with my work, and..." He bowed his head, pain etched between his eyebrows. "No, it isn't that. Kat, I wanted to keep you safe."

All this, for safety? My obsession. The gods had a shitty sense of humour sometimes.

"Locking me up is not keeping me safe. It's torture."

As he met my gaze, every cool edge of Business Bastian melted away. The man standing before me now was pained, contrite, and, judging by the way he clenched and unclenched his hands, torn. "I'm sorry. Truly. I promise I'll fix this first thing in the morning."

"Will I be able to go outside?"

"Yes, of course. I'm..." He shook his head. "Tomorrow, you'll see the city, safely. *I will fix this.*"

The city. Beautiful and dangerous, just like fae.

But it held answers. Someone had to know about unCavendish. I had this necklace, and although it felt like a collar binding me to his leash, it was also a starting point.

Bastian had made it clear he wasn't going to share his work and secrets with me. If I wanted to know who unCavendish was working for—and I needed to for my sake and for Lara's memory—I was going to have to find out for myself.

In silence, Bastian put the decanter away, and I let him usher me to my room. The fae lights dimmed as he left.

The shadow of his feet remained at the crack beneath my door for a long while.

10

KAT

Bastian was true to his word and at some ungodly hour the next morning, I found myself walking through the palace corridors with him. Target practice, he'd said —I needed to be able to protect myself.

I'd take that over being locked in his rooms.

I'd certainly take that over remembering what I said last night.

That wasn't what I really thought about my life; I just needed something to do. I had to think it was worthwhile to have spent so many years clinging on to it.

Or was I just afraid of the alternative?

At my side, Bastian still looked tired—maybe even more so. The sun hadn't yet risen but would soon. He must've already gone to the Night Queen before she sank into her enchanted slumber. He couldn't have had much sleep.

I was about to tell him not to worry, to go back and get some rest, when we stepped out onto a terrace overlooking a practice yard. But the chill of the early morning air wasn't what cut off my words before they began.

Beyond the dummies and targets and other low buildings of the palace was Tenebris.

If I'd thought Luminis beautiful, then Tenebris was stunning.

Dark, glittering stone soared in the same graceful spires, though the golden rooftops seemed sharper somehow. Polished black basalt caught the dim pre-dawn light, contrasting with the cheerful coral pink glow spilling from hundreds of windows. I hadn't worked out why fae fires were pink, save that it was because of some magical property, but now its strangeness seemed perfect against what would've been a sombre city at night.

And it wasn't a dark city. Not at all.

As well as the light spilling from homes, fae lights of a dozen pale colours drifted through the streets. The plants I'd seen climbing up buildings and growing from the rock glowed green and violet.

Around me, the palace rose, darkly glorious. Where the palace in Luminis had flashed with the blue-gold-green of pale moonstone, Tenebris's iridescence was the deep jewel of a magpie's tail feathers. I touched my chest—the stone of my potion bottle matched perfectly.

I'd been so absorbed in my own misery, I hadn't even thought to look out the window and see the city at night. I'd missed all this.

"The first time seeing Tenebris tends to have this effect." Bastian's low voice cut through my awe, and it was only then I realised I'd stopped and my mouth was hanging open.

"It's... incredible."

He shot me a small smile. "I'm glad my city meets with

your approval. I may be biased, but I'm inclined to agree." He set off towards the steps leading down into the practice yard. "Shall we?"

I followed, trying not to stare at the city and palace so much that I fell down the entire flight of steps.

As we walked through the yard, Bastian pointed at the practice dummies. "If you don't have a clear shot to the head, I suggest aiming for the crotch."

I arched an eyebrow. "Isn't that an even smaller target?"

His eyes glittered as he smirked. "Yes. But if a man's in fear of losing his prize jewels, it's an almighty motivation to turn and run."

"Vicious." I scoffed. "I wouldn't expect to receive that advice from a man."

He gave me a sidelong glance, his amusement fading. "Whatever it takes to keep you safe, Katherine."

The look hit me at the same time as the realisation. The old Bastian had woken up this morning rather than the one who was all detached business. A wild and foolish flutter ran through my insides. I swallowed it down and shrugged. "No concerns about honour?"

He made a dismissive sound in his throat. "Honour is a pretty idea. Let me know how relying on it to keep you alive goes."

I found myself smiling up at him. Perhaps fae didn't hold with the same ideas humans had about honour and women's weapons and all that nonsense.

We reached a firing range and I scanned the area, grateful for the distraction. Because the more I looked at him, the less I remembered important things like betrayal and how not to grin like a fucking moron. "So what am I going to be firing to keep myself safe? Do you have my pistol?"

"A pistol is great, but it still can't be loaded as quickly as one of these." From a tall locker, he produced a bow. "And what we don't tend to advertise to humans is that our bows are just as dangerous as our pistols." His grin was vicious and I'd have said it was as dangerous as either weapon. He rolled his eyes. "For some reason your people prefer guns."

I wasn't sure if I scowled at him out of a sense of defensiveness for my fellow humans or because I didn't feel like I belonged with them at all. "Perhaps it's because anyone can fire a gun."

"I'm not sure that's a good thing."

"Aren't you? Said like a man who has the strength to draw a bow with ease."

Bastian's face scrunched up. Combined with his tiredness, his confusion was almost... cute.

I blamed that for my tone softening. "You might feel differently if you were a woman with little upper body strength. Then you'd see the value of a weapon where you only need to pull the trigger."

His eyebrows rose slowly as he nodded. "I hadn't considered that before. Well, you'll be glad to hear our bows aren't as hard to draw as yours." He touched the bow's tip and said, "*Tennacht.*" With a faint creak, the bowstring tightened. He held out the elegantly arched weapon. "Try it."

He was probably basing his assumption on a fae woman's strength, which would be far more than mine. Not bothering to grip it properly, I gave an experimental pull on the string.

The bow flexed. It still gave some resistance—a reassuring kind of feedback—but drew to full extension without much effort at all.

"See?" His grin wasn't even smug. "There's a reason we don't sell our bows to humans." *Now* it was smug.

"Wouldn't want us using them on you." It was meant to be a joke, but even as I said it, I remembered what he'd told me about how close fae had come to being wiped out by war with humans and how slowly their population grew.

His grin disappeared.

"Sorry, that was in poor taste. I didn't mean—"

He waved off my apology. "You need to hold the bow horizontally."

It seemed our lesson had begun, and he'd leapt to the assumption I was a complete beginner.

What would be the best moment to tell him he was wrong? Maybe I'd wait and see how long it took him to realise.

When I obeyed and tilted the bow, he handed me an arrow. "The string goes in the notch, fletching upmost." He moved behind me. "The fletchings are the feathers on the end."

"*Really?*"

"Mm, that's right. Now, take these three fingers." Coming close, he folded in his thumb and little finger. "Forefinger above the arrow, the other two below. Place them on the string."

I was already standing side-on to the targets yet he still didn't realise, so I continued with the charade. "*Then* what, Bastian?" I turned my face away so he wouldn't see my grin.

"Bow upright"—his arm came around me as he guided my wrist—"and draw." He "helped" and I tried to ignore the press of him against my back. "Elbow—oh, it already is up. *Good.*"

That word. Fuck. *That word.*

With my hair braided and coiled around my head, he had to see the hairs on the back of my neck rise. I couldn't summon an overly enthusiastic reply. Not when my stomach was doing odd flippy things like a swallow in the summer sky.

"Make sure you're not locking your elbow."

I wasn't.

"You should feel the pull here." He released my wrist and his palm landed between my shoulder blades. "Then you just need to aim and—"

I let my arrow fly.

It thrummed into the target on the edge of the inner bullseye.

I nodded and rolled my shoulders. "A little rusty. But you're right, that was easier to draw than I remembered."

The air huffed out of him. "You've used a bow before."

I flashed him a grin. "Only a few times. When did you realise?"

"Too late. That'll teach me for not asking, won't it?"

I raised my eyebrows.

He jerked his head towards the quiver mounted to a stake in the ground. "Fire another."

I nocked another arrow and drew. This next part wasn't so different from pistol shooting. Aim, exhale, adjust aim, fire.

Dead centre.

He returned my wide smile like it was infectious. "Another." There was a note of playful challenge in his voice that eased the tension I'd been carrying in my jaw and shoulders since waking in Elfhame.

I could almost forget everything that had happened in Lunden.

Almost.

Maybe this morning, I wanted to. It felt like I had a friend here in this strange city.

Maybe that was what made me cocky. "Name two adjacent colours on the target and a number between one and twelve."

His eyes narrowed and he eyed me with suspicion. "Blue and black. Eleven."

I nocked. I aimed. I fired.

"Hmm. I suppose every shot can't be perfect."

It wasn't in the bullseye, no.

But I wasn't aiming for the bullseye.

"Ah, Bastian," I sighed, shaking my head. "What colours am I on the line between?"

A frown flickered between his eyebrows, and he glanced back at the target. "Blue and black."

I widened my eyes. "*Really?* Huh. Weird. And if the target were a clock face, where would—?"

"Eleven." He exhaled a disbelieving laugh. He looked at me a long while, gaze flicking over my face and down as if he'd never seen me before this moment.

It made my skin burn. That foolish fluttering renewed, fed by his undisguised admiration. I cleared my throat and shrugged like I wasn't so affected. "I told you I was a good shot. It carries over from pistols to archery—that's all."

But it had felt good to prove him wrong, to surprise him where he'd underestimated me. And the look he gave me felt more than good. I couldn't contain my grin.

A slow and dangerous smile inched over his lips, and I found myself preoccupied by his scar. "Fine, so the Wicked Lady can shoot. But what about when she's distracted?"

"You don't think it's distracting to worry about being executed if you're caught? I've been living with distraction for years."

"Very well." His voice lilted, low and teasing. "If you think you're so seasoned, go ahead."

"Where this time?" I drew another arrow and readied it.

"Just the bullseye will do."

"Hmph. Too easy."

"Stop stalling, Katherine."

Fuck. Talk about distraction. The way he said my name in full like that.

I drew a long, slow breath and pulled back the string. As easy as that, I shook him off. He would have to try harder to throw my aim.

I lined up my arrow and exhaled.

Just as I was about to release, a finger traced my temple and down my cheek. I gasped at the resonance humming through my body and the bowstring slipped from my fingers. I didn't even see where my arrow went.

"You bastard!" I whirled on him.

And found we stood toe-to-toe.

My breaths heaved as I glared. He'd use the first touch of the day against me.

But a slow and foolish smile spread across his face. "Say that again."

"*You bastard,*" I said as he watched my mouth form the words. My skin grew too tight under that intimate attention, my annoyance merging with an altogether different heat.

"I normally hate that name," he murmured into the quiet of the practice yard, and I was suddenly all too aware that we were the only ones here. "But when you say it... it isn't the same at all."

I blamed the softness in his voice and his eyes for me dropping the bow and placing my hands on his chest in the same instant his found the notch of my waist.

"Bastard," I whispered.

A soft sound caught in his throat, humming under my palms as he pulled me against him. His gaze was locked on my mouth, and I found my fingers tangling in the soft fabric of his shirt.

Gods, he felt good. Hot and strong and vital. So many

things I was not. We fit together too well for this to be wrong, didn't we?

We could pretend. It was easier to pretend than have the conversation. It was easier to do this than live as I had the past week.

He bowed his head, and I tiptoed up in answer.

Chatter and laughter burst into my ears, into reality, into the practice yard.

Bastian's hands dropped as he backed away, attention shooting up to the terrace where we'd entered. A group of recruits swaggered across it, lit by the sun I hadn't even noticed rising.

"I'll beat the shit out of you today."

"I don't think you could even beat my shit!"

More laughter as they bounded down the stairs. One leapt but landed heavily, a bit like my heart crashing into the pit of my belly right now.

Bastian raked his fingers through his hair. "We should go."

He grabbed my sleeve and marched me inside.

II

KAT

I didn't have the breath or brainpower to argue. Also... maybe he was right.

We'd been about to kiss, and although I was a fool, I still understood that was a terrible, terrible idea. Even if it had felt right for those few fleeting moments.

I needed to control myself. However tempting, Bastian was off limits.

He hadn't even apologised. At least I'd tried to. Getting involved would only lead to more hurt, and I hurt enough.

I needed to get away from him. Not just now but forever. Home was safer.

Eventually, his heaving chest calmed and he dropped my sleeve. After several turns and a flight of stairs, we reached the corridor that housed his office. Coming the opposite direction, almost blocking the hall, was a huge man. His dark grey hair matched his dark glower.

It took me a moment to realise there was someone else at

his side—a woman with strawberry blond hair. Her freckled face broke into a broad smile when she spotted us.

Bastian sighed, shoulders sinking. When we reached them, he turned, but didn't look directly at me. "This is Faolán." He gestured at the giant. "I'm the queen's right hand and he's mine. And this is Rose. Meet Katherine—or Kat."

Somehow, Rose's smile grew broader. "*Katherine.*"

Faolán's eyes widened a touch as he looked down at me, and I realised his lowered eyebrows were more a sign of curiosity than irritation. "Kat." He nodded. "She's so small," he muttered out the side of his mouth.

I couldn't help chuckling.

Bastian arched one eyebrow at him. "And yet she still has ears." He clapped the giant on the shoulder. "Rose works for me and for some reason agreed to marry him."

"Her life *was* in danger," Faolán muttered.

Rose swatted him. "But I chose to stay married to you, didn't I? No danger involved. And as for you..." She pointed at Bastian and narrowed her eyes. Shaking her head, she turned to me. "Anyway, ignore these two. I am so pleased to finally meet you properly."

I threw a questioning glance at Bastian, but he was still studiously avoiding my gaze. "And I—"

"Rose is going to be your bodyguard. I've already briefed her about"—his eyes flicked to my gloved hands—"precautions."

She eyed us, then peered down the hall. "What have you two been up to that's got you looking so flustered?"

"Archery practice," Bastian answered too quickly. "Turns out Kat doesn't need much of it. I'll leave you two to your day." Clearing his throat, he opened the door and I caught a glimpse of Brynan at his desk. He disappeared inside, calling back, "Faolán, my office."

Faolán frowned from the spot where Bastian had stood a moment ago to me. "What—?"

"*Now*," Bastian's voice clipped through the open door.

"Sorry, little flower, duty calls." Faolán kissed Rose on the cheek.

As he held her shoulder, I had to bite back a gasp. At the tips of his fingers instead of nails were claws, short and blunt like a hound's.

Nodding to me, he followed Bastian.

I stared after them. It felt like I'd been hit by one whirlwind after another.

"Bastian... can be like that sometimes." She winced and gestured back the way she'd come. "I'll show you the city. I hear you haven't seen much of it." Her lips pressed together, an expression that ill-suited her. Her face was made for smiles and laughter.

The city meant venturing out from the palace's protection, but it might also give me a chance to find out about unCavendish as well as go to my appointment at the Hall of Healing. At least I'd touched Bastian for the day, so I didn't need to worry about that.

I stole glances at her as we walked through the palace and she explained how the hill it was built on had once been a volcano. Natural hot springs fed the baths in the basement levels and were channelled out into the river that cut the palace off from the rest of the city.

It was only now Faolán wasn't next to her that I could tell, despite what he called her, she wasn't a "little" anything. She had to be six foot tall and well-muscled. And it took a while longer before I realised why she put me at (relative) ease.

"You're human."

She shot me an infectious grin. "Mostly." She peered along the corridor. We were alone. "Until not so long ago, entirely."

I squinted at her in question, but asking what she was had to be considered rude, even for non-fae.

She winked as we turned a corner. A handful of guards waited at the end. "I'll tell you later."

Before we stepped through the doorway, she warned me we were passing into a lodestone, and I steeled myself for the lurch that felt like walking down a staircase with one more step than I expected.

A columned chamber stretched before us, wide and long, the high ceiling showing a sky full of racing clouds and the tinge of sunrise gold. The image moved, and when I gave Rose a questioning look, she shrugged. "Magic. You'll get used to it."

In fact, the buzz on my skin was less noticeable than it had been when I'd left the Hall of Healing, growing clearer when I focused.

Ahead, at the chamber's centre, a fountain glittered, and beyond that stood two huge doors, wide open to the outside. The grand hall Bastian had mentioned. He'd brought me a different route that first day.

I could probably find my way from here back to his offices and the practice yard, even if it wasn't the most direct way. That was progress.

Before we stepped out into the burgeoning day, I glanced back. The door we'd entered through cut off the far left hand corner of the chamber, while another matching door cut off the right hand corner. That had to be Dawn's entrance.

We crossed the same bridge as that first day, and since I avoided looking over its edge (or even acknowledging it had one), I spotted that the sky above matched the one from the hallway. Magic, indeed.

"You'll get used to it all." Rose gave me a lopsided grin. "It took me a little while, but now I love it here. Ari, too. That's my friend—she's one of us." She tapped the rounded tip of her ear.

"Mostly" human—yet her canine teeth were long and sharp like a fae's.

Curiosity ate at me, but the bridge deposited us into a busy street and fae stared as we passed.

So many people—people I could kill with a single touch.

I clutched at the buzzing sensation on my skin, desperately trying to will the magic inside me to be small. I was a girl again, my father rapping a ruler across the table, making me jump.

Sit straight.

Knees together—you're not a whore.

I hated myself for leaning on those lessons—what had they got me? I'd been poisoned—not just by the aconite, but by all the words my father and uncle had dripped into me for so, so long. Except... without those lessons, without their tight boundaries, who the hells was I?

That was too big a question. Far, far too big.

And right now, I needed to keep this magic under control. Much as I hated their rules, they had taught me to be quiet, small, contained, and I needed this power in my veins to be the same.

Still, the fae watched.

"What are they looking at?"

"Us." Rose shrugged. "But mostly you."

I frowned, every inch of me rigid from holding on. "They didn't stare as much when I came this way before."

She gave me a sidelong look. "Were you with Bastian, by any chance?"

"I suppose he's enough to scare the curiosity out of most people."

Another flashing grin. "Mm-hmm. We're human, which is unusual enough. But I'm old news now. You're still fresh and new, and you must know about fae and red hair. I'm sure Bastian's told you the effect—"

"They like it. I know." I didn't want to think about the effect I had on Bastian nor him on me.

"There you go. And, of course, the rumour mill started churning the moment Bastian came galloping into the city with a half-dead woman in his arms and demanded the best healer save her life."

I swallowed down a reaction. *Galloped. Demanded.* I rubbed my chest where my heart dipped.

All of this is real.

Rose went on, pointing out various buildings along the way. Art galleries that were open for anyone to visit. Indoor and outdoor theatres. A school of art, where, through a window, I caught the glimpse of a naked model posing with a pair of weighing scales in her hand and a snake draped over her shoulders.

Music drifted from open windows, a song dropping off as we passed from one street only to be picked up as we entered another. Sometimes the next tune was faster or slower, happy where the last one had been sad, but somehow they all felt akin to one another, like garments cut from the same cloth.

I'd heard in stories that fae loved art and beauty, but this...

It drowned me so exquisitely, I didn't know where to look next, even as I tried to keep an eye on the faces around us. Was that woman following us? Was I just being paranoid?

"I probably should've shown you around the palace first, but I figure you've been cooped up too long."

Agreed. Outside and *doing* something at long last. Speaking of which...

"I have a request, actually." I kept my tone casual, even though a little thrill ran through me. "This necklace—I think it came from the city, and I'd love to get something to match it. Do you think we could find the jeweller it came from?"

She glanced from the pearlwort necklace to a tower topped with a massive orrery. "We have time to visit a few before your appointment, and getting to know the city though jewellery shops is as good a way as any. Though I warn you, there are *a lot* of jewellers in the city. It might take us a while the find the right one."

"I've got nothing but time." I *had* to find out more about unCavendish, and this was my only lead.

So Rose led the way. My head spun a little with her endless chatter about different people and places in the city. It was comforting, even if I didn't fully understand all the references she made, but that comfort was at odds with the looks following us.

I started to build a picture of who was from Dawn and who came from Dusk. As well as blond, brown, and leafy green, Dawn hair colours tended towards the soft tones of a dreamy sunrise, while Dusk favoured deeper colours like the bright ones of a spectacular sunset or the deep dark of midnight. Though a few had starlight hair in pale shades of blue, purple, and silver.

Skin tone varied across both, including the palest and darkest shades seen in humans as well as tinges of green or blue.

Everyone had pointed ears and that same impossible beauty that felt as dangerous as their sharp teeth.

In truth, it was.

Especially in the Dawn fae. As far as I knew, any one of them could be behind unCavendish. True, it was likely to be someone with power and influence, but I didn't know the players yet, nor did I understand how to pick out the powerful fae from the average pawn.

This was a new game.

Still deadly, but with new pieces and new rules, none of which I knew beyond Bastian's warnings.

"Bastian asked me to help train you," Rose said as we turned onto a wide road full of shops with large, curved windows that seemed impossible to make from something as fragile as glass.

I eyed the paired long knives at her side. "To fight?"

She glanced around, then ducked closer. "To use your magic."

Use it? There didn't seem much point, since I didn't intend to have it for long. Elthea had said she was confident she'd find a cure. Fingers crossed, that was why she'd arranged this appointment.

Still, it was a good excuse to pry *a little* about Rose's "mostly" human status. I tugged the cuffs of my gloves. "You have... something similar?"

"No, but I was a human without magic, and now I have it and I have learned to control it. He thought that might mean I could help you."

I raised my eyebrows in question when she met my gaze.

"Oh, you want to know what I am?" She chuckled, then shrugged. "Faolán's a shapechanger—a fae who can shift into another form."

A man passing wrinkled his nose like she'd just said Faolán ate shit.

"And he was able to turn me." She showed me her forearm where an arc of teethmarks showed pale against her freckles. "I'm a werewolf."

I stared at the scar. "You mean... werewolves are real?"

"Oh, yes. Very real." She flipped her arm over, revealing another set of marks, as if that proved it.

Another fae stiffened and hurried across the road.

"Don't worry," Rose called after them, "you're safe. It isn't a full moon. Or—wait—is it? Oh no!" Her back arched and she clawed the air.

I stopped mid-step. Was I meant to get help? I glanced up the hill—I could find my way back to the palace and fetch Faolán.

But... no. Her eyes weren't wide in fear.

"I can feel myself losing control, I'm going to—"

She howled.

Fae scattered.

I was torn between concern about the attention she'd drawn and relief that it kept people at a distance, so I didn't need to worry so much about poisoning them.

Pulling her sleeve down, she rolled her eyes. "Fucking hypocrites."

I raised my eyebrows at her performance. "So... fae don't like werewolves?"

"Or shapechangers. *Even though,*" she added in a voice that filled the street, "the first Day King was one. In case you'd all forgotten that side of your *beloved* hero."

The few remaining fae bowed their heads and hurried past. One clicked their tongue and muttered, "Exactly what I'd expect from such *animals.*"

Rose huffed a long breath out. "I'm sorry, it just really..." She gritted her teeth and shook her head. "Most shapechangers try to keep what they are secret so they don't upset other fae. But I say screw them."

"So I see."

She frowned ahead. "Some think it's just name calling and maybe waiting until last to serve you at a bar, but in some villages, they'll attack you the moment they get a whiff of something animalistic about you."

"You don't need to apologise to me." I went to touch her arm, but the sight of my gloves reminded me why that could be risky. I clasped my hands together. "I can get behind a bit of anger."

Truth be told, I envied her. From the way Faolán had kissed her cheek and called her "little flower" so casually to the way she didn't hide her feelings—I envied her.

"Thanks." She shot me a smile softer than her others, like this one came from somewhere deeper. "Much as I love Tenebris, fae can be so ridiculous sometimes."

"No arguments here," I muttered.

Out the corner of her eye, she gave me a look that felt more knowing that I expected, but when she stopped outside a shop and opened her mouth, it wasn't for a probing question. "Here's our first jeweller."

12

KAT

The fae behind the counter wrinkled her nose as she eyed my necklace. "No, not me."

Not a promising start.

But I was out of Bastian's rooms and I was *doing something*, so even her expression couldn't sour my mood.

"Any ideas who might've made it?"

More nose-wrinkling as she shook her head and wished us a good day.

"Don't worry," Rose told me as we left and started along the road, "there are plenty of jewellers to try." She widened her eyes. "*Dozens*, in fact."

The next place, Clio's, with a moon forming the *C* yielded similar results, though. It was only when I glanced back at the sign as we were leaving that I registered. These were people from Dusk Court. I didn't know who unCavendish had worked for, but since he tried to kill Bastian, it seemed most likely they were from Dawn.

"Maybe the necklace was from a Dawn jeweller, rather

than a Dusk one. We could focus on them instead?" I glanced at Rose, all nonchalance.

Her brow furrowed. "If you think so. Seems weird that Bastian would buy a necklace from a Dawn jeweller."

I barely kept the wince from my face. "It... wasn't from him."

"Oh."

Even though I avoided looking at her, I could feel the closeness of her attention. She expected an explanation that I wasn't going to give.

Still, the weight of her attention pulled on me, especially after she'd been so friendly, so I threw her a quick smile.

"We can go to some of Dawn's jewellers—there are a couple on the next street. But, I warn you, they'll charge us more and won't be as welcoming. Especially when they find out this is to go on Bastian's account."

"What?" My eyebrows shot up. Since I wasn't planning to actually buy any jewellery, paying for it hadn't crossed my mind.

"Anything you want to buy is taken care of. You might want to make the most of that, since it's a deep well you're drawing from." She chuckled.

I frowned and pulled my arms tighter around myself as we passed a large group of fae who watched us. Their darker clothes suggested they were of Dusk, yet their attention prickled over me, unsafe.

"And the price is different depending on who you are?"

"More... Dusk sees you as one of their own—they do with me, too. Dusk looks after Dusk, and Dawn... well, they might turn a blind eye if you were on fire."

I scoffed at the image, and her grin widened. "It's not entirely a joke, is it?"

"Afraid not. Welcome to a city of two courts."

Although the city's appearance changed with the sunset and rise, most streets tended to be dominated by one court or the other. This one we walked down was full of shop signs with constellations and crescent moons, decorated in the deep sunset colours of Dusk Court.

A palace divided by two planes of existence. Two courts divided by day and night. And, so it seemed, a city also divided.

Still, I had a mission, even if it might make Rose believe me a spoilt aristocrat. "Well... I still want these earrings to match, so..."

"Dawn jewellers, it is." She shrugged and led me to the next road over.

Suns and clouds took over the iconography, together with shades of soft pink, blue, and lavender. The change was so stark, I couldn't believe I hadn't noticed before.

More gazes followed us, but here the fae's eyes narrowed. Just a little, almost unnoticeably, but enough that I caught it. Conversations stopped. Folk turned.

I fought to keep my expression neutral.

Never reveal your heart. That included not letting them see I was affected.

We tried another jeweller. This one gave us a stiff smile as we entered, yet her eyes gleamed as she no doubt detected a great opportunity to overcharge Bastian's account. But she shook her head when I asked about the necklace. "I haven't seen it before. Though, I could make something to match."

"Thank you, but I want it made by the same person."

Her stiff smile remained in place, but the skin around her eyes tensed as though inwardly she glowered.

She *didn't* wish us a good day.

"It's probably going to take a few days to get to all the

shops." Rose spread her hands as we left. "And we have your appointment soon, so we should..."

I didn't hear her next words, because amongst all the blond, green, and brown hair, a flash of auburn at the end of the road caught my eye. Tall, lithe, back to me as they moved through the city like they knew it well. Was that the fae I'd seen in Lunden? The one I'd seen at the race?

Pace speeding, I steered that way, but a crowd crossed my path. I craned, trying to peer over them, but at my height it was a doomed effort.

Blinding sunlight flashed off pure, pure white armour, and a low hubbub of murmurs spread through the street.

"Kingsguard," Rose muttered.

It was only when I gave up searching for another glimpse of fox-coloured hair that I registered what everyone was looking at—or rather, *who*.

Resplendent in gold-green iridescent silk, the man working his way through the crowd with a rayed crown atop his head could only be the Day King. His long, pale hair caught the sun, transforming into gilded lengths, so beautiful I couldn't look away.

"The Dawn royals do this from time to time," Rose murmured as we stood back for the growing crowd. "Come and talk to 'the little people,' giving gifts, winning hearts—that sort of thing."

He shook a woman's hand, nodding as she spoke and the man beside her beamed.

"I suppose the Night Queen does the same after sunset."

"Or... never. I don't think she leaves the palace—or at least I've never seen it."

As though he felt my attention, the king looked up from pressing a wrapped gift into the man's hand and met my gaze.

His eyes. *His eyes.*

They weren't just sky blue—they *were* the bright sky overhead, with no pupils. Cocking his head, he surveyed me briefly and said a few words to the woman before turning this way.

The guards hung back as a path cleared for him, and I stood rooted to the spot.

A king—a fae fucking king was walking towards me.

Despite the sun, a chill fled down my spine.

Unfortunately, I couldn't flee with it.

Instead, I stood and waited, taking in every detail I could to help me work out the safest way to respond. Was I in trouble? Or just a curiosity?

The slight lines bracketing his mouth and lingering between his brows suggested he frowned as often as he smiled and made him look older than Bastian and Asher. He seemed to be in his forties.

But he'd allied with the Night Queen in the Wars of Succession a thousand years ago—like many things about fae, nothing was as it seemed.

Beyond him, a woman with hair the colour of summer oak leaves glanced after him, her crown a smaller version of his. His wife, Meredine. A queen, but one without a throne.

She exchanged a look with another man and nodded towards me. Golden blond hair—true gold, not pale like the king's—and a crown depicting a sunrise framed a remarkably handsome face. From his smirking lips and dimpled chin to his hooded eyes, he seemed made of sinuous curves. He raised his eyebrows at me and gestured at what had to be his father, as though reminding me that I was in the presence of a king.

As if I could forget.

"King Lucius." Rose bowed when he stopped before us, and I rushed to follow suit. "An honour."

He sniffed but otherwise ignored her, only looking at me. His mouth curved slowly like a bow I wasn't strong enough to draw. "Well, if it isn't the newest arrival to my city. And, may I say, such a pretty one."

Some compliments made me warm—they were approval, safety. A sign I'd done something right.

Not this one.

Still, I smiled and bowed my head. "Thank you. Your Majesty is too kind."

"The sight of you adorning my streets is thanks enough."

"Then I'm glad to please Your Majesty." My skin crawled at how sincere I sounded, but pleasing a king meant safety, so maybe it wasn't entirely a lie.

He watched me a beat too long for comfort. "Yes, I think you'll do well in Luminis." He glanced at the gathering crowd and spread his hands. "But I must continue with my work—a king is nothing without his people. If you get bored of that shadow, you know where to find us." Inclining his head, he took a step back. "Katherine."

Never before had my name sounded so much like a threat.

It blocked my throat like a mouthful of stale bread, and I had to fight to keep my pleasant smile in place before Rose hurried us towards the Hall of Healing.

My fingers had never itched so much for the comfort of my pistol. Inside Bastian's rooms, I'd felt trapped... but also safe.

I didn't know the rules of this game, but having met one of its key pieces, I was certain of one thing.

Being *noticed* by royalty was *not* safe.

13
BASTIAN

"'When the princess is in power'—that's what they said." The witness held my gaze, not troubled by the unseelie glow.

I shared a look with Faolán.

There were no princesses. Not anymore. Not since I'd beheaded the last remaining heir to Dusk.

Her elder daughter, Princess Nyx, had died in an unseelie attack before I was born.

My fingers tightened around my pen. All the more reason to stop Hydra Ascendant before they became a true threat. The Night Queen had no clear heir. If she died, factions would rise around her distant relatives, like Asher, and those factions would clash in a race to the Moon Throne.

A total fucking disaster.

As was the fact word had got out about Ascendants operating in the city.

The wrinkled woman before us had heard two people outside

her house in the early hours. When she blasted them with a sudden rainfall, they'd fled. Unfortunately, her weather magic had also washed away any evidence, save for a pot of red paint.

"'When the princess is in power this will all pay off.'" She nodded, grey eyebrows drawn together in a fierce frown.

"We heard you." I tried to keep the sigh from my voice.

"Hmph, good luck getting her on the throne," Faolán muttered.

The witness's frown intensified. I liked it, to be honest—it was refreshing for a civilian not to fear me. "Dead women don't make great queens, do they, Serpent?"

I fixed a smile in place, like I found her comment terribly amusing.

But I could feel the blood on my hands, even though it had been long ago. Throwing her head across the throne room had felt dramatic and daring.

Now I knew it for what it was.

Brash and thoughtless.

Not that I wouldn't kill her again if I faced the same situation. But some aspects of how I dealt with it—those I'd change if I had my time again.

The orrery on the mantlepiece chimed softly. Almost time for that meeting. I cleared my throat and straightened. "Was there anything else?"

She shook her head. "That's all I heard."

"And I appreciate you bringing it to me." I stood and gestured for the door. "If you hear anything else—"

"Aye, I know how to find you and your *friends*." She looked at Faolán for the first time since she'd walked into my office. It was the kind of look that made me want to break things. One people gave shapechangers too often.

Instead I squeezed my pen and herded both her and Faolán out the door. Even he couldn't know about my next task.

He shot me a questioning frown after she'd gone. "You don't think Princess Nyx could've survived, do you? No one ever found her body."

"Three arrows *and* a fall from the bridge? I think it's safe to say she's long gone. If by some miracle she survived all that, she would've come back by now."

"Hmm. True."

Once he was gone and the door locked, I approached the far side of my office.

A carved panel showed the planets and the Celestial Serpent threatening to swallow them up as he raged at the loss of his beloved Tellurian Serpent. A pale echo of her coiled between planets and stars—a reminder that they were all made from her body. If only he would remember.

Another panel depicted them in the time *before*. The time before her death. The time before time. In utter blackness, the paired serpents' undulating bodies knotted together to create the universe. One light with dark stars covering her scales, the other dark—her opposite in every way.

The light in the dark. The dark in the light.

The edges of a hidden door disappeared into their scales and stars, invisible, even to sharp eyes like Faolán's.

I stroked the dark serpent's head, drawing upon the magic around me so I didn't have to say the activation word out loud, and the panel glided open. It closed behind me as I entered an unlit passageway.

Even if I hadn't been able to see in the gloom, I knew this route so well, I could've followed it with my eyes shut.

Over the centuries, my office had always belonged to the previous ruler's Shadows. Officially, I was just Braea's representative in the Convocation, a council that helped give continuity and balance between the two monarchs. But everyone knew I was a spymaster. The identity of my Dawn counterpart was unknown, but we had a drop point should we ever need to share information for the good of the realm.

In all my years of doing this job, it had remained empty.

I wondered if they had their own network of secret passageways. There was no record of mine on any plans of the palace, so there was no way of knowing for sure when they'd been built or by whom. But I'd put my money on Tenebris's first spymaster designing them at the same time as the palace. They integrated too seamlessly, taking me to my rooms, to Braea's, and to various other strategic locations, including my destination today.

Ahead, a door awaited me in the gloom. I pressed the ring on my third finger into a tiny indent. The faint thrum of magic signalled the lock opening.

When I stepped through, the world shifted.

A secret lodestone. The only one, as far as I knew, and I'd scoured the palace, searching for weaknesses. No need for guards when our side could only be unlocked with the spymaster's ring.

The afternoon sky opened overhead, bathing the overgrown courtyard and its disused fountain in sunlight. This was where I met with my spy from Dawn, so we could be assured no one would spot us. She'd told me about this next meeting— one I wouldn't take part in so much as *observe*.

I'd reverse engineered my key and had one made for her that opened the door ahead of me, which led into Dawn, but only if I left it unlocked from this side. It had no effect on the door leading to Dusk.

I rarely entered their side, always conscious that the Night

Queen's Shadow being found there could be catastrophic for the relationship between our courts. Frankly, I wouldn't blame them if they considered it an act of war.

But this was too good a chance to miss. Caelus had made little to no effort to win the human queen's hand, and this meeting with King Lucius would surely explain what he'd *really* been up to. For the king to summon him the day he'd returned—it had to be important.

Occasional peepholes covered in spidersilk mesh opened to left and right, and I aimed for the one that peered into Lucius's study. He only used it for more formal occasions—he must've summoned Caelus here to remind him of his own importance.

Lifting the mesh flap that blended perfectly from the other side, I peered through. The king was already inside, sitting at his desk, rifling through papers with his lips pursed. In profile, I could see he slumped a little—his casual pose an odd contrast with the crown upon his head and the regal opulence surrounding him.

Whoever had designed the passages had used this particular peephole a lot, because they'd had a stone seat built into the wall. I'd placed a cushion here long ago, so I settled on that and waited.

No one ever spoke about how the main part of spying was waiting. For the right time. For someone to slip up. For a target to trust you. For the right information to come your way.

A lot of waiting.

But I didn't have to wait too long today, because Caelus was on time to the instant, knocking and entering as the orrery chimed. Classic Caelus—so perfect. So dull.

After bowing, he placed a file on the king's desk.

"It's all there, Your Majesty. Everything I learned in Albion."

My heart sank. Please, gods, tell me they were going to discuss the report and I hadn't come here for nothing.

Nodding, Lucius pulled the file closer and flicked through the pages inside.

Caelus shifted as the silence dragged on, yet he wasn't dismissed.

I smirked at Lucius's use of quiet. An old technique to assert power and encourage the other person to babble just to end their own discomfort.

It had the desired effect as Caelus went on, "We didn't trust another interim report after the last one was intercepted."

The coded message. "We" had to mean him or one of the sisters.

"And where's the part about...? Ah, *there*." Leaning forward, Lucius smoothed his hand over one of the pages, and I pressed against the wall, wishing I could see what he did.

His gaze flicked over the paper, his brow tight with focus until he gave a long exhale. "It's true, then."

I gritted my teeth. *What* was true? Eavesdropping was one thing, but stealing a report from the king—that was another matter. An impossible one.

"Yes, Your Majesty." Caelus bowed his head. "It seems it is possible to end the Sleep."

I froze. The enchanted Sleep that bound my queen to night and the king to day.

If someone managed to break the Sleep, they'd break the balance, too. Night and day gave the queen and king clear lines of what was hers and what was his. They had no choice but to relinquish control as they fell into Sleep.

The only time they were both awake was during an eclipse. A rarity, though we were due one soon. Those rare moments allowed them to meet for the first time in centuries—it was a time for them to appear together before their assembled courts, showing how they each trusted the other to handle the kingdom as they slept.

All a show, of course. Trust didn't come into it—they had no choice but to walk a tightrope, carefully balancing power. If the king broke the peace, the queen could destroy it come sunset and vice versa.

Sleep forced them—and their courts—to hand over the reins. Without it, both sides would vie for power until eventually petty clashes turned into full-scale war.

"If, that is, Your Majesty can get his hands on the relic."

Lucius didn't look up from the report, palms pressed together, fingertips touching his lips.

More silence, though the heavy toll of my heartbeat tried to break it.

End the Sleep. Fuck. *Fuck.*

"But..." Caelus rocked forward on his feet, frowning at Lucius. "Forgive me for speaking out of turn, but isn't the whole point of two courts and two rulers balance?"

"Balance?" Lucius laughed, though it was more sneering than amused. "You think *she* cares about balance? You think *she* wouldn't use this to her own ends if she got her claws into it? Caelus, you are but a child if you believe that."

I clenched my hands at the way he spoke of my queen.

He sighed, shaking his head as if explaining something sad to a youth who hadn't yet been broken by the world. "There is only balance while both sides remain true to it, and that woman hasn't been true to anything since she was a babe at her mother's teat. If we don't secure this thing, she will."

Caelus's throat bobbed. "Of course, Your Majesty. So... the plan is to secure it—to keep it safe."

"You've played your part well." Lucius smiled slowly. "However, my plan is my concern."

With a flick of his fingers, he dismissed Caelus. As the door clicked shut, Lucius sat back, teeth baring in a wide, wide smile.

I knew what that smile meant.

His plan was to use this relic, whatever it was, on himself alone. There would be no sharing. The Night Queen would still be subject to Sleep and Dawn's power would spread, unchecked.

A threat to me. To the queen. To everyone in Dusk.

And it would be my fault.

14
BASTIAN

The overheard meeting heavy in my ears, I stomped back to my office and wrote up a report of everything I'd heard.

By the time I'd finished, the sun was setting, so I stomped to the queen to brief her as she ate breakfast. I left out what I'd just heard—I needed time to process the information and verify it. There was no sense in worrying her if this turned out to be nothing more than myth and legend.

At last, I could turn towards our rooms. I needed sleep. Or to break something.

As if Hydra Ascendant wasn't enough of a problem, now I had Dawn to worry about.

Maybe it linked to unCavendish's plot. Though if he'd known, he would've asked Kat to get the note, and she hadn't mentioned it in her debriefing interview. Assuming she'd been honest with me.

Even a single court had different factions—Dusk and

Dawn alike. It could be unCavendish had worked for one that knew nothing of this rumoured artefact.

I'd know if Kat had trusted me from the start.

"Fuck."

If the king escaped Sleep...

I threw open the door to my rooms and slammed it in my wake. "Fuck!"

Light spilled from the living room door and inside I found Kat curled up on the settee, eyes wide.

"What're you still doing up?" Normally I managed to avoid being alone with her by returning from work so late.

She flinched at my tone, and maybe it was a little harsh, but my muscles were wound too tightly to speak any differently.

Eyebrows raised, she waved a book. "I hadn't realised the time. Is that a problem?"

I made a low sound as I headed to my bedroom.

She had access to the library now. She could read all she wanted. It was fine.

Yet, the closer I got to the door, the tighter my jaw ratcheted. Gripping the handle, I blasted out a breath. "You couldn't have just given me back the damn note, could you?"

It had chewed at me all the way back from the hidden courtyard. The message that had been hidden in my orrery—the one I'd risked leaving Riverton Palace for the night she'd robbed me—must have contained something about this thing that would cure the Sleep.

I shook my head, teeth grinding. "You might've screwed us all by burning it." And it would be my fault for letting her take it and not getting it back sooner. I'd been so confident I could lure her into returning the orrery—and I had. But not quickly enough.

Even now, when I turned and found her wide eyes on me, the green so rich I could pick out the colour from here, I was a fool for her.

A damn fool.

"I..." She shook her head, eyelids fluttering. "I didn't."

She'd lied.

My stomach sank. "So you gave it to him." Of course she did. She had been working for him.

That was worse. So much worse. UnCavendish might've had more information than I'd ever realised. I should've kept him alive for questioning.

But seeing him stand over Kat as she lay dying...

Madness had gripped me.

And because of that, because of a beautiful woman who'd been sent to seduce and spy on me, I risked failing my queen and court—my entire country.

"I suppose you told him about my other self, too."

She'd left that out of her report, but couldn't humans lie? I'd been so ready to believe her, I hadn't questioned the answers she'd given at her debriefing.

Stiffening as if suddenly understanding who I was referring to, she stood and tossed the book on the settee. "No, and also no." Her delicate nostrils flared and her eyes blazed like gemstones catching the light. "I may not have trusted you to keep my court safe, but by the time I got your orrery open, I didn't trust unCavendish either."

Her jaw worked side to side, and the hard pounding of my heart kept me quiet. I didn't trust myself to speak or move—I might erupt and say something I truly regretted. Even if she hadn't given the note to unCavendish, she... I... *we* might've doomed us all.

"You want the damn thing so badly. *Fine.*" She blasted past me, flinging the door open.

I sucked in long breaths in an attempt to regain control of myself. The thud and clatter of her crashing around her room echoed back along the corridor.

She'd been too much of a distraction in Lunden. I'd focused on her, telling myself it was work, when I should've paid more attention to the Dawn delegation.

She came stomping down the corridor and stopped in the doorway, mouth pinched. "I may have spied on you, Bastian, but I told you—it became real for me. I changed my mind." For a second, her voice wavered. "That was why I protected you in this." She shoved my orrery at me.

The contact with her skin rocked through me, our magic searing then sweet.

I held my breath against a reaction, but I couldn't tear my gaze away from the shudder that ran through her.

Instead of looking like she enjoyed it, she screwed her eyes shut and scowled, like she would burn the magic out of her body if she could. I knew it was a pleasurable feeling for her as it was for me, after the pain—I'd seen her pupils blow wide, the flush on her skin.

But tonight, it was as though *I* was the poison and not the antidote.

"I always kept what was yours—what was personal." Possibly oblivious to the fact our hands were still entwined, she glared up at me, yet her chin trembled. "I haven't told a soul about your second self, just like I'd never tell anyone about your nightmares."

Her words were a series of punches I hadn't braced for. She knew more about me than I'd truly appreciated, and when she'd recited her conversations with unCavendish, she hadn't mentioned any of it—not anything important.

The hard edges in me melted as my shoulders sank.

She might've taken the note, but that was as much my fault as hers. In truth, I was a hundred times more angry at myself than I could ever be at her.

She gave a shove before pulling her hand away.

I blinked down at my orrery, which was only half-closed. A screwed up piece of paper fell out.

The note.

She'd kept it, along with my secrets.

Of course she had.

"Shit. Kat, I'm—"

But when I looked up, she was gone.

15

KAT

Yesterday had been a doubly bad day. First my appointment with Elthea had been nothing more than a checkup, taking my temperature, listening to my heartbeat—that sort of thing. No cure.

Then... Well, whatever the fuck that had been last night.

Bastian truly thought so little of me that he believed I'd given unCavendish his secrets.

I stewed over the way he'd spoken to me as I got ready for another day trawling around jewellers. We would come back here for lunch, when I'd have to see Bastian for my antidote, but otherwise I could avoid him. As I smiled at that and slid a star-shaped comb into my hair, a knock sounded at the door to the suite.

Urien, the same dour guard who'd stopped me getting to Bastian's apartments back in Riverton Palace, appeared with a chest—*my* chest. How had that got here from Albion?

"There's a seal on it," he said as he set it down. "It can only be opened by the owner. No one's gone through it." With a nod, he slipped out just as brusquely.

Sure enough, magic hummed under my fingertips when I touched the lid, and it opened with ease. On top of my belongings sat a note with *Katherine* in handwriting that made my eyes sting.

"Ella!" I tore the seal apart and perched on the arm of the settee to read the letter.

My dear friend,

You certainly know how to make an exit, don't you?! Lords and Ladies, you almost gave me a damn heart attack. Kindly don't do that again.

Asher has told me what happened with the mead and "Cavendish." I feel sick for you and for myself. But I shouldn't write too much in here, just in case it falls into the wrong hands. Asher assures me no one else will be able to open this chest, but I'm not sure how much I trust in fae magic.

(As an aside, Perry trusts in it—and him—implicitly. I wonder why. Fairly sure you can picture my expression right now!)

Anyway, I'm being hurried along so this can be sealed and collected. I packed up your things, so you don't need to worry that anyone else went through them. I included all your clothes (yes, the lingerie too), just in case...

(Pulling a highly innocent face right now, just so you know.)

By the time you get this, I'm sure you'll be all healed and well. I hope you're enjoying all Elfhame has to offer—must say I envy you something chronic.

But most of all, I want to give you the world's biggest hug. Don't forget me while you're swanning around Tenebris-Luminis!

All my love,

Ella

x

My eyes were tear-filled by the end. At her thoughtfulness and from longing for one of her hugs. Instead I had to hug the note to my chest and laugh at the ridiculous idea that I could forget about her.

When I rummaged through the chest, I found all my clothes and jewellery, my pistol, and, at the bottom, the box that I'd kept under my bed. It was still locked, the keys tucked into a pocket in the lining of the chest.

Buoyed by the letter, I washed. When I emerged from the bathroom, I found a bouquet of yellow roses in the vase. Every few days, a new bouquet appeared. Until today, they'd always been clean, crisp white. This splash of colour was welcome, and I couldn't help smiling at them as I dressed, ready for another day trawling around jewellery shops.

Today I would get some information about unCavendish. If not for me, then for Ella.

B<small>UT</small> R<small>OSE HAD OTHER IDEAS</small>—<small>WE</small> had to make another stop first.

"Sorry. It won't take long." She winced as she led me along a narrow road. "Bastian was annoyed I hadn't already taken you already."

Shooting her a look, I almost forgot about hiding my frustration at this interruption to my plan. "Did you tell him about the necklace?"

"No." Her mouth twisted. "He didn't ask and I didn't volunteer the information."

I didn't miss what she left unspoken. Not saying something and lying outright were two different things. For Rose there was a line between them.

But she had kept my secret from Bastian, her employer and friend.

Maybe she could be trusted, even if I couldn't expect her to lie for me. Ella's letter had been a reminder of how good it felt to have someone to confide in.

"Here we are," she announced as we reached one of the city's tall marble spires. She led me inside.

Instead of an enclosed entrance hall, the tower was hollow right to the roof, with shops hugging the outer walls. Landings marked every floor, and a small child peered down between a balustrade a few storeys up.

Garlands of flowers and dried herbs criss-crossed the space along with shafts of light that lit up motes of dust. It smelled floral and musky—oddly comforting, like one of Ella's concoctions.

I ached with the wish that she were here. I had so much to tell her. On my bedside table sat a long, long letter to her, and

I was still only halfway through describing everything I'd seen.

"Come on," Rose called, already halfway up the staircase.

I hurried after her, clutching the magic around me. *Quiet. Small. Contained.*

Off the landing, three doors led to elegant shops with equally elegant signs. A perfumer. A leatherworker. A dressmaker.

"Not the best one in town," Rose whispered as we passed. "I'll take you to her later, so you can get something for the queen's ball."

The ball in my honour. I didn't know whether to grimace at the attention it would draw to me or look forward to the opportunity to dig into unCavendish.

Right now, though I huffed, barely keeping up with Rose's long strides as she led us up one staircase after another, not the slightest bit out of breath.

"Here we are." Bright smile in place, she led me into a store whose sign showed a rearing stag. I gave a second glance before I passed beneath it, something about the style familiar.

Inside, various stands held bows of all shapes and sizes. Long and short. Recurved. From dark wood to a material so pale, it might've been bone. One even looked like it was made from a silvery metal.

Along the curving outside wall hung dozens, maybe even hundreds of arrows with fletchings in a rainbow of colours. The air hummed with magic, carrying the scent of linseed and cedar.

"Bastian said you need a bow of your own," she said as she ushered me towards the counter, where a small fae with pale grey hair waited.

"Then you've come to the right place," the fae added,

spreading her hands. I might've wondered whether she belonged to Dusk or Dawn, but now she met my gaze and her eyes...

Black and pupilless, pricked with starry lights. She had to be Dusk.

Rose grinned and gestured around the shop. "They *are* the best bowyer in Elfhame."

The fae's serene expression flashed into a brief smile at Rose. It felt like a reward and I found myself wishing to be on the receiving end. "Now, let's see..." Eyeing me, they stepped out from behind the counter and produced a tape measure. Hooking the end under their toe, they unspooled it and measured my height. Next, they measured my arm span and asked how strong I was.

Gaze turning distant, they bustled towards a rack. "How's your aim?"

"Uh. Good for a human?"

Rose cleared her throat. "Bastian was impressed, so it's excellent. Even amongst fae." At my questioning glance, she shrugged. "He isn't one for exaggeration."

A lick of warmth unfurled in me.

"Try this." Not turning from the rack, the bowyer passed me a recurve bow a little longer than the one I'd used in the practice yard. "Just draw it."

I obeyed and they cast that starry gaze across me. "Mmm." Nodding, they took it back. "I have just the thing." They turned from the rack with a shorter recurve in a deep, rust-coloured wood—yew, perhaps. "This is your bow."

"Don't you want me to draw it first?"

"You can if you like." They shrugged, a faint grin pulling at the corner of their mouth. "But I've been doing this a long time. I know it's the one for you." They held it out with both hands.

It didn't seem a very scientific way of going about weapon selection. But when my fingers closed around the bow, a deep hum resonated through my hands as though its magic woke and reached for me.

The bowyer raised their eyebrows and gave me the same smile they'd given Rose earlier. "See?"

The hum felt warm and right, like approval. I gave it an experimental draw. Full extension easily but not too easily. It gave a little less feedback than the bow from the practice yard. I'd be able to fire this for a long time before growing tired. Its resonance infused me, making me stand taller, feel somehow fuller.

"I... I do."

"It's almost as though I know what I'm doing!" They chuckled and waved off my attempted apologies. "This one has been here a long while waiting for the right person. Too short for most of us, see?"

True enough, they were the shortest fae I'd seen, standing perhaps an inch taller than me.

"I'm only halfborn—my father was human. But I'm no archer. Ironically." When they grinned, their teeth weren't as sharp as Bastian's or Rose's. "This wood came from The Great Yew when it was struck by lightning. I only had a limited amount to work with, hence the size. But I knew one day it would find its hand, and here you are."

Their eyes shone with pleasure, like they'd solved a particularly tricky puzzle that had been plaguing them a long time.

Rose peered at the bow, eyebrows raised. "And you don't mind selling such sacred wood to a human?"

The bowyer snorted. "It chose her. It's going exactly where it wishes."

The Great Yew?

I gave Rose a questioning look, but she shook her head. "I'll show you later."

The bowyer helped me choose arrows fletched with barn owl feathers for silence. "The recurve makes that bow a bit louder than a longbow, but I'll add an enchantment for you—keep it quiet as the grave."

They showed me how to loosen the string for transport by touching it in a specific place and saying *asgal*.

As they wrapped the bow and a few dozen arrows and helped Rose pick some new arrows, I wandered along the glass-topped cabinets that formed the counter. As well as bows, they made pistols and I found a small boot pistol that matched mine—its smaller sister. I decided to buy that, too, since it would be easy to hide.

I pointed at the golden stag decorating the butt. Like the sign over the door. No wonder it had felt familiar. "Is this a common symbol for fae to use on their pistols?"

"That is *my* maker's mark." They tapped a bow behind the counter. A stag decorated its grip, and when I scanned the rack behind me, I spotted more stags—some in brass close to the tip, antlers holding the string in place, others on the grip or decorating the bow's limbs. "You recognise it, don't you?"

"I have a full-size version of that pistol. It's kept me alive on a few occasions."

"Ah, yes." They opened the cabinet and presented the boot pistol. "I made its pair at the same time, but a trader insisted on splitting them and taking it to a rich client of his south of the border. There was a sister piece, too, with a tempered steel stag."

I huffed a laugh, weighing the pistol. "That rich client was my father, and the second pistol went to my sister. I always wondered who made them. And now I know." Warmth filled my chest.

Maybe it was that, maybe it just the fact I had weapons now, but as we left the tower and stepped into the sunshine, the city felt a little less dangerous and a little more like a place I could call home, even if only for a while.

16

KAT

At the next shop, a slender man from Dawn gave us no joy, but at the one after that, when we showed the jeweller the necklace, her eyes widened a fraction. *Recognition.*

"I didn't make it." She shook her head and started rearranging rings in a cabinet.

True, none of the other jewellery here looked like the pearlwort necklace, and she couldn't tell a direct lie. But I'd stake my life she knew more.

"Any idea who did?" I kept it casual, like it didn't matter, even though it burned in me.

"I can't help you."

"Really? Because it's the strangest thing... but when you first saw this necklace, it *seemed* an awful lot like you recognised it." I smiled sweetly, cocking my head.

At my side, Rose straightened and I felt her glance this way.

The fae drew her eyebrows together, expression hardening

as she looked up from fussing over the rings. "I can't help you. Kindly leave."

For a beat, I held her eye. But Bastian's warning that his power was diminished by day came back to me. If the jeweller was of Dusk, she would help me. If this was nighttime, Rose might be able to order her to answer, though I wasn't sure how much of Bastian's sway she held as his employee.

Telling Bastian about my work was out of the question. Last night he'd made it clear he didn't trust me, and he'd proved that he couldn't be trusted. If he found out I was after unCavendish, he'd say it was unsafe and make Rose put a stop to it.

Biting back a sigh, I turned away, Rose's relief palpable as her shoulders inched down.

"Sorry," she muttered as we stepped outside. "That's Dawn for you."

Was it that? Or did the jeweller have a reason to hide the maker and stop me following the trail back to unCavendish's master?

We turned onto the street and with a gasp, I stopped short, a foot away from bumping into someone. I snatched at the poison in me and tried my best to shove it down. *Small. Stay small.*

"Katherine!" Hair glinting in the sunshine, Caelus beamed like he was genuinely pleased to see me.

My throat did something odd as *then* and *now* collided, and for a second I couldn't speak. "Lord Caelus. I thought you were still in Lunden."

"I just got back. But it seems you've forgotten me in my absence. What did I tell you about calling me by my name?"

"Ah, yes." In my surprise, I'd slipped into formality. "Sorry, *Caelus.*"

"Much better." He smiled, throwing Rose a quick glance.

Clearing her throat, she turned and busied herself looking in the window of the shop we'd just left.

He bent closer and went on more quietly, "I hope your belongings made it to you safely."

"How did you...?"

"Who do you think brought them here? Asher and your friend Ella agreed to it as long as they got to pack and lock the chest."

Asher wasn't back in the city yet, so I assumed it had been magically transported. "Then, *thank you*."

"Oh, no." Caelus raised his hand as if to block my gratitude. His mouth twisted to one side as his gaze slid away. "I did it by way of apology. After you... left, I found out about your uncle. I'm so sorry, Katherine. I believed you coming to my rooms was something you'd agreed to. I never would have..."

The rest of his sentence faded beyond the rushing in my ears. I squeezed my fingers and shoved away the image of Uncle Rufus, the feel of his hand around my throat.

Things here and now. The warm sunshine. The scent of baking—sweet and spiced with cinnamon and mace. Finger-nails digging into my palms, muted by the gloves.

I could think of that night purely in words. I didn't have to relive it.

When Uncle Rufus had dragged me through the halls of Riverton Palace, Caelus had believed I was going to him will-ingly. I'd been so knocked off course by the memories that night had unearthed, I'd never thought of his part in it for a second.

For all the city held new threats, at least I was safe from my uncle.

Refocused, I threw Caelus a quick smile. "I'm grateful for

your apology and explanation. My uncle is... a determined man. I'm not surprised he lied in an attempt to win your favour." It was the least he would do.

"I feel..." He shook his head. "Well, not as bad as you must've. He told me Marwood got wind of the plan and that was why you hadn't been able to attend. When I saw you with him at the party, my offer was meant to be an olive branch to show I wasn't trying to tear the two of you apart."

My head spun at the odd way fae relationships worked. My skin burned too, like it was suddenly aware of the fact he'd seen me riding Bastian's fingers to mind-shattering climax.

Knees together—you're not a whore. The words whispered in my mind, my father and my uncle's voices joined in a grotesque chorus.

I swallowed and managed a bitter little smile. "No need to worry about that—we managed it well enough ourselves."

He arched an eyebrow. "You're no longer with him?"

I couldn't bring myself to speak and instead gave the smallest shake of my head.

"Well, that's a shame." The lilt in his voice sounded anything but disappointed.

"I thought fae couldn't lie?"

"I meant for *him*." His smiled gentled as he took me in. "And perhaps for you. Though hopefully not for me." He angled his head a touch, a question there that I chose not to answer.

Perhaps I should tell him about Robin—scare him off. But Bastian's warnings to, essentially, not tell anyone anything chimed in my head.

"I always did like that necklace." It was only when his gaze rested on it that I realised I was pulling on it.

Maybe I could get him to help me find its maker. He might

recognise the style and be able to point me in the right direction. If I could get him to ask for me, the Dawn jewellers would be more likely to speak to him. He was clearly still attracted to me, and I wasn't above using that to my advantage.

Women's weapons. We had to use what we could.

I gave a half smile, letting my gloved fingertips stroke my collarbone. "And here I thought it was *me* you liked."

His sky blue eyes followed the gesture, pupils expanding. "I liked it even before I saw you wearing it."

I drew in a long breath, barely controlling my reaction. He'd seen it before unCavendish had given it to me. Was *he* behind the changeling? But, no, if that was the case he'd be more careful about slipping up.

How to poke without being too obvious, though? I stalled by giving him a flirtatious look from beneath my lashes.

"Looking for jewellery?" A man's voice behind me, smooth and confident.

Caelus's eyes widened and he took a step back, inclining his head.

When I turned, I understood.

Prince Cyrus, teeth brilliant white, golden hair perfectly tousled around his face, eased into the spot beside me. "But such a pretty lady has no need of further adornment."

Caelus muttered a brief goodbye, and my heart sank at losing this opportunity to ask about the necklace.

Yet a prince stood before me, so I bowed. "Your Highness."

"Oh, no, we don't do that here, Katherine." He wrinkled his nose. "Perhaps if you were presented to me more formally, but we're not such sticklers for etiquette as I hear your people are." He cast his gaze over the jeweller's window display, eyes half closed. "Doing a spot of shopping?"

"I wanted something new for a ball." It was easy to shrug

and lie—my name didn't feel like a threat as it had coming from his father. it made sense that he knew who I was, either from the rumours about Bastian arriving with me or from the king.

"Ah, but you're being humble." He chuckled. "This isn't just *any* ball—you're the guest of honour."

Behind the smile, my teeth were gritted. "Her Majesty has paid me a great compliment. I'm sure I don't deserve it."

"I'm sure you must've done something most impressive."

Rose gave me a meaningful look. "We have that appointment."

"Well, I can't have two such lovely ladies late on my account." The prince clutched his chest. "You must allow me to walk you to this 'appointment,' whatever it is."

"It isn't far, you don't need to—"

"I insist." For a second his easy smile hardened, but it was gone so quickly, I questioned whether I'd seen it. He gestured along the street, and Rose and I had little chance but to fall in at his side. He ducked a little closer and raised an eyebrow. "After all, it will give me the opportunity to secure a dance with the woman of the hour."

"A... a dance?" He couldn't mean—

"At the ball in your honour? Or have you forgotten already? I heard you'd been ill, but I didn't realise you'd taken a knock to the head." He chuckled at his own joke, and I forced out a faint laugh.

"I hadn't realised members of your court would be there." That had to be why Bastian had seemed so agitated when he'd told me about it—the dangers of mixing with Dawn.

Yet, they would also bring opportunities. Perhaps Caelus would be there, too.

"Oh yes"—he waved at a man across the street, flashing a

charming smile—"Her Majesty has extended an invitation to us. She's holding it in the shared ballroom. I'm sure you know all about lodestones by now. Will you grace me with a dance, then?"

"I'm..." I couldn't. Not when touching him would kill him. Fairly sure that went far, *far* beyond a diplomatic incident and into all out war. "I'm afraid I'm not able to dance at the moment. My illness, you see."

"Well, that's a shame. We would've looked quite spectacular on the dance floor together." The way he ran his hand through his hair, preening, told me plenty about how to stay in his good books.

"I'm sure Your Highness will look spectacular on the dance floor with or without me." I forced out the honeyed words. If he thought me nothing more than a charming human aristocrat, that would keep me safe.

He made a low, approving sound and straightened, giving me a sidelong glance. "Oh, I *like* you. You can stay around forever if you're going to compliment me like that."

Rose cleared her throat. "We're here."

We stood outside a glass-fronted shop. In the window stood a gown that threatened to make me keel over as it stole my breath so thoroughly. Its glittering skirts seemed to shift colour as I watched, changing from deep purple-black to darkest blue to blackened gold.

"Hmph. Another waste of time." The prince leant towards us and put on a playful tone as he went on, "I'd prefer it if you both came in nothing at all. I'm sure *everyone* would."

He winked dramatically, and I chuckled. Rose made a similar sound—just as forced as mine.

"Ah, but I must be off. Things to see, people to do." He laughed like he had an audience, though this was a street dominated by Dusk and most people only glanced at him as they got on with their days. "I look forward to seeing you at the ball, though I'm not sure how I'll survive until then without your charming company, dearest Rose, loveliest Katherine." He placed his hand over his heart as he backed away.

As I smiled and waved, out the corner of my mouth I asked, "Is he always like that?"

Rose turned and pushed the shop door open with a deep sigh. "Yes. He'll screw anything that moves. Total idiot."

"Who's a total idiot?" As I entered, a young woman with white hair and amber complexion looked up from an embroidery hoop. Her ears were rounded like mine, but that white hair had to be a fae mark, betraying her magic.

Rose closed the door and glanced around the shop. "Cyrus."

"Oh. Yes." The young woman nodded. "*Total idiot.*"

Probably *not* behind unCavendish, then.

As I moved further into the shop, I froze. Next to her chair stood a white hound.

Its eyes burned with red flame. Its ears, paws, and tail, too.

I'd only ever heard of such creatures in stories—the terrifying kind where the Wild Hunt chased unwary souls across eternity, aided by their hunting hounds.

But that flaming tail wagged as it trotted up to Rose and shoved its head under her hand. "Fine, yes, scritches for you. Sorry, I'm neglecting my human duties too. Ari, this is Kat. Kat —Ari. Ariadne, if you're feeling fancy."

Ari's smile had dimmed, but she came and greeted Rose with a hug. "Is this...?"

"Yep. *That* Kat."

"Oh." Ari's dark eyes widened as she surveyed me, her fingers knotting together. "Nice to meet you."

The hound sat, looking up at me with those fiery eyes.

"Don't mind Fluffy." Rose gave me a reassuring nod. "She's such a softy, she was kicked out of the Wild Hunt."

Fluffy? I arched an eyebrow at the hound, whose gaze became twice as beseeching.

"That isn't what happened," Ari muttered.

But Rose shrugged off her objection. "Let her give you a sniff, and she'll be your best friend in no time."

I did as instructed, finding Fluffy's nose was damp, like any other dog's. Ari whispered something to Rose while I stroked Fluffy, setting her tail wagging in double time. Her flames didn't burn.

"Ari wants to know if you'll join us for tea later."

Ariadne gave a shy smile.

"And by 'tea'"—Rose arched an eyebrow—"I'm assuming she means the alcoholic concoctions we make up with fae spirits and fruit juice and so on. It's my new favourite thing."

"I, uh..."

Ari's look matched the beseeching one Fluffy had given me.

I chuckled. "Of course. I'd love to." Even if I couldn't get drunk, Rose was starting to feel like she could become a friend rather than just a bodyguard. Besides, I'd take any excuse to avoid Bastian.

"Good," Ari sighed like she'd been afraid I was going to say no. "Now, dresses for the ball." Stroking her lower lip, she surveyed me and nodded. "I have just the thing."

17

KAT

The next morning, it wasn't Bastian who walked me down to the training yard but Faolán. Thank the gods. I was still avoiding Bastian. Yesterday I'd only lingered to get my antidote before making an excuse to go to my room. He'd muttered something and seemed set to say more, but I didn't want to hear it.

And today, my head pounded too much to even think about it.

"You know, I won't tell Bastian if we skip training today—start tomorrow. You could go and catch some sleep. I'm sure Rose wouldn't mind." I gave Faolán a hopeful look.

He looked down at me out the corner of his eye. "This wouldn't have anything to do with you staying up to an ungodly hour with my wife and Ariadne, would it?"

I'd had a nice time with Rose and Ari. That *nice time* might've involved a few of Rose's concoctions. Turned out fae drinks infused with magic still had an effect on me. I even managed to pocket some *arianmêl*—there was no telling when that might prove useful.

Strategising aside, I had laughed, as Faolán said, and that wasn't only down to magical fae alcohol. Rose and Faolán's home was cosy and simple, cluttered with cushions and little carved knick-knacks that spoke of a happy life. Sure, there were a few more knives slotted in the umbrella rack than I'd expect in the average home, but Faolán seemed the type to want to be prepared.

Although I'd let Rose and Ari speak the most—telling me about their childhood growing up together in a small Albionic town near the border—I'd shared a little about myself. I hadn't told them about Lunden and me and Bastian and they hadn't asked, but it was the closest I'd come to relaxing since waking in the Hall of Healing.

Even so, Ari had all too casually dropped into conversation the fact male fae took "precautions" to prevent unwanted pregnancy. Rose had shifted uncomfortably, and I'd leapt up to fetched more drinks. I wasn't going to be fucking anyone any time soon. I was only taking the preventative because it eased my periods.

As cosy as his home was, Faolán raised an eyebrow when I asked for leniency. "Luckily, enemies are kind enough to only attack when you're well-rested and at peak health."

I groaned, hating him for being right. "Rose said you were gruff, but she didn't say anything about merciless."

"Hmm." The corner of his mouth twitched. "I have plenty of mercy. Just not when the suffering is self-inflicted." He called over one of the fae lights bobbing through the yard, caught it in his palm, and mashed it into the ball. "Especially not when Bastian will inflict even more suffering on me for not doing my job."

So training it was. I tried to hit the balls as he threw them. Once I was even successful.

After, for when I didn't want to kill, he took me through some basic self-defence, which he summarised as "go for the soft bits, then it doesn't matter how strong you are."

Eyes. Ears. Nose. Groin. Throat. Knees. Instep. Not all soft, but places that hurt and would send an attacker reeling—hopefully long enough for me to escape.

As Faolán dodged my attempt to stamp on his foot, I reminded myself that at least I was better at archery than self-defence... or magic.

The past couple of days, Rose had *tried* to teach me, explaining how she turned inward and found it.

But when *I* turned inward, I couldn't find any magic, only my own thoughts. Despite my hard work and her patience, the whole session had been pointless.

Like my poison, magic was something that had been done to me and now lingered, not something I could use.

As Faolán and I finished in the training yard, I wasn't sure if the sweat coating my skin was down to the hard work or my hangover. Why didn't fae, in creating their magically infused alcohol, also make it so it didn't make you feel so shit the next day? Maybe they didn't suffer from anything so mundane as hangovers.

But I would be able to enjoy regular alcohol again soon. On my return to Bastian's rooms, a message waited from Elthea, summoning me for another appointment. So soon after that checkup—this had to be a cure or at least progress towards one.

That hope still buzzed through me later as I squared my shoulders and left Dusk's side of the palace with Rose. She walked me to the Hall of Healing, but even if she hadn't, it felt safer on the streets with the yew bow on my back and the boot pistol at my thigh. I waved her off to wait for me at Ariadne's shop and headed inside.

ELTHEA SAT me in the sparse treatment room I'd woken up in. A thin mask of the same material as the gloves she wore around me covered her nose and mouth. But I knew her well enough by now to know she didn't smile in greeting.

"I have a theory." Straight to it, no niceties.

It was actually refreshing in a way. I knew where I stood with Elthea. I was her patient. That was all. A set of notes in her neat book, a lump of matter to be theorised about.

And she was my healer. The person who could rid me of this accident of magic that left me poisoned and poisonous.

I canted my head when she said nothing more. "Does that theory lead to a cure?"

"If I'm right, yes. I need to know how this affects your body." She nodded at the purple stain on my fingers. Today it had receded to barely lick at the first set of knuckles.

"How do we find out?"

"I need to see."

I bit back an impatient sigh. "Meaning?"

She turned a pointed glance to the low table beside the bed. An array of sharp instruments gleamed upon its surface and a chill as cold as steel whispered through me.

"You need to... cut me open?" I swallowed. I would do it. No doubts there. I would do anything. But that didn't dull the fear.

"That isn't how I would put it, but I suppose in a layperson's terms, yes." She rolled her eyes and motioned for me to place my hands on the bed. "Ready?"

"Aren't you going to... knock me out or something?"

She strapped my wrist to the bed. "That will stop you from moving."

"That wasn't my concern."

"It's better if you're awake so you can tell me what you're feeling. I need to understand how the poison travels through you. If your nerves are the problem, that's different from if it's your veins."

"And you can't tell that with your magic?"

"Not clearly enough. I need to apply this dye"—she held up a small vial of silver liquid—"and see how it travels through your body."

"Fine. Do it."

She acknowledged me with a soft sound as she turned to her tray of blades. "I'd recommend lying down. My magic will prevent you dying from blood loss, but you'll probably feel lightheaded."

"Comforting."

She selected a small scalpel and I lay back. I didn't want to look too closely at the other blades or the strange little clamps.

"Do *try* to stay awake," she said, as though me passing out would be a terrible inconvenience to her.

She ran a gloved hand over my hand and the vibration of magic in the air intensified. "That should numb some of the pain."

Should. Really comforting.

I watched as she pressed the scalpel to my forefinger and blood welled. The pain streaked through me an instant later. My nerves told me to pull away, but I held still, not even straining against the straps.

I'd endured worse.

Long, slow breaths got me through the incision from

fingertip to palm, keeping the worst of the nausea at bay. More magic hummed against my skin, and I dimly registered that there wasn't as much blood as I might've expected, though it felt like I watched from the other side of the room.

She took one of the tiny clamps and used it to hold the cut open.

I caught a glimpse of something yellow and faintly lumpy and something else red and stringy. That was when I decided to lie back and look at the vaulted ceiling.

The pain was bad though not as bad as I might've expected, but I could *feel* her poking around and pulling. At one point, I glanced down and found that she'd peeled the skin of my finger back completely.

Nausea lurched through me.

"There's a bucket on your left."

I barely grabbed it in time to throw my guts up.

Panting, I collapsed back onto the bed and tried not to think about what'd I'd just seen or the continued prodding *inside* my body.

"There. Now we're ready to begin."

"You haven't even started?"

Above her mask, her eyes barely crinkled. "That was just the preparation. Now for the experiment."

I stared up at the ceiling.

This wasn't me. Not my hand. I wasn't here.

It would be fine. Cutting me open had to be the worst part.

Flaying you alive.

I shoved the thought away.

Out the corner of my eye, I caught a flash of silver. The vial of dye. Just a couple of drops and—

My whole body went rigid. The blood roared in my ears.

Every instinct yanked on my arm, screeching that this *was* me and that I needed to get away.

Pain scraped along my nerves like a rusted razor.

I gritted my teeth as a scream scratched at my voice box, aching to be let out. Tears gathered at the corners of my eyes. I tried to breathe—in out, in out, calm and relaxed. Breathe through the pain.

But it was impossible.

"Interesting. Just a little more." I caught her voice between the thundering of my heart.

I wanted to tell her I couldn't take any more, but I had no command over my mouth or my grinding teeth. It was this shaking tension or a terrible scream. There was nothing else.

Over soon. Over soon.

Sentences withered in my mind. There were only those two words.

Over soon. Over soon.

"I wonder..."

Something lanced up my arm, searing and bright, making everything else dim in comparison.

Just breathe. Keep breathing.

Endure.

18

KAT

"There," she said at last.

I blinked in that bright and terrible light and promptly threw my guts up. Bile and blood coated my tongue where I'd bitten my lip so hard.

Somehow, I got it all in the bucket, and as breaths heaved through me, I realised my arm was free of the straps. Not a mark on my fingers, save for the purple stain.

But I could still see my skin pulled back, nerves and veins exposed. With a gasp, I flinched from the cruel trick my mind played on me. Some things were best forgotten.

Calm as ever, mask gone, Elthea handed me a glass of water. She cocked her head as I gulped it down and washed away the mingled bitter and coppery flavours. "Did that hurt?"

"Of course it bloody hurt." I clenched and unclenched my trembling fist. No pain. Truly, no sign of what she'd done. If not for her question, it was like I'd imagined the whole thing.

She scribbled in her notebook. "Then why didn't you cry out?"

I opened my mouth, then closed it when I found my spinning mind had no answer. "Because... Because..."

Obedient. Dutiful. Silent.

"You just pulled a face." Her pen hovered over the page. "What are you thinking?"

"I was taught to keep quiet."

"Hmm. By who?"

"My father." I cradled the glass against my chest and shut my eyes against the room's aching brightness. He'd told me to be quiet. And my mother had modelled it perfectly—the silent ghost in her own house.

"Why? Were you a noisy child?"

"No. Not at all." Even in the time before Avice had come along, I hadn't been a noisy child. I'd... behaved.

"So... why?"

Sipping my water delayed having to answer, but still didn't give me one. "I don't know. So I wouldn't disturb others?"

"Do you have things to say that are disturbing?"

"Probably."

She narrowed her eyes at me, head tilting again. "So you held in the sound of your pain for... my sake? And for the people in the halls outside?"

I shifted, not liking how her questions made me feel foolish or how raw my nerves were in the wake of her test. "I... I suppose so."

Bastian's warnings swam into my consciousness, but too late. I'd already given away so much.

"Hmm. Did it serve you to keep quiet?"

I had no answer.

"Or did your silence just serve others and their comfort?"

I gulped the rest of the water, trying to ignore the way her words crept over my skin like a horrible realisation. The bright lights stung my eyes and kept my stomach tight, like my body expected her to strap me down for more. "Are we finished here?"

"Ah, yes." She sat back, tucking her notebook in her pocket. "I have the data I required. Unfortunately, it means my theory was incorrect. However, there will be more theories..." She patted the pocket. "Especially with what I was able to observe. Fascinating stuff. I've never seen a case like yours." She smiled, and this time it did reach her eyes.

That only made it worse.

My head spun as I rose from the bed and grabbed my coat, but I refused to let that slow me down. I needed to get out of here. Away from the bed, the bright lights, the tray full of bloody instruments, and, most of all, away from Elthea.

I caught sight of myself in the door's mirrored glass. Pale and ashen—I looked like death. And when I put out my hand to open the door, I flinched at the sight of my fingers, seeing the nerves and bare bone overlaid on the purple skin.

It's not real. They aren't like that. She healed me.

Steadying myself on the wall, I nudged the door open with my elbow instead, but her parting words followed me: "I'll send for you when I have a new theory."

What was she going to do next? Did she understand I wasn't fae? What might be normal for them could kill me.

More bile licked my throat as I hurried across the pillared entrance hall. Head down, I tugged on my coat and gloves.

Outside, the overcast day didn't pierce my eyes like the cold light of Elthea's treatment room. Like every other part of me, my breaths shook, steaming. It had grown suddenly chilly, as though autumn had arrived overnight.

I needed to get back to Rose and tell her what Elthea had done. It couldn't be normal—couldn't be all right.

Except then she would tell Bastian, and Bastian... Well, he'd broken a man's nose because he'd questioned me eating cake. He might kill Elthea. I couldn't risk it. Not when she was my only hope of a cure.

I had to keep this a secret. And that meant I couldn't return to Rose trembling and pale, this close to hyperventilating.

But my heart was still pounding and I couldn't control my heaving chest, not as so many people watched me charge by.

I needed to get away. I needed somewhere safe.

Help, my mind cried. *Help.*

I held onto my breath and that let me hold on to a semblance of control, but both were only temporary.

Both would have to burst soon.

I aimed for a park, but as my eyes burned, I realised it was too far—I wouldn't make it that long.

A quiet side street opened up. Its houses had basement floors with staircases leading down.

Quiet, dark, small, they beckoned me.

I stumbled down the nearest one and found a spot between the stone steps and the house, invisible from the road.

Wedging myself in, curled tight and small, it felt like the stone embraced me. I crossed my arms over my knees and sobbed in silence.

Only the gods knew how long I stayed there, but it was enough time to grow chilled and for tears to soak my coat sleeves. I still couldn't look at my hands without being reminded of everything Elthea had done, but I could stand and dry my cheeks, and that was enough.

I kept my head bowed as I took a circuitous route to meet Rose, keeping my bearings using the tower with the bowyer's shop in it.

I managed a smile when I walked into Ariadne's atelier, though I thought it might break me.

Even worse, Rose was already on her feet. "I was just about to come looking for you. I was worried—you've been ages."

"Oh, it just took longer than expected." I waved her off, clinging to my fake smile. "Elthea has some treatments to try now, so we're making progress, but it means my appointments might take longer."

"Treatments?" A wide smile, not even remotely fake, spread over her face. "That's great!"

"Isn't it?"

And it was great. I could almost convince myself.

All part of my plan.

Find out who was behind unCavendish, get rid of the poison and my need for Bastian, then go home.

This was just another thing I had to endure in the meantime.

19
BASTIAN

"Who's the best cryptographer these days?"

Brynan grinned up at me from his desk. "Come on. Surely you know that."

After more than a week of trying to work out the note's contents myself, I wasn't in the mood. I pinched the bridge of my nose but it did nothing to dull the thud of my headache. "Things might've changed while I was away. Just tell me."

"Sorry, Bastian. I was just—"

"It's fine." I patted his shoulder. "The best cryptographer?"

"It's my partner."

"Gael. Of course."

"That's why I was—"

The knock pounding at the door could only be the guards.

We exchanged small frowns.

"Enter."

Led by Urien, a dozen guards filed in and at their centre—

"Elthea? What brings you to Dusk?"

"I'm sorry, Bastian." Urien shot her a glare. "She said she needed to see you at once—something relating to her patient."

Kat. I held perfectly still, but something gripped my throat. "Oh?" I raised my eyebrows like this was only faintly interesting, but inside I burned with a dozen questions. Was she all right? Where was she? What had happened?

"It's a matter of some delicacy. Perhaps your office?" She raised an eyebrow. "I *assume* the queen's spymaster would have wards to ensure privacy."

"I have no such title." Not officially, anyway. I gave her a smooth smile. "But no one can hear what's said inside." I dismissed the guards to wait in the hall and ushered Elthea inside.

"Oh, there's one more joining us," she said as I went to close the door.

"Inviting people to my offices now?"

"This one, I don't think you'll mind." Her eyes glinted as she tilted her head.

Out in Brynan's office, the door opened and a familiar voice drifted through, making my stomach flip. "I had an odd message asking me to come here." I could hear Kat's hesitancy.

"Send her through," Elthea called.

Presumptuous.

Kat didn't so much as glance at me as she stopped in the doorway, pale, her attention fixed on Elthea. She'd largely avoided me since giving back the note. It was probably the universe paying me back.

Once we were all settled, the door shut and thus silenced, Elthea took a deep breath and interlaced her fingers in her lap. "I'm calling in the favour you promised me in payment for saving your human."

Kat's eyes flicked to me for an instant, but otherwise she

kept her surprise hidden. I could've kissed her for not revealing to Elthea that she didn't know.

Yet, inside, I winced. I never intended for her to find out all I'd done in desperation to save her life. Not this, but especially not the deal with her husband—I didn't want to humiliate her.

"I see. Well, I hope it's something good." I spread my hands, inviting Elthea to explain.

"I need you to retrieve an item for me. A box."

I waited, but she said nothing more. That couldn't be it.

"Is that all?" Kat crossed her arms, seeming to shrink under Elthea's gaze. "Why don't you get it yourself? Why waste a favour on something so petty?"

Elthea pursed her lips. "I can't leave the city. As our most powerful healer, I must stay close to my king." She glanced at me. "And the Night Queen, of course."

"*Of course.*" I smiled like she hadn't added Braea as an afterthought.

"And why do I need to be aware of this errand?" The look Kat shot me could've melted steel.

"It's a few days' travel, so you'll need to accompany the Serpent." Elthea fingered her pocket. "Think of it as a chance to see more of Elfhame."

Kat had been pale when she'd arrived, but now all colour leached from her face. She had to be *thrilled* by the prospect of a few days alone with me.

My headache kicked up a notch. Still, I pushed my attention to Elthea. "What's the catch?"

She lifted one shoulder, only half a shrug. "It's in Horror territory."

Ah.

Quite a big catch.

Horrors were difficult to kill, almost always claiming fae

lives in the process. We were too few to make the kind of sacrifice required to exterminate them. Instead, in the days after the Wars of Succession, they'd managed to lure them into one area and use wardstones to keep them there.

What could be so important that she'd want it retrieved from there? Unless... it wasn't for her, but for her king.

My pulse sped, throbbing in my head and ears. If she was invoking our bargain, I had no choice but to at least attempt to retrieve and bring it back to her. There was nothing that said I couldn't then *retrieve* it from her and deliver it to the queen.

"That's quite a big favour you ask."

"It's quite a big favour I did you." She gave Kat a sidelong look.

Without Elthea, she would be dead. Truth be told, a quick jaunt into Horror territory was a small price to pay.

Still, I didn't want her to know that. So I huffed a sigh and stopped just short of rolling my eyes. "Do you know where, exactly?"

From that pocket she'd been fidgeting with, she produced a map and spread it across my desk.

From the other side of the desk, Kat studied the map. This was probably her first time seeing the full extent of Elfhame. We tended to suppress information south of the wall and guests into our realm were by invitation only, their visits accompanied. Even the performing troupe who came every year from Albion were met at the wall and escorted to Tenebris-Luminis. That was the only location most human maps pinpointed, and we allowed no signposts near the border.

Elthea pointed to a small town on the western reaches, barely inside Horror territory. That wasn't so bad. I craned to read the name.

"Innesol," she added.

The name curdled in my stomach like gone-off cream, yet I couldn't say why.

She watched me.

Stars willing, I kept that feeling of dread off my face. "Hmm." I shrugged. "I can do that."

She scoffed in her humourless way. "You say that as if you have a choice."

I gave her a sharp smile. "Allow me that illusion."

"Very well. When do you go?"

Sooner would be better. We'd need to camp, since towns were few and far between out that way—no one wanted to live near Horror territory. I gauged the distance. "We can get there and back before the new moon." I shrugged, like the thought of returning to the city just ahead of the Wild Hunt's ride didn't bother me.

We'd be back in plenty of time, and it was worth it if this proved to be a lead on the artefact Dawn wanted. And if not, it was worth it to pay back my debt with Elthea.

She gave us details of the box's exact location and as part of our bargain included that I couldn't open or tamper with the box. With a pleased smirk, she left.

Kat lingered, picking at the trim on her chair. "Bastian, I think we need to talk about—"

"*Ahem.*" From the door, which Elthea had left open. I knew it was Faolán before I looked up.

I wasn't sure if I should be frustrated or grateful. I owed Kat an apology, not just for the other night, but for so much more. But there was so, so much I needed to explain, and every time I thought about what to say, my mind became stupid, squeezed between Hydra Ascendant, unCavendish's plot, and this object that could end the Sleep.

There was no space left for something as personal and huge as this.

Aside from my father, I'd never given anyone an apology for anything so important, and that one hadn't exactly gone well.

I forced my gaze to hers, brow tight from my headache. "This isn't the time."

Her nostrils flared as she exhaled, and it killed me to watch her reel herself in to something small and contained, hands folding as she left.

"I could've come back tomorrow." Faolán glanced after her, eyebrows crashing together.

"I won't be here tomorrow." From my drawer, I fished out a willowbark tablet. I'd already taken one, but this headache was only getting worse. I swallowed it whole and washed it down with the coffee that had been sitting on my desk for the past hour. "I leave at first light."

20

KAT

We rode away from the rising sun, leaving the city behind. Although I still wore gloves because of the chilly air and the rub of the reins, I felt freer—like I could breathe now I was away from so many people and the risk of poisoning someone unintentionally.

And away from Elthea.

Nightmares had come for me in the night, and I'd woken bathed in sweat, breaths rasping through me.

Thank the gods I wouldn't see her or anyone else from Dawn for a few days.

At least riding had always calmed me—perhaps it was the repetitive motion. Though my stag's gait was different and his back was as flexible as a sabrecat's, this didn't feel so alien, and I found myself watching the rolling hills of Elfhame pass by.

It wasn't as though I had conversation to occupy me.

Bastian might as well have been a solid lump of obsidian on his stag's back for how still and quiet he was. Perhaps he was afraid I was going to try to (gasp) speak to him again.

After how he'd spoken to me about the note and the way he'd brushed me off yesterday? Why bother? He would only find another excuse. Besides, he was the one who needed to apologise to me.

I kept my mouth shut as I pulled my coat tight and fastened the top buttons. I hadn't needed them in the city, but out here, as the hum of magic dimmed, it grew colder. This had to be what Bastian meant about the concentration of magic affecting the climate.

Outside the city, autumn was nearly over, with most trees bare and amber and russet leaves coating the ground of this wooded valley. Trunks crowded close-by, but someone had cleared the lowest branches above the road, so they didn't tangle in our stags' antlers.

We ate in the saddle, not sharing a word, just passing the filled rolls between us, offering a pear, breaking a piece of cheese. Bastian's silver eyes remained fixed on the road ahead, the overcast sky as cool as his gaze and as dark as the scowl he wore.

Off the road, we found a ring of boulders to camp within. Bastian disappeared for a while after setting up the tent, muttering something about "wards." It was the first thing he'd said to me all day. I didn't feel much like replying, and his gloom didn't invite conversation.

We ate, we slept, we rose to another dull day. If anything, this one was even darker, with grey clouds looming above. The weather matched my terrible mood after a night where I woke at least half a dozen times from dreams about Elthea experimenting on me. Travelling gave me no opportunity to sleep in.

When Bastian had sent instructions to pack, he'd told me the town was two days' travel from the city. Halfway there. How much more painful could another day of this be?

Except... we weren't halfway through our ordeal, I realised as I buttoned my coat over my trousers and fresh shirt.

This marked only a quarter of the journey—two days there, two days back.

Great.

Biting back a groan, I mounted my stag.

As it passed noon, our breaths still steamed, drifting away like ghosts that were never really there.

No matter what happens, remember all of this is real.

That damn phrase again. It haunted me, battling with my anger and hurt and the harsh words Bastian had given me. Even now, when I'd sworn I wouldn't bother speaking to him, a question tugged on me, drawn by that inescapable phrase.

"What did you mean when you said...?" But it sounded silly as my words broke the silence. A foolish girl asking for something he couldn't give. "Never mind."

He finally looked at me for the first time in hours; it felt more like days. Not just a glance, either, but a long, deep look. "What were you going to say?"

I gritted my teeth, but it was out there now—or at least half out there. Fine. Better to get this done at last—and better speaking about this than accidentally spilling what Elthea had done. "When you said 'remember all of this is real,' what did you mean?"

His back straightened and the reins creaked in his grip as he turned to the road ahead.

Just when I thought he wasn't going to respond, he opened his mouth. "It was the first time I realised you might some day find out what I was doing."

That was a pretty way of putting it. "That you were using me."

He winced, and I felt a little bad.

But sometimes the truth was less painful than skirting around it.

"It had never crossed my mind before that moment. But having you in my rooms, it hit me all the harder."

"The fact you might get found out."

He turned back to me, shifting in the saddle as though all his attention was on me and me alone. "The fact there was a vast, vast gulf between what we were supposed to be and what we really were."

A shiver ran through me. *What we really were.* I couldn't even summon some harsh truth to push back against him and everything those four words suggested.

"Kat..." He blasted a sigh. "In that moment, I wanted to tell you everything. Why I was there. My plans. How it had started one way, but that we had galloped off course and were out in the wilds with no map."

His gaze might as well have been a grip around my throat for all I could summon any response.

I'd been so lost in my hurt, it had never crossed my mind that he had wanted to share the truth with me. I'd certainly never dreamed that his plans had been blown as drastically off-course as mine.

Our plans that were so similar.

Somewhere, the gods were laughing.

"I wanted to tell you how it scared me," he murmured. "And how it gave me something I'd never had before. But I couldn't." The corner of his mouth rose, but there was nothing happy about it. "I couldn't risk revealing the truth just in case I was wrong about you and you revealed it to unCavendish. And you... I couldn't put that on you when you were in such a precarious condition." His gaze fell to my fingers as they squeezed the reins. "So when I placed my orrery in your hand

and told you to focus on the links, the feel of it, the reality of it... I wanted to help you ground yourself, but I also wanted —*needed* you to know that everything I did for you, everything I wanted for you, everything that happened between us was real, even if you found out the truth later."

My eyes burned.

I didn't want to believe him. I wanted to tell him it was a pretty story. I wanted to shove it back at him.

And yet I believed him.

Not because he couldn't lie, but because it aligned with what I knew, like a constellation mapping out his shape in the sky.

Everything between us had felt real. His outrage on my behalf. His attempts to give me something bright in the bleak grey of my existence. His kindness when I'd been so lost.

Truth be told, I'd known those things were real. Always.

But I'd been in denial, drowning myself in it.

Because if that was all real—if what he'd told me was true... Well, I'd had something precious and beautiful, hadn't I?

And I'd lost it.

They might say it was better to have loved and lost than never to have loved at all.

But *they* were full of shit.

I had to drag my burning eyes away, pretending to scan the countryside for danger.

The only danger was here. Bastian. The fae who had been the biggest danger to me from the instant I'd met him.

Oh, he was a blade all right. A blade to cut my heart out.

"Why did you never come to me for help?" He said it softly, barely disturbing the still air, as though he was afraid of the answer.

Where did I start with a question like that? "I'm not sure it crossed my mind." There had never been anyone for me to go to before. I wasn't sure I even knew how to ask. "If I'd told you that I worked for the queen's spymaster—or at least *thought* I did, it would've been treason. And I had enough crimes."

"You could've told me. I'd have kept you safe." He frowned down at his hands. "You had a choice."

"And yet you judge me for something that wasn't my choice?"

He twitched, eyes widening at me, and I knew he understood I meant my marriage. The muscle in his jaw flexed, and his neck corded.

"I didn't want it, Bastian. I *never* wanted it." Maybe it was my own guilt talking.

His lips paled as he pressed them together. Under this grey sky, it was like he too was becoming grey, like a ghost. His hair could've been the dark charcoal left after a fire. The scar cutting through his lips, silvery. His eyes, moonlight.

I'd have chosen him. If anyone had given me the choice. Hells, no one had and yet I'd still tried to. At that party, I'd *tried* to choose him.

Yet he looked furious at me for it.

"You fucking hypocrite." It burst out of me. I didn't mean to, and yet the words kept spilling—if I kept silent, it would be tears spilling in their place. "You talk so much about choice, and yet you only gave me an abridged one. Was it really a *choice*, when I didn't know what you were doing? Was it a choice when I didn't know you were using me?"

"You were using me too," he rasped.

"Yes, but I never gave you grand speeches about how you deserved more and always had a choice. And"—my words cracked—"and I stopped using you. I tried to get out of the situation." My chin trembled, because some foolish part of me had started believing his speeches.

Maybe I did deserve better. But if that was true, then I also deserved better than what he'd given me.

"You kept going to the bitter end."

He worked his jaw side to side before he spoke. "This hasn't ended yet."

"Hasn't it?" I rubbed my chest where my heart felt as raw as the edge to his voice. "I'm bound to you by some horrible accident of magic. But understand, that doesn't mean I choose to be in Elfhame... to be with you. I don't have the luxury—the power of that choice. *Yet again*." I gave a bitter laugh, but there was no strength behind it.

After several minutes, he bowed his head. "I'm sorry."

I made a low sound of acknowledgement, but I didn't trust my voice to hold together. I'd already surreptitiously swiped away a tear that chilled my cheek.

We rode on in quiet for a long while, the sun setting ahead. Even that was muted by the blanketing cloud—a dull grey sunset.

Still, I felt better for speaking, like a wound had been purged of rot, leaving it clear to heal. At my side, Bastian was no longer wound up so tight, either, and the furrow of his brow was thoughtful rather than angry.

As if the sky had also relaxed its grip, it unleashed a torrent so sudden and absolute, I could barely see beyond my stag's antlers.

I gasped as the chill rain snaked under my collar and down my back. Bastian bared his teeth, nose wrinkling like he could scare off the rain with a snarl.

"Come," he shouted over the gushing deluge, and urged his

stag into a canter. "There are caves in the foothills. We'll make up the time tomorrow."

I followed him off the path, barely daring to blink away the stinging rain in case I lost sight of him. A branch from a tree I didn't even spot scraped my cheek, but I kept on his stag's tail.

By the time we reached the great crack in the side of a granite rock face, I was drenched to my underwear—possibly to my soul. We rushed inside, dragging the deer, who didn't seem so sure about the narrow passage. But it soon opened up to a space plenty big enough for the four of us.

Our panting breaths filled the cave as the frigid air bit through our wet clothes.

Water dripped from Bastian's hair into his screwed up face, and a puddle formed at his feet. A particularly large droplet formed at the tip of his nose.

Maybe it was that, maybe it was the expression that I knew matched my own, but when I caught his eye, I laughed.

It started as a chuckle, but like the rain, it soon became a torrent.

And he laughed too.

I gave my body to it—a release after almost a month of uncertainty. He doubled over, as though the rain had washed away Business Bastian and the tense man I'd ridden out of the gate with.

Also...

"You look like a drowned rat," I wheezed around my laughter, pointing at him, at the clothes stuck to his body and the hair plastered to his face.

He swept that hair back and cast an eye over me. "So do you. Albeit a very pretty rat."

That only made me laugh harder. A few tears mingled with

the rain on my face, but they were good tears. Gods, I hadn't laughed this hard in...

I shook my head and wiped my cheeks as Bastian drew deep breaths, rubbing his belly. "I'm not used to working these muscles."

I cocked an eyebrow at him. "Maybe you should introduce laughter into your exercise regime."

"Maybe you should not argue with trees next time you ride." He bent close and swiped a stick from my hair.

"I was saving that for later." I snatched it off him, like he was trying to steal my most prized possession. "Firewood, you know."

"Ah, yes, that damp twig will warm us right up."

We chuckled. Not the slightly unhinged laugh of moments earlier, but something calmer that lit up Bastian's eyes as they held mine.

"Look, Kat. About earlier..." He shook his head and removed a wet lock of hair from my cheek.

The sun must not have yet reached the horizon, because no magic raced between us, but the way his expression softened and the fact of his skin upon mine still stole my breath.

"I truly am sorry."

I didn't want an apology of obligation. "You don't have to say—"

"But I *am* sorry. I used you. It stopped being just that for me, though. I need you to believe me when I say that." He leant in, gaze so intense it was like a grip on my soul. "It was only when your husband appeared that I remembered what I was meant to be doing to you. And I felt sick to my stomach at that and everything *I'd* done as much as the fact you'd deceived me and were married."

My eyelids fluttered as everything came into new, sharp

focus through that lens. He'd hurt himself as much as me. What a mess we were, inside as well as outside.

"And I'm sorry for what you said about taking away your choice." He caught my chin, stopping me from looking away. "I never thought of it like that before. And this isn't enough for that and for hurting you, but it's a start."

I swallowed, throat thick. "A fresh start."

"Exac—"

Mid-word, he flinched, eyes widening and going distant. "Shit."

A cold even deeper than the rain gnawed my bones. "What is it? What's wrong?"

"They aren't meant to be this far east." His gaze skipped side to side, and I understood—his double had to be scouting ahead as it had in Riverton Palace.

I whispered past the lump in my throat, "Who?"

"Horrors."

21
BASTIAN

Horrors had been confined to their territory for a thousand years.

Or so we thought.

In scouting ahead, my other half had discovered their markings near the road, beyond their borders.

One side of me answered Kat's questions, reassuring her that what I'd seen was hours away, as the other stalked through the darkness.

The thing that was hard to explain—not that I spoke of my ability often—was that both halves were equal. Both were still me—had my memories, my experiences, was aware of the other and everything he sensed. I only referred to "my double" in order to help others understand.

With one of us largely resting on the stag, the other, unburdened by supplies, had made faster time. Out there, magic still pulsed around me. They hadn't yet sucked the place dry.

Meanwhile, inside the cave, Kat and I dried off, but we

didn't make camp until I was sure the marking was the only sign of Horror activity this side of the border.

One must've broken past the wardstones. Somehow.

I would have words with the patrol that was meant to maintain the stones, but it seemed safe enough to sleep —for now.

When we set off the next morning, we—my double and I— watched the road, and Kat shifted in her saddle, unease clear in the way she twitched at every sound, though we were still a few hours from the markings.

"What were these signs your other self saw?" Kat scanned every rock and shrub we passed, as though a monster might jump out from behind it.

"They leave markings. Strange symbols they scratch into rocks and trees or ruined buildings. No one knows what they mean, if anything." I shook my head. "The official story is that the Horrors were created by magic blasting out of control, which is true in a sense, but..."

No fae outside a very small circle was meant to know the rest of that sentence. But Kat wasn't fae.

"You can't tell anyone what I'm about to tell you."

She turned from the tree she'd been eyeing with suspicion and raised an eyebrow at me. "Is the Serpent about to spill one of his secrets?"

"I'm serious, Kat. This is for the stability of Elfhame."

"I won't breathe a word."

"The truth is that the side who lost the Wars of Succession used them as weapons." It made me nauseous to even think about it. Weapons of fear and destruction. Weapons used against civilians.

Something sour coated my tongue.

"If this is too painful, you don't need to tell me." She gathered the reins into one hand, the other clenching and unclenching like she might reach across to me.

The dismay had to be written on my face. At least it was in front of her and not someone who'd use it against me. "It's fine. We suppressed the information to enable the other side to still be part of society and reintegrate. If people knew the truth..." I shook my head.

They wouldn't have allowed a single one to survive. There would have been no truce, only mass execution.

"Wait, 'the other side'—was that the side your father fought on? You told me he was an enemy general and then defected to the Night Queen."

I'd told her that in order to push her away, but as she looked at me from atop her stag, I wasn't sure if she'd ever felt so close. Like I could reach out and hold her.

But this fresh start between us was young and delicate, and I owed her much more than the apology I'd given last night. Actions over words. If I could get her queen to grant her a divorce...

I should just ride back to Albion and kill her husband. It would save us all a lot of trouble.

It would set her free.

And it might lessen the guilt gnawing on me.

But would it cost Kat the estate? I didn't know how their inheritance laws worked. If they were as foolish as their marriage laws, they would probably leave the estate to the nearest human male rather than Kat, just because he had a cock.

I couldn't ask her about it. Not directly. If she got wind of what I wished to to do her husband—well, she already made me swear not to kill her uncle. I wasn't going to let her force me into the same promise about that prick.

"Bastian?"

I cleared my throat and shook off amorphous plans and foolish hopes. "That's right. Both my fathers started on that side. The Horrors were the main reason they turned."

The things they'd made us do. Civilians, children included.

A sea of faces stare back at me, wide-eyed and afraid. A little girl clutches her mother's hand, and I hear her whisper, "Where are we going?"

The way the mother looks at me, hollow-eyed and rigid—she knows. But she pats her daughter's head. "Just a walk, sweetling. Just a walk."

Every hair on my body stood on end, bringing me back to myself.

I took a shaky breath. "The town is just inside Horror territory, but the markings..." I rubbed my head. "Sorry, yes, the markings, I was meant to be telling you about those, wasn't I?"

A deep line was etched between Kat's eyebrows as she watched me struggle to explain something that should've been so simple.

Just facts and ideas. That was all. I straightened in the saddle. "One theory is that they weren't so much created as *brought through* from somewhere else. A sentient species, perhaps, or almost one, sent mad by the magic used to control them. The markings could be the remnants of some kind of language, but no one's ever heard them speak or managed to communicate with them. Rumours say the ones who conjured them could control them... but if you saw them now, you'd see how ridiculous that idea is. They have no control."

That was the worst thing about them. Mindless destruction incarnate.

I'd seen Horrors twice before—sent on patrol at another territory as part of my training. Twice was more than enough.

"Others think the marks are nothing more than shapes they've seen in the flow of magic but don't actually understand." I tried to give Kat a reassuring smile. "We're still a couple of hours away. Keep your bow ready, but if we are spotted by one, our best bet is to run. I'll use my other self as a decoy so we can escape."

Nodding, she squeezed the weapon mounted on her saddle. "Will my arrows harm them as they'd harm fae?"

My hand went to my Shadowblade. I'd traded illegally to get my hands on an unseelie weapon. It had taken years to pay back some of the favours. It was worth it.

"Probably not, but if you hit a weak point, that should slow them down or at least deter them. Their bodies are covered in hard carapaces. The only gaps are the eyes and armpits. I wouldn't bother to tell most people, but I think you could actually hit the mark."

The flush of pleasure that darkened her cheeks warmed the worst of the chill that had lingered in my bones since seeing the name of our destination. She turned away, but I caught the edge of the smile she tried to hide.

We rode on, that warmth growing more and more distant as dread ate it up.

I couldn't shake the feeling something awful was going to happen in that town. Despite eating lunch, my stomach remained a pit, threatening to swallow me up.

Not long before midday, the birdsong stopped. I kept my shadows bound close. There was little magic to draw upon here, and if I let them spread, the Horrors would scent them. A little while later, I pointed out the marking on a boulder a few feet back from the road.

Kat swallowed, gaze tracing over the long upright line

criss-crossed with short diagonals, a circle, and a triangle. "Is there anything else I should know about them?"

"Horrors can smell magic—it's what they feed on." I could barely smell it here, only really noticing its constant presence now it had faded. Kat's was fresh and vibrant, like the first flowers of the year. "Can you sense it around you?"

Frowning, she stroked her arm. "Normally I can. A slight buzz on my skin, but..." She cocked her head as though listening. "It's so faint now."

"They've been feeding. Together with their carapaces, that's what makes them so hard to kill. You can't use magic on them directly. If I tried to attack with my shadows, they'd consume them. Only powerfully enchanted weapons work— something the magic is fixed in. Even then, if they got hold of it for a period of time, they would suck it dry."

She grimaced, squeezing her bow.

The scent of its magic, green growth and leaf mulch, strengthened in response.

I nodded towards it. "Your bow is powerful—it *might* work, but you'd need arrows with a more potent enchantment to be sure."

Her eyes narrowed, and I could practically hear her making a mental note to get better arrows. My billing account winced in response.

Still, knowledge was also power, so I continued feeding it to her in the hopes she wouldn't ever need to rely on it. "The fact there's any magic left tells us they don't come here frequently, but as we go further, you'll feel it less and less. At the centre of their territory, there's none." I shifted in the saddle, the thought of it not just wrong, but terrifying.

Unlike most fae, I drew from the world around me—

evidence along with my eyes that my unseelie blood wasn't just a rumour.

In a true dead zone, I would be powerless.

But that wasn't the only reason my shoulders grew tighter the further we rode. Something else ate at me. Something wrong. Something ahead.

Half a mile on, we found another marking.

It made my teeth grind. "The patrol who's meant to mind this area is going to get a personal visit when they next report to Tenebris. These things are running wild."

"How do they keep them back?" Kat shot me another look, chewing her lip.

"Wards. They're kept stocked with powerful wardstones. They should fucking use them. We embedded them in the wall between here and Albion," I added. "It's to keep our monsters in as much as to keep humans out."

"Why not just kill them all?"

"We tried that at first. It didn't go well. For each one of them we took down, at least two of us died, and with our numbers depleted after the wars..." I shook my head, suppressing a shudder. "Better to sacrifice this area of land rather than more lives."

Then I saw myself in the disorientating double vision that always came when both parts of me reunited. One riding. One walking from an outcrop of rock.

It was like looking in a mirror—his tight movements echoed my own agitation, and when I shifted my attention to his view, I could see how rigidly I sat on my stag. This feeling of dread wasn't just about bringing Kat out of the city or taking her into Horror territory.

It was something else. Something older. Something deeper.

I merged back with my other self, not feeling any stronger for it.

When we reached a copse outside Innesol, that something else hollowed out my insides and I understood.

A ruined tower rose at the centre of the town, but I knew what it had once looked like before its mortar had crumbled and its roof had caved in.

I had been here before.

22
BASTIAN

"Bastian? What's wrong?"

I shook my head and dismounted. Words were suddenly impossible.

As she landed, she stared up at me. "You look like you've seen a ghost. You've gone the colour of one, too."

We left the stags in the copse, and I managed to give them the instruction to stay before entering the ruined town.

My bones itched so much I could've scratched off my skin as I surveyed the road and saw both crumbled walls and pristine buildings, tall and proud. Homes. Shops. Schools. They'd even had two theatres and a gallery.

I could see it all as it had been then and the centuries old ruin it was now.

I wasn't centuries old. I couldn't have seen it.

Yet I *remembered*.

We crouched behind a half-fallen wall, and I scraped my fingers through my hair, giving it a tug to clear my mind. When I peered out again, I saw only the ruins.

A main road led to the town's centre. Where we huddled now was the old school. I refused to look at our feet in case I found broken toys.

Elthea's note said the house with the box was further into the town.

"Ready?"

Kat looked back at me with her eyebrows pinched together and lips thin. Now we were away from the stags, she'd removed her gloves, and her fingers twisted together. The stain covered them completely. "*I* am. Are you?"

I ignored her question and led the way out onto the main road.

Once upon a time, we'd marched through, victorious, so pleased with ourselves to be so close to the capital. Two days' march and we'd be there. True, the combined armies of the Dusk and Dawn Pretenders stood in our way, but we had new weapons my beloved had told us about. He hadn't seen them yet himself, but they were going to be unveiled here at Innesol, and they'd help us journey east and take Tenebris for the rightful queens.

My happily ever after was shame that bowed my back, dragging on each step.

I tried to tell myself that I hadn't been here, it wasn't possible, but I couldn't logic away my feelings or the memories that haunted each view of the town.

We hugged what remained of the buildings, and I had to help Kat cross debris strewn into the road where belongings had been dragged out of houses along with people. I placed Kat's feet on the floor, gripping her waist and squeezing my eyes shut.

Whole families are forced outside. Adults, children—we round them all up now the new weapons have arrived.

The weapons that give me nightmares.

When we're alone, I beg my beloved not to use them, to send them back. I know from the way he's bitten his lips raw and rough since their arrival that he shares my horror at the things, but he insists. Both the Day Queen and Night Queen have sanctioned them. We have no choice.

The night the monsters arrived, one of the younger recruits tried to flee. She was caught and taken to the pens. I know nothing more than that about her fate. I haven't seen her since.

"Bastian?"

Something warm touched my cheek. Like light glimmering through water as I rose from a deep, deep dive, I fixed upon it and emerged, gasping for air.

Green eyes on me. Her hand on my face. A warm body pressed against mine. These things were real. Here and now.

I pressed Kat's palm into my skin, like I could imprint it there and make her a permanent anchor.

"Something's very wrong, isn't it?"

I swallowed, unable to answer when the only answer I wanted to give was a lie. I wasn't fine. Not at all.

She glanced along the road. "We should go back."

"No. *No.*" I squeezed her fingers and tried to smile. "I've just been here... before it fell."

The crease between her brows deepened. "But you said this place was destroyed in the Wars of Succession. Weren't they a thousand years ago?"

I squeezed my eyes shut and pulled away. "You're right." Every thing I saw made it harder to remember logic.

I drew a deep breath. There was barely any aroma of magic left here, but Kat's springtime scent filled me. The air in my lungs was cool. My chest rose and fell, under my control.

I was in control. Not whatever madness the Horrors left in the air.

I had never been here before. I couldn't have memories of this place. It wasn't possible.

"Come on." I took her hand and led her deeper into the town, Elthea's instructions ingrained in my head. We turned one corner, clambered over the rubble of a fallen tower, then turned another corner.

No sign of Horrors, save for the depleted magic. Perhaps they were feeding elsewhere—they tended to move in packs, leaching one area of their territory before moving to the next.

A scrape sounded ahead.

23

KAT

Bastian pulled me behind a tilted pillar, caging me in with his arms. We stood in tense silence, breaths held, listening. I gripped my magic tight—or tried to. If I let go, the Horrors might smell it.

Something scraped over rock, followed by the clack and thud of stone hitting stone and a heavy object landing.

Bastian's moonlight eyes fixed over my shoulder for a long while before he peered out. He eased back into our hiding place and ducked closer. "There's one ahead," he breathed in my ear. "We'll cut through this building. Keep quiet."

Hand-in-hand, we picked through the debris. Sweat slicked his palm, though the day was far from warm. Still, I clung to him. Heart pounding, I tried to place my feet exactly where he did, but my legs were considerably shorter than his, and at times I had to find my own path over fragmented wood and fallen granite.

When I wasn't watching my step, I watched him. All day he'd been even tighter than yesterday, and since we'd spotted the town, the deep gold of his skin had turned ashen. It wasn't fear that marked his movements and expression, but... guilt... shame...

And he thought he'd been here before it had been ruined?

Something was very wrong.

The sounds grew quieter as we emerged on another, narrower road. Bastian looked left and right, then pulled me across the street. We took a right turn and paused in what had once been a doorway, though the timber had long since disintegrated to splinters at our feet.

"There." He pointed out a house at the end of the lane, on a T-junction, set back behind dead shrubs and the remains of a garden.

Despite being abandoned for so long, there was startlingly little life around the town. The copse where we'd left the stags was full of stunted, sickly trees.

Even nature knew to stay away.

He gripped my shoulders. "We go in, find the fireplace. I get the box. You stay close. Understood?"

I swallowed, nodded, then we were hurrying down the lane. We paused at the T-junction, listened, peered around the corner.

Nothing.

We stalked across the road, Bastian's hand tight around mine. No magic surged between us, but his grip still felt like a lifeline.

The way his breaths heaved and his jaw ticked, I wasn't sure whether that lifeline was saving me or him.

No roof remained on the building Elthea had sent us to. The walls were partially collapsed, but thankfully a chimney stack still stood at its heart like a beacon.

As we stepped across the threshold, a low sound rumbled through the air.

I froze, stomach dropping. Bastian raised his free hand, the grip on my fingers tightening. That was the only thing that stopped me fleeing. Head canted, he surveyed the ruined room, then pointed to the far wall.

That was when I heard it.

The crunch of something large moving just the other side of this building.

He pressed a finger to his lips and led the way.

Heart hammering, I tiptoed around broken glass—the shards of a mirror reflecting the clouds overhead. I hardly dared to breathe knowing only an ancient wall stood between me and something the fae found so terrible they called them Horrors.

Great windows had once graced the next room. Now only their metal frames remained, open to the other side.

We crouched below the level of the cracked windowsills and crept along.

The sounds of movement grew louder, accompanied by a series of low, rasping huffs.

Horrors could smell magic.

Was it sniffing the air?

Could it smell us?

A chill sweat trickled down my spine as I followed Bastian dumbly and tried to keep my breathing under control.

We reached the end of the run of windows, and as I straightened, I caught a glimpse of sunlight gleaming on something outside. A rainbow sheen marked the sleek, dark segmented body, like oil on water. I could only see part of it, but...

It was fucking huge.

Bastian's hand on my back urged me through the next door. Despite a crack running its full height, the back wall of this room stood between us and the Horror, tall and relatively complete. My breaths eased a little, though my pulse still throbbed in my throat.

We'd reached the fireplace.

Almost done. Then we could leave this damned place and never return.

Bastian started towards it, but I grabbed his arm. I tapped his shoulders, then pointed out the width of the fireplace—or rather the lack of it. His broad shoulders would never fit, and Elthea had said the box was on a shelf hidden inside the chimney.

He scowled at the narrow opening but that didn't make it any wider.

I pressed my hand into my chest and mouthed, "I'll do it."

His scowl grew sharper and he shook his head.

But he didn't have any other choice. I raised an eyebrow and gave him a look.

On the other side of the wall, the Horror dug through rubble. It had to be searching for enchanted objects to feed on. Its rasping breaths came closer, like it was snorting against the back wall.

The purple stain coated my fingers fully now. Was that what it could smell?

We didn't have long, and I didn't have enough control over my magic to rein it in—not when I was worried about Bastian and terrified by what these monsters would do if they got hold of us.

I pushed past him and into the soot-streaked fireplace. He made a low sound of protest but didn't try to stop me. I turned and raised my eyebrows at him. My hips and shoulders just about fit in—he would've stood no chance.

Brackets fixed in the wall must've once held grates for cooking on, and I made use of them as footholds. Hands braced on the blackened walls, I climbed up.

The narrow space echoed my breaths back at me, making them seem deafening in the darkness. No light filtered through from above—something must've blocked the chimney—so I felt my way.

It was an age before my fingers found the underside of a ledge on the front wall, just as Elthea had described. "Found the shelf," I whispered as quietly as possible.

"Hurry up," came Bastian's tight response.

I slid my hand to the edge, but found nothing. Still, the shelf was deep. I reached for another foothold, toe scraping on stone before I found it. My thigh muscles hummed as I heaved up.

A high, clicking call pierced the air. It chilled my bones as my fingers found something smooth.

"It's caught our scent," Bastian hissed. "Get out."

"Hold on. I'm almost there." Right on the edge of my reach, I couldn't quite get hold of it. But I had it. Almost. I walked it towards me, inch by inch.

Another call. This one sounded like a question. *Where are you, tasty morsels?*

"Katherine, we're going."

"No." Just one more inch. "I've almost got it."

The walls around me rumbled. Outside, something crashed. I grabbed the shelf, only staying up because there was no space to topple backwards.

More clicks, then a piercing screech.

I blinked in the darkness, breaths bursting—shallow and tight. "Bastian?"

Nothing.

"Bastian?"

Every hair on my body rose. I didn't dare call him again. Was I safer in the chimney or should I slip out and run? Where was he? Had the Horror got him?

I reached for the box, needing a distraction from the sudden and terrible quiet and images of Bastian being torn apart.

Something grabbed me.

24

KAT

I t had me by the legs.

I was yanked from the chimney, blinded by the sudden daylight.

A hot stink filled the air. I jolted as the thing carried me.

The back wall was gone. A pile of bones lay on its other side. In the space where the crack had stood, crouched a Horror.

Not a second's doubt. That was a Horror. The name was perfect for the elongated head, the rows of pointed teeth, the void-black eyes that saw right through me.

Dwarfed by its hulking, eight-legged form, Bastian stood before it, drawing a blade edged with shadows.

"No," I cried, reaching for him. That thing was going to kill him.

But I was already being carried into the next room. Carried by—it took me far too long to realise—Bastian. I hung over his shoulder, the box in my soot-covered hand.

His second self stayed behind. A decoy.

Past the windows and over the shattered mirror without so much as a crunch of broken glass, Bastian ran. Faster than I'd expected considering he carried me.

I lost sight of his other self. "What happens if he dies?"

"It's... unpleasant for me," Bastian huffed. "I feel everything he does. But I'll be fine."

Above the crumbled walls, the Horror rose onto its back legs—and rose and rose. Ten feet became fifteen became twenty as it reared onto its four back legs.

With the front section of its torso upright, what had seemed a hulking, squat body, was actually as sleek as its gleaming carapace. The whole thing was like a giant insect, save for its elongated head. That was like nothing else I'd ever seen.

And I couldn't stop staring at it.

Its front legs unfolded, curved and sharp like scythes, while barbs tipped the next pair. Beneath those—that was what Bastian meant by its armpits. A tiny area of weakness that would be near impossible to hit.

More clicking, questing sounds rose from the ruins. More Horrors, the alert spreading.

Bastian leapt over rubble, zig-zagged through narrow streets—too narrow for the Horrors to fit down, I realised as I jostled uselessly over his shoulder.

Useless. You are not a useless woman. Get hold of yourself, Katherine.

Box secure in one hand, I drew my boot pistol with the other.

The first Horror we'd faced slashed with those curved front legs and hissed as it fought Bastian's double, who was hidden by the ruins.

Closer—much closer, a wall crumbled to my right, ripped down by a Horror's claws. "Behind us," I called. "Your left."

Bastian's arm squeezed around my thighs and he turned right, away from the pursuing monster. Below, shadows wisped off his heels.

Twice more, I called out warnings as Horrors came after us, and twice more Bastian took us down side streets.

But as we rounded a corner, one locked eyes with me and shrieked its pleasure. Its strangely bent legs scuttled across the debris-filled street.

"Behind us," I gasped.

"Yep," Bastian huffed. "I noticed that."

It gained, coming closer with each step. My heart beat so hard, my body became one massive throbbing pulse.

As good as my aim was, I couldn't fire with so much movement beneath me, and I didn't dare tell Bastian to stop.

Still, I levelled my pistol. Maybe it would understand the threat. *Maybe.*

But still it closed in. Ten feet away. Eight. Six.

Its shriek pierced my ears. Its dank breath filled my mouth and nose, metallic and sour like vomit and copper coins. Its spittle flecked my fingers, sizzling, and I bit back a cry at the corrosive burn.

But beneath the soot, my purple stains gathered around the spit and the pain faded.

Another bellow from the beast, and more of its spit landed on my fingers, warring with my poison.

Beneath me, Bastian's shoulder heaved, and shadows rose, knocking the Horror away.

We rounded a corner out of sight. I dared a glance over my shoulder. A straight route out of town. The copse lay ahead, almost picturesque in the bright autumnal day.

But picturesque didn't generally involve monsters that fed on magic.

In the distance, another shriek of feral delight tore the air and Bastian grunted. He sagged against a wall, panting. I couldn't see his face, but he doubled over, every muscle clenched. That had to be pain—his double's.

"Put me down, I can—"

"No." He held tight. "I'm faster. I just need a second to catch my—"

The Horror that had almost caught us skidded around the corner, its claws skittering on the cobblestones.

Under me, Bastian shook as he fought to straighten.

"Wait."

I levelled my pistol.

The Horror sprinted towards us, eyes locked on me. Good. Let it focus. Like a hunting sabrecat, that focus held its head still.

I aimed for the empty blackness of one of those eyes.

Exhale. Adjust. Squeeze the trigger.

The shot cracked.

A haze of black liquid burst from the Horror's eye, and its head snapped back.

This shriek wasn't the slightest bit delighted, but the huff the left me was.

It slumped over. I'd stopped it. Killed it.

Bastian pushed himself upright and ran for the copse. Magic hummed over my skin—stronger now we neared the edge of the town.

With a clicking cry, the Horror heaved to its feet.

I hadn't killed it.

Shit.

We burst from the ruins, closing the distance to the copse.

But the Horror closed on us, only fifteen feet away. Even if we got to the stags, it would catch us before we could mount and escape.

My eyes burned as I stared. I reached for my gunpowder, but it would be impossible to reload with this much jostling.

A ragged bellow rumbled beneath me, and Bastian's shoulder squared. Shadows spilled from him, wispy at first, but they thickened and rose, until a wall stood between us and the Horror.

Pale and shaking, he threw me onto my stag and leapt onto his own. "Ride!"

25
BASTIAN

We rode hard.

The Horrors didn't follow.

But I could still feel that place hounding my heels.

Tattered blankets lie in the street where they've been dropped by sleepy children. The silent but leaden footsteps of their parents, aunts, uncles, neighbours as they all file along.

Then and now flickered, overlaying each other and shuffling through my mind.

But one image kept coming back.

Bones piled up in the place where we'd led those people.

I try to stop it, but my beloved grabs my shoulder. Jaw solid, he shakes his head. "They will kill you," he mutters. "We will stop this, but not here, not now. Give me time and I'll save us both."

I squeezed the reins. This was real. This. Now. The breath in my lungs. The sun above. Kat riding at my side.

She watched me, smeared with soot and ash, but I could tell from her crumpled brow that I looked far worse.

Haggard. Exhausted. Gripped by darkness I just couldn't shake.

I should've stayed behind and let those monsters feed on me the same way I'd let them feed on the people of that town.

They struggle when we first bundle them into the pens, but the Horrors hold fast. One by one, the people fall, and the Horrors discard them in neat piles, their magic sucked up, bodies dried out to husks.

Bile rose in my throat.

My shadows curled around my hands, soothing, stroking, a reminder of where I was and when I was... and *who* I was.

They were not my memories.

I wasn't even born when Innesol fell.

I clung to that fact as guilt and shame gnawed at me.

Kat steered closer. "Do you want to talk about what happened back there?"

"No."

I didn't look directly at her, but I heard the sharp breath in and the even sharper one out. She *did* ask.

By the time the thin crescent moon rose, we'd passed the cave, and our stags had slowed to a walk.

Kat's stumbled, and she gripped the saddle's pommel to stay on. "Bastian? I think we need to stop. They can't keep going." She cast her eye over me. "And from the look of you, neither can you."

I wanted to put many more miles between me and that place, but she was right.

Besides, with those bloodshot eyes, she looked exhausted too.

We set up camp beneath a rocky outcrop. My feet dragged as I set the wards. They would keep us safe from most things. A

Horror could break through, given time, but we'd have a warning.

When I returned, Kat was tending the fire, hunched over, face still sooty.

I shouldn't have brought her here. I should have sent someone else. But I'd been so confident—it was only the edge of Horror territory, after all. We could sneak in, sneak out, and never even have to see one of the creatures. Quicker and quieter than a large group.

How wrong could I get?

"Get some sleep." My voice came out husky—I hadn't spoken in hours.

She flinched as though she expected one of the monsters. "Is your double back yet?"

"He's dead." I'd felt it, experienced it, the Horror's slice across his—*our* belly. They'd fed on our magic, adding to my exhaustion. I nodded towards the tent. "Go on. I'll keep first watch."

"But you need sleep. You go—"

"I'll wake you when I'm ready to sleep."

She sighed, shoulders sinking as she glanced at the tent. "I don't want to go in there." She shrank, breaking something in me—something that understood.

"You don't want to be alone." I passed her my blanket. "Sleep here, and I'll keep watch over camp... and you."

Her eyes gleamed in the firelight and for a moment her chin tensed like she might cry. But she nodded and pulled the blanket around herself before curling into a ball on the ground beside me.

Somehow, my fingers found their way into her hair. There was a moment's pain as our magic came together for the first time since sunset, neutralising the poison that would otherwise kill her. But I welcomed it tonight. Pain kept me here and now and out of memories that weren't my own.

Then came the sweet pleasure of it, tight in my spine like a climax building. Eyes closed, Kat made a soft sound, eyebrows peaking. I pulled away, let our magic settle, then went back to stroking her hair until she fell asleep.

NOTHING CAME IN THE NIGHT, but I'd never been so grateful to see the sun rise. Kat woke, bleary-eyed. She frowned from the dawn to me. "You said you'd wake me."

"When I was ready to sleep." Not a lie. I didn't want to sleep and get sucked into that place again. "Now, I'm ready to ride."

She tried to question me and insist I at least nap while she broke camp, but I shook off her protests.

"We need to put as much distance between ourselves and the Horrors as possible."

As much distance between me and Innesol as possible.

Standing by her stag, our bags packed, she pursed her lips.

"*Katherine.*" I held her gaze until she finally huffed and mounted.

We rode. On and on until another sunset came. The stags took a slow pace, exhausted from last night's wild flight. Kat's had developed a limp. Nothing one of the handlers in the city couldn't heal, but at this pace, we were still the best part of a day from the city.

Above, the thinnest sliver of moon remained. It would disappear entirely tomorrow night, and then the Wild Hunt would come.

They hunted the roads of Elfhame and Albion, banished to

ride only under the shadow of the new moon. Those nights, their hellhounds sniffed out quarry—humans and fae foolish enough to be out after dark when there was no moon.

I'd heard the howls once.

They had burned my veins with cold fire, something like terror and desire, an odd energy that had pulsed through me.

That had to be how they tracked you—listening for your pounding heart, scenting your fear. Legend said once the Wild Hunt found their prey, they would pursue them to the ends of the earth. And once caught, they fed upon the poor unfortunate's soul.

I kept us riding hours past sunset to ensure we'd make it home tomorrow. I'd have kept going longer, but I swayed on my saddle and Kat looked ready to drop.

When I led the way off the road into a clearing and dismounted, she didn't land beside me. It was only when I peered past the curtain of hair into her face that I realised she had fallen asleep in the saddle. A true rider, she somehow still had hold of the reins.

It was the first time I'd smiled since before Innesol.

I slid her from the stag and gathered her into my arms. For a moment, she frowned and pushed, muttering, "No. You can't take him." But when I made a soothing sound, she stilled and settled back into sleep.

It saved me arguing with her about keeping watch.

Once I'd made camp, I checked on her—still sleeping soundly, curled up by the fire. I could have carried her into the tent, but I liked having her in sight.

I found the most uncomfortable position I could against a fallen tree, with a broken branch digging in my back, and kept my eyes on the darkness.

A few times, I jolted upright as my eyelids drooped. But I made it through the night and welcomed another dawn.

Kat's eyelids fluttered open, and her gaze fixed on the lightening sky above. "Shit. Bastian?" She sat up, glaring at me as I rose and stretched. "You absolute fucking..." Her hands fisted.

"I can sleep when we get home." I tried to smile, but it was too much effort.

My feet dragged as we broke camp, and I confess Kat did most of the work, muttering about me being an idiot the whole time.

As we set off, a brutal headache buzzed in my forehead and behind my eyes. It was all I could do to keep my stag on the road.

Stay awake.

Awake meant no dreams. Awake meant no nightmares. Awake meant no more of those awful memories.

I fixed my eyes on the hills ahead. Tenebris stood on their other side. We would make it before sunset.

Awake.

Stay awake.

Stay...

26
BASTIAN

There was a soft kind of darkness and something warm wrapped around me. Something warm that smelled good, like the first sunny day of spring. Something I could sleep against.

Sleep.

Wait.

I jolted upright. The stag pranced to one side. I grabbed for the reins, but found a pair of hands already on them. Gloved hands.

"Kat?"

"You're awake then." Her voice hummed into my back. That was the thing wrapped around me—her thighs around mine, arms around my waist.

When I looked over my shoulder, I found her craning around me to peer at the road ahead.

She caught my eye and shrugged. "Not exactly convenient, since you're too tall for me to see past, but as you nearly fell off, I didn't have much choice."

I rubbed my aching head. The pain wasn't as bad as earlier, but my eyes stung. "Thanks. I'm fine, now, though, I can ride."

"That's nice." She made no move to hand over the reins or dismount and return to her stag, which limped along beside us.

"I said I can—"

"I heard you." She flashed me a sweet smile when I looked back. "But you're going to fall asleep again, if I leave you—*fall* being the operative. And in case you hadn't noticed, my stag is lame. It's better if we rest him."

I gave a wordless grumble Faolán would've been proud of.

"I'd have stopped and tucked you in if tonight wasn't a new moon."

"Then I'm glad you realised." If we stopped, we'd never make it to Tenebris before nightfall. "Still, I think your neck would thank you if you moved in front of me so you can, you know, *see*." I cocked my head as she flexed her neck side to side with a wince. "I'll even let you keep hold of the reins."

"Bastian Marwood, letting someone else hold the reins?" Her eyes widened. "Wonders will never cease."

It was the second time I'd smiled since leaving Innesol. "Don't get used to it."

Eventually, she conceded, and we swapped places. True to my word, I let her steer and instead fastened my hands around her waist. She rode with her coat open as the sun streamed down.

I must've still been tired, because the next thing I knew, I woke from the most delicious dream with my head on her shoulder, my arms tight around her, and a raging erection. My shadows had also got in on the act, hazing around her thighs and shoulders, holding her hair back, so I could nuzzle in to her neck.

I held there a moment longer than I should've, guilt quietened by my exhaustion. When I glanced down, I could see her chest heaving and the peaks of her nipples against her shirt. My fingers flexed against her belly as my shadows reached for her breasts to do what I longed to.

No.

I yanked them back and made a show of "waking up" and stretching, pulling my aching cock away from Kat's glorious backside.

"Morning, sleepy head," she said in a voice too light. "Or, rather, afternoon." She nodded at the sun above, turning her head so I caught her tight smile, but not looking directly at me. She'd cleaned her face at camp, and I could see the flush of her tanned cheeks.

Exhaustion had eroded my self-control and let my thoughts ran rampant.

Swallowing, I returned my hands to her hips and thought about boring things like picking apples.

But picking apples became picking apples with Kat. Which became picking apples with naked Kat and feeding them to her as I made love to her in the setting September sun.

My grip on her tightened. Stars above. I was fucked.

My mind skipped from subject to subject, only lingering on a thought for as long as it took to somehow loop around to Kat bouncing on my cock.

Turned out nearly getting killed by Horrors left me horny beyond belief.

The afternoon sun passed overhead and Kat pressed the stag into a faster walk. We should still make it back before dusk, but I didn't trust myself to reassure her.

Eventually she spoke into the pregnant quiet, "So, are you ready to talk about what happened at Innesol yet?"

That was one way to quench my desire. She might as well have thrown me into a freezing lake.

I was about to brush off her question when she looked back at me, brow and mouth tight with worry.

Damn this woman. I couldn't deny her. And... just as my shadows ghosted around her hands and waist, sharing themselves with her, I wanted to share myself with her.

"What do you want to know?"

She raised an eyebrow, then turned back to the road. "What do you want to say?"

Touché.

"You were troubled," she went on. "That much was obvious. And you spoke about things you couldn't possibly know. I was afraid."

I squeezed her hips, tracing circles with my thumbs. "I'm sorry. I didn't mean to frighten you."

"No. You misunderstand. I wasn't afraid *of* you; I was afraid *for* you."

That was the thing that cracked me open.

My throat was too raw to speak for a moment, but then speak I did. "They were memories. That place... It felt like I'd been there. I could've sworn I had, but... You're right—it fell long, long before I was born."

Watching the road, she went very still.

"Those memories aren't mine." I dragged in a long breath. Only Faolán and my fathers knew this, and with *Baba* gone, that left just two people.

But Katherine...

She hadn't spilled my secrets to the changeling, even when she'd had all the reason in the world to. After I pushed her away, she could've gone to him with the note, told him about my double, told him about my nightmares.

"Those memories are my *athair's*. He did some things in the war that... he wasn't proud of." That shame was mine, curdling in my gut. "And it scarred him. He had nightmares and flashbacks, even centuries later, after I was born."

"That's why you knew what to do... when I was lost and afraid." Her voice came out very small.

I leant loser and placed my cheek alongside hers. "I learned from growing up with his trauma."

She pressed into my touch. "Then I'm grateful to him and to you."

"There was an unfortunate side-effect, though." I straightened. "His magic is of the mind, and although he tried to protect us with wards around the bed, his worst nightmares spilled over to those nearby."

"You mean... to you."

"I lived those moments like they were my own. He's the one who helped take Innesol, but *I* can smell the blood of the battle, hear the ring of steel, see the civilians they captured. His memories—his worst memories—are mine."

We rode on in silence for a long while, then Kat gathered the reins in one hand and reached back. Her gloved fingers slid into the hair at the nape of my neck, and she pulled me close. "I'm sorry, Bastian. That sounds..." She shook her head. "That's why you didn't want to sleep—you didn't want more nightmares."

I let my chest press against her back and my arm snake around her waist. I inhaled all the fresh promise of her scent and took every scrap of comfort I could.

Too exhausted to resist. Too tired of fighting. Too broken by all I'd remembered in Innesol.

I didn't deserve her softness, not after what I'd...

I screwed my eyes shut. *I* didn't do that. I didn't take those people to the Horrors.

I had plenty of reasons to feel guilty, but that one wasn't mine.

So I let myself sink against her, and I let her comfort me as we rode away from the sunset.

27

BASTIAN

Kat urged our stags through the city gates as they turned from the clear crystalline of Luminis to the smoky quartz of Tenebris. The lack of moon had us both tense, but I kept my voice steady as I told her the most direct route to the palace.

The streets were empty—any sensible person stayed inside with doors and windows shut to keep out the Wild Hunt. Evergreen boughs decorated archways and the bridges between towers, ready for the coming Winter Solstice.

I found my thumbs circling Kat's hips again, though I'd have been lying if I'd said it was only for *her* comfort.

When we reached the palace, the sunset blazed behind us, and twilight's indigo sky rose behind the turrets and spires. From inside the guard house, a face peered and waved us through. On the new moon, even the guards stayed safely indoors.

We trotted across the bridge, Kat's body thrumming with

tension. River Velos's magic hissed over me. *Stay out.* If I were fully unseelie, I wouldn't be able to cross at all.

The stable yard was empty and silent as darkness closed overhead. We hurried into the covered aisle, led the stags into the nearest stalls, and shut them in safely.

Kat was opening the double doors into the yard when I heard it.

The huff of a stag ridden hard. The clink of armour.

Heart lurching, I grabbed her. One hand over her mouth, I pulled her back. Her body tightened but she didn't fight.

"They're here," I whispered against her ear. I didn't know how. They shouldn't be able to cross the river. Unless they weren't unseelie as we'd always believed, but *something else.*

The pulse leapt in her throat, close enough I could feel it on my chin, but she dipped her head in acknowledgement.

Slowly, slowly, I backed from the door.

Outside, hounds sniffed at the paving and whined, frustrated they couldn't find what they'd scented.

We drew level with the door's hinges and a thin crack looking out onto the yard.

White hounds with burning red eyes circled the yard, like Fluffy and yet not. Her playful bound was nothing like the focused lope of these hellhounds.

Thirteen steeds, some stags, some horses, all skeletal with flesh hanging from their flanks and necks. They pawed the ground and snorted. Steam billowed from their flared nostrils and curled around their riders.

Even my fae sight couldn't pierce the darkness that gathered around them.

Riding the largest stag, wearing a spiked helm, their leader said something in a voice that was ice scraping over steel. I didn't know the language, but each word skittered down my spine like the blade of an enemy I'd forgotten.

Their nearest companion nodded and turned, surveying the yard. Deep inside a hood, a pair of pale, glowing eyes locked with mine. In my arms, Kat went rigid and made a soft sound against my palm.

The hounds lifted their heads, flaming ears pricking as they sniffed the air.

Barely breathing, I eased my shadows to the door and pulled it shut. At the click of the latch, my shoulders sank and Kat sagged.

"Fuck," she muttered when I released her. "Did you see?"

"Oh, was there something out there?"

She spun, then huffed a disbelieving laugh at me.

I grinned back, able to joke now we were safely shut in. The Wild Hunt couldn't enter a building with closed doors and windows.

She glanced towards the yard. "Have you ever known anyone to see them and live to tell the tale?"

"I saw them once. But otherwise... no. I suppose that makes us lucky. Looks like we're in here for the night."

Her eyes widened at me. "You're doubly lucky." She shuddered as if shaking off what she'd seen in the yard. "Well, it's not my first time sleeping in a stable. Though deer smell different from sabrecats."

She took care of the stags, who we'd abandoned into their stalls in our rush, while I climbed into the hayloft and used the blankets from our travels to make a bed in the straw.

When she climbed the ladder after me, I bowed with a flourish. "Madam, may I welcome you to the Marwood Inn?"

She chuckled and took in the blankets and the twinkling

lights I'd gathered under the hayloft's rafters. "And how long have you been in the innkeeping business, Mr Marwood?"

"Not very long. I'd welcome any feedback madam has on my humble establishment."

"Hmm." She patted the bed I'd made from bales of hay before sitting on it experimentally. "The beds are surprisingly comfortable. Sorry, *bed*." She raised an eyebrow at me.

"My apologies, madam, space *is* at a premium." The hayloft was packed with straw and hay, leaving only an intimate corner for us.

"And you don't appear to have any kitchens."

"Ah." I raised my hand and produced a plate with the last of our camping supplies—one apple, a heel of bread, and a piece of cheese.

"I take it back. You're spoiling me with this bounty, Mr Marwood."

"We aim to please at the Marwood Inn."

I sat beside her and we shared the slim pickings in companionable silence. It felt like it once had. Like we were away in Albion where I didn't have to think about the safety of an entire realm, where I wasn't the Night Queen's Shadow, the Bastard of Tenebris, the Serpent.

I could be what she called me: Bastian.

Alone with our teasing jokes, it felt like what she'd said at that party was true. *I'm yours.* There was no husband to interrupt us as I'd been about to claim what she'd said was mine— what she'd given freely.

Or almost freely.

Her words from a few days ago cut me as I sliced the cheese with my dagger. *Was it really a choice...?* Now I was free of my father's memories of Innesol, I couldn't escape everything she'd said.

I'd prided myself on giving Kat a choice, on being a thoughtful lover. Gods, how I'd prided myself. I was looking after her, reminding her of consent, where others had stamped all over it. And yet... I turned away when my thoughts reached that point, too cowardly to face the truth.

"Why do I feel like this isn't the first time you've entertained someone up here?" She eyed me sidelong as she deposited her half of the apple core on the plate.

"I told you I was raised in the stables."

"Hmm. I'd thought it an exaggeration. So, did you live right here?" She patted the makeshift bed.

"Not quite. There are servants quarters behind here for the stablehands. But I shared a room with my fathers, so this was where I came for privacy. I wonder..." I rummaged through the hay bundled against the rafters. "*There.*"

BM. Engraved into the timber.

I leant back so she could see.

Clutching her chest, she gave a mock gasp. "Is that... *vandalism*, Bastian? So you were a rebellious child?"

I grinned and counted the slats up from my initials. "I just wanted to mark something as mine. Now, let's see if my treasure is still here." The rough wood twisted up with a bit of prying, revealing a small alcove beneath the roof tiles. "Jackpot."

"Treasure?" She crowded close, one hand resting on my knee as she peered at the small box I pulled out, her casual contact lighting my nerves.

Three dice—our kind with ten sides, not the odd human sort with only six—a few silver coins, and—

"My first dagger!" I drew the slender blade, scoffing at how the hilt got lost in my hand. "I wondered where it had gone."

At Kat's curious look, I offered it to her, handle-first.

She turned it over, frowning at the fine filigree of the moths decorating the crossguard. "It's so small."

"Hmm." I shrugged, clinking the coins together. "So was I back then."

As she weighed the dagger's balance, I stifled a yawn. "You need some sleep." She covered her mouth, fighting a yawn herself. "And so do I," she added with a rueful smile.

We put away my treasure, though when she tried to return the dagger to the box, I closed her fingers around it. "You keep it. A knife needs to be used to stay sharp, and I couldn't use it for much more than a toothpick now."

She raised an eyebrow as if to call out my exaggeration, but she squeezed the wire-wrapped hilt and nodded. "Thank you. It's a beautiful blade." Her gaze fell away and she shifted. "I'll give it back before I leave."

Jaw tight, I swallowed my reaction. I didn't want the dagger back and I didn't want her to leave. Instead, I busied myself clearing away the plate and returning the box to the hiding place. Maybe some other child would find it.

We settled into bed, and suddenly the hayloft seemed even smaller. She lay on her side, back to me, and I kept to my half of the bed as I dimmed the drifting lights.

"I can't picture you hiding away up here," she murmured into the darkness.

"I was a scrawny child." Something about not seeing her made it easier to talk.

Who was I fooling? The fact it was Kat made it easier to talk—that had been half the battle in Albion. Wanting to share everything with her but knowing she was a spy. UnCavendish had chosen well.

"I was the smallest at school. The smallest in the practice yard."

She made a soft sound of amusement. "I *definitely* can't picture a small Bastian."

I fingered the blanket beneath us, trying to convince myself touching that was an acceptable replacement for touching her. "Believe me, I was. I had my arse handed to me many, many times by every other trainee. Especially the princes, Cyrus and Sepher. They would find me outside the training yard and..."

Cyrus would fist a hand in my hair while he punched me in the gut. Sepher hovered nearby, keeping watch. The younger prince stopped helping his brother after his gift developed. No doubt his tail put him on Cyrus's list of victims

Dawn's dirty secret—a prince who was a shapechanger. Not everyone knew, but when he'd lost the ability to hide his animalistic nature, they'd banished him to a ruined palace outside of the city. The Court of Monsters, he called it.

Last I'd heard—I had spies there, of course—he had captured a human assassin and made her his "pet." I preferred not to linger on what that meant—not when I'd been on the receiving end of his attentions.

"Well"—I cleared my throat and the old memories—"I'm sure you know what bullies are like."

A low grumble echoed from her, like she was annoyed for young me.

"But it made me work harder. I trained any moment I could. I learned the dirtiest tactics. I watched for my class-mate's weaknesses and noted their injuries. I didn't hesitate to use them. The ends justified the means."

She half looked over her shoulder, and I caught the smooth line of her wide cheekbones. "Like aiming for the crotch."

"Exactly. And it paid off. Eventually, I started to win."

"Good." The viciousness of her voice cut through the dark like my Shadowblade.

I could've kissed her for it, licked the taste of it from her tongue, fucked her and begged to hear more of her simmering anger. I had to adjust my trousers around my hardening cock.

Down, I ordered it. Yes, I'd apologised, but words were cheap. I hadn't earned her forgiveness—shown myself anywhere near worthy of it. Not yet.

The story was a welcome distraction. "Then one winter, after I turned sixteen, I shot up. I grew a foot in the space of a few months and bulked out. Everyone else's gifts had already developed, but mine came then."

"So fae aren't born with powers."

"Stars above, no. Can you imagine toddlers with the power to crush bones with a thought? Or babies who can wield the weather?"

The hay rustled as she shuddered. "The stuff of nightmares."

"Not that teenagers are much better. I'm sure my poor fathers would call *that* a nightmare. They suddenly had a moody boy with unpredictable shadow magic on their hands. Meanwhile, my classmates started to pay attention to me, and not just because no one could beat me in the training guard. My hideaway became a different kind of retreat when I brought them up here."

"Privacy," Kat murmured.

"Until I was recruited into the Queensguard, the only privacy I could get." I scoffed at the memory. "I'd wait in here until everyone had disappeared before frantically stripping whatever lover had come to sample Bastian Marwood, the traitor's son. We fucked, they asked me to do all kind of things, like they had a list in mind before they came up here, then they left me in the hay, their curiosity and lust sated."

The silence drew on. I didn't regret my past lovers, but something about admitting this to her felt... high stakes.

"You were... a novelty."

"Not many fae with shadows—not in this realm, anyway. They enjoyed using me, and I had my fun. But... I have different preferences now."

"You like to be the one in charge."

She wasn't wrong, but low in my belly something tightened to hear her say it out loud.

Keeping her hands off me in Albion had been an attempt to remain in control—of the situation but also of myself. But it was a broader preference too. In the bedroom and in life.

When I lost control, that was when things went wrong.

Another yawn dragged on me, saving me from responding.

"Goodnight, Bastian," she murmured.

My hand pressed into the space between us to stop it from reaching for her hair, which spilled over the makeshift pillow. "Goodnight, Katherine."

I DROPPED into the depths of sleep at once, like a stone cast into a lake. At some point I woke. There was no sound other than Kat's breathing, which wasn't the slow rhythm of sleep.

"What's wrong?" I mumbled.

"Sorry, I didn't mean to wake you. I'm just a bit cold."

No fire, like we'd had in camp. And we were nearing midwinter. "You should've told me." I lifted the blankets and wrapped my arm around her waist. "Come here."

With a soft sound that started as surprise and melted into

a sigh, she slotted into the space in front of me. Back against my chest, backside tantalisingly close to my dick, thighs curled over mine. I was too tired and already sinking back into sleep, unable to do anything about it other than squeeze her close and nuzzle against her hair and enjoy that simple, perfect pleasure.

28

KAT

Sunlight crept into the stables, pressing on my eyelids. Below, deer snuffled and rustled through the hay and straw. And closer—much, much closer—at my front, Bastian was warm and solid at my front, one arm around me, his other pillowing my head. Our legs had tangled together in the night.

I kept still, pretending to be asleep. If I pretended, I didn't have to move.

I couldn't name it, but something had changed on our journey. Perhaps it was that he'd apologised. Perhaps it was the time away from his work. Perhaps it was time alone.

Something still felt broken between us—not quite fixed by our apologies, but...

It *had* all been real.

And that changed everything.

I gripped his shirt, heart tripping over its beats, and finally opened my eyes.

I should've known he'd already be awake, though he

blinked sleepily and gave this slow smile like he'd only just woken. It only heightened the impact of his closeness.

Silver eyes that seemed to glow brighter in this dim light. Nose half an inch from mine. Hair mussed in a way that made his beauty less sharp and more human. Like maybe, just maybe, I could reach out and...

My fingers slid up his stubbled throat, rasping softly. His pulse thrummed as I crossed it and continued to the scar running from his chin and up through his lips.

Not just the most gorgeous person I knew but... perhaps the most broken. And yet... he endured. Shoulders set, he pushed on into every day.

My heart ached for him. I wanted to tell him that he didn't have to endure. He didn't have to push. He didn't have to pretend it was all fine—that he was untouchable.

But I didn't want to break the spell the sunrise had cast over us.

So I ran my fingers into his hair, combing it off his face, and arched into his tightening grip around my waist.

"Katherine," he murmured, mouth so close to mine, I could feel the name on my lips.

"... *at all?*" From outside, a woman's raised voice shattered the spell. "What do you mean?"

A low answer I couldn't make out.

"There has to be some sign of them," she went on, something familiar in her tone. "Maybe they stayed at an inn."

"That's what we're going to check, madam." A man's voice I didn't recognise. A guard, perhaps? "If you would just calm—"

"There *aren't* any inns between here and there." Was that Asher?

"I'm coming with you," the woman added, and I could

picture the raised chin that went with her comment. "We'll be able to sniff her out."

"Wait." I bolted upright at the same moment Bastian did. "*Ella?*"

I flew down the ladder and burst into the stable yard.

Ella, Perry, Asher, a handful of guards, and, at Perry's side, sniffing the air—

"Vespera." I half sobbed out her name, rushing forward.

They came. Why? How?

A small voice added, *For me?*

I jolted to a stop, a hand gripping my wrist—Bastian's. The gentle crease of his brow and slight shake of his head smacked into me.

The purple stain was up to my wrists, all the more reminder.

My poison.

I stood three feet from Ella. It felt more like a mile.

Vespera started forward with a chirrup of greeting, but Perry pressed a hand into her chest and gripped the halter, a frown imprinted on her face as though she understood something was wrong. Towering at her back, Asher held her shoulder and placed a hand on Vespera's neck.

Ella's perfect face crumpled in confusion as she looked from me to Bastian.

I shook my head. What was I meant to say? How could I explain? Words were impossible, lost in the hollow ache of my chest.

Bastian pressed something into my hand and it took me a long while of blinking at the dark leather to understand they were my gloves.

"Asher," he said, clapping him on the shoulder, though the rigidity of his smile belied his confidence.

I slid on my gloves, separating myself from the rest of the world. Something else that had changed on our journey—no fear of poisoning anyone.

"Perry, Ella," Bastian continued with his greetings as the guards dispersed. "It's good to see you, though I didn't realise Asher was going to have company."

Ella was still casting a questioning look between me and Bastian.

Perry patted Vespera's shoulder, though her knuckles were white on the reins. "Officially, the pirate queen would appreciate me paving the way for a royal visit."

Bastian cocked his head. "And unofficially?"

"I know Vice would appreciate me keeping an eye on her sister in... uncharted waters."

With a deep breath, I forced a smile onto my face. "Thank you."

These leather gloves were safe—I'd saddled and bridled the stags without harm. One hand on my pendant, I pressed my palm to Vespera's forehead. She pushed back, a purr rumbling in the air around us.

"Hello, my lovely. I missed you. Stags just aren't the same." She butted forward, trying to get her head against my chest, right under my chin, as she always did.

My eyes burned as I had to catch and stop her. "Don't let..." My words to Perry broke. "She can't touch me."

Perry and Asher worked together to pull her back, and I had to swallow down my threatening tears before turning to Ella. "I can't believe you're here."

"I needed to check you were all right." She gave Bastian a meaningful glance. "*Are* you all right?"

"It's a long story," I murmured. "Just don't touch me."

Bastian widened his eyes at me.

"I'm telling them," I shot back at his unspoken warning. "Surely that's safe."

Jaw flexing, he exhaled. "Fine. But wait until you're inside —somewhere secure."

"Our rooms?"

His eyebrows shot up, and a private smile crept over his lips. "That sounds perfect."

The look he gave me was intimate, but I couldn't work out what had surprised him.

"Sorry to leap on you with business first thing in the morning, Bastian." Asher stepped out from behind Perry, though his hand remained on her shoulder. "But we have some things to discuss."

That private smile dimmed a little. "We do," Bastian said, not taking his eyes off me.

My fingers curled as they had into his hair only minutes ago.

As Asher headed inside, Bastian backed away, giving me a slow nod, gaze lingering until he had to turn.

I couldn't touch my friends or my sabrecat until Elthea had a cure for me. And not all things could be cured in the Hall of Healing, but maybe Bastian and I had mended the worst of the rift between us.

29

BASTIAN

Asher led me into the palace, gestures clipped and tight. Bad news.

We kept quiet until we were into our side of the building. "What is it?" I murmured. "What happened?"

"Multiple things. Only one of them good. Things are smoothed over with the human queen, for now. She's sending a delegation to continue the rekindled relationship between our countries."

That was something. "And the bad?"

"His Majesty had several Dusk folk arrested for 'aiding and abetting' Ascendants."

"Fuck. Let me guess—with flimsy evidence?"

"The flimsiest. And Faolán recognised one of the women who was taken—she'd witnessed some Ascendants painting outside her house?"

The woman we'd interviewed. "Her, an accessory? She came straight to us. Reported everything."

"I know. I took it to Braea as soon as I heard. Even Cyrus

tried to speak sense into the king, but..." His head bowed. "He had them all executed."

For several steps, I couldn't speak. Dusk folk who'd trusted their court to keep them safe, killed, and for what? For the king to discredit the queen? To score points over us?

"How many?"

"Twelve."

Twelve more marks on my soul. Twelve more people I'd failed.

I nodded, every movement tight. "What else?"

Asher hesitated. "An attack. Gael."

I swallowed, throat suddenly tight. "Are they—?"

"Injured. But on the mend. I arrived yesterday and checked them over—the healers did a good job. In a couple of days they'll be fine. But they demanded to see you as soon as you returned."

The note. I'd left it with them to decode while I was away. The attack had to be related. There was no other reason for someone to come for Gael. Either the attacker wanted to retrieve the note or silence them from revealing what they'd discovered in it.

I eyed the next set of guards we passed—there were more than usual. Good. They were taking this seriously.

Either Dawn had operatives on our side or one of their people had snuck through a lodestone. I needed to check the courtyard. I'd left threads of spidersilk on the doors so I would know if they'd somehow been opened.

We arrived at Gael and Brynan's suite where we found Gael pale and laid up in bed with their partner fussing around them.

"You're back." Gael's eyes widened as they pushed up on their pillows.

"Don't…" Brynan eased them back, throwing me a tight smile.

"He's right. Don't." I raised my hands and nodded towards the pillows. "I'm sure this can wait until you're feeling—"

"No." They sat up, swatting away Brynan's protests. "I'm not as bad as he thinks. Really, darling, you're fretting now. I can't tell you here."

"You're worried someone may be listening."

"Brynan told me your offices are secure. Once we're there, I'll explain." They swung their legs out of bed, ignoring Brynan's protests.

I would've voiced my own, but Gael moved with ease, only seeming stiff when they bent over and pulled on a pair of shoes. We filed to my office in tense silence.

Once we were sealed inside, I gestured for Gael to explain. "No one can hear us now. What happened?"

"I was working on…" They raised their eyebrows and eyed Asher.

"He knows about the note. Carry on."

"It had grown chilly, so I went to close the window, and… there was someone there. In our sitting room." They pressed their lips together, and Brynan squeezed their knee.

"Go on, darling."

"I caught the movement out the corner of my eye and turned, but it was too late." They rubbed their stomach, pale skin turning even paler. "I barely managed to twist away from another strike. I don't know how long I dodged them, trying to get to a weapon, but they got me again before I could. Then… Then"—they covered Brynan's hand with their own—"he came back early from reporting to Her Majesty."

Brynan's mouth twisted. "I think I pissed her off, so she sent me away. Thank the Stars she did. Someone was standing

211

over them, all in grey, face covered. I couldn't see anything of use."

I worked my jaw side to side. "Let me guess—average height, average build, no sign of masculine or feminine features."

Brynan nodded. "Their dagger had a bronze hilt, that's all I can say."

Asher made a soft sound. "A perfect assassin."

Eyes gleaming, Brynan bent closer to Gael and touched his head to theirs. "They were ready to... finish things. But I..."

Gael chuckled darkly. "You blasted in. I thought someone had unleashed a Horror."

"If I get hold of whoever that was, I'll feed them to one." He scowled. "I only managed to get a slash in."

"*Only?*" Gael raised their eyebrows. "You sent them running. You should've gone after them, though."

Brynan's refined features scrunched up—an exaggerated version of his more customary thoughtful frown. "I had to check you were all right." He shot me a look. "By the time I made sure this one wasn't about to bleed out, there was no sign of the attacker. I'm sorry. I know I should've—"

"It's fine. I understand." If it had been Katherine, I'd have done the same.

Eyebrows rising, he exchanged a glance with Gael. Asher looked away, a smirk edging his mouth.

The old Bastian would've rebuked Brynan for not going after the assassin. Capturing them would've given us vital information. And while many watched my shadows with mistrust and fear, they were weren't my true power.

That was knowledge.

And yet instead, here I was telling Brynan it was fine that they'd put their partner first.

Kat was turning me soft.

"Guards swept the palace, but didn't find the intruder." Asher shrugged. "Not even a trail of blood."

"Of course not." I pursed my lips. "Still, you could've written this in a report."

"Not this next part." Gael sat up and held my gaze—something only those closest to me managed for any length of time. The glow tended to unnerve the seelie. "I finished decoding the note."

I straightened in my seat. "And?"

"I burned my decoding. I don't trust it to paper. If my attacker had got hold of it..."

My money was on the attacker working for the king, their aim being to stop us from uncovering its contents.

"It was just addressed to 'sire'—no clues about who that may be." Gael placed the original note on my desk, unfolded. "This part says the writer went to the Riverton library as instructed and found a book that referenced the 'undesirable situation.' Apparently the humans didn't realise the age of the book they had—it had been collected with writings by other scholars and rebound into a single volume, but the script matched that of a scroll in Dawn's library."

I sat back with a soft huff. "You think it's one of the works taken to Albion as part of the marriage bargain?"

The lord who'd married the human queen a couple of hundred years ago had taken books with him—old books, as Lysander liked to scowl and complain about. The Dawn delegation must've found the information they sought in one of those.

Shit. Why hadn't I spent more time in the library and less time caught up in Katherine?

There had been that one time where both things had

crossed paths. Her thighs in my hands. Her sweet whimpers. Sunlight haloing her blazing hair as my ember had become a glorious flame.

Focus, Bastian. I raked my hands through my hair.

Asher frowned at the note. "That's the only way I can think of humans having something that matched one of our scrolls. Does it say anything about the author of these papers? I wonder if we have a copy."

"It does." Gael swallowed. "The Lark."

I sat up.

Asher's lips parted. "You're... sure?"

"I know what I'm doing. That's what it said."

The sorceress from the time we warred with humans. Considered little more than legend and fable by most, but legends and fables tended not to leave texts written in their own hand. We had a few. Dawn had more. And apparently Albion had at least one. I would have Lysander gather ours. Perhaps my spy could get her hands on Dawn's, but they'd likely be missed.

It would be easier if I could give her more specific instructions of what to look for. "Any indication what this book said exactly?"

Gael drew a deep breath and squared their shoulders. "The book said there was an artefact that could end the Sleep."

Old news. I tried not to let my disappointment show.

"You understand what Dawn getting that would mean, don't you?" Gael sat forward. "If King Lucius isn't bound to daylight hours, he'll push for more power."

Asher's bronze skin lost it richness. He nodded, gaze shifting into the distance. "With only one monarch awake at a time, it's clear who people need to obey, whether their family is tied to Dusk or Dawn. It curbs conflict. But if they're both awake at once things will only grow more confrontational. I can hear Dawn folk now. 'Why would I obey the queen when my king is here?'"

Lips pressed together, Gael nodded. "That's why I burned my decoded version of the note. The king could use it as justification to take over as sole monarch. He wouldn't need the queen. It would..."

"It would be a coup," Asher finished for them.

"*Another* coup." Gael gave a bitter smile. "This one of Dawn over Dusk."

"There would be no more Dusk." Asher frowned at me. "Why aren't you reacting to this?"

I sighed. "I already knew there was such an object and that Dawn was after it."

When Gael turned wide eyes on Brynan, his gaze dropped. "You too?"

"He works for me. I made him vow not to tell you. Thank you for decoding the note, Gael. Thanks doesn't really cover the price you've paid, but I'll see to it guards remain on your corridor."

I'd been so sure the note would give me new information. Still, there were the Lark's texts. Better than nothing.

Clearing my throat, I rose and started towards the door, so I could unseal it and let Gael get back to resting. "I appreciate you understanding this knowledge can't go any further."

"That wasn't all."

At Gael's quiet addition, I spun.

"It doesn't just say there's an artefact that could free a ruler from the Sleep... It names it."

My muscles went taut. This *was* a lead. A name gave us something to look for in the texts, maybe even coded references in old stories. "And that name is...?"

"The Circle of Ash."

Not familiar. "A circle? What could that be?" I glanced at Asher—he was older than me and might've heard of it.

He shook his head.

"A hoop made of ash wood?" Brynan spread their hands. "Maybe it means ring rather than circle?"

"It's unclear." Gael rubbed a fold of their trousers between their fingertips. "I'm working with a coded reference to a spy's translation of an ancient scroll. It may be the scroll is clear but the person who coded the note has phrased it in an obscure way as a failsafe to keep the information secret."

Asher grunted. "Or it may be the text is just as murky."

The bag containing Elthea's box sat at my feet. Was there a ring or disc inside?

I huffed and nodded at Gael. "Seems I owe you an even bigger thank you. This gives us something more to go on with our research."

Brynan rose as I caught his eye. "I'll put together a reading list."

"I'm sure you can do that back in your rooms."

My guests gathered themselves, taking my hint.

"Gael—look after yourself." I patted them on the shoulder as I opened the door. "And maybe let Brynan look after you a little. It's as much for him as it is for you. He thought he'd lost you."

I could picture it. Walking in, finding Kat on the floor in a pool of her own blood, a dark figure standing over her.

I *had* seen it. Kat. No blood, but instead the sharp scent of poison surrounding her. The changeling standing over her, triumphant. My eyelids fluttered as I pulled myself back from the horror of that moment and said my goodbyes.

Once they were gone, I pulled out the box. Kat must've

cleaned off the soot. It hummed with weak magic, but it could be warded to disguise its contents—that would explain why the Horrors hadn't pulled apart the chimney to get at it.

It seemed too great a coincidence that Lucius was on the trail of something important and lost, just as Elthea sent me to fetch a magically locked box from Horror territory. Giving him the Circle of Ash would see her well rewarded, her influence elevated—it would give her what everyone at court wanted.

Power.

With a growl, I set off to deliver the box... and work out how to get its contents back before Elthea could take it to her king.

30

BASTIAN

As soon as I entered the Hall of Healing, Elthea was on me like a fly on shit.

I'd come here along the busiest route possible. If Dawn courtiers saw that I was back, word would soon spread, and with a little luck that would discourage any further attacks. Of course they'd only dared come to our side of the palace while I was away.

Her eyes lit up, skimming over me. "Do you have it?"

I kept my mouth shut and nodded into the depths of the building.

Fiddling with the pocket that held her notebook, she led me upstairs to a tidy office, as pale as her hair. "Well?" She spun as soon as the door shut behind me.

"I have your box." I watched her as I pulled it out.

Her eyes widened as I placed it on the desk. She slid a hand over the box's varnished surface and breathed, "Ooh."

Kat would've known what her every action meant. I could only watch and deduce that she looked relieved.

With a long exhale, she smiled.

Had I fallen into some trap? Had I delivered the very thing that would allow Dawn to destroy Dusk? The rules governing bargains meant I couldn't snatch it away right now, but there was nothing to stop me waiting outside for her to leave.

Bending over, she opened the box.

A delicate chime rang through the room, beginning a soft melody, and as the lid opened fully, it revealed a bird emerging from a tiny trapdoor inside the box. The bird, a swallow, swooped from one side of the box to the other, its movements flowing with the music. Dimly, I recalled the words to the tune—they told about the simple pleasure and perfection of a summer swallow cutting the sky into shapes that she then threaded into garments for the gods. A old lullaby.

"A music box?"

Eyes closed, she raised a hand. The hand stayed there until the tune finished.

I could only stare at the swallow and its forked tail, my tired mind tripping over itself.

"*A music box?*"

"Yes. *My* music box. That's why I didn't want you breaking it open." She held up the little key and smiled, then closed the lid and reopened it, starting the song again. "Do you like it?"

"*Do I like it?* You sent me into Horror territory for a fucking *music box?* I don't believe it." I pulled off its inner lid, but that only revealed the delicate clockwork of the mechanism and the soft scent of old, weak magic.

"You're going to break it." She snatched the box back and set it on the table, stroking the inner lid now it had slotted back into place.

Was she *humming* along with the tune?

Teeth gritted, I squeezed my hands into fists. I needed to pull myself together.

"I thought it was going to be a powerful artefact. Something of use for you or your court. A relic for your king. Something *worth* almost getting us killed."

She huffed. "There's more to life than power and courts and kings and queens. This was *mine*, given to me by my parents. When your fathers marched on Innesol, we fled. My mother wouldn't let me take the box—I had to be practical, she said. We could only take what we could carry. So I hid it and told myself we would be back one day. That was before your father brought his monsters to my home." Her normally calm face had turned hard, her eyes unblinking. "I know they slaughtered everyone there. It was lucky my parents chose to leave. But I still wanted this little reminder of the home I'd once had—the childhood friends who would listen to this song with me."

I held still, every word a grain of salt in the open wound of my father's memories and the destruction I'd seen for myself.

She hugged the box to herself. "I remember those who have been forgotten by all others. And I remember what your family did, Serpent. The queen might have forced me to heal your wounds the night of the coup, but I would never save your life by choice. That was why I left the scar—I followed her orders so you didn't die, but I wanted you to remember."

She didn't shout or hiss—no, this was a quieter kind of fury that paled her lips.

"I pity you. The Serpent who can't understand why I would want something for myself, why I might care for other people. After all, you killed your own father without batting an eyelid." She scoffed, cold as winter. "How sad you are, a Serpent who doesn't realise that not every fae is as obsessed with gathering power as he is."

That was where people misunderstood me. It was never about power.

I didn't set her right. Better that folk didn't know my motivations, then they couldn't use them against me.

Never—never reveal your heart.

I SLEPT the rest of the day. Despite my exhaustion, it was a fitful sleep. Every time I woke, my hand went to the empty space beside me. One time, I woke saying her name. Another, I was reliving the moment when she'd referred to these as *our* rooms.

Part of me was glad we'd spoken. It had certainly created a better atmosphere, and it felt good to be able to speak to her as I had last night.

But it also made things worse.

So much worse.

Now the air between us was clearer, the temptation of her shone all the brighter.

Last night, in the hayloft, I could pretend a little longer. Just us. Just that moment. No messy past.

But pretending wasn't real, and I had a job to do.

First order was asking Braea about the executions. She was meant to soften Lucius's paranoid, knee-jerk reactions, not let him execute anyone. Certainly not innocents. After visiting Elthea, I'd checked there wasn't anyone else in their dungeon. I would have no more executions.

Now, shoulders squared, I entered the small, informal dining room where the queen took breakfast.

The instant the door closed behind me, I knew something was wrong. It wasn't that the air was colder, as such, but the scent of snow filled the room, crisp and harsh.

The scent of my queen's magic.

"Well, look who it is darkening my door." She slammed her cutlery into the table. "The little snake who keeps secrets."

I held my ground and kept my shadows close. Head cocking in question, I raised my eyebrows.

"Don't play the fucking innocent with me, Bastian." She stood, chair shrieking across the floor. "First, it's not telling me about your little friend waking up, then it's this." Every movement clipped and sharp, she approached, black eyes burning into me. "I'm starting to question where your loyalties lie."

My loyalties? I'd killed my own father for her. The man who'd fed and clothed me. The man who'd shown me how to fight, how to beat the bigger children when I'd been so small. The man who'd stood by me even when my unseelie blood had woken and I'd struggled to control my shadows.

I'd killed him.

For her.

And she questioned my loyalty?

Muscles tight, I swallowed the sting of her doubt. "They lie with you, as you well know, Braea."

"Don't you use my name now, boy. I may be fond of you, but even my indulgence has a limit." Her finger thrust into my face, pointed nail half an inch from my chin. "I could understand you keeping quiet about your little indiscretion with the human girl, but this? *This?*"

I worked my tongue around my mouth and drew a deep breath, praying to any gods that were listening that I looked calmer than I felt. "Perhaps if you told me what *this* was, I could explain." Somehow my voice came out level.

"The Sleep." Her nostrils flared and she paced away as though her anger made standing still impossible. "You have discovered there is an object that will end the Sleep *and* that Dawn is after it, yet the first I hear of it is from your assistant."

The air flew out of me like she'd jabbed me in the stomach when I wasn't prepared. Brynan. I'd left him to report to her in my absence. He must have mentioned it, not realising I was waiting for confirmation before informing her.

"Until today, I knew nothing but a faint whisper. I didn't want to say anything until I had details."

She turned, one sharp eyebrow rising. "Today? What happened *today*?"

"We decoded the message I intercepted in Albion." I explained the note's contents, and her shoulders inched down until finally she looked like she wasn't about to put *me* in the dungeons.

When I was done, she leant back on the table, gaze on the window and the dark sky outside. "Find it."

"What?"

"This Circle of Ash. Find it. I want all your resources on this."

"But Hydra Asc—"

"*All of them.*" Her gaze shot to me. "I'm not afraid of some children with a pot of red paint. If my cursed Sleep can be ended, I want it done. *Do you understand?*"

I blinked at her, understanding all too well.

She wanted the relic to end her own Sleep, not just to keep it out of Dawn's hands. What about the balance between us and them?

No, she was just angry. This information was still fresh. Once she took the time to think about it, she'd realise this Circle shouldn't be used by either side.

As for Hydra Ascendant...

It wasn't just vandalism. They weren't just a few kids with a stylish insignia. They were recruiting, spreading. And they hadn't only reached the city—if my hunch proved right, they were coming for the palace.

Meanwhile, *within* the palace we had Dawn—close enough to attack Gael. Connected enough to plant a changeling in the human court.

All of these things needed the Serpent's resources. Any one of them could rise up and bite us in the arse.

But my queen lifted her chin, imperious and unwavering. "Bastian?"

I swallowed and found an answer that wasn't a lie. "I understand."

31

KAT

The week after our return fell back into a routine. Exploring the city (and its jewellers). Training with Faolán a couple of times a week. Attempting to learn some control over my magic... and *failing*.

Rose kept up her hopeful smile, but I sank deeper into despair. I hadn't been able to make contact with any power inside me. I could only unreliably affect the stains on my fingers.

At least Bastian wasn't avoiding me. Not deliberately, anyway—his work just kept him busy, so we only tended to see each other for dinner or lunch.

This all disappointed Ella, who seemed convinced that somehow us spending time alone together on the road would've resulted in us sleeping together. "You, him, a camp-fire... *One* cosy bed in the hayloft. I have no idea how nothing happened, to be honest."

I was just glad to have her back, even if I had to force

myself to sit on a separate settee so I didn't forget myself and touch her.

By the time the ball arrived, Rose and I had visited every jeweller in the city. No one admitted to making the necklace, so my investigation hinged on Caelus. He'd be there tonight—I'd managed to get that piece of information out of Brynan.

Outside, the sun dipped towards the horizon as I slipped a hip flask of *arianmêl* in a thigh garter and dressed in deep, glimmering purple, close to black. It almost matched the stains on my fingers, I realised as I patted raspberry-toned rouge on my lips.

Ari had given me a little pot of powder that disappeared on the skin until it caught the light in iridescent gold and violet, and I dusted that over the high points of my cheeks and my collarbones. A few specks caught in my hair, and I laughed as I watched the effect in the mirror.

I almost looked fae.

Tugging on a pair of sheer black gloves with lace cuffs, I headed into the sitting room. I looked the part. Gods willing, I'd be able to play it, too.

My stomach bubbled with nerves, and I went to poured a glass of brandy to settle myself. Except Bastian only kept regular spirits in our suite. No little drunken buzz for me.

I was putting the decanter back when a knock sounded at the door. Urien strode in, carrying a large case. "Clothing delivery. *A lot* of clothing." He raised his eyebrows, and I suddenly felt self-conscious, so when he offered to take it to my room, I declined the offer.

As soon as he left and I tried to lift the case, I regretted it. Ari had mentioned she was throwing in "a few extras"—she and I had very different definitions of "a few."

I was bent over, half carrying, half dragging it towards my

room when the door to the antechamber opened and Bastian appeared.

His eyes bulged, and when I looked down I realised why—my cleavage was... very cleavage-y—almost escaping my gown's low neckline, in fact.

He cleared his throat as I straightened. "Hiding a body?"

"Just one."

The corner of his mouth twitched. "Oh, well, in that case." He shrugged like it was no big deal and came closer. "I'll take care of it."

I wasn't sure if he was still talking about the fictional body or the case.

"I got you something. Some*things*, actually." He pulled a flat box from his inside pocket.

"You didn't—"

"Are we really going to have this conversation? 'Bastian, you didn't have to.' 'No, Kat, but I wanted to. That's how gifts work.'" He cocked his head. "Anything more to add?"

It seemed the Bastian I knew from Albion had woken today. I wasn't sure what to call him. Playful Bastian? Intimate Bastian?

Devastating Bastian?

Somehow I swallowed and raised one shoulder like he wasn't quite so devastating in his perfectly tailored jacket that he'd left unbuttoned to reveal the sheer black shirt beneath.

"Only *thank you*."

Inside lay a pair of gloves that matched my gown—sheer, blackened purple with flecks that glittered in the light. "How did you...?" I blinked up at him.

"I have spies everywhere. It wasn't so difficult to find out what you planned to wear, and Ariadne owed me a favour, so..."

I removed the black gloves. "I'm sure you could've used the favour on something more worthwhile."

"I'm sure I couldn't have." He kept his tone light and teasing, but an undercurrent ran through it, and I pulled on the first glove, giving it far more attention than needed. "Before you do." He covered my hand, stopping me donning the second glove.

I stilled and stamped down any other reaction to his touch. He'd already eased my poison at lunch time, so this didn't resonate with magic. And yet...

It was Bastian. The one I knew. The one who tangled me up so fucking easily.

"The other something," he murmured and dipped into his pocket again.

This time he produced a ring. Silver toned metal but cooler than true silver. Platinum, perhaps? A clear stone shaped like a star. Smaller stones surrounded it in star-shaped settings. The jewels flashed with tiny sparks of rainbow light—they had to be diamonds.

I was already shaking my head before I realised. A platinum and diamond ring? I couldn't... *I couldn't.*

"It counters fae charm," he went on in that same private voice. "I thought you could get rid of that necklace and everything it reminds you of."

I fingered the pearls at my throat. Their weight dragged on me as though unCavendish constantly had a hand around my throat. I probably didn't need it for the investigation anymore —Caelus knew what it looked like.

Yet, much as I wanted to get rid of it... "I can't accept this. It's too expensive. They're diamonds, Bastian."

"*Are* they?" He gave the ring a wide-eyed look. "Thank the Stars for that, otherwise I'd have to pay the jeweller an unpleasant visit to ask why he didn't make what I asked for. Please, Kat. Take the ring." He held it out. "I had it made for you, so it's not like I can return it."

I tugged at the necklace and swallowed. Perhaps I could throw it on the fire. I should probably sell it—it had to be worth a lot—but I'd rather watch it melt. Did pearls burn?

"I'll... borrow it. You can have it back when I leave."

A muscle in his cheek twitched, and I thought he was going to tell me no. But he snorted a laugh. "Whatever you need to tell yourself, Kat." He placed the ring in my hand. "But I won't be accepting it back."

"We'll see," I muttered as I slid it onto my middle finger. "A perfect fit."

"Of course." His gaze flicked to the necklace. "May I?"

"*Please.*"

He sucked in a quick breath, and I realised what I'd said. But he circled behind me and made no comment about how much he liked that word.

The world narrowed as he gathered my hair and placed it over my shoulder. The movement ghosted over my scalp, sending goosebumps chasing down my arms.

I helped hold my hair to one side and counted my breathing, forcing it deep and slow. Bastian's exhalation tickled behind my ear.

I closed my eyes. I wouldn't shiver. Mustn't. Shouldn't. I was sure the hairs on the back of my neck gave me away, though.

His fingertips feathered over my spine, pulling the necklace tight for an instant. I straightened, taut, breath held, waiting, waiting, waiting.

With a soft click, the tightness disappeared, and he gathered up the necklace.

That terrible weight was gone. I could breathe.

"There." The word skimmed my sensitised skin, and I must've forgotten about control, because I shuddered, eyelids fluttering shut.

When I opened my eyes, he stood before me, closer than he should be, holding the necklace in the scant space between us.

"You're free."

Free.

But, no. I wasn't. Not from my husband. The fact hung in the air, thick and heavy like cheap perfume.

We stood in it a long while, inhaling that ugly truth. Maybe it was its own kind of poison and if I took in enough, it would kill off my attraction to him. It must've destroyed his desire for me. Probably for the best.

And yet.

Neither of us walked away, locked together by our gazes.

Not until a knock sounded at the door, and it was as though my ears popped and I could hear again.

Bastian straightened, a muscle in his jaw rippling as his fist closed around the necklace. "Enter." It was Business Bastian who spoke, all clipped and formal.

I dragged my attention from him and took a long while pulling on my glove.

"Well, don't you two make a gorgeous couple?" Rose surveyed us, smile wide.

"We aren't..." I muttered.

Faolán's gaze flicked across the small space between us.

Bastian backed away. "Right. I thought Katherine would want an escort for the party. But I see she already has company."

"Oh, no. You don't escape that easily." Rose blocked the doorway.

"Faolán." Bastian raised an eyebrow at him.

"Hmm. We've already discussed it, little flower." He disentangled himself from her. "It's best if I escort Kat."

I should've expected it. I shouldn't be hurt by it. And yet the rejection stung me.

It was sensible. All eyes would be on me. Walking in on Bastian's arm would only make it look like there was something between us.

So I plastered on a wide smile and gave Faolán a playful bow before checking my gloves and only then placing my hand in the crook of his elbow.

Without looking at us, Bastian offered his arm to Rose, and we set off for a party in my honour.

I felt a lot of things in that moment. Honoured wasn't one of them.

32

BASTIAN

With Rose on my arm, I watched Faolán escort Kat to the party and slammed every door in my mind against the memory of the last party we'd attended together. Thankfully, she wore more this time. Fine lace covered the low back of her gown, but I'd still seen how she reacted to my touch.

And I'd felt an answering call in my bones.

Our time on the road had made me weak. Giving her that ring had been foolish, filling my head with all sorts of stupid ideas. I could so easily have kissed her.

And she might've let me.

Somehow, despite everything, she wanted me, physically at least. The only thing worse than her not wanting me was the thought that if I asked—if I led her to a quiet corner of this party—she might let us finish what we'd started in Albion.

I wasn't sure I was a strong enough, a good enough man to not follow through with that. But I knew I didn't deserve to. I hadn't earned that right—that forgiveness.

I certainly couldn't afford to let others see how much I wanted it and her.

That left me with only one option: distance.

Chin lifted, eyelids drooping with boredom, I sauntered through the first chamber. In my nostrils, her magic was sweet and sharp, like something delicious that I'd adore right up until the moment it killed me.

Drink of all kinds and the faint woody scent of *sairsa* smoke surrounded us. Thank the fucking gods we didn't have to drink *arianmêl* this time or I really would have been lost.

Someone sang, sweet and slow like honey. Dozens of conversations bubbled below that, low and intimate.

No one announced us, but every pair of eyes in the room followed Kat's path.

In different circumstances, I'd have swelled with pride to be near her in public. Part of me did—a base, instinctual part that didn't give a shit about the past or anyone else seeing how I felt about her. All it knew was that she was mine. *Mine.*

That part could say whatever it liked, but it wasn't in charge. I ignored it and kept my shadows on a tight leash.

The next chamber's dark walls made the space feel smaller. Here, lingering touches punctuated the intimate conversations, heating the space with seductive promise. The base part of me liked the charged atmosphere, telling me it was the perfect place to bring Kat later.

In the third chamber, the honey-voiced singer's voice combined with drum and cello. Dancers filled the main body of the room, but this wasn't the kind of dance we'd done in Albion.

They heaved with the music's heady rhythm as though they were part of it. Bodies entwined, they rocked and wound around each other, laughing, kissing, some biting their own lips in that delicious moment of resistance that came before giving in to temptation.

The dancers parted for us, though they watched. Despite her small stature, Kat's hair was a beacon, and I stiffened, ready in case anyone thought her appearance was an invitation to touch.

Rose squeezed my arm. "She'll be fine."

I scowled at the people we passed. "I hope you're right."

We reached the edge of the dancers and found the queen upon a gilded chair, watching as she stroked the hair of the lover sitting at her feet. We'd discussed the Dusk folk who'd been executed and put in place countermeasures to ensure there wouldn't be a repeat of that. It was almost enough to ease my guilt.

Dark eyes on Kat, Braea smiled slowly. "Ah, and here is our guest of honour."

Rose gave my arm another comforting squeeze before retreating. Faolán nodded to the queen and joined Rose. Just past them, the lush green curls of the Queen Meredine's hair caught my eye as she watched Kat approach Braea. It made my spine stiffen, but I couldn't tell if that was because of some ill intent in the Day Queen's expression or just my protectiveness.

Still, she wasn't the queen who'd summoned Kat here. I bowed my head formally to Braea. "Your Majesty. I present Lady Katherine Ferrers."

Kat swept into a graceful bow.

"None of that." Queen Braea clicked her tongue and waved Kat closer. "Come here, child."

I didn't detect any reaction in Kat to being called "child" but she had to wonder—after all, the Night Queen didn't look much older than her. But Braea had lived many human lifetimes. At thirty-five, even I was a child to her.

Kat approached and I lingered nearby, close enough to hear any quiet conversation and swoop in for rescue or damage limitation, if needed.

"Let me see you properly." Braea reached out as if to turn Kat's head. Her fingers closed just short as she must've remembered my warning. She took her in for a long second before nodding. "Such a sweet-looking girl."

"Your Majesty is too kind," Kat murmured with lowered lashes.

Braea chuckled. "You may look sweet, *sound* sweet, yet you helped my Shadow uncover a plot."

"Luck put me in the right place at the opportune moment, Your Majesty. But I'm grateful I was able to help."

I frowned as their soft, polite conversation drew to a close.

"What's wrong, dear Bastian?" Braea raised an eyebrow at me. "Surely you can't complain about our guest of honour?" Again, that reach for Kat before pulling back. "She is delightful."

"Not that." I shook my head and couldn't help my gaze skipping to Kat. "Never that. But I think she may be thirsty."

"No drinks? We can't have that. Go—get yourselves away. Drink and enjoy all my court has to offer." She spread her arms to encompass the room and dismissed us.

What an idiot, I told myself as we turned away. I should never have underestimated Kat. Of course she knew how to juggle a queen, whether human or fae. Anyone else listening wouldn't be able to guess Kat's skills. What she knew. What she wanted. Her heart.

Even in a strange court, she understood how to keep herself safe.

33

KAT

Not yet familiar with fae drinks, I let Bastian choose me something pale amber and sparkling from the a tray. When I tasted it, the bubbles danced across my tongue. Sweet and sour, like lemons and limes but... different. Brighter—more like sunshine. I made a soft sound of pleasure and let my shoulders ease.

"I think that went well." I raised my eyebrows at him, hopeful.

He eyed me over his drink as he took a sip. "You were perfect."

His words suffused me, and, face heating, I had to take another gulp of whatever it was in my glass. *Slowly*. I had plans for tonight. Not to mention the need to keep hold of my magic.

A moment later, his expression stiffened and he looked away before leading me to a small group including Ella, Rose, and Faolán and introduced his assistant, Brynan, and his partner, Gael. Then Bastian excused himself.

I stood there amidst their smalltalk, tiny thorns pricking my heart. Things between us weren't right, not entirely, but after our travels, I thought they were better. That moment when he'd given me this ring and removed the necklace... it had felt like *something*.

Ella ducked closer, eyeing guests passing. "How's your 'project' going?"

I'd told her about my investigation into unCavendish. She'd given me a fierce grin of approval and offered to help in any way. But she'd endured enough fae intrigue—if I could keep her out of this, I would.

"Mixed results so far." I scanned the crowd, which was as full of Dawn folk as Dusk—their outfits blending to create a full rainbow from rich jewel tones to pale whispers of colour. "I'm looking for Caelus. Think he knows something."

"He's here—I saw him earlier." She nodded back towards the entrance. "Over that way."

Perfect. My first instinct was to give her a squeeze, but... poison. It had been enough of a challenge to trust my gloves and layers of clothing to take Faolán's arm on the way here.

Instead, I blew her a harmless kiss. "You are a diamond."

She primped her hair and grinned. "I know. I'll help you get away, too." She winked before draining her drink and turning to the rest of the group.

Effortlessly, she inserted herself into Rose and Brynan's conversation about the coming eclipse and listened as though rapt.

A moment later, she asked, "And that's the only time the queen and king can be awake at the same time? *Fascinating.*" She went to take a sip but widened her eyes at the empty glass. "Damn."

I bit back a laugh, suddenly filled with fierce joy at having my friend back. "I can get you a fresh drink—save you missing out on any of this *fascinating* discussion."

She touched her chest. "Oh, *would you*? So thoughtful."

"Aren't I?" I gave her a wink, mouthed a *thank you* when no one was looking, then slipped into the crowd.

The folk from Dusk glanced at me and nodded, most of them smiling—I was old news to them. But those from Dawn watched more closely, albeit from behind fans and glasses. They were courtiers, and just like back in Albion, they knew a little about subtlety.

Any one of them could be behind unCavendish. Admittedly, it was *possible* he'd been sent by someone from Dusk—someone who hated Bastian, but Dawn seemed most likely. Poisoning him at the wedding—that felt less personal, more political.

The question was, who had tried to ruin the alliance?

I searched for Caelus in the crowd, careful to keep my gloves up to my elbows so no bare skin peeked out.

Although I searched for one fae, it was Bastian's name I picked out on someone's lips. It was too noisy for me to catch much more than the word "oathbreaker" and I didn't spot the speaker.

As I went on, my thoughts remained snagged on Bastian and his stiff shoulders as he'd disappeared.

He wasn't the same person who'd taken me to the party in Riverton Palace or the one who'd laughed with me in a cave, drenched in rain. This man looked tired all the time. He carried a weight I couldn't fully understand, only that it seemed like a heavier version of the one I'd held when the estate was under threat.

Messages arrived for him in the middle of the night—pounding on the doors woke me. A couple of times I'd padded to the sitting room door to listen to the quiet voices. I'd heard enough to understand that he was about to hurry back to his room and get dressed, ready to deal with whatever his court and queen demanded.

Golden hair caught the light and a laugh rose above the others. Prince Cyrus. Head back, arm around a woman's shoulder, he poured drink from a bottle into another man's mouth.

Mostly in his mouth, anyway—his laughter sent plenty spilling over his chin and cheeks.

As Cyrus lowered the bottle and his friend spluttered, he met my gaze.

I held my face still, not allowing myself to wince as inwardly I chanted: *Don't come over. Don't come over.* After his behaviour last time, I had the feeling he wasn't going to take no for an answer when it came to dancing.

With a smirk, he nodded, but otherwise made no approach.

A total idiot *and* capricious, it seemed.

Lucky for me.

A voice came at my shoulder. "Despite being a Day Prince, His Highness's attentions wax and wane like the moon."

I spun on my heel and found Caelus, chestnut hair gleaming like the sun was upon it, even now in the dead of night. "Just who I was looking for."

His eyebrows flicked up. I didn't miss the pleased smile that ghosted on his lips. "And I was looking for you—the guest of honour. Join me?" He gestured along the loose path that opened up through the guests, and I fell in at his side.

"You know they held a ball just before I left Lunden, but without you there, it was entirely dull."

"Oh, you mean no one interrupted any important rituals or smashed priceless glassware?"

The corner of his mouth twitched. "I believe one glass was broken, but not a single ritual was interrupted by anyone taking poison."

"How *boring*." That's it, put him at ease. I eyed his drink as I swirled mine. Somehow I had to get *arianmêl* in there.

"Even more boring—your uncle spent the whole time trying to ingratiate himself with your queen. Kept going on about how you were his niece and had saved the country. It was quite embarrassing."

My throat tightened, and I went to tug at the necklace that was no longer there. Uncle Rufus could embarrass the Ferrers name for all I cared, just as long as he stayed far, far out of my life.

"I'm sorry—it looks like I shouldn't have mentioned anything." Caelus wore a pained look as we passed a set of doors leading out into the gardens.

You're meant to be tricking him into spilling what he knows about unCavendish, not making him feel bad.

I needed to get the hip flask of *arianmêl* out of my garter and pour some in his drink. Somehow.

So I waved him off and forced out a breezy laugh. "He *is* a fool. But aren't we all fools, sometimes?"

"I think perhaps I was at the last party we both attended."

My breath caught at the reminder of him asking if I would share myself with him as well as Bastian. He'd seen Bastian make me come undone, and that made my face burn, but perhaps it opened up an opportunity...

He winced. "I should never have—"

"Maybe *I* was the fool."

His attention honed in on me, as focused as the pressure at a blade's point. I made myself wait—*one, two, three*—before turning and giving him a meaningful look.

Lips parted he held my gaze and there was such hope in them that for a moment I hated myself.

But only for a moment.

Because I needed to know about unCavendish, and if that meant crushing Caelus's heart—well, so be it.

The changeling had helped destroy my heart—in some warped way, it felt like a fair exchange.

"You know," I went on, voice lower, "we never had a chance to drink one of those shots together at that party. What were they? *Ariammel? Aria—?*"

"*Arianmêl.*"

"That's it!" I touched his arm, my glove keeping him safe. "They had shots of it at the door, didn't they? I swear that stuff was responsible for..." I looked away and focused on the memory of him watching me, hoping the heat in my cheeks translated to a blush. "Well, me getting up to *all sorts* or things. We could remedy that now." Slowly, I bent over, conscious of how it emphasised my cleavage—the only skin I had on display.

Caelus's stare burned into me as I pulled up the hem of my dress and retrieved the hip flask.

I waited long moments before letting the hem down again, letting him get a good view before I waggled the hip flask in front of him.

His eyes narrowed as he eyed it, then me. Not convinced. Suspicious, even.

Maybe if I...

I opened the top and took a sip, keeping it upturned for a while after so it seemed like I drank more than I did. Still, it went down smooth and warm, sweet and lulling, like this was a wonderful idea. I held out the hip flask and purred, "Your turn."

His canines flashed as he gave a short, huffing laugh. "How can I say no?" He accepted, taking a long draught while my head swam.

I couldn't lie, but I could dance around the truth like fae did, and it would make him more forthcoming with the truth. I had this all under control.

He made a soft sound as he licked his lips and passed the flask back. "That's good stuff."

"Isn't it?" I secured it back in place before we set off.

I kept to flirtatious smalltalk initially—no need to make him suspicious by leaping straight to the necklace.

"Look, over there..." He gestured towards a woman with hair the colour of starlight—a silvery blue. "That's Bastian's mother."

I blinked at her, then looked away as she turned, not wanting to be caught staring.

"She was attacked by an unseelie and fell pregnant."

That was how he'd been conceived.

"She gave him up?"

Caelus nodded. "So I understand it. As soon as he was born."

That explained why he'd never mentioned her, only the fathers who'd raised him. If he'd come from that kind of assault, I couldn't blame him for wanting to separate himself from that. I squeezed my glass, overwhelmed by the urge to find him and hold him.

Still, I was meant to be charming Caelus, not reminding him of another man, so I didn't ask anything more and busied my fingers pushing my hair back over my shoulder.

He sipped his drink and watched the motion, gaze catching on my throat. He frowned. "Your necklace—it's gone."

Perfect.

I opened my mouth to say the clasp had broken, but... I couldn't speak.

Arianmêl. No lies.

"I'm not wearing it tonight." Obvious, but true, and a kind of explanation. "It's a shame, since I know you like it so much." I tilted my head, exposing my throat as Ella had shown me, and his attention skimmed down it, continuing to my chest.

Arianmêl plus a distraction—hopefully that would be enough.

"The other day," I murmured, "you seemed like you were about to say something about that necklace, but we were interrupted. I'd love to know what it was."

"Would you, now?" He touched his lower lip, attention dripping down my body.

"*Caelus,*" I said, drawing out his name in a way that had his gaze locking on my lips. "How did you see that necklace before it was given to me?"

"I collected it," he murmured so softly I wasn't sure he realised he was speaking out loud. I had to crane closer to catch each word. "I owed her a favour, so I picked it up when it was ready."

My pulse leapt in my throat. "*Her?*" I softened my tone to match Caelus's.

"Not anyone important." He shook his head and edged closer, making me realise we'd stopped.

"*Who,* though?"

"Adra... His Majesty's assistant. I lost a card game and owed her. That's all. She isn't..."

He went on as though reassuring me I had no reason to be jealous, but my thoughts were louder.

The Day King's assistant. That meant King Lucius was the one who'd sent unCavendish.

The attempt to ruin the alliance between Dusk and Albion had come from the very highest level of Dawn Court. Was that why he'd come and spoken to me in the street? The way he'd said my name felt even more like a warning.

Gods. I needed to tell Bastian. Did he already know? I glanced around, but there was no sign of him.

Eyes glazed with drink, Caelus reached towards me, perhaps for the lock of hair tickling my bare neck, and that was when I remembered.

Poison.

I jerked away, a horrible shock of heat running through me chased by ice. If he'd managed to touch me...

He cocked his head, this small frown on his face. "I don't und—"

"This isn't a good idea."

Flirting with him as Bastian had searched his rooms had felt like it might be dangerous to me. But this, now—it could be dangerous to him.

I wanted his information, but I didn't want him dead.

"I—I'm sorry." Shaking my head, I turned and hurried through the patio doors I'd spotted earlier.

Cool, fresh air. Just what I needed. I sucked it in, greedy—desperate. The world stopped spinning quite so hard, and I clutched the potion bottle pendant. At least I would've been able to stop him dying.

Still, my stomach churned at how close he'd come.

I made it ten paces into the dimly lit garden before I leant over a wall and vomited.

Why had I ever messed with poison? I'd known it was something as likely to hurt the wielder as their victim, and yet I'd still taken the vial from unCavendish.

My hand went to my throat, but his necklace wasn't there. I could've cried with relief.

I used the last of my drink to wash away the taste of bile, and ventured further along the path. The party had grown so loud, my ears still rang with it, but the quiet soothed me.

Silhouetted against the night sky stood the Dawn Court's Great Oak and, beside it, trunk split in two was Dusk's Great Yew. They blotted out the stars in deeper darkness. Rose had brought me here and told me how they represented the Great Bargain—a contract between the land and the fae, granting the latter long lives and powerful gifts.

What the land gained, she wasn't clear on—the fae were tightlipped about that. But the trees' magic rumbled through the air as if they were the source of it all. The yew's felt more powerful—darker, somehow, like a cello compared to a violin.

The intensity of their magic made my stomach turn again, I chose a path leading away from it.

Ahead, pale in the starlight, white roses rambled over an arbour.

And I was still a fool for their beauty, because I found myself drawn to them, tugging off my gloves. Just one touch. Just a texture other than my own clothing. Just the momentary connection with another living thing that wasn't Bastian Marwood.

I reached out, heart already full as I inhaled the rich scent.

For a second—one glorious second—I had that velvety softness against my skin.

Then the white petals shrivelled and blackened. The shrub's leaves curled and withered. The branches dried and snapped under their own weight, and where moments earlier had stood a beautiful plant, now lay a mouldering mound scented sickly sweet with decay.

I reached out like I could somehow pull the pieces back together. But there was nothing. And my touch couldn't fix, only kill.

Death. That was my gift.

I fumbled with my gloves, panting as I fought tears of horror at what I had done—what I could do to anything and anyone with the merest brush of skin. Then I turned and—

And before me stood the man whose entrance into my life had started it all.

34

BASTIAN

The sight of her trembling, with tears on her cheeks, had me on high alert, muscles and shadows ready to rip anything or anyone apart. But when I saw the dead plant in the gloom and the way she yanked on her gloves, I understood.

Her poison.

"Come with me." I had to place a hand at the small of her back to get her to obey. "It's all right."

But she shook her head over and over, staring at the ground a few feet ahead. "The roses. I killed them. That whole plant—gone."

"It's all right," I murmured in the low, soothing tone I'd used with my father on his bad nights. "The gardeners will clear it up."

The sharp creases between her eyebrows cut deep. She held up her gloved hands as though only now truly seeing them. "I am death walking."

She wasn't even hearing my arguments, not in any

comprehensible way. So, I rubbed her back and ushered her along. Maybe showing her would work where telling her didn't.

The palace hothouse loomed from the darkness, a ghostly set of glass towers that glowed from within.

Her breaths had calmed by the time we reached its doors, and, arms folded, she peered up as we entered.

The thick, humid air hit us. Tropical trees with broad leaves soared into the darkness, and around us ferns lined the path. Buzzing insects blanketed the building with their hum, like a calm version of the magic running through the River Velos. Pale orchids grew on the trees, adding their vanilla scent to the air.

Instead of fae lights drifting along to show the way, blue and violet glowing fungus encrusted the trees and fallen trunks, and tiny flowers with nodding heads spilled motes of glimmering pollen. It drifted as we moved, sparking with each step and rising around us.

Her mouth fell open as she took it all in with wide eyes. Her tears had stopped.

Watching her experience it all—the way she took in a long breath of air scented with dampness and growing things, and the sweet pollen—heightened every sensation. She made the tree's shadows darker, the glowing mushrooms brighter, the heady smell more intoxicating.

She moistened her lips, and I found myself caught up in that simple gesture. "What are all these plants for? Do you eat them? Or use them for dyes? Why build this whole glasshouse and go to the trouble of magically heating it?"

There she was. My practical ember. Although, if it distracted her from poison, I would accept practical.

"One thing I realised during my time in your country is

how humans and fae are different." I set a slow pace along the path, keeping my hand on her back, enjoying her warmth through the sheer lace. "We have an inherent cultural appreciation of beauty, in art and nature. It's why we favour human artisans—if they can already create beauty, we want to enhance that and see what heights they can achieve."

She made a soft sound, but said nothing.

"There's beauty in stories, music, song, dance, people... in physical love as well as emotional." Even if it could devastate —I couldn't deny its beauty. "In passion of all kinds."

Her brow creased. "So, they aren't tropical vegetables?"

I chuckled. "If we only grow vegetables, what will we look at while we dine? What will give us a reason to eat? Why bother living for tomorrow if not for things that feed our souls?"

The crease deepened as her gaze skipped from plant to plant.

"There is beauty in the world, Kat. And beauty has a value."

She snorted and eyed me sidelong. "I was asked to spy on you because of my looks. Don't you think I know it has value?"

Was that all she saw? What she had that someone would pay for?

"Not that kind of value. Not the kind that is used or paid for or coveted." I splayed my fingers across her back, enjoying the way it made her draw a quick breath. "I mean, *inherent* value."

She pursed her lips, making a faint sound that said she either didn't understand or wasn't convinced. Yet the hothouse plants still held her attention, so maybe deep down she knew.

"Beauty can keep us going. It gives us a reason to live and

fight." My chest tightened with the heavy truth of it. If not for being able to take pleasure in life, I would've given up long ago.

This was why I needed her to understand.

"It is a balm for the soul." My voice came out rough and raw, and her gaze jerked to me.

Her eyes gleamed with turquoise and violet light. The closeness of her attention—the softness of it—almost silenced me.

"It is a balm for the soul, no matter how broken that soul may be. It is *something*. And when you have nothing left, even a scrap of something is important."

She bit her lip and bowed her head.

We hadn't raised her outburst, but the words surfaced now. *It wasn't worth saving.* I would give her every scrap of everything if it made her realise that wasn't true.

My shadows pooled around her, barely skimming my feet as we walked on in silence. I tried to keep my eyes on the path ahead, but they kept returning to her, gauging her reaction, whether she believed me. Her fingertips toyed with a shadow that reared up at her side. I wasn't sure if she realised she was doing it.

"Why are you being nice to me? Why save my life? Bring me here? Have me live with you? Give me this?" She touched the bulge in her glove where my ring sat. "I spied on you. I lied to you. I tried to poison you, for fuck's sake."

The ghost of a laugh hummed in my throat. "You didn't though, did you? You took it yourself like the wonderful idiot you are."

Her teeth showed for a second before she bowed her head as if trying to hide her smile. She took a long breath before turning back, the smile gone. "I am sorry, you know. Truly. I just... I couldn't escape him."

My teeth gritted together as all the things she'd told me about unCavendish blasted through me at once, a horrible cacophony of every sentence in her report. Listening to her answers, I'd bitten my cheek until I'd drawn blood. If not for the grounding metallic taste, I'd have lost my fucking mind.

"You already apologised." I stroked her back, letting my thumb run along the groove over her spine. It was meant to be reassuring, but I ate up the little shiver she gave in its wake. "And I cut you off. Quite rudely, in fact." Letting her continue would've broken me, and I'd already been dangerously close to that. So I'd pushed her away. "That's on me. You don't owe me anything—apologies included."

I still owed her, though. I'd said the words, yes. But actions mattered more, and this, tonight, was a small thing I could do —a step towards earning her forgiveness.

We walked on, the quiet between us soft and calm until she gave a sudden exhale as though reaching a decision. "I need to tell you something. About unCavendish. I've found out—"

"Not here." I used a shadow to squeeze her hand in reassurance. "It isn't secure and... and unless it's an emergency, can I just be Bastian rather than a spymaster? Just for a little while."

The look she gave me was tender enough to break me. I had to look away and busied myself shrugging off my jacket, in danger of wilting in the heat.

Aside from the low neckline, Kat's gown covered her to elbows and ankles. Since entering the hothouse, a pink flush had crept across her skin, and now she fanned her face with one hand.

"You can take off your gloves, you know. I'm the only person here and you can't poison me." Too late for that. She'd

251

seeped under my skin months ago.

"The plants," she muttered, frowning as she wrung her hands.

I blocked her path and stopped, forcing her to halt. "You're going to melt."

Her lips flattened.

I loved her determination. But sometimes, I cursed it.

Sighing, I pulled one of her hands free. "You can't hurt me, Katherine." I tugged the little finger of her glove, then the next and the next, until I could peel the light fabric from her skin.

It was ridiculous that doing this made the hairs on the back of my neck rise. I'd seen her naked, tasted her, explored her sweet slickness—taking off a glove shouldn't feel this intimate. Yet goosebumps pricked her forearms, so I wasn't alone in this feeling.

I rubbed the dark stain of her fingertips, and shuddered at the sting followed by the heady resonance of our magic meeting. Our first touch since sunset. I hadn't accounted for that and the way it rushed through me, hot and intoxicating.

Kat's nostrils flared as she took in heaving breaths. She watched, eyelids fluttering until our magic faded, leaving a deep ache in me.

I removed the other glove and caught her hands between mine. Eyes closing, she sagged, like my touch was a relief, even without our mingled magic.

Fuck. The way she responded... it had spelled my doom in Albion, and she was no less dangerous here.

I wasn't supposed to be seducing her. This was meant to be a comfort.

"Come," I rasped, and led her to a quiet corner where a glass-walled room stood separate. Vents kept this space cooler than the rest of the hothouse.

Her eyes widened at the tall spikes of deep purple flowers with black centres. "Aconite."

I braced myself for the scent.

Death.

It made the instinctual part of me want to turn and run.

Our own weapons could kill us, yes. But iron and aconite? They *poisoned*. Slow and painful.

A clever joke for the gods to make it such a beautiful plant.

As long as I didn't eat or rub my skin against it, I'd be fine. I planted my feet and nodded towards the hooded flowers. "Try touching it."

"But I'll..." Her eyes widened. "You think I won't kill it because... My poison is its poison." She examined the nearest plant, then took a deep breath.

Slowly, slowly, she reached out. Half an inch from the purple petals, she faltered, and I willed her on.

She straightened her back and crossed that gap.

Breath held, she waited. Glaring at the flowers, daring them to die, I waited.

Nothing happened.

Kat's chin wobbled like she might cry. Then she laughed. A laugh of relief. Of surprise. Of pleasure.

The most perfect sound I ever heard.

She looked up at me as if to check I saw the same thing she did. When I nodded, she flung her arms around me and buried her face in my chest.

I'd have been a liar if I said I didn't love it, seizing the opportunity to hold her close. "You will learn to control this gift, Kat. But in the meantime, you're not alone."

She pulled back, eyes glassy-bright as she looked up at me. In a small voice she said, "It feels like I am."

"No, you're not. You have Ella and Perry, Rose and Ari,

and... And I'm here." I wanted to say "you have me" but stopped myself. If I'd been drinking *arianmêl*, I would've spouted that and all sorts of things I shouldn't. Enjoying myself too much in Lunden had made it harder to keep myself reined in now I was home.

"*Now* you are, but..."

"I know. My work." I sighed and pushed the hair from her face. "I need you to be brave for me, Kat. You can face this. I know you can."

She frowned. "I don't feel very brave."

"You're the Wicked Lady."

"She wasn't brave, just desperate."

I shook my head, not understanding her distinction.

"We needed food. If I couldn't get it..." She shivered against me. "Once, early in our marriage, Robin and I were attacked on the road." She winced as though she hated the reminder of her husband even more than I did. "The highwayman took a tidy sum from us that night. A few months later, I found Robin's papers showing all his debts."

Every muscle thrummed as I held myself very still. After seeing the bruise on Kat's cheek, I'd asked Asher to pay him a visit to make sure he understood that he wasn't welcome in the same room as his wife, whatever he thought his marriage entitled him to.

I hadn't trusted myself to face him. Not with our mission so close to success. Ripping apart one of her subjects with my shadows wouldn't have gone down too well with the human queen.

"His debts?" I prompted her, since she seemed lost in thought.

"I did what I could." She shrugged. "Sold some furniture, the silverware, gilded candlesticks—that sort of thing. But once that was gone... I couldn't sell any land or the house. I couldn't get a job. Robin had already used my dowry to get a creditor off his back... and buy himself a new wardrobe." Her smile could've cut glass. "I had no option. The only way I could see to make money..."

"Was the Wicked Lady," I said into the silence she left hanging.

"So you see, she's an invention of desperation, not a sign of bravery."

I frowned at her until she cocked her head in question. "And yet you faced me down on the road. You spied on me. You let me have you in a number of compromising positions, one time in front of dozens of other people. You rode in that race and kept yourself together when you dangled over the water-fall, inches from death. You shot a fucking Horror in the eye."

Her laugh was dismissive as if *everyone* did such things. "I was terrified the whole time."

"We only get to be brave when we're afraid."

Her face dropped. She blinked, and I could see her replaying what I'd just said.

"You are brave, Kat. Probably the bravest person I know. It's just... somewhere along the way, you convinced yourself that you weren't."

She shook her head and went to reply—to argue, no doubt.

"My father told me that who you really are is what you do when no one else is looking." The words unfolded in me together with a deeper truth. "You, Katherine, are *only* yourself when no one else is looking. The rest of it? It's a mask you wear to keep yourself safe."

Brow creased, she turned to the aconite. "Maybe what you think is a mask is the real me."

But she didn't sound as sure as she had earlier.

I'd take that as progress.

35

KAT

The day after the party, I woke late. Even Bastian did, grabbing a slice of toast off my plate on his way out. A different kind of quiet stood between us—not the stiff silence we'd shared initially or the charged one after our trip to Innesol, but a softer one. A moment after he left, he stuck his head back through the door. "We'll talk later about that thing you wanted to tell me. Wait up for me?"

I nodded, then he was gone, his smile leaving a flicker of *something* running through my belly.

Be sensible, Kat.

That inner voice was right. We'd found a way to live together. I would be cured soon and I'd go home to Morag and Horwich. This was good. I didn't need anything more—I certainly didn't need to yearn for anything more.

I smiled and took a sip of coffee. This *was* good.

Should've known it wouldn't last.

As I finished my breakfast, a message arrived summoning

257

me to an appointment with Elthea. I wrung my hands and didn't dare look at them, but that didn't change what the piece of paper said, so I returned to my room to get ready.

The roses had been changed—today's were a soft lavender hue. I'd learned my lesson from last night and didn't touch them, but I appreciated the servants' attention to detail in keeping them fresh and the scent—gods, the scent! It filled the room and despite the appointment, I found myself smiling as I got ready. A short while later, Rose collected me and we set off into the city.

Where Dusk's side of the palace had become familiar, safe even, now I knew the king was behind unCavendish, it made the city feel more dangerous than before.

That, plus my impending appointment wound my nerves tighter as we wound through the streets. I needed a distraction as I scanned the faces we passed, wondering if any of them were spies. Had I seen that person before? Were they following me?

"What do fae mean by 'oathbreaker?'"

A man passing gasped and shot me a glare before striding off.

I winced, pulling my coat tighter. "Something bad, I'm guessing."

Rose glanced around, but no one else was close enough to hear. "Be careful using that word. It's one of their worst insults. Where did you hear it?"

"Last night. Someone called Bastian one."

Her expression darkened. It ill-suited her but matched the overcast day perfectly. "I can only think of one reason they'd call him that. Word must've reached the city about your marriage."

My stomach dipped like I'd missed a step. "How do you know about that?"

She offered me her arm and bent closer when I took it, protected by her sleeve and my gloves. "Bastian told me. The way he acted when he carried you through the shadow door made it obvious how he felt about you, but he didn't tell me anything else. Clearly something happened in Lunden—I'm just not sure what... *or* what the situation is with your husband." Her eyebrows rose slowly.

I explained the bare bones of my arranged marriage and that Bastian had found out only after knowing me for months. I let her fill in how our relationship had been progressing and the brick wall it had ploughed into with the arrival of my husband.

"Bloody hells, Kat." She shook her head and squeezed my arm. "That sounds... pretty shit, to be honest. At least you're away from him now."

I gave a dark chuckle. "Being away from him has never been the problem. I've been away from him for a long time... and yet I still can't escape him." I held in the sigh that wanted to blast out. It would do no good.

We arrived at the Hall of Healing and I scrunched my toes up inside my shoes against the urge to run away.

I needed a cure. This was the only way.

So I sent Rose to wait for me at Ariadne's, squared my shoulders, and went inside.

I DIDN'T KNOW how much time passed, all I knew was that I staggered from the Hall of Healing, nausea and dizziness warring inside

I turned corner after corner, hoping to find that same side street, but my earlier journey was a blur, and this one wasn't much better.

The image of blood and sizzling skin. The memory of my own sobs in the treatment room, while in reality I stumbled along the road, biting my tongue.

All I could do was avoid the busier roads and keep an eye out for somewhere small to hide while I recovered.

Ahead, a bellow shattered the quiet. "Shut up!"

The few folk on the street swerved to one side, giving me a view of a man on his knees, gathering vegetables and bread from the floor. A basket of food lay on its side.

Someone must've knocked into him. I blocked an apple rolling down the hill with my foot and scooped it up.

Face screwing up, he curled in on himself. "Quiet!"

But the road *was* quiet.

This wasn't so simple as I'd first thought. Was he ill—a sickness of the mind? Or maybe something magical I didn't understand. No one stopped to help. If anything, the one passerby who did look at him wrinkled their nose in disgust.

Wary, I approached, but he seemed lost in his own world, sharp breaths hissing between his teeth. Below his pale violet hair, pain etched his features, and my chest squeezed in response. No sign of blood or obvious injury, though.

"So many," he muttered. "Too many."

One eye on him, muscles tight and ready to dart away, I gathered the spilled vegetables and loaf of bread and reloaded the basket.

My mind whispered, "Unsafe. Keep clear."

Yet my heart answered, "But look at his pain. You know pain."

The practical option would be to place the basket at his

feet and continue on my way. But that felt cruel, especially with such a fresh reminder of agony making my fingers twitch around the basket's handle.

This could be a distraction. If I focused on someone else, I might forget about what had just happened—for a few minutes, at least.

"Hello?" I kept my voice soft—fae hearing was sharp, after all. No response. Lightly, I nudged him with the basket. No chance of poisoning him.

Piercing violet eyes opened, the perfect match for his hair. He stared at the basket, then me as if to ask what the hells I wanted.

"Do you need some help?"

A gaggle of fae hurried past, and his face screwed up again. He gave a soft grunt but nodded. "Home. I need... *Home.*"

Helping the poor man get home wasn't a great risk and hopefully not too great a detour. I'd get rid of my pallor by the time I caught up with Rose.

He stood and hunched into the wall, half-staggering as he gestured ahead.

Besides, he'd have to be a fool to attack me when I was under the protection of the Night Queen's Shadow. And if he *was* a fool, well I had my bow on my back and the boot pistol hidden beneath my skirts... not to mention a touch that could kill.

My throat tightened at the idea of using it. I'd spent so much time worried I was going to accidentally poison some-one, it hadn't crossed my mind to deliberately touch anyone. The rose's death played out in my mind, and I shuddered.

"Is it far?"

He lifted his head, peering up the road. "Not far. Not long."

With a grunt, he staggered as though wrestling some great weight.

It might not be far, but at this rate he wasn't going to stay on his feet long enough to make it, and I wouldn't be able to carry him.

I checked my gloves were securely in place and that he wore a thick jacket. That had to be safe, right? I touched my potion bottle to reassure myself it was there before clutching my magic to keep it small. All that in place, I took his arm.

Trembling, he leant on me. Strange to be the strong one in the equation, but then Tenebris-Luminis was a strange place by night or day.

He made a low sound that might've been a "thank you" or a "bugger off" but didn't pull away, and we made quicker progress.

I took the opportunity to examine him more closely. One of the older looking fae I'd seen, as a human, I'd have said he was almost fifty. His pale violet hair could fit Dusk or Dawn, and his grey clothing didn't help me place him, either.

His jacket was a thick wool but smooth—it probably felt soft, but I couldn't tell through my glove—and the hems were clean and crisp. His leather shoes shone. Although his hair was messy like it had been cut by an eight-year-old, he looked otherwise well groomed and if not wealthy, then comfortably off.

At the next corner, he dragged on my hold and nodded when we turned. A few houses down, he slowed and pulled a key from his pocket. I helped him inside, but had to stop on the threshold as magic rolled over me, thick and smothering like a blanket.

It took a couple of breaths before I could open my eyes. I

went for my pocket, where I'd cut a hole that would let me reach my pistol.

But the fae was bent over the table, dragging in deep breaths, and there was no sign of another soul.

The magic wasn't an attack but... something else. And maybe I was a fool for entering a strange fae's home (make that definitely), but he didn't look in a fit state to attack a plate of food, never mind me.

Beyond the table, a wall of books gave the room a delightfully cluttered feel, and two cosy armchairs sat beside the fireplace. The moon and star decoration surrounding the fireplace answered my earlier question. Dusk Court. My shoulders eased.

A kitchen with cabinets and a stove occupied another wall, so I took the basket over.

"Am I all right to leave you now or...?"

He didn't respond, just continued his long inhale and long exhale, palms pressed into the table.

Maybe I should keep an eye on him for a minute, just to check he wasn't about to keel over.

But standing here just *looking* at him felt beyond awkward, so I made myself useful unpacking the basket. Aside from pots, pans, and plates, the cupboards were bare.

"Looks like you really needed that shopping trip," I muttered as I placed the potatoes in a basket in a low cabinet. Perhaps that was what had driven him out of the house even though he was unwell. "I can get you a healer, you know. I was just at the Hall of Healing—it won't take me long to go back." The idea made me shudder, but if I had to, I would.

As I picked up a blood red apple, I had to close my eyes against the sight of my flayed fingers.

Not real. Not real. Not real.

"What do you think?" I straightened and turned.

And found him *right there*. He grabbed my arm, eyes wide, and I gasped at the biting grip.

"What did she do to you?"

"Don't touch me." I yanked, but he was too strong. At least my coat meant he wasn't touching my skin.

Wait. "What did you—?"

"Uncontrolled magic." His eyes went even wider and he dropped my arm like I'd burned him.

Heart pounding, I checked my sleeve—the cloth was intact. I hadn't accidentally poisoned him. "I don't... I was just trying to help."

My fingers on my sleeve. But open, flesh exposed to the stinging air. I screwed my eyes shut. Last time, the intrusive memories had mostly faded after a while, but going back in that room had triggered them all coming back. I couldn't go through the rest of the day seeing that.

"You're right. You can't."

"Did I...?" I covered my mouth. The horror of Elthea's experiment had me voicing my thoughts—dangerous at the best of times, but here in Elfhame, it had to be worse. Deadly, even.

"No, you didn't say it out loud." His mouth twisted in the ghost of a sardonic smirk. "But you're right, sharing your thoughts with the wrong person could get you killed."

If I didn't say it, that meant... Heart leaping, I scrambled away, banging into the countertop. No. No. Not in my head. That was *my* space. "Get out. Out!"

He flinched like I'd struck him, but raised his palms. "Ouch. Shit. Message received." He pinched the bridge of his nose. "In my defence, you were thinking very loudly."

But he still stood between me and the door.

And he could read my fucking mind.

Despite my shaking, I managed to draw the miniature pistol from my thigh holster. I would shoot him if he tried to stop me. I thought it hard—let him understand I meant it.

"I'm not even reaching for you right now, but I could still hear that."

"Good. Then you know I want you to get the hells out of my way. I don't know why you lured me—"

"Lured?" He laughed. "You stopped and helped me when I was..." A muscle in his jaw rippled. "I wasn't *luring* anybody—I was too busy trying not to lose my mind. There are too many thoughts out there. I'm not what I once was. They break through too easily."

I glanced past him to the door. "So you can hear everyone?"

He scowled. "Unfortunately. Wards make this place my sanctuary... until human women come along with such *loud* thoughts, that is."

Being able to read minds sounded like a great gift, but seeing the shadows under this fae's eyes, I understood.

It was as much of a curse as my poison.

And it made sense. I struggled enough with my own thoughts—I didn't want anyone else's, thanks.

"Fine. Sorry for thinking so loudly." I lowered my pistol, ready to raise it again if necessary. "That means I can go, then?"

He stepped to one side, arms spread. "You always could."

"Perfect." I strode for the door, only looking away from him when I reached it.

"You know, I can help you."

I paused, gripping the handle. "What do you mean?"

"With forgetting."

I whipped around. "What makes you think—?"

"I heard you." He shrugged, looking a little younger now his face had relaxed. "I don't know everything. I only see what someone's thinking at that exact moment. But I know enough. That woman did..." His gaze flicked to my fingers, and I tucked them under my armpits, not wanting to see them even in the periphery of my vision. "Well, I saw it. And I know you can't escape it. But what if you could?"

My pulse quickened. "Are you saying, you can take away a memory?"

"If you want me to."

I narrowed my eyes at him. "And why would you do that? The kindness of your heart?"

Fae were not kind.

He snorted like he found the idea as ridiculous as I did. It was oddly comforting that he didn't try to persuade me. "No. But I owe you for helping me. You're here in Elfhame, so you must know we *love* making bargains."

I eyed my fingers. Jaw clenched, I managed to focus and not see what Elthea had done. Still, my skin crawled, because I *knew*. And there would be more. "I helped you. You help me."

"That's how it works."

"Say it. Say exactly what you're going to do, so I know you're not twisting around some deception."

"You *have* bargained with us before." He flashed a grin. "Very well. In exchange for your help today, I will remove two memories you give me permission to remove. I won't go rooting around in your mind for any other thoughts, and I won't tamper with anything else in there. Two memories of your choosing removed so you'll no longer be troubled by them. That's what I'm offering."

That had to be safe—safe enough, anyway. And at this

point, I didn't care if he could be trusted or not—I needed to escape everything Elthea had done to me.

No more nightmares about her tugging on my nerves—pulling them like puppet strings.

I swallowed back nausea and nodded. "You have yourself a deal."

36
BASTIAN

The night after the party, I caught up with Kat and she told me what she'd discovered about her necklace, though she refused to reveal how she'd come upon this information.

Lucius had sent unCavendish to Lunden. After me, perhaps. To ruin the alliance with Albion, certainly.

He was responsible for that man touching Kat, for placing poison in her hands, and for forcing her into a position where she had to take it or risk war that would've been disastrous for both our countries.

It had crushed me when she'd asked, "Now what?" Like there was something we could do about a king's machinations.

I'd hated myself for replying, "Now nothing. We can't act against him."

We couldn't. Without Braea's approval, the main thing I could do at the moment was be vigilant... and give Dawn a reminder of my presence and power.

The next day, I had a meeting lined up with a visiting merchant who dealt in antiquities and rare books. I could make some veiled enquiries about the Circle of Ash, see if they had any texts that might be useful.

I could've had them meet me in the palace, but this was a perfect opportunity to deliver that reminder. So, shadows on full display, seething around me, I made for the grand hall.

Busy. That was good—perfect, in fact.

I strode through when a stir amongst the courtiers caught my attention. They whispered, and I followed their sidelong glances to that rarest of things amongst the fae—red hair. Not Kat's—this hair was streaked with cream.

Tall and well-built, Prince Sepher prowled through the pillared entrance hall with all the grace I'd expect of a sabrecat.

What the hells brought him here? His tail swished behind him as he walked, so he hadn't rid himself of that. My spies said a curse stopped him adopting a fully fae form and hiding the fact he was a shapechanger. Hence his exile to the ruined palace outside the city. So what had made him break that exile?

Worked well for me. He could deliver a reminder of my presence directly to his father.

Eyelids half-closed, smirk in place, I strolled over. "Sepher."

Chin tilting up, he stopped and cast a disapproving glance over me. His yellow eyes and slitted pupils might've unnerved me if I hadn't been used to dealing with Orpha. "Ah, Serpent. I wondered what that smell was. Thought it stank of betrayal over here."

I chuckled like he was as witty as he so clearly believed. "Not presiding over your little Court of Monsters?"

"Obviously not, since I'm here, aren't I? I thought you were meant to be a spymaster." He rolled his eyes and started past me. "I've come to see my parents."

"Telling them about the human woman you've been terrorising or just taking the chance to see dear ma and pa?"

The way he stopped mid-stride and turned on the spot flushed me with pleasure. Sparring with Sepher was petty, but the irritation weighing on me made me petty. So did the Day Princes.

"Huh. Well done, Serpent. A spy at my court or...?" He narrowed his feline eyes at me, more evaluative this time as he cocked his head.

"You know I can't possibly reveal my sources. Though it's good to have it confirmed—and from the horse's mouth no less. Or should that be the sabrecat's?" I nodded down at his swishing tail, and my shadows flicked in its direction. "By the way, your tail is showing."

He bared his teeth as he chuckled. "I assume that isn't an innuendo but a display of your *masterful* perceptive skills. Yes, my tail is showing, as are my claws." He examined them like someone might examine their fingernails. "Perhaps you'd like a demonstration."

"Only if I get to demonstrate my shadows. They've been waiting years for a chance to say hello to you." They rustled at the hem of my trousers, a reminder that as ethereal as they appeared, they had form and could touch... and tear.

His brother had held me down and told Sepher to hit me to "teach him how it feels to master the small folk." My shadows could hold Sepher while I taught him a lesson with my knuckles.

He made a soft, dismissive sound. "Tell me Bastian, why pay such close attention to little old me? Sounds a little obsessive. Is it because I never went up to that hayloft with you like most of our classmates?"

"You should get your memory checked, Sepher. You were never invited. We both know if you had been, you would've gone, even if just out of curiosity."

He eyed my shadows sidelong. "Perhaps. Freaks together. Unfortunately for you, I've come to deliver the news that I'm no longer available, however obsessed you might be. That human has agreed to marry me."

For a fraction of a second, I held very still. *What?* Then I laughed as if amused by the idea and not shocked. Maybe obsession was on Sepher's mind and he was merely projecting on me: my spy had intimated that he seemed fascinated with the human woman, enjoying her punishment.

"Don't tell me, you gave her an option between marking her as yours with the collar or with a wedding ring. Not sure that's much of a choice."

His nostrils flared and he leant closer, crowding my space. "She chose me freely." A growl laced his words.

But I'd had years of dealing with an angry shapechanger several inches taller than me. I didn't back away and instead smiled wider. "Then let me be the first to extend Dusk's congratulations. I look forward to helping the rest of the Convocation with the royal wedding preparations." And I did, even if it was just to see his shoulders sink as he realised that, as the Night Queen's representative during daylight hours, I would indeed be involved.

"You're too kind." With a low sound, he nodded and swept towards the door to Dawn's side of the palace.

Prince Sepher marrying a human. I stared after him for a beat.

Shock aside, Braea wasn't going to like this. Dawn would

be a step closer to another heir in their line of succession—
Cyrus, then Sepher, then any child from Sepher's marriage.

While she had nothing.

37

KAT

The days after having my memories erased were easier.

It was magic. Literally. I could remember stopping and helping the fae, returning to his house, the details of our bargain. But I had no idea what he had stripped from my mind. There was a blank space between my arrival at the Hall of Healing and leaving again, shaken and haunted.

I just had this uneasy feeling in my gut, like an important task I'd forgotten about.

What could be so bad that I had feared looking at my own hands?

Thank the gods I didn't need to worry about the answer to that question anymore. I could meet my friends for dinner tonight and be normal and happy. After almost a week without nightmares, I felt... well, fucking amazing.

But when a message came from Elthea summoning me to another appointment, a terrible dread stole over me.

AFTER, I somehow managed to stop at a shop on the way to that cosy house on the corner, but gods knew what I bought. The produce spun around and around, making my stomach heave. I had to run outside and throw up before setting off again.

Where I'd grown comfortable in Dusk's side of the palace, I only squared my shoulders when I ventured into areas where Dawn would be. But masking up was impossible with this horror weighing on me. I was barely aware of anything other than the familiar door I kept my gaze fixed on as I hurried down the street.

I knocked and a moment later came the response: "Go away."

"It's me."

"I don't know anyone called me. *Go away.*"

"How bare are your cupboards?"

No answer.

"I have food."

The door inched open and his scowling face appeared. "What do you want?"

I glanced up and down the road. "I'm not telling you where anyone might hear. But I have payment." I hefted the basket.

He eyed it for a long beat, then huffed and opened the door. "I was gearing myself up to venture out again, but..." He grimaced at the door as I shut it behind myself.

This time, as I put food away for him, I obeyed the fae rules and told him my name first and let him give me his. Kaliban.

"Why don't your neighbours pick up food for you?" I asked

as I stood up, swaying. This time there'd been more blood, and I was woozy, swaying side to side like a landlubber on a ship.

"Oh, like they helped me when I was keeling over on the street, you mean?"

The irony. I had Rose, Ariadne, and, most recently, Faolán trying to help me connect with the magic inside, and they'd all failed. While Kaliban needed a much simpler kind of help that no one would give.

"Would you sit down," he grumbled. "You're making me seasick."

I slumped into a chair, pressing my hands into the table in my search for something solid.

"Your magic is still uncontrolled."

"You said you wouldn't read me." I shot him That Look, like Morag when she told me off for drinking too much.

"It's hard when you shove your thoughts in my face so hard. You have a powerful mind."

I scoffed and opened my mouth.

"Don't say it." He eyed me sidelong as he rummaged through the fruit bowl to see what I'd brought. "You think you're powerless. I think that's bullshit. The way you pushed me out the first time you came here..." He shook his head as he buffed an apple on his shirt. "Powerful." He took a bite, with a satisfying crack of the apple's flesh. "I'm not trying to read you. I only caught a glimpse."

I winced and rubbed my temples. "Certain thoughts have been very loud recently."

He watched me a long while as he chewed. "You have a lot weighing on you." His voice was softer than I'd ever heard it before—he tended towards Faolán's gruffness combined with Bastian's sarcasm.

His eyes twitched narrower, telling me I'd thought that too loud.

Smiling sweetly, I batted my eyelashes at him. "You aren't like anyone else. You are a beautiful and unique snowflake."

With a wry smirk, he wiped his hands clean, the apple finished. "Let's clear your unpleasant memory, then I have a suggestion to calm your mind. Perhaps you can quieten those loud thoughts."

We pulled two chairs opposite each other, and he hovered his hands an inch from my temples.

I held still, forcing my breaths slow, all too conscious that if I turned my head, we'd be touching.

"Ready?"

"Ready." Biting my lip, I pushed my thoughts towards Elthea's treatment room. Bright and bloody. The coppery tang in the air. My cries. Leather straps biting into my arms as she poked and pulled at parts of me that were never meant to be pulled.

Kaliban's presence was a cotton swab wiping it all away.

No blood, no fear, no...

I blinked. Kaliban's home. How had I...?

He sat back, nodding slowly.

I'd left the Hall of Healing. There was something in there I wanted to forget; I had no idea what. Rubbing my forehead, I nodded. "It's gone. Thank you."

"No thanks needed. You brought your payment."

"I thought fae liked politeness."

He chuckled. "It's preferred, but not required. Come." He led me to the two chairs before the fire.

Although I'd never seen anyone else here, a pair of tweed slippers sat before each chair—one dark purple, the other the same blue-black that Dusk's guards wore.

"I'll get these out of our way," he muttered.

The purple pair he swept away with his foot, but the other slippers, he scooped up like I'd scooped up Vespera when she was a kitten. He placed them beside the fire, then gestured for me to take the chair they'd sat before.

I had the uncomfortable feeling that I was taking someone else's spot, even though I knew he lived alone. Or at least he did now.

I gave him a small, tight smile.

"Take off your gloves."

"But—"

"I'm nowhere near you," he said, sinking into the other armchair. "We won't touch—I don't have a death wish. But the marks on your fingers are part of your magic. I want to be able to see them."

With a sigh, I obeyed. "I thought this was about my thoughts."

He arched an eyebrow. "You think these things are separate?"

"I think I have no idea what my magic is, just that it's here and I can do nothing with it... except risk killing someone with a careless touch."

"Then listen to me, young human. I've been doing this longer than your people have been speaking Albionic."

My eyes widened. "Wait, how old are you?"

"Old enough that I know what I'm doing. Now," his voice pitched lower, "look into the fire."

I probably shouldn't trust the random fae I'd met on the street. But he'd had opportunities to hurt me or steal thoughts from my mind and hadn't. This couldn't be any more risky than that.

The flames licked in the fireplace with that odd orange-pink hue. The magic meant they could call the fire into being with a word and extinguish it just as easily. It also didn't burn flesh and could only escape its fireplace with outside influence. There were no accidental house fires in Elfhame.

"Now what?" I threw him a glance.

"Now, you learn some patience. Stars above, human attention spans are as short as a gnat's." He huffed. "You *keep* looking at the fire. Focus on it."

I did as he asked, waiting for the next instruction. This couldn't be *it*, right?

"Let your breaths slow," he murmured. "We're not trying to get rid of thoughts or emotions. They are important and necessary."

I wasn't sure emotions were. They were nothing but confusing. Thoroughly impractical.

"But we need some stillness and perspective on them too. We don't want them to control us."

That I could understand. I didn't want *anything* to control me. Too many things had.

Fear. My father. My uncle.

The hairs on my arms prickled, but I kept my eyes on the flames.

"Thoughts and feelings will come, just acknowledge, then nudge them away. They'll soon float off, like clouds in the sky."

Dutifully, I did just that. Goodbye, fear. Goodbye, Father. Goodbye, Uncle Rufus.

"All you need to focus on is the fire. What do you see? What can you feel? Scent, colour, shape—focus on your senses."

Its warmth pushed away the lingering chill from outside. But I'd thought fae fires scentless. I drew a deeper breath. The hint of woodsmoke and something faintly herbal.

The longer I watched, the more I saw. As well as the coral

pink and deep sunset orange, other colours leapt in the flames. Yellow frilled its edges. Sparking green and deep blue tangled at its centre, hugging the burning wood.

There were shapes, too. Just flashing for an instant. Huge hulking beasts with long tusks. The Great Yew, with its split trunk and spreading branches, followed a blink later by Dawn's Great Oak, upright and proud. A couple locked in a spinning dance.

And for a moment.

A fraction of a fraction of a second.

A fiery crown.

Such strange beauty.

I sank into its crackling show, letting it reveal more shapes and colours.

Gradually, I became aware of the way the fire hummed. As did the world around me. Kaliban's magic was a constant presence. There was more in the room, different tones—perhaps magical objects like the fireplace and the fae lights. Outside, other pitches merged together, forming a chaotic set of notes.

But there was the makings of something beautiful in there.

I sifted through the vibrations. They weren't *quite* sounds but close. This note and this note went together. Add in a third and ignore the rest, leaving... A set of frequencies that worked together like a harmonious chord.

"Now look at your hands," Kaliban's soft voice crept into my reverie.

I let my head sink, everything slow as treacle after so long staring into the fire. I blinked at my hands where they rested in my lap. Why was he asking me to—?

I gasped.

My fingers.

The purple stain had retreated, leaving only my nails and

the very tips dark. "I... I did it. It's gone!" I huffed a laugh, heart leaping. "Does that mean—?"

The colour flooded back, covering my skin to the first knuckle.

"Oh." I didn't bother to disguise the way my shoulders sank—my thoughts were probably loud enough for Kaliban to hear my disappointment.

"Not 'oh,' Kat." He sat back, palms pressed together. "You controlled your magic."

"Only for—"

"A moment, I know. But it was a moment more than you've managed before. If you can do it for a moment, you can do it for a minute. And if you can do it for a minute..." He spread his hands and raised his eyebrows, his rare smile infectious.

I rubbed my fingertips together. I still hadn't felt any magic inside myself, but that hum—I'd felt it outside me.

Slowly, I nodded. "It's a start."

38

KAT

That night, Rose walked me through the streets of Tenebris, both of us a little tipsy. We had joined Ari, Perry, and Ella for dinner at Moonsong Spire, a restaurant at the top of one of the city towers, where we'd watched the sunset turn Luminis into Tenebris.

The setting sun's lengthening shadows had spread over the city, bit by bit, turning white marble into black basalt. Alabaster into obsidian. Pale moonstone into dark labradorite. It was like the shadows painted the world from a different viewpoint.

I'd watched from the rooftop terrace, tears streaking down my cheeks. What a place. What a world to grow up in. If I'd grown up somewhere like this, perhaps I would've understood Bastian's love of beauty right away.

Even now, as we reached the bridge leading to the palace, I had to dash my cheeks. Rose opened and closed her mouth like she didn't know what to say before squeezing my gloved hand

and wishing me goodnight. Dusk's guards greeted me, and I set out across the bridge, keeping to its very centre.

I'd left the restaurant early, not wanting to drink more fae wine and lose the memory of this night. It was one I'd hold close and lock in my heart.

What had Bastian said? *When you have nothing left, even a scrap of something is important.*

I may have lost part of myself when I'd taken that poison. I may not be sure of who I was or my purpose. But I had *something* and maybe that would help get me through.

I had to find him, tell him I understood. Apologise for... I didn't know what for, just that it seemed stupid that I had ever *not* understood.

Or perhaps I was just drunk and overcome by the view.

Still on the edge of tears, I didn't want to encounter anyone from Dawn in the grand hall. Even though these were joyful tears, precious tears, they were still a weakness—a badge of my heart. Unsafe.

So I skirted the palace, aiming for the side entrance.

What I'd seen tonight had opened a dam in me, because I had to pause for another glimpse of Tenebris. Below, the water in the ravine glimmered with blue light, softening the rocky outcrops with its dim glow.

As I looked out over it, a prickle worked from the nape of my neck down my spine.

I wasn't alone.

I whirled, reaching for my pocket, ready to draw my pistol.

Beneath a low holly tree, a shadow unfolded.

Bastian?

But as the figure emerged, I realised it was a woman's, curved like a full moon. Tight curls surrounded her face.

"Your Majesty." I bowed, getting my hand far from my

weapon. One thing Albion and faerie had in common— monarchs and drawn weapons didn't mix. At least, not if you wanted to keep your head. "I'm sorry, I thought I was alone."

"So did I." She smiled, and the soft light from the crescent moon above caressed the fullness of her cheeks and lips. "But it seems the Stars have gifted me tonight. It's past time we got to know each other better." She beckoned me closer.

Perhaps it was my poor track record with queens... Perhaps it was just the fae alcohol. Either way, I hesitated, my feet wanting to continue indoors. But, another commonality between us and them—you didn't deny a queen.

So I approached, trying not to fidget under her scrutiny, which left me feeling like a child being checked for flaws in their attire.

Her head tilted as she narrowed her black, pupilless eyes at me. "What sort of woman has so bewitched my Shadow that he'd break a sacred contract?" A momentary flicker of tension around her eyes and mouth. Was she irritated? And if so, at me or Bastian?

I swallowed and bowed my head.

Sacred contract? What was sacred about a lifetime chained to a man with no choice and no escape? Fae really were full of shit.

Good gods, I had drunk too much. I was in danger of my tongue running away with me. After pressing it to the roof of my mouth for the count of three, I trusted myself to speak. "I didn't know how Your Majesty's people felt about marriage contracts, and Bastian didn't know I was bound by one."

"Hmm." She nodded and settled back against the tree trunk, indicating I should join her.

I obeyed, looking out over the River Velos, the bridge over to our left. "I must thank you for the ball. I never dreamed I would have a royal event thrown in my honour, never mind by the Night Queen herself."

She chuckled, soft as the dark clouds skimming overhead. "Did you enjoy yourself?"

"It was... enlightening."

Another low laugh, then we stood in silence for a while.

She wanted to get to know me, yet she wasn't asking many questions and I knew better than to volunteer information. Even though she was Bastian's queen, I still heeded his warning.

"Did you know rings have a symbolic significance to fae? I'm not sure it's the same for humans."

Under my glove, the ring Bastian had given me weighed suddenly heavier. "Really?" I kept my tone light. Had she spotted it?

"Circles have no beginning or end. Like the Celestial and Tellurian Serpents biting each other's tails in their mating dance, they stand for eternity. We give them as a token of love everlasting. As a mark of belonging."

My throat went tight and I barely stopped myself tugging on my collar. "*Really*? How fascinating."

Out the corner of my eye, I could see her studying me. My pulse grew heavier, harder, like a drum marking time for an army. Why did this feel like a battle?

"I suspect that's what Bastian thought of you. A fascinating, flame-haired human. Even better that he was away from home and most of his usual responsibilities. I dare say he saw the whole trip as a chance to relax... blow off some steam."

Meaning *I* had been a chance to blow off steam and nothing more. Yet he'd had ample chances to take his pleasure with me and hadn't.

Still, what she said (and presented as her opinion, so not a lie) had an undercurrent of truth. Now I'd seen how Bastian lived here, I understood that Lunden had given him some measure of freedom.

"Maybe he needed the break from such heavy responsibilities placed upon him." Subtle enough to not get me in trouble, but with all her centuries of court life, she had to understand that I meant *she* placed too much upon him.

She exhaled a soft sound, a shade thoughtful, a shade amused. "To think they say humans are stupid."

"And they say fae are polite above all else. I think *they* don't know what they're talking about."

Her chuckle rose, then fell into a thoughtful silence. We stood there a long while, the lights and life of Tenebris playing out before us. I wondered if I could excuse myself or if I had to wait for her to dismiss me as I would in Albion.

"I come here some evenings." She spoke quietly, gaze on the bridge, a crease between her brows. "More so since this news of Dawn's royal wedding."

Prince Sepher and his human bride. They'd chosen the eclipse for their wedding day so the queen could be present alongside King Lucius. I hadn't thought of how she might feel about it.

"I think of my daughter," she added.

The princess Bastian had beheaded?

"Did Bastian tell you I had two daughters? Once upon a time, anyway."

I shook my head.

"And now I am left with none." She snorted, a bitterness to the sound. "The younger, Sura, was... *foolish*. She brought on her own end, and I thank the Stars above that Bastian was there to save me from her plot. The elder... my heir... my Nyx... That bridge was the last place I saw her." The furrow of her brow deepened. "Months earlier, unseelie had broken through the veil, no doubt with some foul blood ritual. That was the night Bastian's mother was raped. They must've worked together to come through to this realm and take whatever they wished." Her jaw squared as her attention returned to the bridge.

So Bastian's mother wasn't the only one attacked that night. How many unseelie had come through?

"One took Nyx. My poor girl. In her own bed." Her nostrils flared and those dark eyes gleamed in the dim fae lights.

This wasn't the Night Queen speaking, but a mother whose daughter had been assaulted. I squeezed my hands together.

"After that, I knew they'd return. As sure as the sun setting and the moon rising, they would be back. That was when I enchanted the river to keep *him* out of the palace. And of course, I was right." She bared her teeth, fury in her gaze. "All those months later, he came back for Nyx to take her away forever but couldn't cross the bridge. Somehow, he found a way to lure her to it. I saw her, but I couldn't save her from crossing. I watched in horror, knowing that once she did, she would be in his clutches and he would take her to the Underworld."

I could picture it—the queen helpless as her daughter approached the bridge and the unseelie man waiting on the other side.

"He'd done something to enchant her and despite my cries telling her to turn back, she stepped out onto the bridge. I saw her fighting when she was halfway across. A battle for her own will. He must not have liked that. Perhaps he decided if he couldn't have her, no one would." She swallowed and my throat ached in sympathy. "The next thing I saw was her blood... an arrow in her chest... and her body falling into the river."

I rubbed my chest, which had grown tight with her sorrow. She might be a queen, but in that moment she'd been powerless. Even queens were only pieces on the board.

"I searched the banks myself, sent every guard I could... but no one found her, only the grave of a deer calf stillborn with two heads. An ill omen."

Exhaling, she pressed her hands together and shook her head at the bridge, as though that was the source of all her sorrow.

"I'm sorry," I murmured into the quiet space she left.

"So am I." She lifted her chin. "Now you understand why Bastian is so important to me. And why I cannot allow him to become distracted from his duty."

I went still as stone, not even daring to breathe.

This story... it wasn't about "getting to know" me, it was the backstory to a warning.

She had no heir. No princesses to rely on. She had Bastian. And between her words, I heard what the Night Queen didn't say.

She would do whatever it took to keep him.

39

KAT

The queen's unspoken warning followed me back to
our rooms. The lights were on when I entered, and in
the sitting room I found Bastian, head in his hands
before the fire.

I stopped in the doorway, struck by the collapsed lines of
his shoulders and back.

Who you really are is what you do when no one is looking.

This was Bastian.

How had I ever questioned it?

The bored aristocrat who'd practically rolled his eyes at the
idea of dancing with me. The stranger I'd seen in Albion after
Robin had appeared. Business Bastian.

The cunning Serpent. The Bastard of Tenebris. The Night
Queen's Shadow who would go to any lengths to get what he
wanted.

They were the masks.

This man—the one who came out when it was just the two
of us—the scarred man, bent by responsibility, haunted by

guilt from actions and memories that weren't his own. This was the real Bastian.

The man I'd known in Albion—*he was real.*

It burned my eyes and throat.

"Bastian," I said softly as I approached.

He swallowed as though gathering himself.

In this moment when he was vulnerable and soft, I ached to tell him about Elthea and the fact I'd had to get the memory of her treatments erased.

I ached to tell him *everything.*

But he didn't need my pain on top of his own, and he was soft now, but he was also the man who'd broken bones for me. I needed Elthea's cure, and to get it, I had to suffer in silence.

So, I took the chair next to his and curled up on it to face him. "What's wrong?"

With a deep breath, he pulled his attention from the flames and swept his fingers back through his hair. "It's been a long day." One side of his mouth rose like he was trying to give me a comforting smile... and failing.

"What, in particular, made it so long?"

"Putting it diplomatically, the queen is not in the best of moods. Prince Sepher's wedding has reminded her of... everything she doesn't have." Another attempt at a comforting smile. (And another failure.)

Very diplomatically put.

"The king had several Dusk folk executed while we were away. If I'd been here..." He shook his head and his frown pierced my heart with thorns. "Then there's..." He huffed out a long breath. "A list of things I can't tell you. State secrets, etcetera."

I tugged off my gloves and wrung them with both hands. "Does any of it relate to unCavendish?"

"Perhaps. It's... unclear."

"Is there some magic that could... I don't know... Pull any knowledge from my head that I might've missed?" That had to be something Kaliban could do.

Bastian flinched and shook his head. "Not that I would risk using on you."

I waited, but he didn't elaborate. "There must be something I can do to help. Something I've missed. Maybe if you interview me again, I'll—"

"I'm not putting you through that, Katherine. Not again." His jaw rippled as he stared into the flames. "And even if I would, I don't think there's anything you missed in your report. You were perfect."

I swallowed down the pleasure that word gave me. This wasn't about me—this was about trying to pry some of that weight off his shoulders. "Then put me to work for you."

"What?" He turned a fierce frown on me.

"I got that information about the necklace, didn't I? I can be useful, and I can do something none of your kind can."

"Lie." His gaze flicked down to my mouth as though he could see every lie I'd told as a stain upon my skin.

"Even if you don't need me as a spy, there must be something I can do. Plus, it sounds like you could use the help."

His lips pressed together and he sat back. It felt frustratingly like a dismissal.

"Put me to work, Bastian. I don't like being useless. And right now, with my inability to control this magic, I feel pretty damn useless." Granted, I'd used Kaliban's fire trick to help me keep it calmer, but it still didn't feel like it was mine to control.

Bastian's gaze skimmed over the rug. Thinking about it, perhaps.

"*Please.*"

Growling, he gave me a sidelong glare, which was fair.

Using that word was a low blow. But didn't he advocate so-called dirty tactics?

His jaw feathered as he folded his arms.

Perhaps he wouldn't be so easy to manipulate in this matter.

Fine. Logic, then.

"We made a good team in Lunden."

He raised an eyebrow in question.

"We stopped the changeling, didn't we?"

"We weren't exactly working together on that."

"No. But we were *both* working on it, albeit separately. And we stopped him just in time." Lifting my chin, I met his gaze squarely. "Imagine what we could do if we *did* work together."

Several things flickered over his face, each too quick for me to dissect. But they amounted to one, important outcome: he was thinking about my proposal.

Eventually, he drew a deep breath. "Fine."

I shot upright, grinning. It had worked.

He raised his hands, frown deepening in response. "But you're not a spy. I won't be sending you out as one of my operatives. It'll be desk work. Research. Very boring. No sneaking around or trying to get information from anyone."

I didn't care. It was something. A purpose. Maybe even a tiny chip of stone taken off the weight he was carrying.

"Whatever you need, Bastian."

The way his eyes widened told me something that dimmed my smile.

No one had ever said that to him before.

I spent the next week reading old books and calming myself by focusing on the fire each day. Forcing the stains small had become increasingly exhausting and they bubbled back once my attention waned, but focusing on sensory details as I did with the fire seemed to help.

As for my reading, it turned out the language that was similar to Latium was High Valens—one of the old fae tongues.

Bastian claimed they'd shared it with humans and that was how Latium had been born. If he hadn't been fae, I'd have called him a liar—Latium had originated around the Central Sea, not Albion.

Then again, he'd told me fae had once inhabited the whole world, only pushed back into Albion because of human expansion and their own dwindling numbers. The inhabitants of Elfhame certainly looked more diverse than the humans of Albion.

I shelved his claims as "maybe true." At the very least, he believed them.

Now I worked for him, he'd told me the contents of the note from his orrery, so I searched for mentions of a Circle of Ash or anything that might be similar. The more I read, the less I had to refer back to the book of High Valens grammar Brynan had provided.

It felt good. I was being useful. I was learning. Maybe we'd get somewhere and find the Circle of Ash before Dawn and keep the Sleep in place.

One morning, Rose walked me to an appointment with Elthea. We stopped at the bottom of the steps and she cocked her head. "Lunch at Moonsong after?"

I glanced at the orrery tower—Rose had taught me how to read the time from it. I needed at least an hour for the appointment—some stretched on longer. Then I could go to Kaliban's with supplies, get my memory cleared, and get to the spire in perhaps forty-five minutes.

"Perry and Ella are coming," she said with a playful lilt.

"Sounds great." Once my memory was wiped, I would be able to stomach food in blissful ignorance of whatever Elthea was about to do to me. "I'll meet you there."

Inside, I found Elthea waiting in her treatment room. With only the briefest greeting, she waved me onto the bed. "This one..." Her fingers fluttered over her notebook with a kind of excited energy. "This might be the one, Katherine." She smiled. Actually smiled—it sparked in her eyes.

My last treatment. I'd be able to go home.

Great. Awful. Did I really want to?

I swallowed down the knot of feelings and questions. Of course I wanted to be cured and go home. I would be able to hug Ella and stroke Vespera. I wouldn't need to fear accidentally brushing against someone in the palace halls or on the street. I wouldn't need to arrange to see Bastian every day to get my antidote.

He would be free of me and me of him. It was what we both wanted. An end to this awkward entanglement.

I gave Elthea a tight smile and sat on the bed. She strapped me down—ankles as well as wrists. That set my heart pounding harder, faster.

Just one more treatment. Then this would all be over.

Her gaze flicked over my fingers. "What a pretty ring."

Bastian's ring. *Never reveal your heart.* Nor his. "Thank you. It's new."

She held still and watched me, no doubt waiting for me to answer her unasked question—where did it come from?

I smiled blandly at her. Let her think the human too stupid to understand subtext.

Eventually, she huffed and opened the glass-fronted cabinet. Inside sat a smaller case that she unlocked and opened, revealing row upon row of tiny vials. Some glowed. Some glittered. One was a black void as though it sucked light out of the very world.

I didn't see which she selected, but she approached with something held tight to her chest.

"It was a challenge to get hold of this. One of the hunters died. But I'm sure we'll see results."

I swallowed. It was as though my heart was trying to beat its way up my throat and out. "What is it?"

She held up a tiny vial, only an inch long, the top sealed with black wax. Its contents moved sluggishly around, not responding to her movement but... as if it had a life of its own. It licked the top and bottom of the vial where she held it, perhaps drawn to her flesh. As it slithered and moved, it caught the light, gleaming a dark, yellowish green.

"This"—she held the vial up and examined it—"is manticore venom."

"Venom? You're going to poison me? That isn't—"

"Are you a scientist, Katherine?"

"No, but I have a brain." The harshness in my voice and the fact I questioned her—not bravery but desperation. I yanked on the leather straps but they held fast. She was insane. Why had I sent Rose away?

I tried to contain myself, but my breaths heaved. "I'm already poisoned and poisonous. You're going to kill me if you—"

"No, I won't. I have done the research. You yourself should know that." She gave me a thin-lipped smile as she approached the bed. "And if, somehow, I am wrong, well, I have the antidote to manticore venom right here." She held up her other hand, revealing a larger vial full of translucent yellow liquid flecked with gold. "I promise this won't end your life, Katherine."

"Is this... all this really going to heal me? Or am I just an experiment?"

"Can't both be true? This has all been a path towards a cure. What happened to you was unique. My methods must be similarly... unorthodox."

I might not trust her, but I could trust in her inability to lie. I told myself that a dozen times as she cracked open the wax seal and bent over the bed.

"Now, drink up."

For all I knew, this might not be any worse than the other things she'd done to me. It would be fine.

And if it was bad, Kaliban would be able to scrape away the memories so it would be like it had never happened.

I opened my mouth.

She tilted the vial of green liquid. At first, it didn't pour, throwing itself against the glass sides, but when she lowered it to my waiting lips, it twitched and dropped from the vial.

Cold.

So cold. A refreshing, iced drink.

The flavour was coppery and sour, like someone had mixed lime juice with blood... but it had none of the pleasant zesty flavour of lime. This tasted of... dank forest floors... or perhaps the rotting smell of swamps.

It writhed on the tip of my tongue, and I flinched at the strangeness of that sensation. This stuff had a mind of its own.

Eyes wide, I stared at Elthea.

"Close your mouth and swallow."

Every single hair on my body stood on end as the stuff slithered over my tongue, growing warmer by the second.

Just this one thing. Then it would all be over.

I clenched my hands into fists and forced my lips together.

The thing snaked its way over my tongue, and now I could feel it on the roof of my mouth too. Every instinct said I should spit it out. I'd accidentally put something *alive* in my mouth. Spit it out.

Spit. It. Out.

I swallowed.

I gagged. Because the writhing didn't stop once it was in my throat. It twisted, either fighting not to go down or eager to get inside me.

All I knew was that this—*this* was the most wrong anything had ever felt in my life.

But if it would cure me...

I choked the stuff down.

That was when the burning began. On my tongue at first— threading along the route the venom had taken. Then down my throat. Every place it had touched was now on fire.

Gasping, I strained against the leather straps. "Water. I need water."

Goosebumps pricked my arms and sweat broke out on my brow, but Elthea shook her head. "You can't." She sat back and pulled out her notebook and a pen.

The burning hit my stomach, scorching now, and I arched from the bed, biting back a whimper.

"Still fighting it." She made a thoughtful sound and shook her head as she wrote in the notebook. "I wonder what will be the thing to make you scream at last."

"How long?" I managed to rasp between panted breaths.

She shrugged, eyes widening. "We shall see. The next phase should hit you right about..." She glanced at the orrery mounted on the wall. "Now."

Next phase? I huffed through gritted teeth, spit flecking my lips.

Was this a fae joke? A horrible one, but the stories said they were cruel and loved to toy with—

White hot pain shot through every nerve. Chest. Back. Arms. Legs. Even my throat and face. It was like a lightning bolt, gone just as quickly.

I blew out a breath, almost laughing in its wake. Not funny but relieved. If it only lasted a fraction of a second, I could take that. It wasn't so—

Again. Brighter. Hotter.

This one lasted longer, too—a full second.

I collapsed back into the bed, eyes stinging with unshed tears.

"Almost," Elthea murmured, watching me over her notebook as she wrote.

What a fool. What a fucking fool. That stuff crawling down my throat wasn't the most wrong thing. This was—my body burning from *inside*, limbs spasming out of control, muscles tight and twitching after. And her watching like this—my suffering—was merely *interesting*.

It had to be almost over.

Had to be.

Another streak lanced through me, arching my back, muddling my brain until all I could do was grit my teeth and wait.

Any second now, it would disappear.

Any second.

I reached out like I could pull time to me, make it move faster.

Please. Please. Help me.

My vision hazed purple. Blood, maybe, with pain affecting my sight.

A sound came from Elthea. On the edge of my tunnelling vision, she stood and backed away.

I tried to turn and ask if it was nearly over, but my body wasn't my own. I could only wait for the lightning lick of pain to fade.

And wait.

And wait.

Then, like someone had broken a barrel, letting the contents burst out, the pain doubled, tripled, quadrupled, exploding into every fibre of my being, tearing my mind to tatters.

There was nothing. I was nothing.

Only pain and purple haze and a terrible, terrible scream.

40
BASTIAN

My office door flew open, ruffling Orpha's report. I'd sent her with a group of guards to find the patrol who should've been checking the border of Horror territory. They hadn't found them yet but had replaced some missing wardstones.

I frowned up from the report as Rose burst in, panting. "You need to come. Quickly." She was already backing out. "It's Kat."

My whole being—maybe all of reality lurched. I tossed the papers on my desk and ran after her. "What is it?"

"She's with Elthea and... I've never heard a scream like that. It sounded like she was killing her." She shook her head as we sprinted down the corridor. "She'd forgotten her scarf... went to take it to her. But I couldn't get in. Door must've been sealed magically."

Kat screaming.

Despite our pace and the blood pumping through every part of me, my body went cold.

She hadn't screamed when she'd dangled over the waterfall; she'd only called for help.

As poison had worked through her system, dragging her to the floor, she hadn't screamed. That had only come in its advanced stages. Her initial quiet had worried Asher, in fact. He'd thought her too far gone to save.

What was Elthea doing to her?

Fuck manners—I shoved folk out of the way as we crossed the grand hall. The bridge was a blur. I didn't slow to greet the guards.

I just ran.

As we raced through the city, dozens of looks followed us. The Night Queen's Shadow didn't race headlong anywhere.

Shadows swarmed around my feet, like they could speed me along. Anything to get me there faster. If I was too late...

"Oathbreaker," someone shouted, emboldened by my uncharacteristic display.

Lucky for them, I didn't have time to stop.

We skidded around one corner after another, until we were finally on the Hall of Healing's street, my heart ready to explode.

Folk fled from our path as I put on a burst of speed, every part of my soul's attention fixed on the white marble columns.

At the top of its steps, a splash of red interrupted the hall's pure white. Hugging the wall, Kat stumbled from the building.

I flew up the steps. "Katherine?"

She trembled, hunched over, not looking at me.

"Kat? What did she—?"

Then she looked up.

Pale, hair plastered to her forehead, blue-ish shadows beneath her eyes—I hadn't seen her look this bad since she'd taken the changeling's poison. She reeked of sweat and fear and rotten plants, though beneath that, the sweet scent of her magic seemed stronger.

What the fuck had Elthea done? My teeth ached as I clenched my jaw.

Rose caught up, gasping as she took in Kat's state.

"Take her back to our rooms. Get Asher to look at her." I held Kat out by her shoulders as she muttered something. "I'm going to have words with Elthea." There wouldn't just be words. I was going to tear her apart.

I started into the Hall of Healing, but Kat's gloved hand landed on my stomach. "I'm fine," she whispered between heaving breaths. "She tried a cure. It didn't work. That's all." Eyelids fluttering, her gaze sank, and she frowned as she rubbed her chest. Right on the edge of hearing, she murmured, "I think my heart stopped." She swayed, and I caught her as she fell.

Every muscle vibrated with rage as I eased her into Rose's arms. "Take her back to her room."

Eyes wide, skin pale between her freckles, Rose nodded.

I charged inside.

I think someone tried to stop me, but my attention was fixed on the door to Elthea's treatment room and nothing else could break it.

She was putting something in a small case inside the cabinet, glass clinking on glass.

I let my shadows go.

They streaked across the room and closed on her wrists. She let out a cry that I barely heard over the rush of blood in my ears. "You should've saved your favour to stop me tearing you apart." I spat the words, every part of my face too tight to even attempt the appearance of calm. My blood didn't just boil

—it had evaporated, leaving me dry and sizzling like a pan about to burn.

My shadows turned her, so she'd be able to see me as I killed her—as I paid her back for whatever she had done to Kat.

I think my heart stopped.

Elthea's chest heaved as my shadows tightened around her arms, cutting off the blood flow. "I'm her best hope of finding a cure, and you know it." She lifted her chin, expression barely on the edge of calm.

"A cure? You're going to fucking kill her." Hands fisting, I sent shadows down to her legs. I wanted to rip her apart with my bare hands. Maybe I would.

A vicious smile tugged on my mouth. Muscles humming and hot, I crossed the room.

Her fingers were turning white, now. As I told my shadows to pull, she let out a whimper.

"You kill me and that's it." An uncertain waver entered her voice. "N-not to mention the repercussions for our courts."

My shadows paused.

It was about the only thing she could've said to get through to me. We'd only just smoothed things with Dawn after the executions and freeing the remaining prisoners.

Blood still roared in my ears, though. Fuck Dawn. Fuck the balance. End her. She'd hurt Katherine. She'd killed her, even if only for a moment.

I saw Kat's face, so pale.

But then I saw it crumpling, her eyes glittering with unshed tears as she'd pushed away Vespera.

That was what the cure meant to her.

I pulled myself straight and released Elthea. My teeth ground. I'd let Kat down by not making Elthea suffer as she had. But I would let her down more by robbing her of any chance at a cure. I swallowed down my frustrated rage and let it attack me instead.

Elthea huffed out a long breath and glared at me. "You can't make an omelette without cracking a few eggs." Swallowing, she straightened her sleeves. "Curing her is going to require a lot of experimentation. There's no avoiding it."

Kat wasn't an experiment, but I couldn't push words through my tight throat.

"Either you want her cured or you don't." Elthea canted her head, casting her gaze down me and back up. "Though I can imagine you might like having her bound to you for the rest of her life, even if she is married."

I clenched my hands at my sides—it was that or grabbing her. "You hurt Katherine again, and I won't just kill you. I'll fucking destroy you."

As I stalked out, her reply followed me: "It isn't up to you, Serpent."

41

KAT

It was dark when I woke, no light pouring in through my bedroom windows.

My bedroom? I was...

I grabbed my wrists. I wasn't bound. And this wasn't the Hall of Healing.

"Kat?" A deeper shadow in the darkness bent closer, two dimly glowing eyes on me.

"I'm awake." I swallowed, rubbing my throat as the ghost of the manticore venom crawled down it. "*Lumis*," I said, thinking of low level light.

Three fae lights blinked on, drifting overhead.

Bastian sat at my side, knees touching the bed, brow furrowed as he eyed me. "How do you feel?"

"Tired, though it looks like I've been asleep for hours." I nodded towards the window. "What time is it?"

"Past midnight." He covered his mouth, stifling a yawn.

I failed to stifle mine, stretching into it. The moments before I'd passed out came back—him, Rose, trying to stop him barging into the Hall of Healing. "Elthea... what did you—?"

"She's alive." Any slackness in him shut down as his eyebrows clashed together.

I sighed my relief. The manticore venom had failed, but she was my only hope of a cure. Not to mention the fact I was fairly sure the Night Queen would blame me if Bastian lost his mind and killed her. His eyes had blazed with murderous intent on the hall's steps.

"Good," I murmured, eyelids drooping.

"You should sleep."

"So should you." I gave him a half-hearted grin as he pulled the blankets around me.

"I can sleep here just fine." He settled back into his chair.

I meant to argue, but my mouth wouldn't open and my eyelids sank shut.

THE NEXT DAY I woke late, finding Bastian in the chair by my bed. The only sign he'd moved was that his hair was damp and he wore a fresh outfit—shirt and trousers in charcoal grey.

As I bathed and dressed, body sluggish, he brought breakfast to my room, pushing the vase to one side. Today it contained a fresh bouquet of white roses, petals edged with fresh green. Their soft scent drifted through the room alongside the array of pastries he set out.

"Dessert for breakfast?" I eyed the options—puff pastry folded with chocolate and hazelnut, lemon tarts made with flaky pastry, little egg custards, almond and raspberry frangipane, slices of apple in a pastry nest topped with apricot jam, and a bowl of fruit to one side. I didn't know where to start, but my mouth watered.

He shrugged and poured coffee for us both. "The kitchens must've been baking today."

Something about the way he said it—too light, too casual—made me give him a sidelong look. "They just *happened* to be baking a batch of various delicious pastries? Total coincidence."

His mouth twisted to one side. "You know I can't say yes to that. Fine. I requested them so you'd have something pleasant to wake up to. Happy?"

I grinned as I selected an almond and raspberry frangipane. "Ecstatic." I didn't know whether I was more pleased by the pastries or the fact I got to have breakfast with the real Bastian rather than his business façade. Gods knew how he felt about me—he did sweet things like this, but I still caught signs in him that might be guilt about the past or over my marriage. But it felt good to see *him* rather than his mask.

I ate more than I needed, using each mouthful to wipe from my mouth and throat the sensation of the manticore venom.

After breakfast, when I stretched to try and give the obscene amount of pastries and one lone apple space to move down my stomach, he watched me, lips pursed. Did even he think I'd eaten too much?

He frowned. "You look like you're gearing up for something."

"The start of my day?"

"I was hoping you might rest."

"That sounds an awful lot like sitting here *bored*." Which would give me time to think about the appointment. At least if I went out, I could see Kaliban.

Shoulders sinking, he sighed. "I should've known you'd say that. How about I bring the work to you?"

I gave him a mutinous look and opened my mouth to argue.

"I'll give you space in my workroom."

I clamped my mouth shut. "Access to Bastian's mysterious workroom. Now that's an offer I can't refuse."

The corner of his eye tensed, like he was trying not to wince, but he led me into the hall and unlocked one of the few rooms in our suite that I hadn't yet seen.

Light streamed through the floor-to-ceiling windows, hitting drifting motes of dust and...

And a fucking mess.

A grandfather clock missing its pendulum. Cracked vases and bowls. A teapot with no spout. Canvases stacked against the wall, their images jarred by rips. Various blades without hilts and hilts with no weapons. Glass-fronted cabinets filled with broken mechanisms and cogs. Stacks of books so tattered, I feared touching them would make the whole pile crumble to unreadable fragments.

Clearing his throat, Bastian brushed past me and gathered assorted tools and a pair of goggles from the large central table. It had been so piled high with *stuff* I hadn't even realised it was a separate surface from the side boards and shelves around it.

On the table sat a collection of cogs and gems and the jumbled insides of a broken orrery. The subtle hum of magic whispered over my skin.

"This is..."

As he cleared the table, Bastian's shoulders hunched, like he was bracing himself.

"Not what I expected from your workroom." I gave the

space another inspection. It was hard to tell how large it was with *so much* clutter.

He made a soft sound and scooped the broken orrery onto a velvet-lined tray.

I craned over his arm as he carried it away. "Are you... fixing that?"

"Trying to," he muttered.

The fragments of vase I'd found in his suite in Riverton Palace. My fence's off-hand comment about him buying broken things from her. "You're fixing it all, aren't you?"

Brow low, mouth tight, he turned and glanced over the collection. He wrinkled his nose and sent a shadow to swipe dust off the grandfather clock's face. "*Trying* to. But there are more broken things than I can keep up with."

"Has it crossed your mind that they aren't all your responsibility?"

He ignored my comment, still focused on the assembled items. "Besides, I don't have time. Not for hobbies and tinkering, anyway."

I bit back a laugh—not at him, but of disbelief. "Bastian Marwood's hobby is collecting broken things and trying to fix them."

He picked up a piece of vase and peered at it. "Just seems a shame to see it all thrown away. So when I find it, I rescue it." He scoffed and screwed his eyes shut, dropping the pottery shard back in the pile. "That sounds ridiculous, doesn't it?"

"No." I touched his back. "It's... somewhat ambitious— over-ambitious, even. Kind of sweet. But not ridiculous."

He gave me a long look, as though waiting for me to add something. When I didn't, he nodded with a soft sound and ushered me to a chair he'd uncovered.

I could feel his discomfort. He didn't let other people in

here, and I wasn't about to mock him for such a noble pursuit... even if it was doomed.

So when he brought me a stack of books and a pot of tea, I smiled and set to work.

THE NEXT FEW days went much the same. I lived in this contradiction, trapped between exhaustion and nightmares about my last appointment. I wanted to eat everything, like my body needed the energy, but certain food textures reminded me of the appointment, forcing me to leave the meal uneaten. Bastian hovered nearby, only letting me out of his sight to sleep, wash, and go to the toilet. Thank the gods for that, at least.

It felt like the time I'd spent in his rooms in Lunden, but I wasn't in nearly such a bad place. Maybe he feared I might fall into that pit. At least I could function and spent my time reading through books and scrolls, searching for reference to the Circle of Ash. (Not the most catchy name, but who was I to question ancient fae spellcrafters?)

I tried to persuade Bastian to go back to work. Instead, he brought his work to our rooms, and invited Rose and Faolán for dinner, Ella for lunch, Perry for a late breakfast. Our suite went from a private space to one for entertainment, and having visitors made the place feel homely. Bastian didn't even comment when I added little touches like potted plants and cushions on the settee.

One night, Perry and Ella came for dinner. After several hints that she wanted to catch up with me without the far-too-attentive fae—hints that were ignored—Ella eventually raised her eyebrow at Bastian over her glass. "Is there a reason you won't leave us alone with Kat? Something you don't want her to say?"

He blinked and straightened, and inwardly I winced. "No, I just…" His expression tightened, shadowing his eyes. "You know she died. I'm merely—"

"Only for a moment." I sat forward and wiggled my fingers. "See? Still alive."

Bastian clenched his jaw and inclined his head, then left the room.

His silence cut deeper than his words. He was trying to care for me. Perhaps he hadn't realised just how tightly he was holding on.

"Are you really all right?" Ella surveyed me.

"Still a little tired, but otherwise…" I spread my arms and smiled like I wasn't haunted by nightmares where my heart stopped and left an echoing silence that I couldn't escape. When I held out my glass for a top-up, she placed the bottle of fae wine out of reach. I gave Perry a beseeching look, but she shook her head. Traitors, the pair of them.

"And you two…" Ella arched an eyebrow at the door Bastian had disappeared through. "Have you resumed things again?"

I scowled and upturned my glass, catching the very last drop on my tongue for a disappointingly brief flash of fruity sharpness. "It's… complicated."

"Hmm." Perry swirled her wine glass, its fullness mocking me. "But you said he apologised while you were away."

"He did." I frowned at the glass.

"And I've heard rings hold *special* meaning to fae." Ella eyed the slight bulge in my glove where the enchanted ring sat on my finger.

"I don't think it applies to *all* rings." And even if it did, what was the point of possessing something if you weren't going to claim it? Despite every lingering look and almost kiss, Bastian had left me thoroughly *unclaimed*.

"You've forgiven him, though." Perry gave me a long look. "And he doesn't *seem* angry at you about the marriage thing."

I shrugged. "I apologised. And I think he's forgiven me."

"So, what's the sticking point?"

How was I meant to explain that while I wanted him, something still felt wrong between us?

Ella narrowed her eyes. "Why are you sitting here with us rather than fucking him until you both die in a haze of exhausted bliss?"

I huffed a laugh and toyed with one of the fine seams of my glove, trying very hard not to imagine how much sex that would require.

Perry screwed up her face. "You want them to fuck themselves to death?"

"I don't *want* it." Ella spread her hands. "Though as deaths go, it's definitely not the worst. I just... well, it would be better than whatever *this* is." She gestured from me to the door. "Because the tension between you two is..." She exhaled, cheeks puffing out. "It's heady. Every time I leave the room, I feel the need for a cold shower."

After sighing and shaking her head, she turned back to me with a glint in her eye. "Have you *tried* seducing him?"

The conversation turned to well-meaning advice for doing just that before dissolving into some highly detailed descriptions of how to ensure a lover was well satisfied. I'd never sucked a cock, but after Ella's explanation, it felt like I had a wealth of experience. Not that it seemed I was ever going to get to use this new knowledge.

But I noted how pink Perry's cheeks went as she gave a private smile behind her glass.

Ella and I exchanged looks, and I knew she wondered the same thing I did. When was Perry going to tell us about her relationship with Asher?

Not tonight, it seemed. And I wasn't going to push.

Many hours later, I went to hug them goodbye and remembered myself. Gloves firmly in place, I squeezed their shoulders and blew harmless kisses.

No hugs. No touch. Distance. As I waved them off at the door, I prayed my broad smile disguised my tears.

42

KAT

I needed a cure.

Desperately.

I couldn't keep living at arm's length from everyone. Perry had reassured me that she'd given the stable hands clear instructions on how to care for a sabrecat, since they were used to deer. Before my latest appointment, I'd gone to visit Vespera every day. But it wasn't the same.

So, the next morning as Bastian sat by the sitting room window and read through reports, I looked up from selecting my next research book, an old, old volume of stories—the fae equivalent of faerie tales. "Has Elthea sent word of my next appointment?"

He blinked, stared at me, blinked some more. "*What?*"

"I thought she might've made some progress after the other day."

The crawl of the manticore's poison echoed through me and I shuddered. I'd scratched my chest raw, waking from nightmares where the poison was many, many times bigger, wrapping around me, consuming *me* rather than me it.

Still, however horrible Elthea's methods, they were my only chance at a normal life. Gathering myself, I gave a firm nod. "I'm ready for another treatment."

His mouth dropped open as he squinted. "Absolutely not. She killed you."

"Only temporarily."

"*This time.*" He tossed the report on the table. "What if your heart doesn't restart next time? Not that there's going to be one."

I pursed my lips. Old Kat wouldn't have dared risk it. Nothing that threatened survival. But... "Going around afraid to touch anyone is not living, Bastian."

Sucking in a breath, he rose. His eyes were so wide, so fixed on me, I wasn't sure he realised he moved. "It—it isn't. But..." He shook his head. "She is out of control. And the fact you won't tell me what else she's done has me terrified—*terrified* that it's even worse." His chest rose and fell like he fought to contain himself.

I squeezed the book to disguise my discomfort. I hadn't told him about the memories I'd traded out of my mind. He'd berate me for being foolish enough to let someone in my head. But Kaliban had heard my thoughts whether I liked it or not—letting him wipe them away wasn't revealing anything new. But it had given me a chance to live—and *sleep*—without the intrusion of unwanted memories.

I touched my chest, wincing. Bastian had given me a salve and dressings to stop my clothes rubbing on the raw skin, but it was still sore.

I needed a cure, but I didn't need the memories of how it came about.

Bastian was already trying to stop the former. If I told him about the latter, he'd try to stop that, too. Then I really would lose my damn mind.

"It's fine." I gritted my teeth. "Nothing I can't handle."

Liar. It was his voice in my mind.

"Katherine." He raked his fingers through his hair. "I don't know how to make you understand—"

"It's my body."

He stopped, mouth still open mid-sentence.

I raised my eyebrows. "You said it was always my choice."

He exhaled, shoulders sinking. Giving in.

I didn't just want him to give in, though. I needed him to understand. "I've suffered for far more pointless things than this. At least this has a purpose and I *choose* to endure it. I won't be bound to you like this forever, Bastian. It isn't fair on either of us."

Lips pressed together, he clenched and unclenched his hands. After a moment, he threw them down at his sides and started towards me. "But I don't want you to—"

A knock echoed through from the main door to the suite.

His eyes screwed shut as he called, "Enter."

Brynan filed in, followed by Asher, Rose, Faolán, and a man with black hair that gleamed purple and blue when it caught the light.

The meeting. Of course. As part of bringing his work to the suite, Bastian had arranged for us all to gather here to discuss the Circle of Ash.

I gave a tight smile as Rose caught my eye and raised an eyebrow. Meanwhile, at her side, Faolán gave Bastian a similar, questioning look.

"This is Lysander." Bastian ignored his shapechanging

friend and gestured towards the stranger. "Better known as Ariadne's husband."

Lysander shot him a frown. *"Thanks,"* he drawled before approaching me and offering his hand and a smile that dimpled his cheeks. "Ari's told me a lot about you."

I looked from his hand to my gloved one. It was safe. I shook it, hoping my smile didn't look too rictus. "And she's told me all about you, too." It was sweet how smitten she clearly was with the fae who had "stolen" her, setting in motion Rose's journey into Elfhame and subsequently meeting Faolán.

As we sat and Bastian summoned tea and coffee with a word, I wondered whether the Night Queen realised the chain reaction she'd caused by demanding Lysander enact the Tithe.

Faolán poured coffee for Rose and himself before offering the pot to Lysander, who produced a notebook from his pocket and declined the coffee. I ran and fetched my notes, returning to find everyone seated and a space left on the settee next to Bastian.

"How's Gael?" I asked Brynan while Bastian poured coffee for me and himself.

Much-needed coffee. I couldn't get through the day without several cups, thanks to my nightmare-interrupted sleep.

"Better." He sighed and nodded. "Thanks for asking. I hope you're..." He raised his eyebrows. *"Recovered?"*

Bastian cleared his throat. "So, the Circle of Ash."

Brynan nodded and rolled a large sheet of paper out over the table, pinning it down with the cups and pots. He sat poised with a pen.

Bastian took us all in. "What do we know so far?"

"It's rumoured to end the Sleep," Brynan said, writing as he did.

"Dawn is on its trail." Rose sat back, both hands wrapped around her drink, but her tense expression belied her apparent calm.

At her side, Faolán growled.

"And they gained information from a text in Albion," Asher added, stirring honey into his tea. "A text written by the Lark."

"Then there's its name." Lysander wrinkled his nose. "Though I wish I could get hold of the original text. I'm sure Gael decoded it correctly, but whoever wrote the note must've mistranslated."

I scoffed. "Agreed. The Circle of Ash isn't much of a name for a grand and powerful artefact."

Lysander flashed me a smile. "Exactly."

Bastian made a low sound that was almost thoughtful, but it reminded me of Faolán's growl. "Well, that name is all we have so far. I know Katherine's been conscious of anything circle adjacent in her reading." He gave a smile as warm as my coffee. "I trust you've been doing the same, Lysander." This smile was much, much cooler.

A certain tension around Lysander's eyes suggested he was struggling not to roll them. "*Of course.*"

"So..." I sat forward, reaching for the cream. Bastian grabbed it for me, along with the sugar, and added a generous amount of both to my cup. "What might this Circle of Ash actually be, then?"

"A ring?" Rose shrugged.

"A ceremonial platter. A wreath. A carved disc of wood with some ritual use." Lysander ticked off the possibilities on his fingers, while Brynan wrote them down one side of the paper.

"Might not be an item but a place." At Faolán's gravelly voice, I sat up.

"What do you mean?" Bastian asked, mirroring me.

"Could be a circle of ash trees. You know, *growing*."

"You mean, a specific grove somewhere." Bastian's eyes widened as though he hadn't considered that possibility. He nodded slowly, gaze distant and thoughtful. "We've been so focused on the circle... what about the ash? It could be the tree itself, but what else?"

"The wood from the tree, obviously." Rose rubbed the edge of her cup.

With a nod, Bastian smiled at her. "Let's not assume anything is obvious. What is ash wood used for?"

"Axles." Faolán nodded. "It's strong."

"Healing and protection." Asher tugged his lower lip.

Rose pointed her cup at him. "There's also *you. Asher*."

A ripple of laughter ran through the group, easing the sense that we were missing something. Of course we were—that was why this relic or grove or whatever it was had sunk into obscurity.

"Ash is the best firewood," I murmured as my gaze landed on the fireplace.

Every pair of eyes turned to me. All but Rose frowned. "Fae fires don't consume fuel in the same way, so I'm not sure you'd realise, but ash burns for a long time with intense heat." I'd rarely been able to afford it, but one cold winter, when I brought Vespera inside to stop her freezing to death, I'd gone through the house and picked out every item of ash furniture and chopped it up for firewood. That was the main reason we'd survived.

"She's right." Rose nodded. "Ma and Pa use it if they need

the ovens burning for a long time." No surprise she knew about fires—she came from a family of bakers.

"Then there are ashes," I added, lifting one shoulder.

Faolán's eyebrows lowered. "But a circle of them wouldn't last long."

"True." I laughed at myself. "Sorry, I was caught up in ideas."

"Don't apologise." Bastian's warm hand closed on my knee, the unexpected gesture making my heart trip. He didn't seem to notice Faolán's frown deepening as his gaze fixed on that contact. I wasn't sure he even realised he was touching me. "Nothing is obvious and no idea is foolish. Not while we're still groping around in the dark."

Rose jabbed an elbow into Faolán's ribs and he looked away.

"And some of us are groping around in the light." Lysander arched an eyebrow.

When Bastian turned to him, he jerked his chin at my knee.

Throat bobbing, Bastian slid his hand onto his own knee.

"She *is* married, if you recall."

My blood simmered. Was Robin destined to dog my steps, even in Elfhame? I shot Lysander a sharp smile. "And she is *here*, if you recall. My marriage is none of your business, but if it was, I'd tell you that I didn't choose it. An arranged marriage might've worked out well for you and Ari, but we aren't all so lucky."

An icy silence froze the room.

I bit my tongue. Too late, though, wasn't it?

At my side, Bastian's knuckles were white on his own knee. I'd let him down, stamping all over the fae rules of politeness. I should've stopped after my first sentence—that would've put Lysander on notice without causing this awkwardness.

I cleared my throat. "Sor—"

"Don't," Bastian gritted out.

"It could be made from one of the old Guardian trees," Brynan piped up.

Lysander nodded, eyes downcast. "Three of those were ash."

The meeting went on, discussing a plan of action. Bastian would send operatives to a remote library. Lysander would trawl the libraries of friends outside the city. I would continue working through Dusk's library. I kept quiet and drank my coffee, not wanting to cause any more problems with my simmering anger. I tried to put a little distance between Bastian and me, but the settee wasn't very big, and our legs brushed every time one of us moved. No one made any more comments.

When they left, my head swam with possibilities, but I braced myself for Bastian's reaction to the tongue-lashing I'd given Lysander.

He leant against the door as he closed it. "Are you all right?"

I blinked at him. "You're...? You're not pissed off at me?"

"Should I be?" He canted his head.

"I just..." I gestured towards the armchair Lysander had vacated. "What I said."

The corner of Bastian's mouth twitched as he stalked closer. "He had it coming. And I have to admit, I enjoyed seeing him on the receiving end of your fire."

Burn for me, my ember.

He spoke in the same tone now as he had then, and the way he crossed the floor with predatory purpose put me right back in Lunden.

I stood there, breaths a little too fast, tongue stuck to the roof of my mouth at the memory of everything Ella had described last night.

He reached me, eyelids heavy as his gaze raked over my face. "Your anger is a beautiful thing, Katherine. You are allowed to have it, and you're allowed to show it."

I gripped my gown's skirts, though I bent towards him as I'd seen Brynan bend towards Gael. Ella had been right—the tension between us was enough to set the world ablaze.

But I was married. His friends and employees cared about that fact. His queen cared. Maybe he did, too. He might want to fuck my brains out, but if he gave in, he'd only regret it after.

I didn't want to be anyone's regret. Certainly not his.

Eyes burning, I arched a brow at him. "Even if I'm raging about my marriage?"

His neck corded as a muscle in his jaw twitched. He exhaled, shoulders sinking, and took a step back. "Especially then," he muttered.

"Perhaps we could both use some space." I swallowed down the sickly feeling rising from my stomach. "I appreciate you looking after me, but I'm not in the same place I was after..." I gestured vaguely, searching for the words that would tell him what I meant but wouldn't put me back there. "When my uncle grabbed me."

"Maybe you're right." Gaze to one side, he nodded. "I'll go and work in my office for a few hours."

43

KAT

A soon as he was gone, I hurried out. I didn't have Rose, but I didn't care. She couldn't know about Kaliban—I wouldn't put her in a difficult position of choosing between me and Bastian.

But I desperately needed my memories gone.

Once I cleared the palace grounds, I breathed a little easier —less chance of Bastian or Rose catching me. The scent of roasted nuts coated in sugar and spices tinged the air, a sign of the coming Solstice festivities.

But my relief was short-lived, as the Hall of Healing's white marble pillars caught the midday sun.

Throat closing, I scratched my chest, snatched back from the edge of that memory by the streaking pain of my raw skin.

Head bowed, I trotted through the streets, only looking up when I needed to get my bearings. Each time, the sight of the hall put me right back in that white room. I couldn't remember the pain. But I remembered the horror. The choking poison writing in my throat. The twitching of my body out of control. The fear it might never end.

My breaths sped as I turned onto Kaliban's street.

I didn't stop to buy him food. I would have to owe him.

I needed this memory gone. *Now.*

My mind played yet more cruel tricks on me, as my sight hazed, everything taking on a purple cast. Was I going to pass out? Then someone would stop and help. They would *touch* me.

Fuck.

I locked my eyes on Kaliban's front door and sprinted. The heaving breaths in my lungs. The sweat beading my skin. They were real things. *Just hold on to them and don't pass out.*

I hammered on the door again and again and again until it opened.

"All right, all right. Stars above, I'm coming. I'm..." His eyes bulged and he backed away. "Get in."

Panting, I sank into a chair and fisted my hands in my hair. "Get it out. Get it out of me. *Please.*"

He coughed. "Control your magic, Katherine. It's humming around you."

When I looked up, I found him on the far side of the room, sleeve over his mouth and nose, the air between us tinted purple.

That was real? Not just a memory?

"I—I can't." I tried to grab for it, reaching out with my will, hissing at it to come here. Only my skin was meant to be poisonous, not the fucking air around me. "I can't!"

"The fire," he choked, opening a window and half hanging out it. "Focus on that. Get yourself under control."

"I'm sorry." I clutched my necklace, its hard stone reassuring, even through my gloves. I had the antidote.

With a deep breath, I turned to the fireplace where the cheerful pink flames leapt. Coral pink. Orange. Flecks of yellow, red, and violet-blue. The scent of the lavender and lemon candles he liked to burn. The time-worn surface of the table, smooth in that way fresh varnish just couldn't replicate.

The purple haze faded.

Kaliban huffed and bustled around, opening the other windows. "Thank the fucking gods that's over." He clicked his tongue like I was a naughty child.

Exhaustion swept over me, a wave that threatened to drag me under. "I did technically die for a minute. You'll forgive me if I'm not entirely under control."

His eyebrows shot up. "You... died?"

I hung my head, wishing I hadn't burst out with it so easily.

"No use wishing that. I'll see it when you let me take the memory, anyway. Come on, then." He took the seat next to mine and gestured for me to sit up.

I called the memory afresh, gripping the table's edge as I battled nausea.

Hmm. Kaliban's voice reached into my mind as he wiped away the start of the appointment. *Do you want this part erasing, too?*

He pulled a memory to the surface...

My throat is hoarse. My breaths wheeze. But most importantly, when I open my eyes, the burning in my body is gone. Every muscle aches, weak and trembling.

No more pain.

From the far side of the slowly spinning room, Elthea watches me, head cocked, a slight crease between her eyebrows. She's wearing a mask now. She didn't have that before.

She approaches and makes a thoughtful sound. "Interesting."

"*Interesting?*" It bursts out of me as I fight to control my breathing and the spinning of the room.

"*Very interesting.*" She nods, examining my hands.

I'm still strapped to the bed, or else I'd be mighty tempted to wring her bloody neck for calling this "interesting." Somehow I would find the strength to do that, despite my limbs feeling like liquid.

"The manticore venom had the usual effect, but then... it was like your body began to process it. It caused a lot of stress to your system, and there was a strange reaction from your skin—like the aconite hazed out of you." She pulls up my sleeves, pinching the skin and nodding.

"Your heart stopped for a while. But then it restarted on its own. And"—she ducks close, peering into my eyes—"I didn't need to heal you, but you're clear of all effects."

I shoot upright—or as upright as I can with the straps biting into my wrists. "I'm cured?"

"What? Oh." She laughs. "No, not that." Another laugh that makes my fingernails cut into my palms. "The manticore venom. It didn't work as a cure, but..." She frowns and unbuckles one wrist. "It seems you might be immune to poisons."

I can't do anything but stare at her, too exhausted to process, too drained to reply.

She flashes me a smile. "Like I said: interesting."

I pulled back to the here and now. *Take it.* I offered the memory to Kaliban and sagged when he swept it out of my mind, even though I didn't know *why* I felt so relieved.

"Thank you," I murmured, scrubbing the heels of my hands into my eyes. Despite the coffee I'd had at the meeting, exhaustion came crashing over me. I could sleep now. And I needed to rush back so Bastian wouldn't know I'd snuck out.

Kaliban made a low sound. "You should be careful of the Serpent, Kat."

"Sorry." I gathered myself. "I didn't mean to think so loud. I'm just so tired." But I frowned at him as I processed what he'd said. I thought he might've had sympathy for someone else who was disliked by society.

His lips set in a thin line. "Not for him."

"Bloody hells." I squeezed my eyes shut. I was used to controlling my actions and my speech—today's outburst to Lysander being a rare exception. But my thoughts were the only place I got to be free. At least, *usually* they were.

When I dared to look again, I found Kaliban watching me with a thoughtful frown. "Do you ever let go?"

"What do you mean?"

"You're trying to hold tightly on to your feelings—to *yourself*. The tighter you squeeze a bird, the quicker it dies."

Rising, I snorted. "What a cheerful image."

"So is the image of what that healer has done to you."

I flinched, folding my arms.

He grunted as I made for the door. "You might want to reconsider pursuing a cure, Kat."

I paused, hand on the handle. "Why?"

"I can't keep taking your memories forever. It damages the mind to have gaps."

I laughed darkly. "You're telling me."

Hadn't I lived half my life with a yawning gap in my memories? The empty space had haunted me, little shards of that night poking through until it had all come back.

What I'd forgotten had haunted me, and now the memory of Elthea's treatments did the same. I couldn't win.

44
KAT

Despite Kaliban's warnings, the next few days were good—great even. My routine resumed. Archery and self-defence with Faolán. Magic training with Ari. What she tried to teach me didn't work, but I took what Kaliban had shown me with the fire and applied it to whatever was nearby. It calmed my mind and made the stains on my fingers recede. Much better than trying to squash the power down.

It made more sense that his comments about letting go. That sounded a lot like losing control, and the haze had come off me when I'd been utterly out of control. Daily practice with the fire—that seemed my best bet. Maybe this was as good as it got, and I just needed to hold out for a cure.

In the afternoons, I read and took notes, searching for anything that might be related to the Circle of Ash. It shouldn't matter, but the new bouquet of roses in my room were a rich, deep pink that made me smile every time I saw them. *A scrap of something.*

Meanwhile, things between me and Bastian were... complicated.

Shocking, I know.

We weren't arguing. In fact, we were playful and friendly—flirtatious even—but there seemed to be a forcefield around us that neither of us dared cross. We sat on opposite sides of the table in his dining room. We took separate armchairs in the sitting room. He didn't enter my bedroom and I had yet to see his.

It was all perfectly safe.

Though my body grew tight and empty at once, like I wore an ill-fitting skin.

To combat that, the day before the Solstice, for Ella's birthday, I arranged a lunchtime poker party, followed by an afternoon theatre trip and dinner at Moonsong Spire. A fun distraction with my friends and no Bastian.

Although he had the afternoon off ahead of a busy Solstice festival, he gave me space and went to Rose and Faolán's. Meanwhile, I put the finishing touches to our suite and waited for Rose, Ella, Perry, and Ariadne to arrive.

I decorated the space with oversized playing cards and red, white, and black flowers from a florist near Kaliban's. (I'd also taken the opportunity to drop off food for him and the new tin of shoe polish he'd requested.) I placed the last lemon tart on the cake stand, stirred the jug of fruit punch and stood back.

Too much food for five people.

Probably more decoration than a card party required.

But... I kind of didn't care.

The frothy white hydrangeas made me smile. The card designs were silly—I'd copied them from the deck of cards we would play with tonight, but I'd added little touches that made the different characters look like people we knew. I hadn't really thought about it when I'd made Bastian the King of Spades and me the Queen, but...

It still looked good. And tonight, I was going to have fun.

ELLA SQUEALED and begged to have the picture showing her as the Queen of Hearts. Perry laughed, especially when she found herself as the Knight of Diamonds. Ariadne cooed over the stack of macarons. And Rose stared at it all, smile the broadest I'd ever seen it.

As we sat with plates piled high with cakes (the best I'd ever eaten) and the golden-brown sausage rolls Rose had brought, Ella cleared her throat. "We need a toast."

Rose paused with a sandwich halfway to her mouth. At Ella's nod, she placed it back on her plate.

"We may have both been fooled by someone we trusted..." She held my gaze as her chin dipped, and the gleam in her eye said she was thinking of unCavendish and what he'd done to us both. "But that prick brought us two together, and if not for that, I'd never have met all of you, either." She turned her smile upon the rest of the table, infecting us each in turn. "To friend-ships forged in shitty circumstances."

Laughing, I clinked glasses with everyone.

Between eating sandwiches and cakes and toasting to the birthday girl, the poker began and Rose told us about the first fae party she'd attended—in a haunted house, no less. Ella grilled her about everything she'd seen.

Eventually, she sat back. "Toes? Really? I don't believe it's possible."

Rose chuckled. "I suppose it depends how long his toes are."

A pink cast to her amber-toned cheeks, Ari placed a bet. "Do you think those two are talking about this stuff, too?"

"I can't picture Faolán talking about sex." I raised an eyebrow at Rose.

She huffed out of her nose as she matched Ella's bet. "There's a little tension between them at the moment, so I hope they're talking about *that*. Knowing them, though, they're probably drinking and complaining about work."

"Tension?" Perry cocked her head, cards forgotten.

Rose shot me a quick, stiff glance. "Oh, you know how it is. They're just—"

"It's all right." I shrugged. "You can say it. Faolán's grumpy —well, grumpier than usual—because of what happened in Lunden between Bastian and me and the fact I'm married."

Ari's eyes went wide. "Oh."

"Bastian told me when you woke, and... I may have deliberately not mentioned it to Faolán." Rose winced. "I knew he'd react that way. It's a strange hangup—treating marriage as sacred."

"Hmph." Ella glared at her cards. "If only human men did the same."

She'd mentioned her marriage only in the most general terms. I got the impression she was sadder about her husband's death than I would be about Robin's.

I eyed her as the conversation went on.

"It applies to engagement, too." Ari nodded, closing her fan of cards. "I managed to capitalise on that to get Ly out of some trouble." Her gaze skipped to one side as she gave a small smile.

"Where do they stand on divorce?" A frown scored its way between Perry's eyebrows. Her eyes were on her cards, but didn't rove across them, as though she didn't really see them.

"Kat's already tried for a divorce." Ella huffed. "Are you sure we can't just kill him off?"

"I didn't mean Kat's," Perry murmured.

Every pair of eyes turned to her.

I lowered my cards. "Are you married?"

"I was once. Not anymore." She chewed her lip, and Ella pulled the cards from her hands and placed them on the table. "Who's been topping up my drink?" She frowned at the half-emptied glass of shocking orange punch.

"You've already started spilling." Ella shrugged. "No sense in stopping now."

Perry snorted and drained her drink, then held out the glass. "Well, I'm going to need more of this."

Rose obliged while Ari fetched a cake stand and placed it before Perry. I clasped my hands, conscious that I wasn't wearing my gloves, since they'd stopped me from shuffling the deck.

"My mother was from Noreg, and after my father died, she moved back there. I would visit from time to time—this was long before I sailed with Vice."

Ari murmured at the mention of Avice. As far as she was concerned, the Pirate Queen was a living legend, even if, to me, she was the little sister whose snot I'd wiped away.

"You can guess the next part..." Perry arched an eyebrow.

"Don't tell us"—Ella cocked her head—"you met a dashing Northman who treated you like the queen you are?"

Perry scoffed. "Something like that. We married. We were happy. We had a child. We were even more happy."

I swallowed, my half-finished drink forgotten as I waited for the *but*.

"There was an attack." Perry's brow pulled low, and my heart squeezed for her. "Our girl... I say 'girl'—she was fully grown by then. A young woman. Some were killed. Some were taken. We couldn't find any sign of her."

Eyes burning, I thrust my hands in my lap so I didn't reach out to her.

"She was gone. We searched, but..." Perry shook her head. "It took a long while, but eventually I accepted it. My husband, though..."

Ari scooted to the edge of her chair and slid her arm around Perry's shoulder. Ella stroked her hair, while Rose reached across the table and squeezed her hand. I sat on mine, the need to comfort her scouring my heart.

"He sank and sank and sank... I tried to pull him out. I knew it would take time, but... he never accepted it. He raged and drank and raged, and one day I realised I hadn't seen my husband for years. Instead, I was married to someone bitter and vicious, and despite every attempt, I couldn't bring him back."

With a sad smile, she squeezed Rose's hand and tilted her head into Ella's touch. "And finally, I understood—if he didn't want to come back, I couldn't make him. I wasn't making him any happier—if anything, I just reminded him of our daughter, since she looked so much like me. And he certainly wasn't making me happy. We were locked in misery. Thankfully, divorce is a lot easier in Noreg than Albion." She shot me an apologetic smile. "We parted ways, and I set sail, met a pirate named Vice, found Ser Francis Drake's treasure, etcetera, etcetera, and wound up here."

A heavy quiet filled the room, punctuated only by Ari sniffing.

"Not the best adventure story, I know." Perry gave us a half-hearted smile. "But there is a lesson to be learned from my misfortune. Things outside our control can rob your happiness in an instant. You can't stop it. But don't let the things that *are* in your control do the same." She gave me a long look that made me gulp down the last of my drink.

Memento mori. Death comes for our lives... but also for our happiness.

"There's something you're leaving out of this tale." Ella topped up all our glasses and narrowed her eyes at Perry. "Why would you be concerned about *fae* caring that you're divorced?"

Perry chuckled. "I'm sure you can guess."

"I did hear certain *sounds* on our journey from Albion. Late at night when we were all meant to be sleeping. And that innkeeper commented on your bed not being used that time..."

"Nothing gets past you, does it?" Shaking her head, Perry scooped up her freshly filled glass. "You're going to have to get me a lot more drunk before I tell you more."

Ella took that as a challenge, and for the next couple of hours the room filled with laughter and secrets and the warmth of friendships forged in shitty circumstances.

"It made me so happy to see you laugh today." Eyes bright, Ella stood in the antechamber, hands clasped while Rose yanked coats down from the hooks.

"You do know I'm coming with you, right?" I chuckled as Ella stood there like she was saying goodbye. "We have a play to get to."

"This one's yours," Rose slurred as she held my coat out to Ariadne.

"Oh, gods." Ari tiptoed, replacing my coat. "No, no, no. Let me do that."

Oblivious, Ella shook her head and studied me. "You looked so tired last week."

Perry turned from smoothing her hair in the mirror and nodded. "We were worried about you."

"I'm fine." I shrugged. "I—"

"Stop saying that, you big... something." Ella giggled and grabbed me in a hug.

I laughed. I hugged back, cheek tingling.

She went stiff.

And I realised.

Her warm cheek was on mine.

The gasp tore through me as I shoved her away. Perry caught her rigid body.

Rose guffawed. "Didn't know you were that drunk."

Ari squeezed her arm, staring.

From Ella's cheek, blackened tendrils spread across her skin. Her whimper woke me from my horrified stupor.

The world pitched like someone had pulled the ground itself from beneath my feet.

I'd poisoned Ella.

I'd...

My heart leapt, like it just needed one great beat to force blood into me and make me move.

I tore off my necklace and fumbled with the lid, my shaking hands useless. Perry went to help. "Don't touch me!"

Ella wheezed, fingers clawing as an awful high-pitched sound came from her throat, like she was trying to scream but didn't have breath to.

Quickly. Quickly.

My vision tunnelled to the potion bottle, and I dragged in a breath, held it, and gripped the lid. I turned it, chin wobbling as Ella went silent.

She was dying. Maybe already dead. I'd killed her.

Oh gods, I'd killed her.

"How many fucking times does this thing need to turn before it comes off?" My voice broke as I shouted, every part of me raw.

Then, with a soft clink, the lid dropped to the floor.

Ella lay still. So, so still.

My ears roared, leaving only muffled sounds in the rest of the room.

Move. Fucking move, Katherine.

Holding the precious bottle in both hands, I bent over Ella and tipped the antidote into her gaping mouth.

"Please." I didn't know who I begged, but I did. "*Please.*"

I waited.

She didn't move.

It was just a hug. The thing I'd wanted from her for so long. A *hug*.

On the edge of my awareness, Rose held Ari, who buried her face in Rose's chest. Perry sat back on her heels.

"Do something," Ari sobbed.

There was nothing more I could do. The antidote was supposed to work. I'd left it too late. I was too slow. The lid.

It was just a hug.

I covered my face and shook my head, taking a long moment to realise I was still whispering it over and over again: "Please. Please. *Please.*"

A choked cry filled the antechamber.

"Ella?" Perry's low voice barely registered over my begging.

Ella sat up, clutching her throat, sucking in great lungfuls of air. Pale, yes, but the dark veins had gone.

Rose laughed, and Ari launched at Ella, flinging her arms around her.

"I'm sorry," I whispered.

"Good fucking gods," Ella rasped. "Fuck. *Fuck*." She looked up at me and chuckled. Maybe relief. Maybe hysteria.

I fell back, pressing myself against the wall, like its solidity might bring sense to the world.

I'd almost killed Ella. For a few seconds, I had.

The knowledge crashed into me, a boulder dropped from above.

All for the sake of a hug.

How had I been so stupid? So selfish? So... uncontrolled.

"Get out."

"It's all right." Ella smiled the same smile that had been so infectious earlier. "I mean, it hurt like hells, but, I feel fine now."

I would never have seen that smile again if...

The low-level hum against my skin intensified.

"Get out."

"Kat." Perry reached out before snatching her hand back and giving me an apologetic smile. "I know you're afraid, but—"

Everything hazed purple.

Perry's eyes widened.

I scrambled for the sitting room, crying, "Get out!"

45

BASTIAN

I burst into the antechamber. Coats littered the floor and amongst them, glinted the lid of Kat's potion bottle pendant.

As soon as Rose had appeared at the door to her and Faolán's home, face tear-stained, I'd known something was very wrong. Thank the Stars, Ella was alive and apparently fine. I'd left Rose in Faolán's arms and raced back to the palace. A guard was fetching Asher to have him check on Ella, while I'd sprinted down the corridors to get back here.

My chest was too tight, and not because of the run.

"Kat?" I called into the dim living room. No sign of her, though the scent of her magic hung in the air, thick and sweet.

I tried her bedroom next, then her bathroom, half expecting to find her throwing up in the toilet. I even checked my room, thinking perhaps she'd be curled up in my bed, sobbing. She wasn't.

It was only when I went into the dining room that I found her in the midst of her party decorations. Afternoon sun spilled through the window, lighting up a small shape at the wall's base—knees hugged tight, face pressed against them.

"Kat." I sighed out her name, unspeakably relieved to find her. The fear she'd run had been a tight knot in my belly that only now untied. If she was here, I could help her. If she'd gone...

"I poisoned Ella. I—"

"I know." Crouching before her, I placed my hand on her head. That only made her pull tighter. "It's me. You can't hurt me, remember."

Her shoulders shook, and I couldn't tell if the sound she made was a sob or bitter laughter. My shadows caressed her hands and feet. Eventually, she lifted her head, pushing into my touch.

"I nearly killed her, Bastian." The desperate look she gave was a sledgehammer, breaking every part of me.

I had to swallow and take my time stroking her hair before I could pull myself back together and reply. "You didn't, though. Rose told me. You gave her the antidote, and Asher's checking her over now. She's all right. Everything is going to be all right."

"It isn't. You call magic a gift, but this is a curse. I'm never going to be able to touch anyone. I'm never going to be able to control it." Her chest heaved, and her lip wavered for a second before she clenched her jaw and drew herself up. "If there's no cure... I'm going to have to live alone for fear of hurting someone."

Despite her straight back and set jaw, I saw how fragile she was beneath it, how ready to fall apart. I wanted to take her to my workroom and try every trick and technique I knew to put her back together.

"She hugged me. And I wanted it so badly, I didn't..." She

shook her head, gaze dropping as she frowned. "I didn't even realise. I forgot about my poison. When she arrived in Tenebris and I had to tell her she couldn't touch me, she looked like I'd punched her the face. And it felt like that to me too."

"I know." It was a shitty, useless response, but I had no other words.

I'd seen her reaction and Ella's. I'd seen how hard it was for Kat to push away Vespera. It had broken my fucking heart.

Kat stared at her hands, clenching and unclenching her stained fingers. "My skin feels wrong and tight, like it needs life the same way plants need water. People aren't meant to be alone, are they?"

"You need touch. We all do. Come here." I pulled her against me, delighting in how perfectly she buried her face in the crook between my shoulder and neck. I skimmed my hands over her back and pulled her to her feet, so I could hold her full length against my body. The hairs on the back of her neck rose and her arms tightened around me.

Heart beating a heavy rhythm, I brushed my lips over her ear and dipped my fingertips under the edge of her dress, skimming her skin.

She drew a shaky breath against my throat, lighting up my body in a dozen different places. "But...."

"This isn't..." I swallowed, edging closer to a lie. "I'm just holding you. It's only touch. Not breaking any rules." True enough—barely. "I can't stand the thought of you trapped in this invisible bubble, afraid to go near anyone. Let me do this for you, Katherine," I murmured against her hair, high on her springtime scent. "You're dying of thirst."

She lifted her head, eyelids heavy. "And you have water."

I inclined my head, inches away from a lie. Because whatever I told myself, that wasn't the only reason for this. The main reason, yes. But not the only one.

She pulled her hair over her shoulder and nodded.

In silence, I unbuttoned the back of her dress, inch by frustrating inch, letting my fingertips trace circles and spirals over her spine as it was revealed. Once it was open to her waist, I slid my hands under the silk and pulled her tight against me. Her warm, soft skin was a wonder I could lose myself in. The only thing I could possibly like more was the little sigh she gave as she melted into my hold.

I was so lost in every touch, every scent, every sound of her heavy breathing, I didn't realise her. Hands were skimming up my chest until she reached my nipple, stealing my breath.

"Katherine," I murmured, not quite an admonishment, but low enough to make her questing fingers fall still. With a gentle shadow, I guided her hand away and pulled it around my back. "This isn't for me."

She lifted her head again, lips parted, and I was ready to pull away if she tried to kiss me. "Is that what you told yourself when you didn't come in Albion?"

Of course she realised. She was no fool.

"Yes."

"And when you told me about the coup, you deliberately painted the worst version of it so I'd think you were a selfish traitor who killed his father for his own advancement."

To hear her say it hurt—physically hurt. Yes, preventing the coup had improved my position—made me the Night Queen's Shadow—but that had never been my motivation.

"You neglected to mention the lives you saved, the war you prevented."

Fuck. She saw. She saw *everything*.

Her eyes were tired, her voice dreamy, but she drove right

to the centre of who I was.

Hands on her waist, I turned her. Safer without her looking at me. I caught my breath and managed to answer, "Yes."

The dim light picked out the curve that swept from her back into her waist and out over her backside, and I ate up the sight as I peeled off my shirt.

We stood on the edge of madness. But I could keep myself on the ledge, and I'd hold her there, too.

I pushed her long-sleeved gown over her shoulders, letting it catch on her breasts, and crushed her against me.

Her whimper almost destroyed me. The feel of her hot skin against my chest was its own kind of sweet torture. But it was touch, and I'd promised to give her that.

"Katherine," I said against her ear. I couldn't stop saying her name—my damnation, my salvation, my everything in between. "I knew that with you, I risked spilling dangerous secrets. If I kept my desire leashed, I could keep control. I started off telling myself that touching you, teasing you was all part of luring you in. When I realised that was a lie, I told myself it was for you. And it was." I swept my lips down the column of her neck—close to a kiss but not quite.

"Yet it was for me, too. All these years of loyalty to a realm that looks upon me as the man who killed his own father, and there you were treating me like... like a person. You reacted according to how I behaved. When I was an arse, you treated me as such. When I touched you, you reacted not to a reputation, but to *me*. Stars above, that was a heady combination. So when you looked at me differently... even though I intended to push you away, it was still a knife between my ribs."

My eyes burned with that image. It was seared in my soul. Her face, hurt and tearstained, the shock, the confusion, the re-evaluation of the man she'd shared so much with.

"I hated myself." I didn't mean to say it out loud, but it rumbled out from somewhere deep inside. "Hurting you like that. Being that person." Eyes screwing shut, I buried my face in her hair.

"I know." She squeezed my arms around her waist and reached back, cupping my cheek. "I know."

We stood there a long while, this embrace somehow turning into something that was soothing me instead of her... or perhaps *as well as* her.

Eventually, I had the strength to straighten and pull back.

By the time she turned, holding her gown over her chest, I was on my knees.

"Katherine." My heart was in my throat, finally able to spill what it needed me to say. "I kneel for no one, but here I am on my knees for you. I am sorry."

Her eyelashes fluttered. "You already apologised. I forgave you."

"Not like this. What you said about choice has been on my mind, burrowing into it, like you planted a seed and now the roots are in my system. I hadn't thought about it like that. All I could see was how horribly you'd been treated, how much you held back, and how much *I* wanted to give you some spark of pleasure to counter it. I decided I would treat you like the precious flame you are and pile fuel upon you until you were truly ready." I shook my head, queasy with how blind I'd been.

A frown pressed between her eyebrows, and she shook her head. "You don't need to—"

"I do." I hung my head. "*I do.* Because you were right. Was it really a choice if I didn't give you all the information? If you didn't know what you were getting into? All I thought about was how I was giving you something more than you were taking for yourself... That *I* was being better than those other men who'd used you. But..." My breath failed me, trapped in horrible, harsh guilt that I'd been battling for months. "But I did use you to my own ends. I manipulated and tricked you even as I was trying to 'free' you. I was no better. I see that now."

When I looked up, her frown had gone, and now her lips had parted as though she meant to speak but words evaded her.

So I pressed forward with mine before my bravery fled. "I may not ever deserve your forgiveness, but I need you to know that I am sorry, and I swear I'll never do anything like that to you again. I swear on everything that I am." I placed a hand over my heart, shadows pooling around me as I pressed my other hand to the floor at her feet. "I swear it on my magic."

The stone floor answered, old, old power lifting its head from a long slumber, and I could feel the land, the Great Yew outside, the very soul of Elfhame listening.

Kat's gaze raked over me, passing from one eye to the other, to the hand over my heart, to my knees digging into the polished floor and the hand placed between her feet.

"Do you accept my vow?"

Slowly, she nodded. "I do. That and your apology."

The land's magic touched us, sealing it. Kat shivered, rubbing her arms, frown deepening. A profound exhaustion settled over me as that great power ebbed away and with it went the gnawing guilt. Kat's blood-shot eyes reminded me of the ordeal she'd been through today.

I had no more words left, so I rose and, palm on the small of her back, I guided her to her room and to bed.

Heart full, arms empty, I stood outside her door a long while until there was quiet.

She slept soundly, and so, at last, could I.

46

KAT

The next morning, I woke from the best sleep of my entire life. Every muscle felt loose. My eyes were sore from last night's tears, but in the morning light, I could remind myself that Ella was alive. A note that had been pushed under my door revealed Bastian's handwriting.

Asher says Ella is fine. No lasting effects. I hope this puts your mind at rest.
B

It was only after I read it that I spotted another piece of paper barely poking out from underneath the door.

Please, please, please don't beat yourself up over this. I've woken up feeling fine—incredible, in fact. Wonder if there's something special in that antidote. Think we could get the recipe?

You'd better bloody come out today! No excuses.

Ella—who loves you most, even though you poisoned her.

She'd drawn a heart at the end of the last sentence.

She was all right. And joking about me poisoning her—not angry. I owed her an apology, but it felt like I was already forgiven.

I hugged the note to myself, fingertips relishing the paper's rough texture... tingling with the memory of Bastian's rougher stubble.

He'd certainly dosed me up on touch last night.

Not to mention his apology. The most heartfelt apology I'd received in my entire life. I felt like less of an idiot for believing the moments between us in Lunden had been real.

I was smiling to myself when the clock chimed.

"Eleven?" I stared, but the traitorous hands confirmed it. I was late. "Shit."

Still, there was one vital thing to do first: top up the potion bottle pendant.

After that, I got ready in record time, pulling on woollen leggings so I wouldn't freeze to death in the pretty silvery white gown Ariadne had made. Hair clasped with silver snowflake clips and a touch of rouge pressed to my lips, I grabbed gloves and the celestial cloak Blaze had made me.

Opening the door, I focused on the humming magic around me and made it small and neat before hurrying out. Ella may have forgiven me, but I needed to be careful.

Bastian was working and would meet us later this afternoon—not even the Solstice dragged the Night Queen's Shadow from his work. Ella and Perry waited for me in the grand hall, while Ari and Rose would meet us in the city. Perry wore icy blue and Ella pure white, and several fae shot them admiring glances as they passed.

I confess, I dawdled a little once I spotted them, a sudden knot in my belly.

"There she is," Perry called out and waved.

No backing out now.

Hands clasped, I crossed the hall. "I'm so sorry, I—"

"Shut your pretty little mouth, Katherine Ferrers." Ella fisted her hands and wrinkled her delicate notes. "Damn it, woman, now I want to hug you even more. You have nothing —*nothing* to apologise for."

"But I—"

"*I* hugged *you*. I was drunk and for a second I didn't think of anything except how much I love you."

That stung my eyes more than if she'd told me off. "I love you, too."

"Good. Or else you'd be in deep trouble." She shook a finger at me, then dashed tears from the corners of her eyes. "It was a mistake. No apology owed. Got it?"

"I already gave one," I muttered. "Not taking it back."

"I heard that," she growled as we set off.

We crossed the bridge, which thankfully didn't get icy even in the coldest weather. Tinkling music that reminded me of frost chimed through the city, and everywhere drifted the scent of roasting nuts and spiced cakes. My stomach growled, reminding me that I'd missed breakfast in my rush, so I bought a bun swirled with brown sugar and cinnamon, topped with icing and ate that on the way to Rose's house.

Waiting outside, Faolán looked smart in a dark grey coat that matched his steel-coloured hair. He nodded at us.

"Too hot in there with this on and Rose is dawdling." He tugged at his lapel before banging on the door. He eyed me, then Ella. "You two all right?"

Ella eyed the giant and nodded, suddenly quiet.

I'd spent so much time around the shapechanger, I'd forgotten that others saw him as this massive, scowling fae. Smothering a laugh, I smiled up at him. "It was a more eventful day than I'd planned, but we're all right. Thank you."

Other than that customary scowl, Faolán's expressions tended to be quite subtle, especially when his beard disguised the movement of his jaw and mouth. But I spotted the corner of his lips rise.

"I knew you'd forget, so I picked these up for you." He reached inside the door and produced my bow and quiver.

I eyed them, then raised an eyebrow at him. "Do I really need a weapon on the Solstice?"

He canted his head.

"But..." I gestured at my dress and cloak. It wasn't exactly an outfit for accessorising with a bow.

"Luckily—"

"Don't say it." I cleared my throat and lowered my voice, making it gruff like his. "Luckily, enemies are kind enough to only attack when your outfit matches your weapon."

"Hmm." His lips pressed together, and from the doorway came a laugh as Rose emerged. But she was wearing a pair of long knives at her belt and Faolán had his, too.

With a sigh, I strapped the bow to my back.

We bought mulled wine and toasted to "surviving the dark," since it was the shortest day of the year. Wandering the city, we stopped to listen to singers and watch dancers. In one square a troupe wearing skin-tight shimmering outfits performed with flaming staves and hoops. I stood breathless as they dared to dance with fire, letting it lick their bodies. *That* was bravery.

In a park in the lower city, we caught the tail end of a play. The Winter King took the Summer Queen to his bed, bringing a long, deep winter to the land, just as he—the villain—had intended. But what he hadn't counted on was the Summer Queen melting his heart of ice and emerging, pregnant with spring and all the newness of a fresh year. Different from the tale they told in Albion—that one contained less sex but a lot more bloodshed as the Holly King and the Oak King battled for supremacy.

I think I preferred the version with seduction.

"What is it you keep smirking about?" Ella eyed me side-long as we left the park, caught up in the crowd.

"Smirking?" I touched my mouth—my traitorous mouth—and pushed my expression to something more innocent. "I'm sure I wasn't smirking."

Rose ducked in. "You absolutely were."

"I noticed it, too," Ariadne murmured.

From ahead, Faolán cleared his throat as he made space for us to pass through the crowd. "She's been doing it all day."

Asher had "just happened" to bump into us shortly after we left Rose and Faolán's house, and he and Perry were off to one side, too wrapped up in their own conversation to join the judgement of my facial expressions.

"See?" Ella widened her eyes at me. "Spill it. I can tell something happened."

At the shapechanger's growl, I dawdled to put a bit of distance between us. Even though Bastian and I had only hugged, I had a feeling he wouldn't approve of it. Just in front of me, Rose and Ari angled their heads in a way that said they were listening.

"He apologised."

Ella frowned, then dipped her head as though prompting me. "Right. He already apologised though. On your trip. Is your memory all right?"

I huffed out a soft laugh. What a complicated question. "This was different..." I summarised the conversation, the fact he'd taken what I'd said on the road and had thought it through and not simply said the word sorry. He understood exactly what he was apologising for.

The thing that had felt wrong between us. It was gone.

"He *what*?" Rose spun, eyes wide. "He swore on his magic? He said those words?"

"Is that... bad?"

Ari sucked in a breath. "Not bad, but... they aren't just pretty words."

"That vow"—Rose hung back, letting Faolán get several paces ahead of us—"is literal, not metaphorical."

I blinked from her to Ari. "Meaning?"

Ari cleared her throat and leant in. "If he breaks it, he loses his magic."

I missed a step. Bastian had tied his magic to his vow. I'd felt power on my skin but hadn't realised it was *that*.

Suddenly my eyes burned. Because that wrongness wasn't just gone, it was...

It was *right*.

The last crack sealed. The last seed sprouted. The last bit of distance between us closed.

My heart kicked to life like it had been dead until now, filling me with warmth.

I wanted Bastian. Not just to kiss him or fuck him—not the

temptation against better reason we'd battled since I'd woken in Elfhame—but something bigger.

"I need to find him." He was due to meet us later—the Serpent might work most of the Solstice but even he was allowed a little time to celebrate. But I couldn't wait until then. "I'm going to the palace."

"Yes, you are! *Memento mori*, my friend." Ella clasped her hands and gave the widest smile I'd ever seen. "Go get that idiotic Shadow."

Rose and Ari shooed me away, and Perry and Asher shot me curious glances.

Pulse leaping, I dived into the crowd.

As I wound towards a wider street leading to the city centre, I tried to think of what to say when words seemed pathetic and small compared to how I felt.

That was when the screams began.

47

KAT

Distant at first, I thought the screams were part of a performance. Folk continued milling along the roads, but then they grew louder, closer, more numerous, and the crowd responded. Tension thrummed as people lifted their heads, frowning, listening, turning towards the sounds coming from the city walls.

I craned and tiptoed, trying to spot something, *anything*, but all I could see were the backs of fae much taller than me.

Unsafe.

My rushing blood knew it a split second before the crowd turned.

Like a tidal wave, they surged.

They carried me along, faster and faster, a frightened buzz of questions and warnings swallowing me up.

"Did you see?"

"My boy! Where's my boy?"

I pulled my coat tight around myself and checked my sleeves overlapped with my gloves as I fought to keep up.

Looking back, I couldn't spot anything, but their panicked eyes and the screams that came ever closer told me enough to know that *away* was the right direction.

"What is it?" I tried to ask, but people pressed in from all sides. I used my elbows to keep enough space around myself to breathe in the hot, stuffy air and keep one foot in front of the other.

A terrible stench rose over the smell of sweat and fear and forgotten spiced buns. It blocked my throat, and as the crowd surged, I lost my footing, lifted in the swell of bodies.

I wasn't touching the floor anymore. There was no space to breathe. My bow dug into my spine—if it had been a human-crafted weapon, it would've snapped by now.

Panting, I lifting my head and tried to keep my face above the smother of coats and backs and away from grasping hands. I stretched my feet down. I needed control. Needed solid ground.

If the crowd dropped me, I'd fall, and then I'd be crushed.

Elbows jabbed my ribs, pushing out the little air I managed to suck in. Magic hummed around me, aggressive and dangerous. I didn't need to see my hands to know they were fully stained. I could *feel* the haze threatening to break my skin—my poison ready to spew out.

No. Not here. Not now.

Whatever was back there would be nothing compared to the devastation I could cause if I lost control.

I gave up reaching for the floor and clung to the thick, woollen coat before me, gambling on the tall fae to keep me upright.

What do you see? What can you feel?

Green wool flecked with lavender. The stink of sweat. The acrid stench of something familiar, just on the edge of recollection. They weren't comforting, but they were real and grounding.

My panic and my poison ebbed.

I pulled myself up and found space to draw a full breath. The fae grunted and frowned over his shoulder. I was too busy gasping to apologise.

A terrible clicking rose over the crowd's fearful chatter.

I knew that sound.

From a turning ahead loomed a huge, dark shape. Sunlight rainbowed on a black carapace as the Horror's scythe-like front legs reached into the crowd.

Screams. So many screams.

I couldn't make any sound as I stared at the thing. How? How was it here? How had it reached the city? *How?*

Its claws emerged with a figure dangling from them.

Like we were one organism, the people charged right, and suddenly there was no press of bodies. The woollen coat slipped from my fingers, and the crowd spat me out. I stumbled, fell, wrapped my arms around my head as I rolled.

Somehow, no one trod on me. I scrambled to my feet, finding the street empty, save for me and the Horror and the terrible sucking sound of it feeding.

At the crossroads, it crouched over its victim, body wrapped around them so I couldn't see.

Bile rose in my throat and goosebumps prickled across my body as I fought to breathe slower, deeper than this shallow, desperate panting.

Pull yourself together, Katherine. It was the practical inner voice that had kept me alive for thirty years.

I needed to move or else that winning streak was going to come to an end.

The crowd had gone right. They were as dangerous as the

Horror, as two bodies splayed in the street could attest. Their broken shapes and staring eyes said there was nothing I could do for them.

I could only try to stay alive.

The Horror had come from the main street on the left. Likely that way would be clear of people and I wouldn't get caught up in another deadly crowd.

It lifted its head from its meal and sniffed the air.

Nothing to smell here. No magic. No tasty morsel.

Slowly, slowly, I backed away. A narrow alley opened to my left. A few paces more. *Quiet, now. You can make it.*

As the Horror turned its head, I dived down the alley.

48

KAT

Hurry. Pause at the corner. Listen. Check over my shoulder. Hurry again.

That was how I threaded through the city. The Horror didn't follow, but I heard more clicks and screams. This wasn't the only one in the city.

How had they got here? How *the fuck* had they got here?

I kept tripping over the question, but that wasn't going to help me—not right now. It was for after—for *if* I survived.

Yet once I quashed it down, a dozen more gushed into its place. Were Ella, Rose, and the others all right? Did Bastian know about this? Could the fae fight the creatures? During our trip, he'd suggested powerfully enchanted weapons could kill them, but how many such weapons were there in the city?

And how many Horrors had found their way inside the walls?

I shivered even though fear and running had me bathed in sweat.

A fresh clutch of screams split the air, and ahead, a

couple of dozen people sprinted across the road, followed by a Horror. I hid in a doorway, heart hammering so loud I was afraid the monster would hear me and turn this way.

But it disappeared after the group, spit sizzling on the paving stones.

I had my bow and my boot pistol. I'd seen how little the pistol did and I didn't dare hope the bow would do much more. If I could get a clean shot, I'd slow it for a little while but that was all. I couldn't save those people.

As I worked my way towards the palace, zig-zagging to avoid Horrors and crowds, the questions fell away.

Fear pared back everything.

There was only sight and sound and the terrible tension of my muscles on high alert.

I kept to alleys and small side streets, banking on the size of the Horrors keeping them to larger roads.

Frightened faces peered out of windows, but no one opened their door when I knocked.

I couldn't blame them.

Couples and small groups sometimes slipped past me, coming the other way or crossing my path. Eye contact, a nod, then they were gone. No offers of help.

Survival was a solitary pursuit.

As I rounded the corner into a small square around the back of some elegant townhouses, I stopped short.

Back to me, a Horror hunched over an upturned cart, clawing at its sides as if hungry to get in.

Keeping my panting breaths as quiet as possible, I ducked into a doorway and peered out.

Magic hummed on my skin.

A glimmer of light seeped from a crack in the cart's side,

pooling and gathering until it formed the shape of a woman and two children.

They ran from the cart and the Horror lifted its head, sniffing the air. But as the light-people disappeared down an alley, it clicked and resumed its assault.

"Bastard!" A woman's voice came from under the upturned cart and I understood. That light had been her magic.

Shit.

I gripped the edge of the doorway, throat clenched. She was trapped. And that Horror wasn't going to give up. But I couldn't help her. Still, my fingers closed around my boot pistol. It wasn't enough. Too small, not enchanted. It would be no more use than her gift.

Fae carriages were sturdy—the monster hadn't yet broken through. Thank fuck. Still, it was only a matter of time.

Then came the wailing sobs of children.

Shit.

Of course. The shapes she'd conjured matched the figures the Horror had chased here—her and her children. But her gift hadn't fooled it.

I tried to turn around. I wanted to turn. I *should*.

Somehow my pistol was in my hand.

Fae children were a rare blessing. Many fae never managed to get pregnant, and there were fewer than a hundred children in the city. That was why they'd struggled to rebuild their population after their wars.

I checked my pistol—loaded and ready. Though I couldn't get a shot from here—not with its back to me.

I could distract it, make it turn. With a little luck, my shot would drop it long enough for the family to escape and for me to get out of sight.

Or not.

It might charge at me immediately, giving me no time to get a clean shot on its eye.

Unless...

Unless.

The woman's magic hadn't worked, but mine might.

Every hair on my body strained to attention as I slipped from the doorway and, instead of running away, *approached* the Horror.

It was stupid.

Not safe.

So fucking monumentally *not safe*, I couldn't believe I was actually doing it.

Yet here I was, placing my feet in careful silence as I eased off my gloves and placed them in my pockets.

I hardly dared to breathe.

Somehow I closed the distance and the Horror didn't turn.

Unblinking, I watched as the details of its segmented body became clearer and clearer, revealing faint streaks in its carapace.

Almost there.

Then I was.

I swallowed down every instinct screeching at me to get the fuck out of here.

Trembling, I reached out and touched the Horror.

It wasn't cold. Smooth, but not cold, like polished wood.

The poison in my skin tingled as it had last night when Ella's cheek had touched mine, and I waited for the dark tendrils to stretch over the Horror's body.

And waited.

And waited.

My heart lurched into my throat.

My poison wasn't... poisoning.

There had to be...

I tucked away my pistol and tried both hands.

The breaths twitched in my chest, fighting to become over-whelming gasps, but that would be too loud. The thing would hear.

Still nothing.

Then the Horror moved.

It didn't collapse as Ella had, overcome by my poison.

It rose on its back legs, turning.

I looked up and up and up.

And found its void eyes looking back.

49

BASTIAN

Strange looks followed me to my office that morning. But did it really matter after last night? I could still feel her skin against mine, her hair tickling my face—could still smell her if I inhaled deeply enough.

Fuck, she was intoxicating.

Even better was the fact that, at last, I truly felt like she'd forgiven me. Maybe I'd even gone a small way towards earning that forgiveness.

There was more I could do. And I would.

"What's put the spring in your step?" Brynan looked up from his desk, eyebrows raised as I entered his office.

Ah. That explained the odd looks.

I smothered a smile and shrugged before disappearing into my office. Not even the stack of reports on my desk could sour my good mood.

That didn't happen until Brynan appeared at my door, ashen-faced.

An attack.

Horrors.

Here in the city.

On the busiest day of the year when folk had gathered from nearby towns and performers filled every theatre and square to celebrate the Winter Solstice.

When Kat was out in the city with our friends.

I was moving before I fully took it all in. I didn't need to know more than that.

Sword. Leather armour. Gauntlets. With those in place, I gathered guards outside the palace. None questioned my orders, even though the sun was high and half their number was Dawn rather than Dusk. There wasn't even a whisper of "oathbreaker."

The swiftest I sent out on foot to gather intelligence from the rooftops. How many Horrors? Where were they? Their orders were not to engage but to keep eyes on the monsters.

And to watch out for any sign of Kat. I shouldn't have mentioned her, but... I couldn't *not*.

The others I led towards our stables.

Emerging from Dawn's stable yard came Cyrus on a huge golden stag followed by his elite guard on marginally less impressive steeds.

"Don't worry: I'll kill them all." As his stag reared, he raised the Brightblade, Dawn Court's ancestral sword. He tilted it to catch the sun's rays and set its magic ablaze. "On me!"

Cerulean blue cloaks streaming, he and his guards charged away.

The Dawn folk around me faltered, glancing back after their prince. But he had no plan and no interest in leading. He wanted only glory. *I'll* kill them all. Not *we*.

I continued into Dusk's stable yard and left them to decide whether or not to follow.

Stags and hinds snorted and pawed the ground, picking up on the fear and anticipation. With low words in the ancient tongue, stable hands calmed the creatures and warned them of what was to come.

Trainees and those with only basic weapons, I ordered to help civilians. Panic was as much our enemy as the Horrors themselves. They would help get people indoors to safety, coordinating with the lookouts to keep them away from the roaming monsters.

I barked order after order, muscles tight and ready. I should be out there finding her, not here dispatching units to different quarters of the upper and lower city.

The Head of the Palace Guard, Evin, arrived and I gestured for him to take over, but he shook his head and motioned for me to continue.

Those with enchanted weapons, I split between him, his first and second in command, and myself—a dozen per group.

The Queensguard and Kingsguard would keep to the palace—a last line if it was needed.

I prayed to every last god that they wouldn't be.

We mounted and rode out. I flew across the bridge, barely registering the sheer drop.

How did the Horrors get past the wardstones? Past the patrols? The questions burned in me, but they would have to wait until the threat was neutralised.

We passed abandoned stalls, chestnuts burning on portable stoves. The smoke blotted out most scents, but they wouldn't be enough to cover the stink of Horrors once we got close.

One stove had been tipped over, and I jerked my chin for a guard to speak over the fire and quench it. They weren't meant to spread, but if Horrors sucked up the magic, it might turn into a normal fire—as hungry and deadly.

We had enough to deal with for one day. Let's not add inferno.

We aimed for the screams coming from the lower city. In a neighbouring quarter, it sounded like the monsters had breached the upper city, but that was Evin's problem to deal with.

As I rounded a corner, I picked out a flash of red hair against a wall. Kat? My heart leapt.

But when I slowed, I saw it was lighter—strawberry blond rather than rich red. "Rose?"

She slipped from the doorway, a larger shape unfolding behind her—Faolán. Just the two of them. Kat had to be safely indoors somewhere with Ella, Perry, and Ariadne.

"Stars above, am I glad to see you." I flashed them a grin, which neither returned. "You're both all right? No injuries?" I examined them more closely. No sign of blood.

Rose kept her eyes downcast, and Faolán edged forward, placing his shoulder between us.

"What's...?" I frowned between them. "Where are the others?"

His nostrils flared as his raised his chin. "Ari, Ella, and Perry are holed up in the shop. Asher's stationed himself there healing folk who need it. They're assisting with bandages, triage, that sort of thing."

"Ari, Ella, Perry, *and Kat*, you mean."

My heart beat harder with every moment it took Faolán to reply.

His throat rose and fell in a torturous swallow, but it was Rose who looked up, eyes wide, and asked, "She isn't with you?"

The street tilted. For a second, I thought I was falling from my stag.

But no. It wasn't me falling. It was the entire world.

"Why would she be with me? She went to the festival with you. You were meant to be—"

Faolán's growl made my stag toss his head. "She headed back to the palace to find *you*."

She hadn't made it.

Rose's eyes filled with tears. "It... it was just before the attack began."

More screams pierced the air. They could be Kat's. And even if they weren't, they belonged to people relying on us —on *me*.

I urged my stag towards the sound.

Faolán loped beside me, claws elongating. "We're all worried about Kat, and she clearly cares about you." He shot me a look, brows drawn low. "But you need to make a decision —*do* something. Because at the moment she's still—"

"If you're about to mention her marital status, Faolán, we're going to have a problem. Should I not care if she dies because she's married to someone else?"

"No," he growled. "It's just... be careful, Bastian. You're on the edge of something here."

"Yes, I'm on the edge of fucking reason because you're lecturing me about the fact Kat is married *when there are Horrors in our city*."

"I thought you needed the reminder."

Like I didn't remember it every single day.

I bared my teeth at Faolán, every part of me tight and sharp. "I didn't expect you to be so invested in rules handed down by the same people who consider you an abomination."

At once, I hated myself for saying it. But I hated the world more for this situation.

And a Horror rose ahead.

No time for apologies, I spurred my stag onward and rode to face it.

50

KAT

Down one alley, darting into the next, I ran and ran and ran. My legs burned as breaths tore through me.

It hadn't worked. The carapace must've protect the Horror from my poison as it protected it from weapons. Shit.

I turned again and again, trying to lose the skittering sound of the Horror's feet.

The fact I'd drawn it away from the woman and her children was the faintest glimmer of a silver lining.

The next corner brought me to a long lane with no turnings and a wide set of gates at the end. If those gates didn't lead out onto a road, I had just found the cloud for that silver lining.

A thick, black dead end of a cloud.

I pushed, sprinting with every ounce of energy I had.

Questioning clicks echoed from behind me as the dank stink grew, invading every sharp gasp for air.

I didn't dare turn. If I did, I'd trip or just plain lose my nerve in the face of those flat, void-like eyes.

Just a little further. Just a little faster.

Acidic spit sizzled on the stone behind me.

Then my hands were on the gate, shoving it open.

Once I was through, I flung my body against it and dropped the bar. Not that it would keep the thing out for long —not when it could climb over.

A stable yard. Stalls with upper doors open, deer snorting as they scented the monster running up the lane towards us.

Not long. Not long at all.

I slammed shut the nearest stalls, but they wouldn't last if the thing tried to get in. I needed something sturdy or small— somewhere to hide.

In a corner, I found a shelter full of tack and hunting weapons, but one side was open to the yard. Still, soft magic hummed over my skin. Some of the saddles and spears had to be enchanted. That would attract the Horror and give it something to feed on. It might also mask my scent.

There was nothing else here—no route out.

The gates rattled in their hinges. The bar holding them groaned.

The Horror slammed into them again. They wouldn't last long.

Why bother climbing over when you could go through?

It almost made me laugh, but my pulse throbbed in my throat, constricting like a tight grip.

Behind a saddle stand, I spotted a door handle. A way out?

But inside there was only the scent of saddle soap and leather. A cupboard.

I had no other option—I darted inside and shut the door as the gates crashed open.

In the darkness, I found a leather strap—an old halter

perhaps? Trying to keep my breaths quiet, I tied it around the inside handle and a hook on the wall.

The yard erupted with throaty bellows from the deer and the Horror's echoing clicks.

Trembling in the cramped space, I managed to get the bow off my back, tighten the string with a whisper, and nock an arrow. If the monster opened the cupboard, I would fire off a shot and surprise it. Then I might manage to slip past it. Or I might die.

Not the most comforting set of options, but I didn't have any others.

Outside, the bellows turned to screams and the sound of rending flesh.

I covered my mouth, holding in my fear as tears streaked down my cheeks. Those poor creatures. I couldn't help picturing Vespera in their place. I thought Horrors only fed on magic, but...

My chest grew tighter and tighter with each cry.

Then there were no more.

I had no idea how long it took. The darkness of the cupboard felt like the darkness of eternity.

More crashing and a grunting sniff that came closer.

Breath stilling, I drew my bowstring taut. The leather shoulder pieces of my cloak dug in, but I was firing this arrow the instant that door opened.

Scratching and scraping, then the sucking sound of it feeding.

Then silence.

Gone, or...?

I let the bowstring slacken and pressed my ear to the door.

It could be waiting out there. Or maybe it had forgotten about me.

Waiting this whole thing out in a cupboard might've been an option if not for an inconvenient truth.

I needed my antidote before sunset. And a wonderful bonus of the Winter Solstice was that sunset came *very* early.

To surviving the dark, indeed.

I counted to a hundred like this was nothing more than a game of hide and sneak.

Still no noise.

Heart in my throat, I untied the broken halter and readied my bow. When I nudged open the door and peered out, there was no sign of the Horror, though upturned saddle stands blocked some of my view.

I waited. I saw nothing.

I crept out.

Saddles and tack littered the floor. It hadn't been torn apart, but the leather had gone pale and dry, and when I nudged a harness with my toe, it disintegrated into fragments.

I picked my way through the debris in silence. Even the steel tips of the hunting spears were dull and grey like lumps of ore rather than the polished steel they'd been when I arrived. They didn't flake apart with a nudge, but I tested one under my foot and it crumbled like charcoal.

Then I realised.

No magic vibrated against my skin.

The Horror had fed on every enchanted object here. Did that make it stronger? More dangerous?

Bastian had told me they'd been used as weapons in the war, but I hadn't asked for specifics, especially not when he'd been in such distress from his father's memories.

I edged out of the shelter and...

Every part of me froze.

There was no sign of the Horror, no, but I stood in the midst of its aftermath.

Blood pooled across every inch of the yard. Entrails, legs, antlered heads—they lay strewn over the ground. Bodies sat in the doorways of their stables, like they'd been dragged out and torn open.

I couldn't do anything more than stare, but as I did, I realised... nothing was missing. The Horror hadn't killed these stags and hinds to eat them. And their remains weren't sucked dry as the saddles had been. It hadn't fed on their magic.

It had just... torn them apart. For fun? Out of anger at being unable to find me?

Was this my fault?

My legs wobbled and I fell to a crouch, covering my mouth to try and hold in my gasping breaths. A dozen deer. Gone because I'd led that monster here.

"I'm sorry." It came out again and again, then I threw up as the full stench of death and blood and the Horror filled my throat and somehow made this all the more real.

I vomited until there was nothing left but to spit bitter bile on the ground.

Emptiness felt better.

Numb and no longer trembling, I pulled myself upright. In the cupboard, I found some leather scraps and used one to tie my hair back. I deposited my cloak inside, remembering how it had interfered with my draw.

Clear water sat in a trough at the far end of the yard, untainted by deer blood. I rinsed out my mouth and washed the sweat from my face. As the ripples stilled, I caught my reflection staring back at me.

Afraid and yet determined. Practical. Ready.

Was this who I was?

I touched the surface and let her dissolve into ripples.

Squeezing my bow, I straightened. By Horror, crowd, or poison, I was not dying today.

Overhead, the sun began its descent to its early solstice evening.

51
BASTIAN

Nine. That was how many Horrors had entered the city.

It had taken us what felt like a lifetime to fell the first one we'd found, and we'd lost two guards to it.

Lysander had caught up to us not longer after, shadow-stepping here from his estate, bringing the hellhound Fluffy.

Now we closed in on two more Horrors and the hound stuck to me like a pale version of my shadows, even though Lysander was at the other end of the road. On foot, I led half the unit and Faolán the other half, cutting in from both sides as the monsters sniffed and scratched at a brazier that had been used to roast nuts and marshmallows. Archers crept to position on the rooftops.

Movement from above. I raised my sword on instinct but recognised the darkly-dressed woman as one of the guards I'd set on watch. I lifted my eyebrows in a silent question.

"The two ahead are the last in this quarter. Two more are

down, leaving one in north and east and two in the south quarter."

A third of them dead. I nodded, but her report didn't bring as much relief as it should've. "Any sign of the red-haired woman?"

"There was a sighting in the southern quarter, but they lost her before they could extract her."

I gritted my teeth, eyeing the Horrors as they jostled over feeding from the brazier's scant magic. We'd head south as soon as these two were taken care of. It sickened me not to go now, but...

Duty called.

I nodded to the lookout, dismissing her, and signalled for Faolán to continue advancing. Once we were thirty feet from the Horrors, I raised my hand and the archers fired their first volley.

A dozen arrows glanced off the monsters' carapaces, but they were never meant to be anything more than a distraction.

While the Horrors looked up, screeching at the archers, we moved in.

Fed by the city's abundant magic, my sword was at full power—a pure void with shadows dripping off its edges. I bared my teeth as I reached my enemy, the darkness inside me ready and eager to strike.

I sliced the monster's leg. When I met its chitinous shell, there wasn't even an instant of resistance. My Shadowblade cut clean through, and a buzz of magic funnelled into me, stolen from my shrieking enemy.

The long head swung to me, black eyes unblinking.

It snapped, row upon row of teeth closing on the space where a split-second earlier had been my shoulder.

I rolled across the paving, its stone surface digging into my shoulder and ribs.

Muscles roaring with the simple pleasure of battle, I landed on my feet behind the Horror. The remains of its severed leg bled foul ooze onto the ground, flailing as it reacted to another strike.

Growling, Fluffy bit one of the legs. Her teeth sank into the exoskeleton, her magical flame unleashing an acrid smoke that smelled of burning hair.

I battered into the monster's back, the thicker shell resisting my blows, but making it twitch and start to turn— distracting it for the rest of my unit.

Russet fur darted between the other Horror's legs—Rose. She snapped at its clawed feet, blinding fast in her wolf form, always staying inches ahead of its strikes.

One of the guards wasn't so lucky. He flew back with a grunt, clubbed by one of the legs.

With the monster chasing Rose, Faolán leapt onto one of its legs. His fingers elongated into vicious claws.

I grinned as I blocked a strike, clipping the end of my Horror's leg. I knew exactly where he was aiming.

Back arching, I dodged, then sidestepped, drawing my Horror away from its partner. If it spotted Faolán's progress, leaping from one leg to the next, further forward, it might try to stop him.

Acid sizzled against my gauntlet as the monster snapped at my hand.

Two inches. That was all I dodged by.

But two inches or five—it was all the same. I still had my hand, and the Horror had its back to Faolán. With a roar, he reared and drove his claws into the spot behind his monster's front leg.

Dark blood spurted.

The Horror shrieked, splitting the air and my ears. I staggered as the sound lanced through my skull, an instant of blinding pain.

I kept my sword high, but as the other Horror fell, mine lunged.

The world lurched as I fell back, driving the air from my lungs. I couldn't do anything else but roll as my pulse roared, like it was a beast trying to scare off the Horror bellowing inches from my face.

Somehow I managed to jab as I rolled. Even more miraculous, I hit something, and the monster reared back with a scream, bleeding from a ruined eye.

But it kept fighting. My chance jab hadn't gone deep enough to hit the brain.

Still. One leg missing. Blind on one side. It couldn't last much longer.

I scrambled to my feet as a horn blasted through the air and hooves clattered across the paving.

Light filled the street as a golden stag galloped in.

Cyrus bared his teeth in a wicked grin and raised the Brightblade.

I didn't have time to stand and stare—the Horror had realised I'd taken its eye and must've decided that made me the biggest danger, even as the full unit hacked at it.

Blow after blow I blocked, dodged, feinted to make the thing pull back an inch. I kept to its blind side, taking every opportunity to swipe at its face as it lunged for me, ignoring the acid burning through gaps in my armour.

"Don't worry, Serpent." Cyrus's voice cut through the sound of my own pulse. "I've got this foul beast."

A flash of light arced in from the right, and mid-lunge, the Horror crashed to one side.

There was no screech, no more blows, just the thing lying on its side, the Brightblade embedded in its eye.

Hands on my knees, I caught my breath, ears still ringing from the death cry of the first monster. With a couple of gestures, I had someone take the injured guard for healing. Getting tossed across the street like that, he'd have internal bleeding.

Meanwhile, Lysander arched an eyebrow as, looking like smugness incarnate, Cyrus dismounted and strode over.

Faolán appeared at my side, giving me a once-over. "We had it," he grumbled as Cyrus drew his sword from the Horror's head and raised it with a flourish.

The effect was slightly ruined when he turned and eyed Faolán's claws, a sneer marring his victorious grin.

Cyrus was a prick. But I didn't give a shit who killed the beast or got the glory. As long as these things were killed and the city safe, anyone could finish the damn things.

As he remounted, waved, and returned to his elite guard, someone tugged on my sleeve.

"Bastian?"

My eyes skipped over her at first, that wraith magic at work. But I knew Orpha's voice, and I followed it, however much my gaze tried not to. Mouth pinched, she looked up at me.

"What are you doing here?" I'd sent her to catch up with the patrol who should've been guarding the edge of Horror territory.

"We found that patrol. They're dead. Looks like Ascendants got them."

What the fuck were they playing at, interfering with something that kept us *all* safe?

"On our way back, we found the Horrors. We've been trailing them the past day, trying to stop them or overtake them so you'd at least have a warning." She shook her head.

We could've prepared. Stopped the festivities, ensured people were evacuated to safety.

"All the wardstones on this side of the territory had been removed. We replaced what we could, but..." Another shake of her head as her eyebrows clashed together.

I wiped off my sword. "Why do you think it's Hydra Ascendant and not just an accident?"

"I caught one of them moving the wards to line the road. He's here. Though not in the best shape." She smiled, sharp teeth glinting as she nodded towards the city walls. "I tried asking him a few questions myself. Didn't want to talk, though. I'm sure the Serpent can persuade him."

An Ascendant. And she'd caught him interfering with the wards designed to keep the Horrors away from civilisation. Lining the road...

Funnelling them here.

My blood ran cold.

This was a deliberate attack, using Horrors as weapons, just like the Wars of Succession.

"Get him to Asher or the Hall of Healing. I need him kept alive. I'll speak to him later."

Once the city was safe.

And—my gaze skimmed up into the orange sky and I froze.

The sun was setting and we hadn't touched today. Once it hit the horizon...

I needed to find Kat.

52

KAT

I worked my way uphill, aiming for the palace. Bastian
might not be there, but they had to know where he was.
If he realised the time and came looking for me, it
seemed the most likely place he'd start.

My calves burned as I pushed up and up, one eye on the
road, one on the setting sun.

Questioning clicks echoed from a lane to my left, and I
hurried the opposite way, taking a winding alley that cut
through to another street. I hugged the walls, gripping
my bow.

My touch hadn't worked, so an arrow to the eye was my
best hope. If I was lucky enough to get a clear shot on both, the
monster would be blinded. Would that make a difference
when they could sniff out magic? I tugged the cuffs of my
gloves like they might stifle my scent.

The palace grew larger and larger, and my hope unfurled.
Another ten minutes.

I turned a corner and stopped dead. A gasp caught in my throat.

Ahead, perhaps forty feet away, stood a Horror.

Maybe it hadn't seen me.

Swallowing, I eased back a step.

The thing's clicking sped as it rose, front legs coiling as if ready to grasp.

Oh, it had seen me.

It had *definitely* seen me.

I turned to run, but more clicks skittered off the walls of the alley behind me.

Shit.

Head low, the Horror that stood between me and the palace prowled closer, its eight legs moving with hypnotic slowness. It was like a sabrecat approaching its prey—slowly, slowly, then in an instant, it would explode into movement.

My stomach roiled, liquid.

No turning back.

But no going forward.

Closer, the Horror came, void-black eyes locked on me.

I nocked an arrow.

Pure desperation drove me. There was nothing else. Well, I could curl into a ball, I supposed, but... No. That wasn't an option.

Maybe Bastian was right. Maybe I was brave. I certainly stood here facing a magical beast, lining up my shot.

That *sounded* brave.

Pulse pounding in my throat, face, temples, I exhaled and aligned my arrowhead with the creature's eye.

I didn't need to kill it. I just needed to buy myself enough time to get to the palace.

I loosed the bowstring.

The arrow flew.

And skimmed off the monster's brow.

Fuck.

I'd rushed and missed in my fear. Under my gloves, the stains had to be covering my hands—a marker of my out of control emotions.

Another arrow. Deep breaths. Calm. Focus.

The orange sky turned the Horror's carapace into a fiery rainbow. As if it understood what I meant to do, it hissed. Acid sizzled and pitted the stone paving.

If it could corrode granite, what would it have done to my skin if not for my...?

"Poison."

Touching it hadn't worked, perhaps because of the carapace, but...

I yanked up my sleeve. If I delivered my poison directly...

Twenty feet away now.

I still had time to run.

But I would have to run away from the palace. And then I'd be dead, anyway.

Desperation. Bravery. It didn't matter what it was—I sliced the arrow across the back of my arm, gritting my teeth at the streak of pain. One eye on the Horror, I let the blood well and coated the arrowhead.

Fifteen feet.

There was no time to think.

Draw. Aim. Exhale. Fire.

Every part of me stiffened, trained on the arrow's arcing flight.

Please. *Please?*

I didn't see it strike, but I saw the Horror's head snap back. Its shriek split my ears.

It stumbled, my arrow buried in its eye.

Had it worked?

Maybe more poison...

Another arrow. Quickly. Quickly.

I smeared it with blood as the Horror slowed and tossed its head side to side like it might be able to throw off the one already embedded in its eye. When that didn't work, it lowered its head and roared.

Its acrid breath burned my eyes, the stench choking.

But I drew and lined up my shot, stilling every part of me save for my leaping pulse.

I fired.

Deep down its throat, past the rows of sharp teeth, my arrow buried itself inside the monster. Its roar cut out.

I already had another arrow out of my quiver and was coating it in blood, but...

The Horror gave a high-pitched wheeze, like it was trying to scream but couldn't. It took a step closer, but its front legs crumpled, and the monster slumped.

Its remaining eye stared on and on.

Was it...?

I nocked my prepared arrow and edged closer, ready to fire again if it moved.

But it didn't.

Dark blood oozed from its mouth and the eye I'd pierced, but it didn't so much as blink.

I'd done it.

I'd killed a Horror.

Maybe there was something good to come from my magic.

I laughed and circled around the monster's massive form so I could get to the palace and, hopefully, find Bastian. The sun had dipped below the buildings around me. It wouldn't be long before the poison in my system would reset and start—

Clicking.

Behind me.

I wasn't even past the dead Horror, but the sound gripped my heart and it felt like I took an hour to turn and...

Another Horror. Charging. Screeching now it had lost the element of surprise.

I backed off. I just needed to run for the palace. I just needed to—

Something snagged my heel and the world lurched.

Somehow, I caught myself on the dead Horror's legs. Coppery blood flooded my mouth where I'd bitten my tongue.

And the charging Horror was almost here.

No time to run.

I drew, aimed, fired in a single breathless moment.

The shriek told me I hit, but I was already bloodying another arrow, gasping as tears stung the corners of my eyes. Tears weren't useful, though, so I gritted my teeth and straightened, bowstring taut.

This Horror had to be tougher than the last, because it was still bearing down on me, sharp teeth bared. Fifteen feet away. Ten.

I fired.

A shriek that cut off as the monster's neck arched.

It fell silent and I sagged with relief.

But its legs were still moving, even as its head slumped, like its body hadn't quite caught up with the fact it was dead.

Five feet.

I ran.

Tried to.

Tripped.

Scrambled to my feet.

Then a terrible weight crashed into me.

My muscles jerked, burned, but... I couldn't move. Cold stone pressed into my cheek, and something lay across my back. My bow sat several feet away, rocking on the ground.

When I looked over my shoulder, I understood.

The Horror lay across my back, pinning me to the ground.

And the sky deepened to twilight as a tingling began in my fingertips.

53

BASTIAN

Reports came in on our way south. Most of the Horrors were down, but my lookouts had lost sight of the two in the southern quarter after they'd stopped to help a family who'd become trapped.

Thankfully, I had Faolán and Rose. They picked up the foul stink of Horrors and followed the trail towards the palace. The closer we got, the harder my heart pounded. They couldn't make it across the river. Couldn't.

But a chill trickled down my spine.

And it grew worse as I blinked up at the darkening violet sky.

The sun had set.

Dread gripped my heart, a solid stone fist, and I spurred our group on. Elthea had said aconite took up to an hour to kill. How much time did Kat have left?

We hit a main road leading to the palace and found the way blocked. The bodies of two Horrors lay on the ground, and Rose huffed as if clearing the stink from her nose.

"Who took them down?" I turned my stag, searching for any sign of Cyrus and his guards.

Faolán shrugged. "The lookout said they'd lost them. The unit for this quarter was scouring the lower city. This couldn't have been them. There's an arrow in its eye. Could be a civilian?"

Rose lifted her head and sniffed the air. Frowning, she pulled ahead, approaching the fallen monsters.

I growled, strangling the reins. "I could've started searching for Kat twenty minutes ago if I'd known they were already down." She might be at the palace or Ariadne's shop. The Hall of Healing didn't seem likely—not after what Elthea had done to her. I wheeled my stag around, ready to ride for the palace. "Check on the other patrols. I'm going after—"

"Wait." Nostrils flaring, Faolán started after Rose. "Is that...?"

Picking her way between the Horrors' limbs, she nodded. "I can smell her."

I leapt from my stag just as Faolán sucked in a breath.

"The fletching on that arrow." He nodded towards the ruined eye of the Horror facing us.

"Barn owl." My heart leapt as my stomach dropped, like I didn't know whether to be hopeful or horrified. "She shot it?" I hurried closer, trying to ascertain whether the shot to the eye was what had killed it.

Something pale stuck out from its mouth. A second arrow. Definitely's Kat's.

She'd killed it. But there was a second—had she taken them both down and continued to the palace searching for me?

I turned on my heel. "I need to get to—"

And that was when I saw.

A spill of red hair snaking across the ground.

I didn't remember moving, just that I was at her side. "Kat?"

Face down, horribly still and pale. She looked too much like she had at unCavendish's feet, dying. Yet the only injury I could see was a cut on her arm, and her skin wasn't dried out like she'd been fed upon by a Horror. Her bow lay nearby covered in bloody fingerprints. Her blood—*poisonous* blood.

This *was* her work.

Her genius fucking work.

"Get this thing off her," I bellowed as I yanked off my gauntlet. The instant I could, I pressed my palm to her ashen cheek, refusing to so much as blink at the sting of her poison, while Faolán, Rose, and the guards heaved the Horror to one side. "Katherine?"

With the softest sound, she frowned. Slowly, like waking from a deep, deep sleep, she stirred and her dark lashes fluttered against her cheek.

"Katherine, love," I murmured, cradling her head, keeping my skin against hers. "It's time to wake up. You've got two kills to celebrate."

Two Horrors. Her incredible aim and her magic. A fucking miracle.

As her eyes opened and focused on me, the dread unclenched in my chest and pride surged in its place, hot and bright. "There you are."

"I am." She gave a tired smile, blinking slowly. "You found me in time. My poison..."

"Thank the fucking Stars."

She touched my cheek, the leather of her gloves not nearly as soft as her skin. "Thank *you*."

I scoffed but pulled her closer, desperate to reassure myself

A TOUCH OF POISON

that this was real. "You're the one who survived—who killed two Horrors. I could kiss you for it."

For a second she bit her lip. "Why don't you?" She tilted her head, mouth coming closer to mine, so I felt her next words. "*Memento mori.*"

Yes. *Yes.*

Time opened up. I bent in. My body throbbed with each heartbeat.

But then that heartbeat lurched. Something wrong. I jolted upright, on instinct searching for another Horror.

There was none.

Yet my gut said something was wrong. That had to mean danger. It usually did.

Before I could shake it off, Kat pulled from my hold, a tight, false smile in place as she yanked her sleeve over the cut.

Rose helped her to her feet. "How did you...?" She eyed Kat, then the fallen Horrors.

The guards turned on her, gaping. As she explained that she'd shot them with poisoned arrows, I became aware that my gaze skipped right over something on the periphery of the group.

Make that some*one*.

I steeled myself and turned to Orpha. "This is about your prisoner."

She bowed her head. "He's woken up."

54

BASTIAN

Orpha had already tried to get him to talk the messy way.

Granted, things could get messier, but that didn't necessarily mean he'd talk.

But I had another way, potentially.

After I ensured Kat was safe and we received a report confirming the last of the Horrors had been dealt with, I apologised to Faolán for how I'd spoken earlier. I was about to march headlong into a quagmire of guilt—I needed to get forgiveness where I could. He shrugged and clapped me on the shoulder in wordless acceptance.

That was one of the comforting things about Faolán. Simple and straightforward where so much of my life was... *not*.

With a heavy step, I set off for a small house on a side street and steeled myself to face the last person in Tenebris who wanted to see me... who just so happened to be the only one who could help.

I knocked. There was no answer.

Of course not. He probably knew it was me.

"Let me in," I called, knocking again.

Nothing.

"I'm not going until you do."

I could hear the sigh in my head a moment before he opened the door.

Chest tight, I faced my father.

Stone-faced, jaw set, he stood in the doorway. "What the hells are you doing here?"

Oh good, so it was going to be as friendly as usual. I pulled myself tight and straight, masked with professional detachment. "It's for the security of the realm. I wouldn't have come otherwise."

"Of course it is. What else could the Serpent of Tenebris possibly be interested in?" His smile wrinkled his nose, sardonic and sneering.

"I'm not discussing this on the street."

"And I'm not discussing this at all—not with you."

But when he went to close the door, he found my foot in the way.

"Three minutes. Let me in. Let me talk. And then tell me to fuck off."

He exhaled through his nose as he stepped back. "Two minutes."

I gritted my teeth as a dozen familiar scents and sights hit me. I couldn't let myself focus on them. I wasn't his son—not right now... maybe not anymore. If I allowed myself to see the books on military tactics that had been *Baba's* or his carved deer on the shelf, I would be that boy in the stables again. Their scrawny child who adored them for teaching him, for laughing at his jokes, and for the simple fact that they loved him.

And the Serpent of Tenebris couldn't afford to adore anyone.

So I screwed my eyes shut and turned as he closed the door. Arms folded, he raised his eyebrows. "'The security of the realm'—is that how you describe what you did to your father?"

His hurt hurt me, as painful as the slice that father had delivered across my chest and belly—an injury I'd been lucky to survive.

"I'm not going to get into another cyclical conversation with you, *Athair*."

His jaw flexed and I thought he was going to tell me not to call him that, but his gaze flicked over to the orrery on the mantlepiece. "A minute and a half."

Had he looked this cold as he'd led those families to the Horrors in Innesol? Or had his dismay shown? He'd always been the one to express his emotions, where *Baba* hid everything behind a stoic mask.

Athair's face dropped. "Innesol. You went there. You... you saw." Back bowing as if all his vitriol turned inward, he spun on his heel, and once again, his hurt hurt me.

"You were in an impossible situation with only terrible choices." I wasn't sure if I was telling him that or myself. "It meant you survived long enough for you and *Baba* to—"

"Don't lecture me on terrible choices, Bastian. I could've chosen to die rather than..." He shook his head. "Rather than doing what I did. That is always an option."

One I'd considered for a moment during my battle with *Baba*—for as long as it had taken him to cut me from collarbone to bellybutton and step back, eyes wide at the blood spilling from me.

"Die and give up any power you have to affect the world for better or worse, you mean?"

"Exactly," *Athair* rasped. "Some people shouldn't have that power." He turned and I understood what he was thinking.

I shouldn't have that power.

If I didn't, *Baba* would still be alive.

His expression hardened. "What did you come here for?"

"I need a favour."

He scoffed, raising one eyebrow. "You have fifteen seconds before I tell you to fuck off."

"The attack." That would be enough to tell him how important this was—not to *me*, but to Elfhame. "I have one of the people responsible. He won't talk. But you could scrape his mind, find out where their base is, how many there are, what they really want." His gift was a rare one—there was no one else in the city who could do this.

His lip curled. "You might be willing to do anything for your queen, but I am not. I don't toy with people's minds without their consent. Not anymore."

"But—"

"*No.*" His voice boomed in my head as well as around the room, silencing my arguments. "You'll have to find someone else to do your dirty work." He opened the door and gestured out into the night. "Now, fuck off."

55
BASTIAN

Folk swept the streets and set to work on repairs while flow laments drifted through the crisp night air. They nodded as I passed, and some placed a hand on their heart as they did.

Even though I wasn't deserving, I touched my brow in acknowledgement.

I still wore my bloodied and acid-pitted armour. There was a good chance it was about to get messier, too.

My jaw tightened the closer I got to the Hall of Healing, and when I entered and spotted Elthea, my blood boiled.

"He'll live." She indicated a door at the far end of the wide entrance hall—one I'd never entered before.

I arched an eyebrow at her as she fell into step beside me. "No favours this time?"

"This isn't for *you*. It's for Elfhame."

The sun had set now, but it had still been high when Orpha brought the man in—Elthea was under no obligation to help. Useful to know she would forego a favour for the realm's sake.

"Who's with him?"

"No one, currently. I was just in there making sure he was… comfortable."

"Good." I went to open the door, but she hung back. "Not joining me?"

Her usual calm stiffened—not quite a change in expression, but almost. "I'd rather not. There's nothing for me to learn about his health from your… activities."

My teeth ground behind my smile. "Ah, so you like torturing human patients, but when the subject is a traitor responsible for dozens of deaths, suddenly you can't stomach it. Noted."

She backed off a step, perhaps mindful of the fact we were past sunset. Dusk was ascendant now and I could order her to accompany me. For a second I was tempted, but this would be easier without any interference, so I dismissed her and entered.

Another bright space, like her treatment room, but this one had a chair at its centre and a slumped figure strapped to it. Blood and dirt caked the Ascendant's dark hair and clothes. It had once been a smart uniform but from the tattered hems and tears on the knees, it looked as though he'd been dragged across the ground for miles. Maybe that was how Orpha had brought him here.

This was one of the mechanised chairs that allowed healers to tilt the patient back or straighten their legs or arms for treatment. That could be useful for my purposes.

This had gone beyond defacing vandalism and theft. Civilians had died. I needed to know who was behind this and put a stop to Hydra Ascendant once and for all. No matter my queen's wishes that I focus on the Circle of Ash. No matter the cost. Even if my soul and this man were the ones paying.

393

Orpha had said he was awake, but he looked unconscious now. It was only once the door clicked shut that he lifted his head. His eyes went wide when they landed on me, and he pressed back in the chair like he could escape.

"Good." I smiled as I approached, letting my shadows unfurl across the floor. "You know who I am. That will make this easier."

His nostrils flared as he watched me, but he pressed his lips together. Whatever Orpha had done to him, Elthea had healed now with no sign except for the blood. Some crusted on his lip and beneath his nose.

Circling, I lifted his chin with a shadow. He tried to turn his head to keep me in sight, but I held him in place.

Let fear rule him. The anticipation of pain sharpened the mind. With any luck, he'd understand he had two options: speech or silence. Both ended in death, but one would be much, much more painful.

I ignored the tightness of my stomach at the thought. My discomfort was not important. My country was.

"I hear you were moving wards." I cleared blood from under a fingernail as I circled back into his view. "Using them to channel Horrors here. *Why?*"

He pulled against my shadow, trying to dip his chin, and I pulled away suddenly, making him gasp.

"It was an order." I spread my hands. "I understand. Sometimes we must do things we don't like. I'm sure you didn't want to hurt anyone in Tenebris."

He hunched over, shoulders curling in.

His hair suggested he was originally from a family aligned with Dusk and his shame when I referenced our city supported that. The dirt made it impossible to tell what colour his uniform had once been, but it looked dark enough that I'd guess it was one of our colours. A torn insignia of the three-headed monster covered his heart.

So the Ascendants were Dusk rebels. And, what? They wanted to replace the queen with one of their own?

I'd been worried about the possibility of civil war if Braea died without an heir, but here they were trying to bring one even earlier.

I pulled my anger tight and kept my voice light. "Just like I hope you'll understand, I don't want to hurt you."

His head lifted, eyebrows raised in hope. His mouth even dropped open as though he breathed a soft sigh of relief.

"But I will." My shadows coiled around his ankles as I gave him a slow, slow smile. "What does Hydra Ascendant want?"

That was the best way to understand how to guard against them, and it would seem innocuous to him. If he believed in the cause enough, he might even relish the opportunity to share their mission. Once I had that information, I'd find out who led them. And once he'd grown used to spilling secrets, I would ask where they were based and how many they were—the details that would allow me to annihilate them.

"No answer?" I cocked my head. "That won't do."

My shadows tightened and tightened. They'd be bruising now. Cutting off the blood soon. And when I pulled them tighter still, there would be the crunch of breaking bone.

"What does your organisation—?"

The door sprung open and in swept a blaze of light. "This is the one who did it?" Cyrus glanced at me, fury in his eyes.

"We're in the middle of—"

"Dawn needs to be here too." His lips went pale. "They killed my people as well as yours, Bastian."

The prisoner flinched as the prince stormed towards him.

"Traitor," he bellowed, gripping the man's throat. "All

those people dead. My father's subjects. Who do you work for? Where's your base? We'll send an army and destroy them!"

Fucking idiot. He was going to bloody kill the man before I got anything.

"Cyrus," I snapped, letting my shadows brush his legs—a reminder that it was night and Dusk's time.

The fact I used his name and not his title must've got through to him, because he straightened and pulled back, chest heaving.

"You can stay—it affects Dawn too. But this is my prisoner, and you will not touch—"

Steel flashed. The Ascendant's hand—free somehow—held a dagger.

My shadows arced towards him.

If he killed the prince on my watch...

But instead of reaching out, the Ascendant raised the blade to his own throat.

"No!" I reached with every part of me, but blood sheeted down his chest, spurting over my shadows as they gripped his wrist an instant too late.

I called for Elthea as I tried to staunch the blood from his gurgling throat. But it flowed and flowed, and he slumped, no longer making a sound.

The knife clattered to the floor.

Fuck. *Fuck*!

Cyrus gasped, hand going to his belt and the empty sheath there. "My dagger."

The strap on the chair's arm hung loose, its edges sliced. He must've taken it when the idiot prince leant right over him, placing the hilt in reach of his bound hand. A simple flick would bring the blade against the leather strap and a moment later—free.

Free to ensure he could never be made to speak.

Elthea burst in. Her eyes only widened a touch as she took in the blood pooled around the treatment chair.

I whirled on her. "Did you strap him in tightly?"

Her expression tightened. "I did my job, Serpent," she spat. "You failed in yours."

I held very still so she couldn't see how her blow landed as she went to the prisoner.

"Well," Cyrus growled as he retrieved his dagger and cleaned it on the Ascendant's trousers. "He can't talk now. I should've stayed away and left it to you." He shook his head. "I'm sorry."

Even my self-control wavered at that, making my mouth drop open. Cyrus. Apologising to *me*?

He frowned, returning his weapon to its sheath. "Did you get anything from him before I arrived?"

I gave Elthea a questioning look as she straightened from inspecting the prisoner. She shook her head. He was beyond even her powers.

Shit.

I sighed and shook my head at Cyrus. "No. Nothing."

Elthea was right. I had failed.

56
BASTIAN

It was almost a week after the Solstice, when Rose knocked on my open door. "You wanted to see me?"

I looked up from my desk where I'd been poring over reports from witnesses and spies from that day. Nothing groundbreaking, but if I went over them enough times, I surely find the vital clue I'd missed.

"Not for another..." I blinked at the orrery on the mantle-piece. "Oh, now." I rubbed my eyes with and gestured towards a chair by the fire. "Shut the door." That would stop anyone hearing this awkward conversation.

As I stretched, shoulders aching, she edged in and took the offered seat.

With a sigh, I sank into its twin. "You know this mission I'm going on tomorrow?"

Her eyes narrowed and she fidgeted. "Yes." She drew out the word.

"I need to talk to someone about something personal

before I go and you're the ideal candidate... the *only* candidate, actually."

"Oh!" She flopped back in the seat with a chuckle. "I'm here as your friend, not employee. Thank fuck for that! I thought you wanted to send me and Faolán instead."

With a laugh, my tension melted. "You're safe. Her Majesty doesn't trust this to anyone else." Partially true, but also, no one else could know the true intent. But that was a headache for another day. Between the Solstice attack and this, I had enough to deal with.

"I'll be gone a while and... obviously, I'm not going alone... and this is sounding all the more stupid the closer I get to saying it. Let's just forget—"

"Bastian. Please. Spit it out."

I huffed and closed my eyes. "It's Katherine."

"I should've known—I've never heard you babble so much before."

That sounded about right. In Lunden, hadn't she and a single shot of *arianmêl* turned me into a babbling idiot?

Pinching the bridge of my nose, I shot Rose a pointed look. "*Thanks*. The problem is we're going to be alone for the whole journey and... I don't know what's wrong with me."

After several silent seconds, Rose shook her head. "I still don't know what you're trying to say. What's so bad about time alone with Kat?"

"I want her, Rose. More than... more than is sensible. And yet..." I raked my hands through my hair, because I didn't know what the *yet* was, just that there was one.

"You know, when we found her on the Solstice and you touched her and she woke... I thought you were going to kiss her."

"So did I."

"But you didn't." She cocked her head. "You've pledged your magic to her. She wears your ring. Yet kissing her is out of the question."

Groaning, I scrubbed my hands over my face. "It sounds even worse when you say it. I... I don't understand it myself. And that's the problem. I hoped you might have some insight, since you've managed to successfully..." I gestured like there was an amorphous form before me. "Make a relationship happen."

Her gaze skimmed away as she gave a private little smile, and I wondered how that must feel. To love and be loved. To not be torn apart by your feelings but made whole by them.

I gave a bone-deep sigh. "It's like my mind isn't my own, and I don't want to go away with her while I'm feeling so... unsettled. Logically, I know she's forgiven me, and now I feel like... like I've not just *said* sorry but *shown* it. But something inside me..." I pulled on my lower lip as though I could pluck words from this nameless feeling. "At the Solstice, when she and I were about to... it felt like something was wrong. I thought it was my instincts warning me of danger. Then when I thought back on it later, all I could hear was 'oathbreaker.'"

"I didn't think you'd be so bothered about her marriage considering what her husband's like." Her normally bright expression darkened. "And by that I mean, a total fucking prick."

"He is. You should meet him, Rose—*he really fucking is.*" My blood boiled at the fact of his mere existence. "I thought it was just that finding out was a painful shock. I knew so much about the situation, but I hadn't seen that coming. I've had time to get used to the idea now, to understand why she never said. People have shouted that word at me, and it isn't as bad as I expected. I'm willing, but part of me... *isn't.*"

Her lips flattened as she pulled her eyebrows together. "And it goes back to the 'oathbreaker' idea?"

"I'm well aware how ridiculous it is. All the things I've done and yet this is the line some part of me can't seem to cross."

She made a low, thoughtful sound—the cousin of one of Faolán's *hmm*s. "I don't think it's ridiculous at all. In fact, it makes a lot of sense."

"Then please explain, because I don't understand."

"You've told me before that you've broken laws and... people, right?"

Wincing, I nodded.

"Have you ever broken a contract?"

"No," I snapped. "Of course not."

The realisation was like being run over by a whole herd of deer. "Oh. *Oh.* Fuck."

Killing. Torturing. Manipulating others. I'd done those things because I had to. The realm was more important than a stain on my soul.

The lives of hundreds of thousands of fae were more important than my father's.

I'd weighed those things against each other and made my decisions accordingly. One fae was not more important than *all* fae.

So when they'd called me Serpent, I'd gladly stepped into that role. The snake who had helped create the world, then tried to destroy it. The betrayer.

It had pushed back my father's death, made it something ordained by fate. It had made me a villain not to be crossed so my queen could be her people's heroine.

If I had to destroy in order for others to live, so be it.

I wore the name Serpent as a badge of honour. A necessary darkness in the light.

But *oathbreaker*?

Not that. *Never* that.

I'd held on to a single ideal, kept every bargain and contract to the letter. I rarely even tried to twist them to my advantage. It was like inside, deep beneath everything else, part of me believed I could be honourable in this one area and that would go some way towards counterbalancing all my wrongs.

Not redemption—I was beyond that—but a dream of it.

I lifted my head, gaze skimming over the panel that hid my secret door. "My speck of light in the dark."

Slowly, Rose nodded. "A speck you've been clinging on to for a long while. Long enough that it's sunk right down to your subconscious. Deeply held beliefs aren't easy to escape."

"But logically—"

"We can't just logic them away." She gave a sad smile that said she spoke from experience.

"Hmph. Then, what *can* I do?"

"Be aware of it. Start arguing back. Decide whether you truly want to give up this belief—whether you're ready to do that hard work on top of everything else. It will take time, if you do. Well, time or traumatic events." She spread her hands. "Or, if you want to keep hold of that glimmer of light, you could try plan *B*."

"Give up a belief. I'm not even sure how to do that. What's this other option?"

"Solve the external issue. Resign yourself to waiting until Kat isn't married. You could help her get a divorce."

"Or rip him apart with my bare hands."

She chuckled. "Normally I'd be against casual killing but

after what I've heard about him? I can get behind team murder."

Murder or divorce. Or battling a deeply held belief. Nothing in life was ever easy. But Kat was worth it.

We sat a while longer, talking, and while I didn't have an immediate solution, at least I understood what was holding me back and had a path forward.

Being with Kat wasn't a case of *never*, just *not yet*. I could remind myself of that as we travelled north—just the two of us.

57

KAT

"**P**eople of Tenebris, night owls of Luminis, we have endured much this past week." From the royal balcony, a lodestone, the Night Queen scanned the crowd, Prince Cyrus at her side.

A show of unity, Bastian had called it.

Numerous folk from Dusk and a handful from Dawn gathered in the square opposite the balcony, eyes on the Night Queen.

Bracketed by Rose and Faolán and wearing a voluminous hooded cloak, I stood amongst them. Though, between the cloak and my friends' large forms, no one would've realised it was me. I was supposed to be tucked up in bed, "ill."

"My heart aches for you and for our losses. But know this —we have not been idle in our sorrows. No." Even from here, the ferocity of the queen's frown was impressive. The Crown of Night caught the light, glinting like moonlight on a blade. "We have captured an enemy operative."

The crowd stirred and murmured, and the queen paused.

Technically, she spoke the truth. An enemy operative had been captured. She was just leaving out the part where he was already dead.

I'd seen his bloody uniform in Bastian's office yesterday when I'd stopped to drop off some notes and pick up a new stack of books. A grisly piece of evidence, but the way he'd glowered at it had told me he got no information from it. His frustration had pressed on me—I could *feel* the weight on him. An extra load for every soul who'd died in the attack. So I'd peered at it over his shoulder.

Torn, muddy, and bloody, the thing was a mess. The only part that stood out was the embroidered insignia, still glinting gold despite its ill treatment. So I'd asked if I could take the patch.

"For some gruesome collection I should know about?" Bastian had asked as he'd cut it from the uniform.

"No, but there's an expert who might be able to tell us something about it."

For the first time in days he'd smiled and I'd never been so glad to be in possession of a piece of bloody cloth. "Ariadne."

I'd taken it to her late that afternoon. It hadn't led to any great breakthroughs, but she'd been able to tell us a few things. Expensive materials. Expert stitching. Silk thread, except for the Hydra, which was picked out using a distinctive two-ply thread made up of red silk twisted with real gold.

That had been the last of the leads—or the last dead end as Bastian had grumbled—so here I was, ready for another journey out into Elfhame.

"As a sign of how seriously the throne—*both* thrones"— the Night Queen gestured to the prince at her side—"take this attack, I am sending my most trusted advisor on a vital mission."

Bastian stepped forward, his black clothing and black hair absorbing the fae light. Shadows flowed from his shoulders, heightening the effect, and the crowd strained forward, many nodding at the show of power.

"Bastian Marwood, I charge you to uncover the foul villains acting against us."

Also technically not a lie. But not the whole picture, either.

When Bastian had tabled the idea of venturing to the oldest and most powerful of the Ladies of the Lake, she'd only agreed to it if, instead of asking about Hydra Ascendant, he used his one question to ask about the Circle of Ash. She didn't know that we planned for him to obey, while I would ask my own question about the Ascendants.

The way she described it to the approving crowd made it sound like she was working for them rather than for her own desires to lift the Sleep.

A masterclass in fae deception.

I took in every word, and once her speech was done, I travelled with Rose and Faolán down to the city gates and rode out to a copse of cedars. Five minutes later Bastian arrived on his stag.

All this so folk wouldn't know I was travelling with him.

I rolled my eyes as I pulled off the oversized cloak and handed it to Rose. Beneath, I wore much more practical clothing—shirt, trousers and a close-fitting coat that Ariadne had made for me, sewing magical warmth into its fine wool, so I'd be cosy in the cold north.

Bastian's back stiffened, but he turned to Faolán, giving him some last instructions for while we were gone.

We said our goodbyes, and I patted my stag's shoulder. Bastian had suggested I bring Vespera, promising that he would take care of tack and grooming. But she was too fond of butting her head into me, and I couldn't risk her touching me. The idea of poisoning her as I had Ella made me feel sick. The stags weren't so affectionate.

Bastian barely looked at me as we turned and rode out.

He'd been wound tight since the attack with more and more weight upon his shoulders, not to mention busy.

And, frankly, I was a coward. I hadn't raised the question of us, not after the way he'd rejected my advances. Either I'd misread the meaning behind his vow, or it was merely that he didn't want to kiss me in front of everyone.

I kind of didn't want to know which.

If I didn't know, then there was always a possibility. As we left the others behind, it struck me that on the road, just the two of us, there would be no escaping the question.

Fear, anxiety, excitement, and other feelings I couldn't name all blurred together, fluttering in my gut. Maybe I would bring it up. Not straight away, but at some point. Or maybe not.

Coward, a corner of me muttered.

Once we were on the road, trotting at a good pace, Bastian cleared his throat. "You're wearing those boots again."

I glanced down at the thigh-high leather boots—the ones he'd admired in Lunden. "I am. Is that a problem?"

He eyed me—or rather, *them* sidelong. "They're very... distracting."

The fluttering inside me warmed, and his attention flushed my cheeks. I lifted my chin like I wasn't affected. "That sounds like a *you* problem rather than a me problem."

But I swallowed and had to turn my head to hide my smile. Perhaps I was brave enough to ask. And perhaps it would go well—maybe *very well indeed.*

Ella must've had the same idea. Bastian and I reached our first stop at the edge of a small town that reminded me of Innesol, and when I rummaged in the bottom of my bag, I found one of the lacy nightgowns from Lunden. Ella had been fussing with my bag as we'd said goodbye and must've snuck it in. I laughed to myself and threw it back inside.

Over the following days, we rode west, then north into the foothills, and as the weather grew colder, things between us grew warmer. We talked about our work, the city, the circle of friends that had built around us. We talked a little about his childhood, and I burned for how he'd been bullied. I shared my own stories, and noted how he squeezed the reins when I told him about my father's aggression, even though Avice had borne the brunt of it.

On the third night, as we sat in the private sitting room of our inn suite, sharing a bottle of wine, I even told him about Fantôme and what had happened after. The grave my uncle had dug. Dia's body already in it. The way he'd made me lie there, burying me a little more each time I moved.

Things between us were whole now, and it felt like the right moment to share it and he was the right person to share it with.

It was the first time I'd described the experience out loud, and I didn't get through without tears. But in solid silence, he held me through them, and when I tugged on my necklace, suddenly hating having anything near my neck, he removed it and placed his orrery in my hand.

With that, I got through the whole story and felt a little

less broken for it. Maybe his hobby applied to things outside his workroom.

The next day, we rode through a wide, dry mountain pass. Shrubs and grass poked through the recent light snowfall, and at first glance I thought brown shrubby trees grew in the distance. Then they moved.

Bastian didn't seem concerned by the creatures—didn't even mention them—and as we got closer, I picked out their sloped backs and long tusks. "Mammoths," I breathed, the word steaming into the air. I'd read about them and seen pictures in books, but I never dreamed I'd see one.

"Our lands were once connected to the mainland by ice. When it retreated, they were stranded. My people were here; they remember."

I watched as we rode closer. They moved in a herd, with fur varying from reddish brown to almost black. Two animals—a smaller adult and a calf—had lighter brown coats.

I pressed my hand to my chest, which suddenly felt very full. "Were humans here then, or hadn't we yet arrived?"

"You had, though I'm not sure you had writing to record seeing them. Eventually, you hunted most of the mammoths on the island to extinction. Remote populations like this one survived."

"To extinction?" I frowned at the creatures as they used their trunks to tear up clumps of grass and place them in their mouths. "That was short-sighted. If they'd limited their hunting, they would've still had more to hunt in the years to come —for their children and grandchildren."

He snorted and lifted a shoulder. "I'm not going to argue with that. But I suppose only living a short life makes you not consider much beyond its end."

I arched an eyebrow at him. "Whereas fae are *so* far-sighted."

This time he laughed fully. "No. Not at all. I take it back—it's nothing to do with how long the life is. People just want something that will benefit them *now* rather than enduring the pain of wanting."

That made me huff out a breath. *The pain of wanting.*

Stars above was that a pain I knew well.

It was an endurance sport we'd grown good at. I returned my gaze to the mammoths. "Not everyone."

"No," he murmured, "not everyone."

We didn't speak much more for the rest of the afternoon and we found a sleepy village with an inn at the base of the next mountain pass. Tomorrow would take us up into the pass and to the lake.

Polite chit-chat punctuated dinner in our two room suite, and I felt like my chest might explode with all the things I didn't know how to say. But I piled roast chicken and crispy potatoes on top of those unspoken words and swallowed them all down, finished off with a slab of gooey chocolate cake.

I might not be able to speak about my feelings, but I could damn well eat them.

58

KAT

The next day we rode up into thick snow. Vespera would've huffed about the cold and kept her head hunched low. The stags weren't so bothered, but despite my poison, part of me wished she was here. Bastian seemed unaffected.

In the afternoon, we passed a cosy looking inn nestled against the mountainside. Hunting parties sometimes came up this way, Bastian told me, though they were banned from hunting the mammoths, and many stayed at the Fallen Star Inn.

As we rode higher and the sun set, the cold bit deeper into my face and hands, despite the warmth enchantments Ariadne had sewn into my coat.

"So, this Lady of the Lake." I dipped my chin into my upturned collar and frowned over at Bastian. "Ari mentioned she's met one, but is it really worth all this?"

He chuckled, canines bright in the moonlight. "Well, your King Arthur certainly thought so."

I gasped, even though the air felt like it was made of tiny needles. "You mean... this is *that* Lady of the Lake? The one who gave him his sword?"

"The very same. She's the eldest of the sisters and the most powerful. If anyone can tell us about the Circle of Ash, it's her." His brow tightened. "At least I hope so."

"You're... not sure?"

"There's a reason I didn't do this straight away." His mouth twisted. "If you go at the right time, give a satisfactory offering, and declare your 'truest desire' a Lady of the Lake must answer your question."

I canted my head. "That sounds like a good thing."

"It would be, but they are known for... cryptic answers. I can't blame them—otherwise they'd be constantly harassed. But it does mean we're only bothering with this because..." His eyebrows pushed together as he pursed his lips.

"Because we're out of options."

"Exactly."

We rode on for another hour before we reached a rocky crest and below us stretched a large, round lake of milky turquoise water with three small islands at its centre. A faint waft of steam rose from the lake's surface, surrounding it with mist.

"Warm water?" I shot him a questioning look. "Like the hot spring baths at the palace?"

"It used to be a volcano, once upon a time. The water is acidic and sometimes there's a plume of gas coming from the north edge—it's not safe to go close then. I suppose technically it still *is* a volcano."

"An acid lake. Poisonous gasses. You bring me to all the best holiday destinations."

He smirked. "I know, I spoil you."

We rode down a rocky path to the lake's edge. I caught the faint, eggy scent of sulphur as we dismounted.

Bastian placed his offering—something small I didn't catch sight of—in a fine mesh bag and used that to dangle it in the water.

"The moon is high, and this is my offering. Lady of the Lake, I call to you." He said it three times, frowning at the water.

Just as I thought nothing was going to happen, ripples radiated across the lake's glassy surface. Within seconds they'd formed a bow wave like the front of an invisible ship coming towards us.

My heart thrummed against my ribs, matched by the magic vibrating harder and harder against my skin.

At last, a dark, slick head of hair broke the surface, followed by a face as pale as freshly fallen snow. Eyes of ice, unblinking, watched us as the woman's naked body emerged. No water dripped from her, but rather seemed to drip from the lake *up* to her clawed fingertips and sheeted up to her midnight hair, breaking every law of gravity.

The back of my neck prickled and the magic around me suddenly felt beyond powerful, like I could take her strength and make it my own. I trembled at the idea.

She stood on the lake's surface and lifted her chin, taking us both in. Her skin was unmarked by the lake's acid, though Bastian's mesh bag was already fraying. "You summoned me, Serpent and..." She canted her head at me and raised her thin eyebrows. "Interesting."

She probably didn't see many—if any humans. Maybe none since King Arthur. I bowed my head.

"I have an offering, Lady." Bastian raised the bag a little, and she snatched it up just as the threads left in the lake dissolved.

Long fingers uncurling, she peered at what he'd brought for her. With a surprisingly gentle smile, she exhaled what might've been the cousin of a laugh. "Treasure."

Before her hand closed, I caught a glimpse of three small objects—the dice from the box hidden in the stables. A meaningful offering.

Her smile widened, revealing sharp teeth. Not just sharp canines as Bastian and most fae had—every tooth was sharp and jagged "And do you have a truest desire?"

He dipped his chin, jaw twitching tight. "I do, though it is only for your ears."

"A secret, even from your companion." She chuckled at me and sauntered closer to Bastian, her wide hips swaying.

I clasped my hands together to hold in my reaction. I shouldn't be surprised. Hadn't he warned me to never let anyone know what I wanted? Despite how close we'd grown over our journey, he still wanted to maintain that distance.

I swallowed down my hurt.

"Tell me," the Lady went on, "and I shall judge whether you want it utterly. If you do, I shall answer your question."

She bent closer, and he whispered in her ear. Her eyebrows rose as her icy gaze flicked to me.

As she straightened, a private smile flickered on her mouth. "You *do* know your own heart. I was expecting denial from the Serpent, but..." She spread her hands. "Turns out even one who knows all can be surprised."

Bastian's nostrils flared and for the briefest instant, I swore his lip wavered. It was as though he'd just had something terrible confirmed. What was so terrible about his truest desire?

The Lady clicked the dice around in her hand. "Ask your question and I shall answer."

"There is an item that will lift the enchanted Sleep of the thrones. I've heard it called the Circle of Ash."

I nodded as he gave the exact wording we'd discussed. The Lady of the Lake was still a fae, and this ritual was still a bargain. If he left any loopholes, she would slip through them and give an answer that wasn't to the question he meant to ask.

"I seek to find it. Tell me how."

With a long breath in, the Lady lifted her chin and narrowed her eyes. "You have another question, though, don't you?"

About Hydra Ascendant. I fingered the drawstring of the bag containing the flowers I'd brought as my offering, though my gloves dulled the sensation.

Bastian pressed his lips together. "This is the question I'm asking, though."

"Lucky for you, the answers to both mysteries lie in Ashara... as does your salvation. Take the path through the Asharan Forest, and aim for the old palace in the hills. You will learn far more than you ever dreamed."

Was that it? A vague set of directions?

But Bastian inclined his head to her, hand over his heart like he was satisfied.

Her gaze flicked to me. "Your human is interesting. Not... wholly human. At least, not anymore."

A shiver chased down my spine as though her gaze was a touch as cold as this snowy volcanic peak.

"Don't you want to ask me a question, girl?"

I swallowed, working my tongue around my mouth. "I have an offering." I fished the flowers from the soft drawstring bag and held them out, feeling suddenly foolish as moonlight hit the hot pink petals. They were a violent gash of colour against this grey and white landscape, clashing with the turquoise lake. "I—I thought you might not see flowers very often, they're—"

"Not in years," she breathed, and when I dared to look up, I found her staring at them, hands outstretched but not quite touching them, as though she didn't dare to. "So many years."

Her longing squeezed my heart—a longing I understood—and I edged the posey a little closer. "They are yours, my Lady."

Eyes closing, she shuddered as she accepted and held it close. "Ah. That smell." She exhaled, shoulders sinking, then drew an even deeper breath. "Life." Shaking her head, she opened her eyes. "Well, aren't you both just full of surprises for an old thing like me? Tell me, child, what is it you want most in all the world?"

I shot Bastian a glance, throat suddenly tight, but he nodded in encouragement.

"To be safe."

Her eyebrows pulled together, forming a deep crease on her ageless face. "You do. Though I fear it's an impossible desire."

The words clanged in me like a foul note in middle of a beautiful song. "Impossible?"

One corner of her mouth rose, gentle again. "That's not necessarily a bad thing. Many a great deed was done while striving for the impossible."

I wasn't interested in great deeds.

"Don't despair. You still have your question."

"Ask whatever you want," Bastian murmured. "We have a lead on Hydra Ascendant now. The Lady won't tell us anything more about them, so don't waste your question."

She flashed him a smirk of confirmation. She'd told us everything she was going to about the rebels and the Circle of Ash. So, what did I want to know that was worthy of asking an ancient fae who knew all?

I clenched and unclenched my fingers, gloves creaking. "My power... Your kind call it a gift, but it doesn't feel like one. I almost killed a friend." My eyes stung as I met the Lady's gaze. "How can I control it—keep hold of it so I don't accidentally poison anyone else?"

Stroking the petals of her flowers, she looked at my hands as though she could see through the gloves. "Green fingers. Purple fingers. A touch upon the throne. Death for life. Life for death. A journey into the unknown." Her voice was as distant as her gaze, then she blinked and returned to here and now. "Your question contains the problem. Control. You hold on too tight. No grip can stay closed forever. You try to push it away. Neither can work."

I waited for an explanation.

But she raised her eyebrows and dipped her chin and skimmed away across the lake. Her toes dipped beneath the surface, her feet and calves.

"Wait." I started forward, boots an inch from the lake's edge as her thighs disappeared from sight. "Is that it? There has to be more! Tell me how to—"

Bastian's hand closed over my shoulder. "She has."

The Lady of the Lake smiled again, hugging her flowers close before sinking into the pale water.

I opened and closed my mouth. What the hells did she mean? I needed another offering—to call her back. I'd try again. I'd—

"That's all she has for you." Bastian gave me a little shake. "It's your job to work it out."

As we mounted and rode back down the mountain, I played her so-called answer over and over in my head. *You hold on too tight. No grip can stay closed forever. You try to push it away. Neither can work.*

Kaliban had referenced letting go. I sat and focused on the fire every day, letting go of thoughts and feelings, but I still didn't really have control of this power in me.

By the time we reached the mountain pass and the cosy inn, I had no better understanding of the Lady of the Lake's message, but it was near dawn and the stags' heads drooped, so we led them into the small yard and gave their sleepy stable girl a handful of coins. When she peered at them, her eyes popped wide. Moments later, she had the stags in stalls, while Bastian went inside to get us rooms.

Or, as it turned out, *room.*

As he unlocked the door and revealed a small table and settee in front of the fire and a large bed against the wall, I raised an eyebrow at him. "Are you trying to tell me they're fully booked? I didn't see many deer in the stables."

"No, but I want you in my bed."

My step into the room landed heavily. "*What?*"

He cleared his throat, dropping our bags at the foot of the bed. "Security. It's not the same as we have in Tenebris."

I frowned, closing the door behind me and leaning on it. Walking further into this room felt like a trap. Possibly one I'd like to get caught in, but I wanted to be sure of that before the jaws closed around my ankle. "But... the other inns we stayed in didn't have security either."

"Our suites always had a single entrance, and only a wall stood between us. The rooms here are all individual. No shared entrance."

I made a sound, trying not to swallow my own tongue as I eyed the bed.

No grip can stay closed forever.

Cheeks warm, I edged into the room. Maybe tonight I could ease my grip on the words I'd held in for too long.

59
BASTIAN

We took it in turns to bathe and don fresh clothes before eating breakfast, though it felt more like dinner to us. I drank more than I should as the Lady of the Lake's words circled my thoughts.

Frowning, Kat ate, but she barely sipped the magic laced brandy, and it was only when she went into the bathroom to get ready for bed that I realised how quiet she'd been.

Fuck, Bastian. Pull yourself together.

The admission of my true desire and knowing it was what I wanted most in the world had me shaken, but clearly our encounter with the Lady had affected Kat, too. I needed to comfort her when she came back. My problems could wait.

I cleared the plates with a word and called for the fire to burn warmer. With the curtains drawn, it felt intimate, like this was the middle of the night and not morning. I scoffed when I found candles and matches, and set to work lighting them the old fashioned way. To think humans did this all the time.

The bathroom door clicked open, and I smiled. "Look, they have candles. How quaint." Grinning, I turned. "I thought you would like—"

Finishing that sentence was impossible.

Because in the doorway stood Katherine, hair loose over her shoulders like a spill of fire, a sheer nightgown skimming over her perfect curves.

My head spun as all the blood rushed to my cock, and I had to squeeze the mantlepiece to stop myself tearing across the room and devouring her whole.

It didn't help that as she sauntered this way, the nightgown opened revealing one of those thighs I'd so thoroughly worshipped.

But for all that she moved so confidently, I couldn't miss the little note of uncertainty in the rise of her eyebrows.

Toe-to-toe with me, she stopped, and my heart thundered, demanding to know why there was *any* distance between us. I had to yank my reaching shadows close—they wanted her almost as much as I did.

She took a deep breath and raised her hands. I knew she was aiming for my chest, and it was easy to catch her wrists. Her poison-darkened fingers curled, and my ring on her finger glinted.

Mine. Yet part of me still flinched away.

"Katherine?"

The light hairs on her arms rose as she met my gaze and pulled against my hold. "You swore on your magic, Bastian. And I understand now—I know how much it means."

She understood the depth of what I'd pledged to her. Maybe she even had an inkling what I'd told the Lady of the Lake. My heartbeat was the thundering hoofbeats of a whole herd of deer.

"*Please.*"

It was a miracle I didn't lose myself right then and there.

That word. What it did to me, coming from her.

Fuck.

Drawing a steadying breath, I stroked the inside of her wrists and watched the goosebumps rise on her skin. "You want touch."

She bit her lip and it took me right back to every time she'd tried to bite back her cries of pleasure and I'd made her fail.

Oathbreaker, part of me whispered.

"I shouldn't..." I gave a shuddering exhale like I could blow her sweet scent from my lungs. "I shouldn't touch you except to give you your antidote." It felt like someone else was speaking, reading from a script of everything I *should* and *shouldn't*.

"You held me before. Didn't you say you were just giving me water when I needed it?" She gave me a wide-eyed look and in that one second I almost—*almost*—believed her innocent.

But she asked me *please* and now watched my lips, waiting for my response.

This was not the innocent Lady Katherine Ferrers.

This was my ember.

Mouth suddenly dry, I barely managed to swallow. "I was wrong. There is no 'just' between us. Only everything."

With a little breath out, she lowered her gaze. Ashamed? Regretful? Didn't she want the same thing, after all?

I released her wrists and took hold of the mass of her hair, finding it still damp at the nape of her neck. Slowly, I wrapped it around my hand until she was forced to lift her chin and look me in the eye. "Is touch all you want?" I gave a gentle tug as her hands planed up my chest, sending a streak of need through my nerves. "Don't lie to me."

422

"No," she whispered. "I want you and yet I shouldn't. Every part of me calls for every part of you, and yet I don't want you to regret anything between us." Her eyebrows crashed together. "How can I want such contradictory things?"

I huffed, letting myself sink into her space, mouth only a few inches from hers. "Isn't that what life is?"

Mine had spent the past thirty-five years tearing me apart. I wanted peace and yet I wanted my father alive. I wanted a life and yet I wanted to keep my hands on the reins of court. And just as I'd told Rose...

"I want you, Katherine. Yet part of me can't bear the thought of becoming a person who breaks a contract. Not now I know."

And that was the contradiction that tore me in two.

Because I had fallen for her. Irrevocably. Helplessly. Perfectly.

Not just on this trip. Long before that. But... these days spent alone enjoying each other's company, working together to look after our mounts and on our questions for the Lady of the Lake... it had broken down every attempt I made to deny it or downplay it. It had made answering the Lady's question easy, albeit terrifying.

Kat's lip wobbled before her chin jerked upward—as far as she could with my grip on her hair. "But it's not your contract to break. It's not even one I chose."

I sighed even as I pressed into her touch and my free hand slipped around her waist.

She saw me as putting her contract before her, but it wasn't like that at all. Not once I'd got over the initial shock.

"I have killed, tortured, deceived without lying. I've broken so many things, I lost count, but never a contract. That was one thing I could still hold sacred. I want to tear that damn marriage contract apart and take you so thoroughly, you don't even remember his name. And yet... yet part of me still clings on to the idea that I have this one thing I haven't broken."

Her eyes glimmered in the candlelight and it felt like she saw me. Not the Shadow or the Serpent or the Bastian, but *me*.

I pressed my forehead to hers, sharing breath with her, for a wild moment wondering if I could just push her against the wall and sink into her.

Oathbreaker. My insides shrank away from that word, easing my throbbing cock.

She squeezed the front of my shirt. "I understand. It's the only part of yourself you haven't surrendered to duty."

I wanted to surrender it to her, though. Or at least my conscious self did.

She gave a slight smile, stroking my collarbone. "You need a scrap of something to hold on to."

I almost laughed with relief, but my throat was too tight. "I do. We will free you from this contract, Katherine, I promise. One way or another. Then my subconscious can shut up, and I will make up for every time it's denied us. In the meantime..."

Releasing her, I backed off.

She swayed towards me. "What are you doing?"

"Obeying the letter of the law, if not its spirit." I sat at the centre of the settee. "Come here."

She approached so quickly, she couldn't have taken a moment to think of it. Because she was that sure or because she wasn't thinking? But she'd only had one glass of brandy, even though it was good stuff—rich and smooth the way she liked.

Still, considering her past, it didn't hurt to check.

"Will you do as you're told, Katherine?"

Her cheeks flushed a deeper pink. "I will."

"Will you tell me to stop if you want me to?"

"I *will*."

"Are you my ember?"

"Yes," the word spilled from her on a breath.

My blood roared, cock stiffening in anticipation. I patted the settee on either side of my thighs. "*Good*. Kneel with your back to me."

There was no danger of kissing her that way.

If I kissed her, I'd be lost.

No kissing. No touching her anywhere forbidden. And definitely no fucking her—not with any part of my body, anyway.

As she obeyed, I pulled open the hem of her nightgown, the slit allowing me to bare her to the waist. Her breath caught as she held her weight on her knees.

"You are safe with me," I murmured, telling my writhing shadows to pull the hair away from her neck. They did at once, glad to touch her. "This... all of this is my responsibility." I placed my hands around her ankles and gave a reassuring squeeze. "That is why you obey. That is why I hold you. You have only to surrender." More shadows snaked around her wrists and lifted them. "Do you understand?"

She nodded, hair spilling free from my shadows, but I think they let that happen deliberately, so they could gather it all up again and whisper over her neck, making her shudder.

"Use your words, love." I used the opening my shadows created to brush my lips across her skin, enjoying the way it set on end the delicate hairs of her nape. "Do you understand?"

"Yes."

I huffed at the desperation crackling through her voice, at how it mirrored my own. "Such a good ember." Biting my lip, I allowed myself to lift her nightgown rather than having my shadows do it. I edged the outside world's rules. We were playing by mine today.

I ate up the sight of her backside, the dimples above it, the stretch marks silvery on her tan skin, the curve of her spine as each inch became visible. Once she was fully, perfectly naked, the nightgown slid from my nerveless fingers, pooling beside us on the settee.

"That's it, love, now *come here.*" I couldn't help the growl that came out with those last two words as I looped an arm around her waist and pulled her against me.

Fuck, even through my shirt, she felt perfect—hot and soft with this little sound of surprise reverberating into my chest. Without being told, she rested her head back on my shoulder when my shadows released her wrists. I squeezed, simply enjoying her closeness, even if the voice inside warned me of danger.

From this angle, I had a view of her peaked nipples and the fullness of her glorious thighs, taut as she held herself up.

That wouldn't do. And neither would this restricted view.

I was denying myself some things, but not that.

My shadows brought over the mirror from beside the armoire, and I bit back a moan at the full sight of her. Knees planted either side of mine. Thighs open so I could see a hint of her pink slickness. Heaving breasts begging to be held.

I caught myself before I obeyed that instinct, and let myself squeeze her thigh instead. Still, it was a reminder of how dangerous a game we were playing.

"Fuck. Don't you look incredible?"

In the mirror, her need-hazed eyes met mine, eyebrows peaking above them. She didn't understand that I expected an answer. Though I wondered if the words of men like Langdon who would rather she only looked at cake instead of eating it made it hard for her to reply. We could build to that.

"Are you sure you want to do this?" She tilted her head and met my gaze directly instead of through the mirror. "You've been drinking."

I scoffed and touched my nose to hers. "I haven't drunk that much. Just enough to make myself weak, not to blur what I truly want. Now"—with the arm wrapped around her waist, I pulled her tighter to me—"give me all of you." She gave a delightful little huff of surprise as I took her weight. "I can hold you just fine," I murmured in her ear and parted my knees just enough to leave her pussy over the gap.

And then I set my shadows to work.

I let them have her tits first, kneading and cupping them as I soaked up the way that made her back arch. When they slid around her nipples and squeezed, she moaned, and I soaked that up too.

This grip was too tempting, too risky. If I moved my hand just a little, *I'd* be pinching her tight nipples, and then I'd lose all semblance of control. Instead I guided her arms behind her back and held her wrists with one hand. The other hand I fisted in her hair and tilted her head back, just enough that I could meet her hooded gaze in the mirror and see her parted lips but still graze the point of my canine down her leaping pulse.

Then she said the word I'd been waiting for.

"Please."

I watched in the mirror as she arched and spread her legs, making my pulse roar, urging me on even as the warning voice shouted in alarm.

But *I* was in control.

So, like I wasn't one slip away from yanking my trousers

open and driving into her, I smirked and murmured against her ear. "Please, *what?*"

"Please touch me *there*, I need..." She twisted her wrists in my grip, but I was only letting go if she asked me to stop.

"What is it you need, my little ember?"

She made a little whining sound as I had my shadows form a hand and slide down her belly at a speed I knew would feel agonisingly slow. "I want you to touch me. To make me come."

I teased the edge of the auburn hair over her mound. "You want to burn, don't you?"

"Yes."

I let the hand dissolve into tendrils and sent them between her legs.

Her head fell back against my grip as her breath eased out.

I didn't need to feel to know she was slick and wet—I could see it glistening over the shadows as they teased her.

She tensed, trying to press into their touch so the tease would end and she could get what she wanted.

But that wasn't the game we were playing today.

With a sound of gentle admonishment, I sent more shadows around her thighs and gripped her in place. The sight of their darkness squeezing her gave me an even better idea.

"Since you cannot restrain yourself..." I bit her ear, making her jolt as shadows snaked around her, criss-crossing her stomach and between her tits. They pulled her taut, making her soft flesh spill between their cords. My chest tightened on the verge of pain. "There. Stunning, aren't you?"

"I don't..." She frowned at me in the mirror.

"Look at yourself, Katherine. *Look.*"

Arched and spread, bound and spellbinding with the lick of my shadows between her legs. How could she see anything but beauty?

"Do you see?" I whispered against her flesh.

"You make me beautiful."

"No, love. You do that all yourself. It is simply who you are. All those facets of you coming together to make a brilliant gem. I've done nothing but give you a setting." I squeezed with the shadows binding her, grinning a little at my own metaphor. "It's you. *You* are beautiful. Do you see?"

She watched for a long while as I told my shadows to tease closer and closer to her clit. Her cheeks deepened to that rich pink shade I adored, and her chest heaved against the bindings.

Just as I thought she'd forgotten my question, she answered. "I do. I see myself. Please, I need you to fuck me just as beautifully."

Stars above, she couldn't touch me, but she didn't need to when she could drive me to insanity with her words.

I was meant to be setting her alight, but it was me who burned as my shadows coiled around her tight bud and she pulled taut against me, a bow drawn to full extension.

"Come for me, ember. Let's burn this whole world and build a new one."

Eyebrows peaked, breath snatched and fast, she trembled like she might snap.

And then she did.

Pressed into me, she cried out, every part of her body straining on the bindings and my hold, like she could break free of the grip of the very world and all its inconvenient truths with the force of her will.

"So perfect," I murmured as she panted and sagged against me. "I want to see that again."

Without relenting the circling of her clit, I drew more shadows into solidity and slid the form along her. I didn't even try to pretend it wasn't meant to be my length made of pure darkness. If I couldn't have her, I could at least imagine it.

I pulled a smaller tendril through her wetness and pressed it against her back passage. "Do you want this?"

"Yes."

"And this?" I positioned the shadow cock at her slick entrance. "At the same time?"

She nodded, hair yanking in my grip.

"So bold. That's the flame I remember. Go on, then. Take what you want." I eased my grip just enough that she could lower herself.

My dick strained as I watched her sink onto my shadows with a breathless moan.

Bit by bit, the shadow cock disappeared, until just shy of two inches remained and the smaller extension in her back passage held still. I only wanted her to feel the fullness this first time.

Panting, thighs trembling as she held her weight up, she leant back on me.

"Do you think you can take it all, love?"

"I don't... I don't know..." Her gaze darted down in the mirror and the moment she saw my shadows inside her, her eyebrows peaked and she made a wordless sound. Eyelids fluttering, she gave a small nod. "Maybe?"

"I think you can." I slid the shadows out, letting her lift her head a little so she could keep them in sight. "Will you try for me?"

Her throat bobbed and she nodded.

She eased onto me—no, onto my shadows, as I reminded myself with gritted teeth and the ache of my raging hard cock. They rose, meeting her efforts until they disappeared entirely.

"That's it, my perfect one."

As she lifted herself again and rode my shadows' length, it made my head spin.

I could have this. Have her.

The wild panic of that seized me, making my pulse spike. I could have what I wanted.

The distraction loosened my shadow grip on her thighs, giving her more movement, which she took full advantage of. Hips rocking, she went from tip to base again and again.

She whimpered as I reminded the shadows around her clit of their task: making her come completely undone.

"My sweet ember takes it all so well, doesn't she?" I didn't know what I was saying anymore. I was drunk. A little on the brandy; mostly on her.

On her scent. On how close she was. On how very near I was to all I wanted.

So while all my willpower occupied itself with keeping my hands on her wrists and hair, I sat here weak and foolish, spilling nonsense praise into her.

And I didn't even care.

Not with the sight of her tits bouncing with every thrust. Not with her pussy dripping for me. Not with the rising cries telling me exactly how close she was to another climax.

I drove into her, chasing that for her.

Not me. *Not me*, as the tight frustration low in my spine reminded me.

This didn't count, I told the part of me that cared. If it was my shadows touching her, making love to her, wrenching such sweet music from her lips and the little wet sounds, it didn't count.

If I was doing it for her, to make up for all her husband and her country had taken from her, to make up for my own failings, and if I didn't come, it didn't count.

I told myself all that.

But it was a lie.

Fae couldn't speak them out loud, but Stars above, could we lie to ourselves.

It counted.

And I took pleasure from it, even if I didn't get to drive my cock into her. Her pleasure was mine, and each sound, each writhing movement, each trembling orgasm was pure joy in my nerves.

Even as I drove her to a third and fourth, I knew—*knew* this was a prelude to doing it for real, with my body and not only with my shadows.

I'd known since first spotting her in that maze, her skin flushed in the darkness, her body taut with fixed attention. I'd known that I needed to have her and one night would.

Just not this false night, with the curtains drawn and the sun outside.

After the fifth shuddering time I broke her apart, she sagged completely, putting no resistance against the bindings or my hold, and I knew she'd taken enough.

"There," I murmured against her ear, taking in the sight of her sweat-slicked body and rosy cheeks. I caught her as the bindings faded out of existence, leaving pink marks on her soft skin.

I held her to my chest until she stirred.

"Am I dead?" Her eyelids fluttered as she touched her cheek. "Not complaining if I am, just... want to be sure."

I caught her fingers—her unmarked fingers—and kissed the tips, even if it did break my own rules. "Not dead. And look." I held out her hand—only her nails were purple.

She huffed a soft laugh, turning her hand over. "You've exhausted even my magic."

Chuckling, I rose and carried her to the bathroom, then to bed. My shadows brought over her discarded nightgown, and I tried not to watch as she slipped it back on. Tried and failed.

"Any..." She swallowed and licked her lips as I pulled off my shirt.

The trousers were staying on. I didn't have *that* much self-control.

She cleared her throat and started again. "Any regrets?"

I stroked her hair to see if my instincts pulled away. But even that voice that called me an oathbreaker was silent. Perhaps it approved of me skirting the rules.

The candles winked out one by one, smothered by my shadows, but before the last of the light faded, I gave her a smile. "No regrets."

60

KAT

I woke at some odd twilight hour feeling full and heavy and light and free all at once. Bastian pulled me close and insisted we had more time before we needed to ride out. I wasn't about to argue.

Taking advantage of the comfortable bed and the fact he'd wrung me into such delicious exhaustion, I sank back into a sleep free of nightmares.

The Lady of the Lake might've called my desire for safety impossible, but in those hours, I *felt* safe.

We rode out before dawn, and Bastian explained that the Asharan Forest wasn't too far away—if we took a different route back to Tenebris, we could explore the palace ruins above it and find our answers.

As we took a mountain pass inland, I couldn't help my furtive glances at him and the shadows ghosting around his thighs. Just as I'd learned to read people's body language, I felt like I had an idea of what the movements of his shadows meant too. Now they drifted, slow and hazy as if caught on the breeze. I took that as contentment.

Was he thinking about what he'd done with those shadows? How I'd ridden them?

I shifted in the saddle, thighs clenching as the echo of his touch bit into my wrists and waist.

His touch. Not his shadows.

Yes, they had destroyed me beautifully, but... It was him I wanted.

This—whatever "this" was—it was only temporary. Eventually I would be free of Robin, right?

Right?

What if I wasn't? And what if Bastian was never ready to break that contract?

Not that I could ask him to. Not now I understood. I'd begged him not to kill Uncle Rufus, despite all he'd done, because he was family—because that was a line I wouldn't cross. This was the same for him. A blot on his soul he couldn't take.

And I wouldn't ask him to.

Despite that, I couldn't get him or his shadows out of my mind—what he'd said as much as what he'd done.

It cast everything in a new light.

The bindings had put the responsibility on him—or so I'd told the old lessons that tried to tell me that my body was my husband's and no one else's. They were full of *shouldn't*s and cruel words, yet I could shake them off and point to Bastian and say *he* was the one in charge. I had only to obey.

His searing gaze in the mirror had been much louder, saying that I was desirable and wanted—wanted for *me* not for my family name or to fulfil wifely obligations.

Riding his shadows had felt potent, and stronger still with his urging voice hot in my ear.

It felt nothing like obeying anyone else. My queen or society's rules or my family.

It felt *powerful*.

These ideas shouldn't fit together. Yet as we rode and I pondered, I understood the factor that resolved the apparent contradictions.

Will you obey? He had given me the option.

I had *chosen* to do as he told me. I always had the power to stop it at any time.

In the rest of my life, I had never had those things.

"Obedience is power," I murmured, "when it is a choice."

"What's that?" He raised his eyebrows at me, and I clamped my mouth shut.

"Uh. Nothing."

"Just because you *can* lie doesn't mean you're always good at it."

My face flushed. "I was just—"

He stiffened, gaze drifting to one side. "Don't react, but we're not alone."

A chill raced through my veins, yet I made myself chuckle as though he'd said something funny. "What should I do, then?"

"Subtly check past me, behind and to the right."

I nodded and scratched my forehead, using the opportunity to flick my eyes in that direction.

A shape briefly visible between the trunks, but soon gone. "I saw it. A person."

"Hmm." His jaw tightened. "We keep going. I'll listen out for them. As soon as we're out of sight, I'll send my double out."

Throat tight, I loosened the buckle attaching my bow to the saddle.

At the next fork in the road, he steered us left, away from our unknown tail.

Bastian cocked his head as we rode on and murmured that they'd swapped to the other side. We turned right at the next opportunity.

"Shit."

"What?" I asked, eyeing his fingers squeezing the reins.

"They switched again. They're herding us west."

Cold crept through me. "If they're fae, they could've moved so quietly you wouldn't be able to hear them, right? They made that sound on purpose."

"Yes." He steered closer, letting his knee brush mine as he gave an encouraging nod. "We'll be fine. We're going to give them a little surprise. On my signal, turn left and ride hard. I'll be with you. But we're going to race past them, stop them controlling our path. All right?"

My pulse sped, but I nodded and patted my stag's shoulder. If this was Vespera, it would be like a night as the Wicked Lady. A shady forest. An enemy to evade. I flashed Bastian a cocky grin. "I got away from you, didn't I?"

He snorted and shook his head.

I hung on his every gesture and breath, waiting for the signal. As we crested a low ridge, he pulled on his stag's reins. "Now!"

Thighs squeezing, I steered into a tight turn and urged my stag into a gallop.

We sped through undergrowth and dodged tree trunks. My heart roared to be racing through the forest, and I ducked closed to my steed's back. "Come on, stretch your legs."

And he did.

The world blurred by, and soon enough a cloaked form rose from the undergrowth.

In a blink, I steered past them. I peered over my shoulder with Bastian on my tail, the stranger spinning on the spot but left behind. They wouldn't be able to outrun our stags.

Grinning, I looked ahead, but another figure blocked the way. A fae woman, bow drawn.

"Kat!" Bastian's voice at my back.

With a gasp and no conscious thought, I steered into a dense clump of trees.

An arrow thrummed somewhere near my shoulder.

Close. Fuck. And two of them.

Then came the sound of thunder.

Could a storm cover our escape? But I heard no rain on the canopy.

When I looked over my shoulder, I understood.

Deer.

Dozens of them. Hinds, mostly, all with riders.

They galloped after us and pulled alongside, their lack of antlers allowing them to cut beneath the lowest branches with ease.

I shot Bastian a wide-eyed look. Who the fuck were they?

He shook his head, as clueless as I was. "Stay with me."

They forced us west, not responding when Bastian demanded to know who they were.

As long as we travelled *with* them, they kept their distance, but as soon as we tried to break through their moving block-ade, they closed ranks and fired upon us. My stag grunted as an arrow clipped his leg.

Ahead the trees thinned out. We'd be at the advantage then—on a clear course, our stags could outrun the smaller hinds. "Come on." I patted his shoulder, urging him towards the forest's edge.

We broke free of the trees, sunshine piercing my eyes.

"Shit." Bastian wheeled his stag around.

My stomach dropped as I pulled to a sharp stop.

Ahead rose a craggy cliff face. To our left, another. And to our right, another.

A dead end.

61

KAT

"Think we can climb?" I eyed the rocks—they seemed craggy enough for footholds.

"That, or fight." Bastian dismounted, shooting a glare back the way we'd come. "Your choice."

The thunder of hooves shook from the forest, thrumming into my feet as I landed.

Not long to decide.

Climbing would leave us as easy targets against the grey cliff face. No cover whatsoever. They'd pick us off in an instant.

Not much of a choice.

Swallowing, I unclipped my bow and quiver from the saddle. Not a choice of bravery. Just desperation.

He drew his shadowy sword and sent the stags back into the forest.

"*Tennacht,*" I commanded, and my bowstring pulled taut, the magic humming in my blood. My pulse leapt at every point as we took cover behind some boulders at the foot of the cliff. For half my life I'd carried a pistol, but I could count on one hand the number of times I'd fired it *at* someone. And only once had I killed.

"You stay under cover," Bastian gritted out, shadows unspooling around his feet in a dense clump as he watched the forest's edge. "If... if you find yourself alone, surrender. Then, the first chance you get, poison your guards and run. Understood?"

"But—"

"*Understood?*"

If you find yourself alone—he meant, if he was dead. I swallowed and strapped the quiver to my back. I wasn't going to let that happen, so his plan was purely hypothetical and I felt no guilt in replying, "I understand."

He blurred and I had to blink away the uncomfortable sensation of seeing double as he split in two. Cloaked in shadows, one part of Bastian crept into the trees.

I nocked an arrow and waited.

Blood roared in my ears like the fight had already begun. My palms sweated into my gloves.

"You can do this, ember."

I jolted at his use of that name here and now.

"Your fire isn't just for me." His teeth bared in a vicious smile. "I look forward to seeing it destroy them all."

A muffled cry came from the forest to the right where his double had gone. I had no time to peer over and wonder what had happened, because an instant later, a wave of arrows flew from the trees.

We hugged the rock as they clattered against it. Bastian held my gaze, a determined frown in place. "Wait for it," he whispered.

I squeezed my bow, watching arrows skewer the ground

just beyond our cover. If my supply ran out, I might be able to use some of them.

The moment the clattering eased, Bastian nodded and broke for the trees to the left.

Drawing, I stood. It took a second to spot a fae amongst the trees.

Aim, exhale, release.

A cry said I'd hit.

I was already nocking my next arrow, searching for my next target.

I fired and fired in that pattern, ducking back as stray arrows clipped the boulder and flew inches from my face.

It didn't seem real that a lucky shot from one of these could kill me. And yet...

I tried to swallow down my fear, but it had already clawed its way into my throat and latched on. I could only work around the thick mass.

Bastian was a dark shape on the edge of the forest, void-black blade sweeping through our enemy. Darker today than at Innesol—odd, but I had no time to wonder about that.

Thank every god I'd practiced so hard with Faolán, even when I'd hated him for adding to my hangover headaches. Readying a fresh arrow was easy, something ingrained in my muscles, and it let me convince myself that this was just a training exercise.

Almost.

Because there were never screams when we practised.

They rose from left and right. Bastian's first kills must've been caught by surprise, but now our enemies knew he was amongst them.

Near one of my early shots someone groaned in pain.

The arrows clacking against rock slowed. How many had we killed? Enough to make them retreat?

I used the lull to gather a handful of arrows from the floor, but when I looked up, that fear in my throat seized me entirely.

On silent feet, fae slipped from the trees.

It was worse than if I heard the pound of their footsteps—that would've been a warning.

For long and stupid seconds, all I could do was stare.

Move. Fucking move.

I had no idea if Bastian shouted it or some part of me thought it or if I said it out loud. But the words reached me, a slap around the face.

I scrambled for cover.

We're going to die.

I grabbed my bow.

Maybe, but let's try not to, eh?

I fired faster than I ever had before. I had a wealth of targets, after all.

My arms should've been aching by now, even with my bow's lightness, but if anything I felt stronger.

Shadows spilled from the forest, tugging on ankles, as two Bastians broke from the trees. He sliced and parried, rolled under someone's guard, clipping the back of their knees so they dropped with a shriek before he rose, sword thrusting through another fae's gut.

Blood. Shadows. Screams. The thrum of my bowstring.

But it wasn't enough.

Breaths heaving, I fired and fired, trying to keep them back from me, back from both Bastians.

But we were only three and they were still dozens and dozens.

I didn't want to die today. This wasn't a day when I had to

weigh the safety of thousands against my own life. I didn't choose this.

But sometimes it didn't matter what you chose. Sometimes death chose you.

I reached for the next arrow. And found nothing.

Before I could break cover and gather more, a louder, harsher cry rose above all others.

Bastian.

62

KAT

I took too long to find Bastian in the melee. When I finally did, I understood why. He wasn't at his normal height but down on one knee, blood spilling from his thigh. Too much blood.

Pulse pounding not just at my temples and throat, but in my face, I felt as though it was taking over my entire body.

Still, he blocked one blow and another.

Unable to look away, I stumbled from behind the boulder and groped on the ground for one of the enemy's arrows. Every strike upon his sword shook my bones.

My fingers closed on an arrow shaft and I nocked it, drew, aimed.

I didn't get to exhale, calm and ready to fire.

A sword erupted from Bastian's stomach as he parried the warrior before him.

Crimson. Glinting metal. His face dropping.

I let out a cry, went to shoot, realised the arrow I'd picked up was broken.

But not as broken as Bastian.

The blade wrenched from his stomach.

The shadows of his sword vanished, leaving only steel. The glow in his eyes went out.

He fell.

"No. *No.*" The bow fell from my trembling fingers as panic buzzed against my face harder and harder with each frantic heartbeat.

Not this. *Not this.*

Not Bastian.

A terrible heat engulfed me, like pressure that needed release, and when I yanked off my gloves, my hands were black. Not purple—*black.* And something dark spilled from them.

That trembling... it wasn't fear but rage.

That buzz... it wasn't panic but power.

You hold on too tight.

Then I would let go. Truly let go.

Skin prickling, poison hazing from me thicker than it had in Kaliban's house, I straightened my back and reached out.

I gathered the magic vibrating against my skin, and purple mist rolled off me. There was only me and the power that consumed my entire focus.

Once I'd used up the nearby magic, I reached out with my mind. I grabbed the rocks and their low resonance, the land's heady hum, the pine trees' higher, more complex vibrations.

Sometimes the power tried to slither away, but I gritted my teeth and yanked it to me.

You are mine.

My poison formed a low mist over the ground, thickening with every second.

It seeped out of me like every angry word I'd only thought and not been able to say.

It deafened me like every scream I'd ever held in.

It rose and rose like a flood fed by every emotion I'd locked inside and poisoned myself with.

Except now, that poison spread out, filling the space at the base of the cliff.

Dimly, I registered that there was still a fight. Bastian. Alive. Only one half of him had been killed.

But I'd seen it. I'd felt it—a fissure in my fucking soul.

And I wasn't about to let it happen again.

I clawed more power to me. The trees on the edge of the clearing turned brown, their branches wilting.

You are mine. You will see to it that I don't die today—that he doesn't die today.

He turned wide eyes upon me, a cut on his chin dripping, more blood on his cheek.

Around us, fae stumbled, their attack forgotten. They clawed at their shins, first, then the dark tendrils reached above their collars and up to their faces. They scratched at their cheeks and throats, like they could scrape my poison out.

Bodies arching, eyes screwing shut, the fae opened their mouths in cries I couldn't hear over my own roaring rage.

One by one, they fell, disappearing in my poison's haze.

Only Bastian and I remained standing.

He was alive. I'd saved him. *My magic* had saved him.

Lips parted, he regarded me. "That was... incredible."

Needing to touch him to be sure he was really here and really all right, I started towards him, but my foot hit something. The mist swirled and revealed a body.

A woman, curled up, her face contorted in death.

It was the easiest thing I'd ever read.

Pain.

Terrible, terrible pain.

That I had caused.

I swallowed and edged around her, but there was another. A young man, this time, scratches down his cheeks from where he'd tried to rid himself of the creeping agony.

My rage evaporated.

All these people. I'd killed them.

How many? Twenty? Thirty? More?

Lives ended in agony.

I stared at my hands stained deep, dark purple, the poison still rolling off of them.

Stop, I told it. *Stop.*

But it didn't... I couldn't...

I'd let go and now I couldn't control it. Panic filled my throat, pounded in my chest, painful and tight.

"Kat? Are you—?"

"Don't." I shook my head, stomach churning. "Don't look at me. I'm a monster."

He caught my shoulders like he wasn't horrified by the death dripping from my fingers. He met my gaze and cupped my cheek, his warmth only dimly registering through the tingling magic. "You're not a monster. You're *glorious*."

He was wrong.

I was out of control. I was a killer. A—

Something smacked into me and I stumbled forward into his arms. I tried to draw breath to speak, but... couldn't.

Bastian paled, eyes wide, jaw slack.

Now he looked horrified.

Sluggish with grey blotches pressing at the edge of my vision, I followed his gaze down to my chest.

Blood. Steel in a familiar pointed shape.
An arrow head.
Pain choked me.
Then darkness.

63
BASTIAN

I killed a dozen of them before they managed to knock me out.

The whole thing was a tangle in my mind. Snatches of moments. More fighters pouring from the forest and down the cliff. A body sliced in two, slumping to the floor. A neck in my grip as I squeezed and squeezed and squeezed. A man clutching his thigh as his life seeped out.

And Kat's blood on my hands.

Standing over her, I roared through it all, more animal than man. More broken than the bodies scattered at my feet.

The empty space in my chest echoed with the memory of a heartbeat.

I wouldn't let them have her. I wouldn't let them live.

But my will was not enough and the universe had other ideas.

I woke with a terrible sickness roiling in my stomach. Someone thrust a bowl before me just in time for me to throw up until there was nothing but bile.

Gasping for breath, I gripped the edge of the bowl. My hands had been cleaned, but there was still something red caught under my nails.

Kat's blood.

Was she...? The arrow sticking out of her chest. She was. Had to be.

My eyes burned as the truth crept through every vein and nerve. It choked me.

I would kill them all. Even if this bowl was my only weapon, I would destroy every last one of them.

I shook, but not entirely with anger. Weakness seeped into my very bones, cold as iron. And my shadows...

No shadows.

I knew what I would find before my gaze trailed down to my wrists.

Iron manacles.

Unless it was alloyed and thus rendered safe, iron was technically illegal in Elfhame and hard to get hold of, but I owned a similar pair of cuffs. I hated using them, but it was the only way to deal with prisoners whose magic made them dangerous.

They'd been wrapped in felt so they wouldn't burn my skin, but their poison still radiated into my body, killing my magic and slowly killing me.

Be smart, Bastian.

Survive a little longer so you can take revenge for her. Then join her.

One breath, two, I gathered myself and gradually became aware of something other than my own body and the horror of what had happened. Rows of beds. An armoured woman with silver hair stationed at the end of my bed. Gilded constellations clustered around a grand chandelier.

An infirmary inside a ballroom.

At my side, a man in a bloodied apron watched me with narrowed eyes before holding out his hand for the bowl.

So long as I had these manacles around my wrists, I wasn't strong enough to kill anyone with the bowl, so I returned it.

He gave me water and a piece of hard cheese. There was no point in worrying about consuming poison—they already had the stuff wrapped around my wrists.

"Get up," the guard bit out once I'd forced the food down.

Standing felt like lifting three Faoláns. My thighs didn't burn like I'd worked them hard, they just strained as though they'd never had any strength to begin with.

I was a boy again. Weak and helpless.

I *would not* remain that way.

Following the guard and flanked by two more with a fourth behind, I pulled on the manacles but in this state, I had no chance of breaking them.

Kat was... She was gone. I'd been an idiot, thinking we had more time—*all the time in the world.*

But *memento mori*, like she'd said. And like a fool, I'd forgotten. Forgotten how delicate life could be, how short it was for humans. *I thought we'd have more time.*

We passed down a long corridor. Its rich decoration and sleek furniture matched my earlier assessment of the infirmary. This was a grand manor house, though cracks marred the walls and windows.

It was nothing compared to what was missing inside me.

"The woman—the human woman I was with. Where is she?"

"I was just ordered to bring you once you woke." The silver-haired guard didn't turn to me, just marched ahead.

"To bring me where?"

She didn't reply.

Dimly, I noted the turnings we took and the ones we didn't and counted the doors until we reached a large set of double doors with guards stationed on either side.

I frowned at their deepest blue uniform—the same colour as the armour Dusk's guards wore. And on their chests...

Red, outlined with gold—a hydra.

Fuck. The iron was making me stupid. And Kat's... *absence* had occupied the thoughts I had left. I hadn't even considered who had attacked us.

Hydra Ascendant. And they had the Night Queen's Shadow as their captive. Either I was on my way to my execution or they were going to torture *then* execute me.

I was still staring at the insignia when a tight knot of guards reached us and one stepped aside revealing—

"*Katherine.*" My legs gave out, and I didn't even care that one of my guards had to catch me.

Because *she was alive.*

Pale and wearing manacles as well as a shirt several sizes too large instead of her own, but *alive.*

She eyed me, frowning. "Are you all right?"

Of all the things when *she* had been shot through the chest.

"I thought you were dead." I finally let myself think the word I had been avoiding since she'd been hit.

She flashed a small smile. "So did I. They have healers who operated on me." Her gaze fell to her hands, now unstained, and the smile faded. "Someone touched my blood and died."

There she was, thinking of herself as a monster again.

I reached for her. "It's all—"

"Silence." A guard blocked me, then the doors swung open.

A long space. Originally a formal dining room, most likely. Glazed doors lined one side, facing the setting sun, casting the room in an orange blaze. I catalogued it all as the guards hustled us inside.

Kat was alive. That meant my plan wasn't one for revenge anymore, but escape.

Even with the weakness in my limbs, I carried that idea in my chest, a beacon that filled me.

Gardens outside, but overgrown with ivy and shrubs that might have once been clipped into topiary. They'd provide cover.

"Well, look who it is." A woman's voice rang out across the room.

The blood in my veins froze.

That voice. Like Braea's but higher pitched.

I knew that voice and the laugh that followed it.

The world shifted in and out of focus as I blinked at the table the guards led us to.

Behind it sat Princess Sura.

64
BASTIAN

"I killed you." I didn't mean to speak, but the thought came out as though saying it would remind the universe that fifteen years ago I had beheaded her. I swayed as a cold weight dragged on my stomach and the world spun out of control.

"Clearly, you didn't do a very good job of it." She bared her teeth and shrugged.

Wide-set black eyes like her mother's with paler golden skin. She'd tied her midnight curls into a high ponytail—a style I'd never seen her wear in Tenebris. Other than that one detail, she was just as I remembered.

That was the same head I'd taken. How? A changeling? Something else? Maybe this wasn't even her. My mind tripped over itself, sluggish from the iron.

"Are you going to stop staring and introduce your little friend—bring her up to date?"

I swallowed and worked my tongue around my mouth,

that sick feeling still coating my throat, thanks to the iron. "Katherine, this is Princess Sura."

Slowly, her eyes widened and she dragged in a breath. She understood.

"Such a pleasure to meet any friend of Bastian's." Circling out from behind the table, Sura's smile was too bright, too cruel.

I knew the kind of "pleasure" she meant. Chest squeezing, I tried to stop her reaching Kat, but a guard grabbed my shoulder.

Kat looked from the princess to me, head cocking. "How are you alive?"

"*At last* someone's asking the important questions." Sura clicked her tongue at me. "Really, Bastian, I always thought you were so bright."

"Remove these manacles and I'll show you how bright I still am."

"Hmm, no, I don't think I'll take you up on that offer. We need to keep those pesky shadows in check, don't we? Not to mention, *someone's* poison." Eyebrow arched, she surveyed Kat. "An interesting little trick. One you won't be repeating. The instant either of you try to escape, I've ordered my archers to concentrate their fire on the human. They'll aim to kill, but with that many arrows, I don't suppose it'll matter. They'll make a pincushion out of you. And humans are so delicate, even ones with poison in their blood." Another bright smile. "Understood?"

With a glower, Kat inclined her chin.

I gritted my teeth, seething. "Why not just kill me?"

Her eyes narrowed on me, a long look of calculation. "Maybe I want you alive."

They'd herded us. A good archer could've picked us off

before I realised they were there. She'd had her healers save Kat's life when it would've been significantly easier for them to let her go.

My lip curled. "And you want to use her to control me."

"Ah, there's some of that cunning I expected from the man they call *the Serpent of Tenebris*." She spread her hands as if it was written on a banner before her.

"You heard about that, then." I had only been called Serpent after her coup.

"Of course. Just because I've been absent, doesn't mean I haven't been *listening*. But, I forget my manners—I was answering dear Katherine's question." She perched on the table and waved the guards to one side.

With us both shackled in iron, she was safe.

For now.

One leg crossed over the other, she watched me closely. "A changeling worked for me. Caira. I loved her, and the damn fool loved me enough to die for me."

Somehow that made it worse. In my childish act of swaggering victory, I hadn't just thrown a head at my queen's feet. I'd thrown *the wrong head*. That heaviness in my stomach expanded until I could barely breathe.

"And this is why you attacked the city?" Kat frowned. "How does killing civilians give you revenge against him?"

"What?" Sura glanced at the guards who waited off to one side.

"You didn't know?"

Oh, she knew. She was just a good actress. Good enough to fool even Kat. I sneered, using anger at what she'd done to squash down my shock. "We found your people redirecting the Horrors to the city, so you can save yourself the performance."

"Not my people." She jerked her chin towards the doors,

457

and two guards hurried out. With a deep breath, she gathered herself. "Look, this isn't what I intended when I heard we'd captured you."

"Believe me, this isn't how I saw my day going, either. How about you let us go, so we can all carry on with our days."

"So you can report back to my mother and bring her full wrath down upon us? I think not." She huffed and scowled. "But it is a difficult position you put me in. I'm not ready to unite the thrones yet and—"

"Unite?" Kat raised her eyebrows. "Bring Dawn and Dusk together?"

Sura sighed. "I forgot how impatient humans can be. Bring together... in a manner. When I take the throne, it won't be divided."

"You want to rule alone. You're not going to Sleep."

The Circle of Ash.

Hadn't the Lady said we'd find the answers to both problems together? That meant this palace had to be Ashara.

And this had to be our execution. We knew the location of her base. It was the only logical course.

If I could make her believe we were more useful alive, that might buy us some time. But that was our only hope.

"Now, how did you find out about that?" Sura canted her head at Kat. "This is another reason to wait—I need more spies in the palace."

More. Meaning she already had at least one. I bowed my head to hide my reaction. She must not realise how much information she was letting slip. She had been away from court for fifteen years, surrounded only by those she trusted. She was out of practice.

"Regardless"—she shrugged—"the split system is broken."

"Why not marry Prince Cyrus, then? Rule together."

Sura wrinkled her nose. "It had crossed my mind—a long, long time ago. But you've met the Day Prince. You understand why that's not my preferred plan. Besides, there should be only one monarch. One queen. One court. One nation, together."

Exactly the instability I feared Dawn causing with the Circle.

"Only one queen, but three heads." I nodded towards the banner hanging behind her table, the hydra's eyes picked out in gold thread.

She sucked in her cheeks and looked away. "How well do you really know the queen you serve, Bastian?"

Deflecting.

I raised an eyebrow, refusing to take her bait. She wanted to sow a seed in my mind, make me wonder what she might be referring to. She really was out of practice if she thought that would work on me.

"Do you understand the lengths she'd go to in order to protect herself?"

"She protects *Dusk*."

Brow set in a determined line, Kat leant forward. "Are you going to just hint that she's done something terrible or actually tell us what it is?"

"There isn't anything," I gritted out. "She's trying to change the subject."

"You wouldn't believe me. Even if I took *arianmêl*, you'd say I was evading the truth." The princess gave a humourless laugh. "Ask your father if you really want to know."

More bluffing.

She rolled her eyes at me. "Stars above, are you predictable. Loyal to the queen. 'She elevated me to her second in command, and all I had to do was kill my father.' It's so boring."

Trying to make me angry. Almost succeeding. Maybe she was warming up.

"Since you went to such trouble to save Kat's life, I assume you're not going to execute us right this second. What do you want? If you get on with it, I can stop boring you."

"I haven't decided what to do with you two. Execution isn't off the table yet." She smiled sweetly. "But for now, I'll take a bargain. My guards will take you to your room and remove your manacles. In return you and Katherine will not in any way harm me or any of my people for the duration of your stay."

She'd already threatened Kat's life if we made an escape attempt. Perhaps she didn't trust me not to take that risk. It had crossed my mind—there had to be a way we could get out and keep her safe from the archers.

Still, bound in iron, I would only grow weaker and weaker. At least this way, I stood a chance of recovering while in our room. She had to mean cell, but I supposed this way it would be a "fun surprise" for us when we arrived.

"No manacles, no one hurts Kat, *and* we get a nice suite with a bed and bath—something fitting of a diplomat from Dusk."

"No one hurts her as long as you don't attempt to escape or unless I decide on execution. That's non-negotiable. You want a bath, you'll have one room. There are no spare suites." She shrugged. "But 'nice' I can do."

"You have yourself a bargain." I raised my eyebrows at Kat, since she would be bound to it, too.

"And no one hurts Bastian."

Sura rolled her eyes. "If it wasn't so sickening, it would be sweet. But yes, fine. Happy now?"

It wasn't going to get any better than that, and I intended to escape before they had a chance to execute us.

We agreed, and the princess and I sealed our sides of the bargain. Kat flinched away when she went to touch her.

"Relax, the iron nullifies your magic. Can't you feel how wrong that is, even for a gifted human?" Sura shook her hand and spoke the words of power. "It is so."

Kat stared, and I could see how she squeezed back. Her little exhale hollowed out my chest. Aside from poisoning Ella, this was the first time she'd touched anyone other than me in months.

And today she'd almost died.

The horror of that followed me through the corridors as guards led us away.

65

KAT

"Nice," it turned out, was an understatement.

Our room was large and furnished in Dusk colours, with a canopied four-poster bed and sunset painted across the ceiling. Granted, it was missing a window and ivy grew in through cracks in the wall, but roses climbed over the windowsill and somehow the room wasn't cold. Bastian muttered something about it being magically sealed. The guards removed our manacles and deposited our saddlebags—they must've found our stags. They left, locking the door behind them.

Bastian drew a long breath like it was the first he'd taken in minutes, and the colour flooded back into his skin.

The purple stain rushed back into my nails and fingertips, too, much less welcome.

He shuddered as if shaking off the iron's effects, and then he was towering over me, cupping my cheek. "Are you all right? Are you *sure*?"

I rubbed my chest. "The healer said it just missed my heart.

That's the only reason I survived long enough to get here. But I'm fine." I closed my fingers around his wrist. "Are you? You looked so ill."

"A little nauseous and weak, but I'll be fine. As long as the exposure isn't prolonged or in the bloodstream, iron poisoning wears off eventually."

"So... since I'm not fae, if I wore something made of iron, it would cut off my magic but otherwise I'd have no ill effects?" I felt tired and queasy, yes, but not so long ago, I'd had an arrow sticking out of my chest. I'd take queasy over that.

His expression closed down into a frown as he slid his hand to my shoulder. "Why?"

I cleared my throat and backed away, slipping from his grasp. "Don't you want to discuss what just happened? The princess—she's *alive*."

"No. Not yet." Absently, he touched the scar on his chin.

I couldn't argue—he had a lot to process.

He canted his head. "I'm much more interested in you explaining why you want to know about iron."

"Do you really need to ask?"

"I want to hear you say it."

I pointed towards the door. "That is the first time I've known peace in months." Except for when I'd sunk into his arms, utterly torn apart. "I poisoned Ella, and then I killed all those people. Even the Lady of the Lake said I can't control my magic."

"That isn't what—"

"You don't know what she meant, Bastian. Maybe that's exactly what she was saying. I seek to control it, but I never will. Doesn't that fit her answer?"

His mouth flattened, scar going pale.

"I can't control my power, so I need something that will

shut it off. I couldn't live with myself if I killed someone by accident." I swallowed, eyes burning. "I'm not sure I can live with myself after..."

Those bodies at my feet. So many of them.

He gave me a gentle shake, bringing me back. "They were going to kill us, Kat. *Maybe* she wants me alive, but..." The muscles in his neck corded. "As far as she is concerned, you are expendable. At best, you saved both our lives. At worst, you saved yours. Both are worth whatever bodies you left on that battlefield."

"But the pain—"

"Do you think they'd have given you a painless death?" He splayed his hand over my chest. "Did that arrow hurt?"

Not at first, but as oblivion had rolled in, yes.

I bowed my head. "I still can't control it. I'm a danger to everyone. That's why you have Rose guard me all the time, really, isn't it?"

His silence was enough of an answer.

No one in the city was likely to harm me. Not while I lived under his protection. But I was a danger to them.

"Not... solely," he said at last. "I want to keep you safe, whether that's from attack or from how much it would harm you if you inadvertently hurt someone."

"Then you understand why I need iron."

"It will make you sick. It nullifies your ring and fae charm itself, but it blocks *all* incoming magic, including healing. It's not the solution is seems to be. Maybe you didn't feel too bad just now, but you were only wearing it for half an hour. Over time..."

"But I'm not fae."

"No, but you heard the Lady of the Lake, and Elthea, too." His faced tightened at her name. "You're not entirely human—

not anymore. Iron makes gifted humans sick after a while. Who knows what it would do to you in the long term?"

"And what about the constant fear of poisoning someone? Isn't that enough to make me ill?"

His hands fisted as he huffed. "Iron is a punishment, not something you do to someone you love."

My next argument died on my lips. *Love?* No, he... he just cared about me. But my chest was doing something strange, like my heart danced, forgetting entirely about its normal beat.

"We'll find another way." Jaw muscle twitching, he backed off and turned away. "I'm running you a bath."

I swallowed, searching for my voice as he threw open the bathroom door. "That isn't going to fix me."

"No." With me following, he stalked into a bathroom with no ceiling. Above, the evening sky lit up with the first stars. "But it will get rid of the stink of whoever's shirt that is."

I sniffed the shirt. "Are you saying I smell?"

"Of another man."

I sat on the edge of the large bath as steaming water ran into it. He glowered, looking between two bottles of bubblebath.

"You know I don't need your permission to do this, don't you?"

"You don't need my permission for anything. But I hope you'll reconsider." He showed me the labels, and I chose the hyacinth and amber scent over the lilac one. "You've been making progress," he muttered as he poured a generous dose into the bath. "If *I* help you, you'll be able to use it. I felt you drain the trees—your magic is unseelie, like mine."

Use it? I'd done enough with this power. Nausea rose in me, and I distracted myself by asking, "So... I didn't poison the trees, I... drained the life from them?"

"Sort of. Their magic, not their life. But they're connected —all living things has some link to the power that runs through the universe."

"Ariadne said something like that. She feels it when she uses her magic—threads connecting everything."

He made a soft sound of amusement. "Of course a thread-witch would see it that way. But I'm sorry. I sent you to all the wrong people for help and... it's taken me embarrassingly long to realise."

"Well, you *were* avoiding me a good portion of that time." I arched an eyebrow at him and grinned when he looked up from frothing the bubbles.

"I was a coward, I confess, afraid of being alone with you too much." His gaze drifted away, following the scented steam. "What a waste of time." He seemed distant for a beat before shaking it off. "But *you* avoided me, too."

"Fair point."

We chuckled, and he left me to bathe. The water was hot and wonderful, the sunset beautiful, and there was no scar on my chest. I could almost persuade myself that although we were captives, this space was a haven from the outside world rather than a prison.

Overhead, the sky darkened to night, and when I emerged, I found Bastian already sprawled across the bed, asleep. I wasn't surprised after the battle and the iron.

He thought he could help me, but it was better if I had no magic and couldn't hurt anyone. I would get hold of iron. Somehow.

66

KAT

The next morning, guards woke us and led Bastian away for a meeting with the princess. They left breakfast, which I nibbled on as I paced the room and brooded over the bargain we'd made. It had to be enough to keep Bastian safe, didn't it? Unless she decided to execute him. Surely she'd warn us.

It was past midday and I was half sick with worry by the time he returned looking pale and tired but otherwise fine. As soon as the guards removed the manacles and left, I flung myself into his arms.

"Hey. What's wrong?" He stroked my back, pulling me close.

"I was afraid she was going to have you executed and I wasn't going to have a chance to say goodbye." I squeezed as tight as I could, burying my face in his chest and inhaling. A little sweat from the iron sickness, but there was also bergamot and cedar and *him*.

"Maybe tomorrow." His chest vibrated with a soft laugh.

"But for today she just asked about Tenebris and the courts. I kept it general—things you could hear on most street corners. Nothing to worry about."

"Good. *Good.*"

When I pulled back, I found him giving me an odd look—brow creased, gaze soft and skipping between my eyes. "Not so long ago, you said to me *memento mori.*"

My cheeks warmed at the reminder of having my kiss rejected.

"It isn't a phrase we use—mortality isn't really a concern for fae. But now I understand. Katherine." He said my name with a shiver, making my breath catch. "*Katherine.* Yesterday, I—"

The door opened and the silver-haired guard from yesterday entered with a tray of food. Another remained at the door, bow trained on us—though I suspected their aim was centred on me after what the princess had said.

"Your lunch," the silver-haired woman said as she placed the tray on the table.

With a deep sigh, Bastian released me from his embrace. "Only one plate?"

"The human dines with Her Highness today." She beckoned me with a jerk of her chin.

His jaw clenched, but I smiled and touched his arm. "Looks like it's my turn for questions."

He caught my fingers as I turned away. "Remember what I told you about Tenebris being different from Lunden."

Different rules apply. Never reveal your heart.

"I'll be careful."

Wrists in manacles, I followed the guard on a different route from the one we'd taken yesterday. The iron was no worse than when we left it late in the day to touch and my

468

slumbering poison made me nauseous. Periods were more uncomfortable.

We passed through narrower corridors—this had to be a private area of the palace. Just as we stopped at a door, it opened, and a girl pulled up short as if leaving. Fourteen or fifteen years old, she had golden brown curls that wafted from the movement of the door. Her black, wide-set eyes narrowed as she gave me a long look. Not a cruel one, but curious, like I was a strange and unusual creature.

I knew those eyes—their match watched from the table further inside. She had to be Sura's daughter.

Already taller than me, the girl craned to one side. "Are your ears really blunt?"

Sura cleared her throat. "Don't you have somewhere to be?"

The girl huffed a breath out of her nose and inclined her head. "Of course." She passed us.

Before we entered, I glanced down the hallway and found her eyeing me.

"You'll have to excuse her," Sura said as I took a seat and the guard unfastened my manacles. "She's never seen a human before."

A pair of gloves waited with my table setting, and I pulled them on, glad to not have to look at the purple stain returning to my skin.

How many of her people had I killed? I didn't dare ask.

I swallowed as the guard took up a position by the door. "Your daughter?"

"What gave it away? The eyes or the attitude?"

"The eyes—just like your mother's. Though her hair isn't a colour I'd expect from Dusk."

A momentary stiffness flickered over her features and she

looked away. With a quiet word and a tap on the table, she summoned a platter of meat and cheese with pickled vegetables, and a board laden with steaming bread and a pat of butter.

The scent had my mouth watering. Perhaps she hadn't fed us last night so we'd be all the more eager to eat—and talk—today.

"Like my grandmother's, too. My sister was the only one who didn't have the same eyes. Hers were like starlight. A pale violet blue shade."

Nothing about the golden brown hair. Sometimes what a person didn't say revealed as much as what they did.

"Please"—she gestured to the platter—"eat. No poison. No ill intent." As if to illustrate, she took a little of each item on her fork and ate it.

So, I loaded my plate and noted that the princess served herself rather than having someone wait on her. While we ate, she asked about Tenebris, seemingly innocuous questions, but I measured my answers. As Bastian had said—things you might hear on any street corner.

Once the table was cleared, she signalled to the guard, who ducked out. Sura sat back, swirling a class of crystal clear wine, watching me.

I had chosen water—there was no telling how strong their wine was, and I needed a clear head if I was going to avoid spilling any secrets. Busying myself topping up my glass from the jug, I refused to take the bait and ask what she wanted.

A moment later, the guard returned with another fae. His shaved head was covered in celestial tattoos, with a thin crescent moon on his brow.

Something in the room changed—a subtle shift in the air. Magic.

I squeezed my glass and smiled at the princess, though inside, my heart beat harder.

"I'm trying to work out what kind of person you are," she said at last. "Bastian is... what I expected. Loyal to my mother. Convinced of the virtue of the split courts. Committed to peace, no matter the cost."

I raised an eyebrow. "You think peace costs as much as war?"

"It isn't free. It costs whatever is sacrificed to maintain it. You must know some of what he's done."

Torture. Killing. He carried that price. I raised a shoulder and sipped my water.

"A cost to him," she went on. "And a cost to those whom peace doesn't serve. The ordinary folk caught in the crossfire between Dusk and Dawn. You must've heard about the executions."

They didn't execute people publicly as we did in Albion, but the fact they'd been killed based on such paltry evidence was bad enough. A dull headache hummed behind my eyes.

"The shapechangers shunned by both sides. Bastian's *peace* requires the silence of all these people—their complicity in their own oppression. That doesn't sound like much of a peace to me."

"How noble." I smiled sweetly. "You missed out the princesses desperate to take the throne. I'm sure whatever plan you're trying to convince me of will help them a great deal."

She snorted—a genuine sound of amusement and surprise. "I think I understand why Bastian likes you enough to become an oathbreaker. I knew it wasn't only the hair."

So she'd picked up that piece of information from the capital, but she didn't know about the attack. There was a delay in her lines of communication. Another note for Bastian.

"The system is broken, and I had hoped Bastian would help me fix it now he's grown up, but…" She sighed into her glass, shoulders sinking before she took a long draught of wine. "He's too convinced by the pretty picture my mother paints— that she wants *Dusk* to be powerful and not only herself. That she's committed to the balance of the courts. It would be lovely if it wasn't bullshit."

She *had* ordered him to focus on the Circle of Ashes rather than Hydra Ascendant. He seemed to believe it was so Dawn couldn't get their hands on the relic and use it first, but… what if it was purely for her own benefit? The woman who'd used the story of her daughter's death to warn me away from Bastian—I could believe she would do that.

But I rolled my eyes as though unconvinced. "And don't tell me—Your Highness knows the truth and has evidence of how evil the Night Queen *really is*."

"Not evil so much as… self-interested."

I cocked my head. "Isn't that what evil really is?"

"A little self-interest is no bad thing. But it comes down to the lines you're willing to cross. The price you're willing to pay."

I twisted the stem of my glass between finger and thumb. What price had the Night Queen paid to improve her own position? Allowing those people to be executed. Perhaps she could've saved them. How did it benefit her *not* to? It made King Lucius look paranoid and unreasonable—killing folk with little evidence. I'd heard whispers since, even from Dawn folk.

"And whose lives you're willing to pay with," I murmured.

"Exactly." She exchanged a glance with the tattooed man

before leaning forward. "Have you heard about my sister's death?"

"I've heard a version of it. But I'm guessing you're about to give me yours."

"I'm about to give you *the truth*." She set aside her glass and took a breath as though steeling herself. "No doubt you've been told vaguely that an unseelie broke through the veil and touched my sister, the implication being that she was taken against her will."

One took Nyx. Yet the queen had used the word rape about Bastian's mother. I'd carried over the assumption from one to the other, encouraged by her vague phrasing.

But Sura was trying to manipulate me with her own version of the truth. Perhaps she thought I'd help her persuade Bastian.

So the Night Queen didn't want to use that word when referring to her dead daughter—hardly surprising. It didn't mean she'd deceived me.

"My sister was in love with the unseelie man she invited to her bed. She helped call him through the veil that night as she had other nights, so they could be together rather than talking through an old scrying mirror she'd found."

Frowning at the table, she ran a finger over its smooth surface. "She didn't know unseelie men don't use a contraceptive like our men do, and she found herself pregnant, with her lover back in the Underworld."

I clasped my hands in my lap to keep them still. Pregnant? The Night Queen had left that part out of her story. But, again if her daughter had been violated, I could understand her not wanting to dwell on the idea.

Sura hadn't explicitly said her sister *wasn't* attacked.

I clung to every word, the exact turn of phrase and cast my

mind back to that conversation with the queen.

Somewhere, growing between the cracks was the truth.

"Our mother wasn't pleased." She scoffed. "An unseelie in the line of succession? Not acceptable. She locked her away and tried to persuade her to get rid of the baby. In secret, I helped my sister, while she pretended to consider our mother's demands. I even took her the scrying mirror with its frame of crows and spears. How my sister didn't know what it was when she first found it, I never understood. The Morrigan's sons rule the Underworld, and those are her symbols. Of course it was going to form a connection to that place."

The goddess of death and war. I fought a shudder at the idea of getting caught up with her or her sons.

"They used it to plan her escape. The night before the new moon when the veil wore as thin as the crescent moon and a storm made the night dark and loud—the perfect cover. But our mother had enchanted the river to keep him out. Everyone thinks it's unseelie fae in general, to keep the palace safe, but it's actually one specific unseelie to keep her and what belongs to her safe."

Of course, it would benefit her to have everyone believe she'd acted to protect all the palace's inhabitants.

I frowned as I realised—she never crossed that river, though I'd seen her wistfully looking out over the city. Was she afraid of him? Was that what kept her bound to the palace?

"My sister was heavily pregnant by that point—a couple of months from giving birth. She tried to run, but..." Frowning, she shook her head. "I discovered later our mother had been feeding her mugwort to get rid of the child. That together with the stress of the escape must've brought on her labour early. I can still hear her screams. She broke two of my fingers from squeezing so tight through the pain. I didn't dare visit a healer

474

—they'd have told the queen." When she lifted her hand, her third and fourth fingers were the slightest bit crooked.

"I did what I could to get Nyx to the bridge, but she told me to keep out of sight—she'd take those last steps alone." Her head bowed, but not before I caught the gleam of unshed tears. "She was protecting me. If the queen found out I'd helped her..." She shook her head.

I slotted everything the princess said between the queen's words. They fitted. So far.

"It was a battle for her to cross that bridge. Every step." Her voice cracked.

I saw her fighting when she was halfway across. A battle for her own will.

The queen's version, that he'd enchanted her, had made it sound like the unseelie was magically manipulating her into crossing the bridge, but... couldn't enchantment be love or at least infatuation? And couldn't the battle be to enact her own will rather than succumbing to the queen's?

The hairs on my forearms rose with the possibility.

"But she was fierce. For all her sweetness, Nyx would crush me in the training ring every fucking time." Sura smiled, but it was a brittle thing like spun sugar. "With her lover waiting on the other side and rain lashing down, she made it halfway, and that was when I knew she was going to reach him and they would escape and all would be well." Her smile broke into bitter splinters and a tear escaped down her cheek. "I was wrong."

She dashed the tear away along with any softness, scowling. "Someone fired upon her. Someone from the palace. A black arrow with white fletchings. She stumbled but kept going. I tried to get to her, to shield her or pull her back into cover or carry her to him—I still don't know what I planned to do. But she used her gift to push me back. All I could do was watch as with a fucking arrow in her chest, *she kept going.* Lightning flashed and a second arrow struck her. She didn't stop."

My heart pounded. I could see it. The long arc of the bridge, its lack of handrails, the storm breaking overhead. Below, the river would be swollen from the rain, crashing through the ravine.

The princess's bowed figure pressing on, one foot after another as she clutched her round belly.

Gripping my glass, I held my breath.

"I couldn't get to her," Sura went on. "But from my hiding place, I could follow its trajectory back to a figure on the royal balcony. A figure I knew well, even in the rain and dark, one whose black arrows had white fletchings. Our mother. As lightning cracked the sky, I watched her fire the third arrow. The one that stopped her."

Goosebumps chased over my skin as another tear slid down her cheek.

"I turned just in time to see her topple off the bridge." She wiped away the tear and frowned like she was angry it had escaped. "Whatever story the queen told you, understand that *she* is the one who killed my sister. No one else."

I sank back in my chair and clutched my head, which buzzed with two radically different versions of the story. The implications if this was true...

"You believe me, don't you?" She raised her eyebrows. "You know I can't lie."

"With fae it's hard to know what to believe. You speak of vague words, but I note you never said that he *didn't* rape your sister."

The way she clenched her jaw and swallowed made my

476

own throat thick with grief. It wasn't a conversation I would ever wish to have about my own sister, and I felt sick to ask, but... if she was manipulating me and the truth as much as her mother had, I needed to know.

Eventually, she shook her head. "That unseelie man didn't harm my sister in any way, including assaulting her. He loved her and she loved him. When she fell, he tried to throw himself into the river after her, but of course, thanks to Mother's enchantment, he couldn't. Does that satisfy you?"

I drained my glass, trying to wash away my empathy. Wrong, perhaps, but practical.

"Why did you tell me all that? When your mother told me her version, she had her own agenda for doing so. What's yours?"

"My mother is not what Bastian believes her to be. That story is the best illustration I know. She killed her own daughter to ensure she couldn't escape her control or bring an unseelie child into the world as her heir. *Her own daughter.*" The intensity of her gaze was enough to silence me for long moments. "Why do you think I tried to take the throne? If she can do that, she isn't fit to hold so many lives in the palm of her hand."

"Why wait so long to stage your coup? That had to be almost twenty years later?"

Her jaw twitched. "I was pregnant. With my daughter on the way, I knew I could secure the Moon Throne with myself and an heir. And... although she's not unseelie, I couldn't risk the queen deciding she wasn't good enough for the line of succession."

Everything about this felt unsafe. I had a feeling the queen would consider merely knowing this story some form of treason.

"Did you tell Bastian?"

She huffed, looking away. "No. He isn't ready to hear it. He'd find some way to disbelieve me. Accuse me of using some spell or illusion that showed me lying to him." She rolled her eyes. "Anything, however unlikely, to make it so his queen is what he believes."

My throat tightened. I'd picked up on things about the queen that had made me uncomfortable, but this story? It was a lot to take in, and I wasn't even as invested in the Night Queen as Bastian was.

He needed her to be this great queen, because if she wasn't, what had he spent all these years loyal to? What had he killed his father for?

I rubbed my throat, though my necklace was far from it. "If you want me to convince him to betray the queen, I'm afraid this is has been a wasted afternoon." That had to be what she was driving towards.

She gave a stiff smile and poured herself another glass of wine. "That's not why I brought you here, but I understand. I hear you have a sister of your own—a queen, no less. Tell me about her."

I delayed answering by taking a long sip of water, but I couldn't see any danger in giving her a few of the public details about Avice. She seemed satisfied with that and asked me a few questions about her adventures and gift, but nothing that seemed probing. No doubt she wanted to remind me of my sister while the tragedy of hers was still fresh in my mind.

It was hours before she dismissed me, and I left in shackles, thankful for a lifetime of hiding my feelings. I would certainly need it next time I faced the Night Queen.

Assuming I lived that long.

67

KAT

When I returned to our room, I found Bastian by the windows, looking out over the gardens. Perhaps it was the angle of his head or the way he leant against the window frame, but I knew he was thinking about escape. Assessing the route, watching for guards, weighing the risk.

The man who'd given so much of himself for others—his queen, his court, me.

The man who carried someone else's traumatic memories and all the guilt that went with them.

The man who knelt for no one, but had for me.

It hit me with all the force that arrow had, and perhaps a little more accuracy, because this pierced my heart right through its centre.

I knew him.

And I loved him. Gods, *I loved him.*

And maybe he knew me too, because he turned and gave

me this look—*this look*, so intense it stole my breath before I could get a word out.

So, instead of speaking, I acted, crossing the room with a determined frown. I wasn't sure what I meant to do, exactly, when I reached him, but he must've understood, as he came this way, shadows at his heels.

There was a moment when his arms closed around my waist and mine looped around his neck. A moment that strung out for hours, days, months. A moment empty of breath but full of wild and reckless hope.

Then, somehow, my lips were on his.

At last. At long fucking last.

Not almost. Not interrupted. Not stopped by the realisation that it was a bad idea.

Because it wasn't.

It was warm and soft and yearning, like neither of us quite realised it was truly happening or we both expected it to be snatched away in an instant.

Then he smiled. I felt its angles, felt the soft huffing laugh on my lips, lighting me up like embers breathed back to life.

He was kissing me.

Kissing me like there were no regrets. No reason not to. Just a lot of wasted opportunities he now wanted to make up for as he gripped my hair and angled my head and deepened what we shared.

I lost myself in exploration and being explored, taking his tongue, curling mine against it, swiping into his mouth and running the length along one sharp canine. I whimpered at that last part, the scrape of pain bright and beautiful.

At the sound, he crushed the air from my lungs, and I had to pull away just to catch my breath.

All of this is real.

Fuck. It was. *It was.*

"Katherine," he murmured, an inch away.

"I'm sorry." I swallowed and tried to step back, but my feet weren't on the floor. "I shouldn't ask this of you. I just... The way you looked, it..." I couldn't tell him how I felt. That would be unfair, just like running across the room at him had been. Hadn't I said I wouldn't take this from him? "You told me where you stood, and I need to respect that."

"No, you don't. Shouldn't. In fact, I'm begging you not to."

"Oh." Bastian begging and asking me *not* to respect him.

"I have been a fool. A fucking fool. Trying to resist. Pretending that if I don't kiss you and that if only my shadows have you, then I'm not breaking any rules." He ran his fingertips over my scalp and I shuddered at the whispering touch. He made a soft sound, part pleasure, part amusement.

"You do remember that I'm... married?" I couldn't help my nose wrinkling at having to bring it up. But I was committed to not being a regret—not for him.

He made a low sound, a glower shading his eyes. "I was planning to wait until *that man* was out of the way, but... I can't wait—not anymore. Not when I've been waiting a lifetime for you."

I opened my mouth but couldn't speak. What he was saying—it felt big. Too big to contain in a moment. Too big to hold in my skin. So big and bright and precious, I might explode with it.

"I was trying to say this morning... The race, the poison, the Horrors—every other time you've faced danger, there's always been something you or I or *we* could do about it. But yesterday... I thought we'd run out of chances." His silver eyes gleamed as he went on in a whisper, "I thought you were dead."

"I'm not, though." I tugged on the collar on his shirt and skimmed a kiss over his mouth.

"No, but you could be." He touched the point on my back where the arrow had entered. "An inch lower and you would be. When I woke, I was convinced you were and I realised—I believed... *fuck them and their rules.* You didn't enter that contract willingly, so why the hells should I give a shit about it? If it means nothing to you, it means nothing to me. Even if that makes me a villain, an oathbreaker, all the very worst things people say." He shrugged, bringing me closer with the arm around my waist. "It doesn't matter. *You* matter. You matter more to me than I do. And I surrender this last thing to you."

I wasn't sure I wanted that level of responsibility. Yet hadn't I lost my mind and control of my power not because *I* was in danger, but because he was? The sight of his double dying had broken something in me. Nothing else had mattered. *Nothing.*

So maybe I was already right there with him.

I gave the slightest nod.

Like that was permission, he walked me back until my shoulders hit the door. He tilted my chin up so there was no escaping his gaze. "I want you, body, heart, and soul. I want to worship you as you deserve to be worshipped. Adore you as you deserve to be adored. Love you as you deserve to be loved."

Goosebumps flooded my skin. He said that word. The one I'd thought wasn't possible for people like me—not until Avice had returned with so, so much of it. The one I thought I'd seen a glimmer of and lost. The one I felt for him.

Dangerous. He was always so damn dangerous.

So I retreated, raising an eyebrow like the Wicked Lady would, like I wasn't afraid. "I thought you said 'fuck deserve?'"

He scoffed, touch tracing down my throat to the neckline of my gown, forcing a snatched breath through my lips. "At your feet, all rules kneel. I'm no hero, Katherine, but, *please*, let me be your villain."

And I understood then the effect of a well-timed *please*.

It reached every part of me, warming like a glass and a half of brandy, but instead of dulling the edges of the world, it made it all sharper. The edges more crisp, the colours brighter, the hard planes of his body against mine all the more perfect.

I drew a deep breath, pressing my chest into his fingertip, soaking up that point of contact. "I've had enough of heroes." Like my heart wasn't thundering, I took my time tracing the scar that ran through his lip. "I dreamt of those as a girl. I consumed stories about them and sucked out the marrow. But no hero ever came. No hero took me from my husband or broke a man's nose because he called me fat. No hero gave me his own blood. No hero made me his as you have."

Because I was.

I was his in every way that mattered, in every sense I knew.

"I want you, whatever that means, whatever you may turn out to be." I planted a long, slow kiss on his mouth. His stillness hummed into me like he was holding on until I unleashed him. "I want you, Bastian," I whispered. "Give me everything."

And he did.

The kiss might've killed me, and everything that came next was in the Underworld, because it was deep and consuming like he really had waited a lifetime. He crushed me against the door as he had in the library, and it had my centre throbbing and my legs looping around him.

His body on mine. His hardness pressing between my legs. His hands on my cheek, in my hair, sweeping down my sides and hips, almost ticklish. He was everywhere, everything, all that I needed in this moment.

I was so absorbed in the kiss, I only registered we'd pulled away from the door when he squeezed my thigh. "Feet down, love."

Dazed and breathless, I obeyed and found myself standing by the bed, its canopy drifting in the breeze from the open window.

With a slow smile, he did nothing but watch me for a moment, then rubbed his thumb across my lower lip. It tingled, swollen from our frantic kissing, and his gaze lingered there like he enjoyed the fact he'd marked me, even if only temporarily.

"Beautiful," he murmured so softly I wondered if he realised he said it out loud. He fingered the curve of my collarbones next, until he caught the gathered shoulders of my gown.

It ached how slowly he eased them outward. My pulse throbbed, counting the moments until at last the dress fell over my arms and the silk pooled at my feet, leaving me in my underwear.

His chest gave a heavy rise and fall as he took me in. His gaze on my breasts might as well have been a touch, furling my nipples tight. "*So* beautiful."

"Please, Bastian." I clenched my hands into fists. "Just take me. This is torture."

One side of his mouth rose in the most diabolical smirk I'd ever seen. "I told you—there is no 'just' for us. And you asked for everything, so..." He spread his hands as though he had no choice but to obey. It tilted the scales between us, shifting power, or at least my perception of where it lay.

Then his hands were on my waist and I forgot about scales

or power or anything other than the heat of his skin sliding down my hips as he pushed my underwear off.

Utterly naked, I stood before him.

He'd seen me before, of course, but... now my heart was bare.

For a moment, my arms tensed, ready to shield myself, an old voice telling me this was wrong that I should be ashamed. *Knees together—you're not a whore.*

But I met Bastian's gaze and my arms eased to my sides.

He looked at me like I mattered. Like I was important—as vital as air, as sacred as a bargain. Like there was nothing in me that ever warranted shame.

"There." He narrowed his eyes and cocked his head. "That —*that* is my ember." He nodded to the bed. "On your knees."

I obeyed, but every ounce of my focus was stolen by him peeling off his shirt, and I found myself staring, biting my lip. Outside, the sun had set and its rays spilled through our windows, edging his muscles and scar with fiery light. It glinted on his piercing, and I reached for his nipple as he approached the bed.

"Uh-uh." He shook his head as a shadow caught my wrists and lifted them above my head. More curled under my thighs and backside, lifting me into the air. He glanced outside as if checking, then nodded to himself. "Sunset."

My poison had reset.

His next touch...

My mouth went dry as, with a gesture he commanded his shadows to spread my legs. They dimpled my thighs, baring me even more thoroughly. If I'd been the old Katherine Ferrers, I might've died of shame or embarrassment, but I wasn't. Not anymore.

This version of me, whoever she was, arched into his

hungry gaze, made powerful by it, and bit her lip waiting as he bent closer, closer, closer.

In one long lick, he cut clean through me, through the world, through the entire fucking universe.

I bucked in his shadows' grip as magic surged between us, from his tongue into me, along every nerve, blazing and beautiful and obliterating.

My cries tore my throat raw as wave upon wave of pleasure broke me, put me back together again, and broke me once more. There was no end to the climax or start to the next, just a rolling, drowning eternity.

When I could open my eyes, he had my thighs over his shoulders, one hand splayed over my belly, and his lips fastened around my bud while his tongue flicked over it.

That was enough to send me over the edge once more—this orgasm not powered by his antidote and my poison coming together, but still sublime.

As I sank from it, he lowered me to the bed and gave a self-satisfied smile. "I've missed that. Sounds like you have too."

What would the guards make of my cries? My cheeks warmed, but before any old voices could whisper in my head, Bastian kissed me, long and deep, and I forgot there was anything outside of these cracked walls.

When he pulled away and unbuckled his belt, I sat on the edge of the bed. At last it was my turn to see him. Somewhere along the way, the sun had set and fae lights drifted through our room, gilding his body. I bit my lip as he unbuttoned his trousers, revealing trimmed, dark hair, and when he lowered them, his cock sprung free, thick and hard already, and—

My eyes widened. "Oh." On the underside, behind the flared head, sat another piercing. A barbell, like his nipple, but instead of small spikes, a steel ball sat at each end. "*Oh.*"

"Is that a good 'oh' or a bad one?" He stroked a hand down his length, pulling back the skin so I could see how the bar pierced a fold of skin Ella had told me was highly responsive.

"More... intrigued. Is it like your nipple—more sensitive?"

"A little. But lovers like it too, especially in certain positions." I could hear the smirk in his voice.

I glanced up at him, one eyebrow raised. "I hope you're about to show me those positions."

He made a low sound as his pupils grew wide.

I had that effect on him. *Me*. Not my weakness or my silence, but my desire and the promise of sharing myself with him. It was powerful.

And maybe *I* was powerful.

Perhaps that was what drove me as, on impulse, I darted forwards and ran my tongue along his underside. Soft, warm skin, followed by the uncompromising hardness of his piercing.

"Fuck," he blurted, grabbing the upper crossbar of the bed like he needed it for balance.

I grinned up at him. My turn to be self-satisfied, especially with his salty taste on my tongue.

Narrowing his eyes, he crowded me. "You need to warn a man before doing something like that." A growl edged his voice.

I blinked, all innocence as he forced me back onto my elbows. "Where would be the fun in that?"

"Wicked Lady, indeed." He kissed me, body pressing mine into the bed.

My heart hammered. Faster. Faster. Faster.

Not with climbing pleasure but with a need to break out from his weight. I screwed my eyes shut and went still, going through the motions of kissing him back. *Keep him happy. It will be over soon. It will be...*

But, no. This wasn't *him*, it was Bastian.

"Stop."

He did. Instantly.

Lifting his weight onto his hands, he widened his eyes. "Kat? Are you all right? I'm sorry, I—"

"Just"—I caught my breath and gave a reassuring smile—"not like that. Not on my back under you."

He eased onto his side, not withdrawing but also not touching, leaving me space. "It can be not at all, if you want. We don't have to do this tonight."

I stood, and I could breathe again. "I want to." With my panic subsiding, the need was still as sharp as it had been moments ago.

"Are you sure? We can just—"

"Shut up and show me, Bastian."

With a low sound of warning, he rose from the bed and strode into me. Without stopping, he lifted me against him, kissing my lips, my jaw, my throat as he carried me across the room, only stopping when my backside landed on a narrow sideboard.

This. *This* was what I wanted.

Legs around him, I kissed the line of his scar and chased the angle we'd found before when fully clothed, letting his cock slide along me and over my clit. As one, we groaned.

He palmed my breasts and nipped at my throat, tangling me in so many sensations it felt like I was losing my mind.

With the scrap of sanity I had left, I trailed my fingertips along the edges of his ears and smiled as his moan hummed over my skin. "Please," I breathed into his ear.

He pulled back and caught my hand, pressing it against the wall. "You're going to finish me before I even begin."

I bit my lip and shifted my other hand to his cheek, enjoying the scrape of stubble over my palm.

He slid along me once more before pulling away. I made a small sound of complaint before he placed his tip at my entrance.

We paused there, chests heaving, eyes locked.

Despite how huge this moment felt, pulling on every strand of my being, for once in my life, I was not afraid.

"Don't close your eyes, Katherine," he murmured. "Keep them on me. This is real. *We* are real. I swear it on all that I am."

Yes. I knew it. Felt it. *Believed* it.

Then, slowly, slowly, he sank into me. Tension thrummed in every inch of his body, a tightness that told me just how much he was holding back, easing the cool ridge of his piercing inside.

Drawing a shaking breath, I savoured the way my body stretched for him. Like the wild drumming of Calan Mai, my pulse pounded in my chest and throat and around his length.

A question raised his eyebrows, and I nodded. I was fine—more than fine. I could take more. With a low groan, he slid that last inch home.

"Bastian." I pressed my forehead to his, catching my breath and adjusting to the sensation—the pleasured fullness that was not quite pain.

"You feel..." He shook his head and kissed me. "Incredible. Impossible."

Gradually, he withdrew, and I whimpered at the contrast of how empty that left me. His piercing sliding out seized my breath, pleasure streaking through me.

He wore a pleased smirk. "You like that?"

I nodded and edged closer, aching to have him back inside me.

"Tell me. I want to hear you."

"I like it. Give me more."

A soft laugh, then his gaze slid to my fingers, which were pale against the dark wall. "Hmm." He nestled at my entrance. "Let go, love." His voice went raw as he thrust into me, faster but shallower this time. "Let go of everything else and just be here with me, now." He gathered my hand and kissed my fingertips. "There is nothing else. Just this. Just us."

I hadn't even realised I'd been holding on until with his next thrust I gave a moaned exhale and the purple stains crept over my fingers. For the first time since waking up in Elfhame, I gave up even trying to hold them back.

"That's it. You can be yourself with me—all of yourself." With another kiss, he drove into me again.

Each time, a little deeper, a little harder—letting me acclimatise, I now understood. The feel of him skimming along my clit, filling me before pulling out again sparked along my nerves. So bright, it was as though part of them had been consumed with trying to control my magic but now they were free.

My body tightened, muscles coiling as they readied for that strike of bliss. I held his shoulders, using them to help me rock with him, chasing his full length with every thrust.

Breathless cries huffed from me with each drive as I spiralled higher and higher.

The way he watched me only heightened every moment as I tried to keep my eyes open for him. He panted now, gripping my thigh as his other hand palmed my breast. "You're perfect, ember. Fucking perfect."

With his praise, I teetered on the edge, barely in control of my body, a shuddering gasp away from breaking on him. It filled my heart, sudden and stunning—after all this time, after everything, we were finally not just fucking, but making love.

Like he knew my thoughts, he nodded and grazed his thumb over my nipple. "Go on, love. Come for me."

I did. Stars above, I did.

Crying out, I surged around him, muscles pulling tight. I tried to keep my eyes open but gods knew if I succeeded, because everything went dark with lights sparking like the entire universe was bursting apart and not only me.

Blinking into the dim room, I sagged against the wall, though some part of me kept my hips rolling with his thrusts, and more pleasure seared through me.

With a dazed smile, he cupped my cheek. "I've wanted to feel that for so long."

"So have I." I wrapped my arms and legs around him more tightly, eager to feel every part, to make us one as thoroughly as I could, and he kissed me, sweet and deep.

But that was the problem.

Gripping his hair, I pulled away. "You're holding back," I huffed with his steady rhythm. "You told me not to, and yet..."

He frowned, slowing.

"Yet you don't hold me down. You haven't dominated me. You've been perfectly sweet. But I don't want perfectly sweet, Bastian. I want *you*."

His throat bobbed as he slid his fingers down my hair and pulled from me. "I didn't want to frighten you."

Of course not—not after how I'd reacted lying beneath him. But that hadn't been about him, just the past. "You could never frighten me." Yet my heart hammered. "What I feel for you—that scares me sometimes, yes, but... not you." I released his hair and cupped his cheeks. "Never you."

He bit his lip, eyebrows tight together. "I thought after your experience before, this would be better."

And I loved him all the more for it.

So I pressed a kiss to his lips and nodded. "You have eased me in beautifully, love. But now I'm ready for my bastard."

He sucked in a breath, gaze skipping to my lips, dick twitching against me. "Say that again. Call me your bastard."

Like in the training yard, but now I understood.

He'd been called bastard like it was the worst thing—the marker of a man who'd never known the one who sired him and who'd killed one of the only fathers he had known. Not a name he deserved, but one he'd been given anyway, and if the way I said it reframed it for him...

"You're my bastard, Bastian. My beautiful fucking bastard. *Mine.* And now I want you to show me everything that means."

He smiled slowly and caught my wrists. "Are you saying you'll obey me?"

A thrill chased through me. "I will."

"What is off the table?"

I swallowed. "Nothing. I said to give me *everything.*"

Grip tightening, he made a low sound that rumbled into me. "I'm not sure you understand all the possibilities, love. There are more than I could fit into this one night. But we can make a start. What will be your code word if you want me to stop?"

It was an easy answer. "Orrery."

He huffed, eyes glinting. "Perfect." Then there was no more amusement, just a glint of a different kind—dangerous and predatory, like when I'd stolen from him.

But I knew him now, and that predation was thrilling rather than frightening.

"Very well. You asked for it." He scooped me over his shoulder and teased between my legs as he carried me to the bed.

My heart hammered in anticipation, and I took advantage of my position to pat his backside.

"You won't touch me without my permission." The warning rumbled through me, another thrill that sent my nerves fluttering.

"But what if I want to touch you?"

He sat me on the bed and stood over me. "Are you going to be disobedient, Katherine?"

With his silver gaze boring into me, insolence suddenly felt a lot less appealing. I wanted to earn his praise... for now, at least. Perhaps I'd push the boundaries another day.

Swallowing, I shook my head.

"*Good*. Now, on your knees, back to me."

I obeyed, pulse kicking up once he was out of sight. The uncertainty of what he would do sent my body into high alert, hairs raised, skin humming in the cool air of our room. I tried to breathe slowly so I could hear his approach, but it was pointless with his fae silence.

At last, the bed dipped behind me, and my breath caught. Then came the heat of his body upon mine and his hard length against my backside. I couldn't help sighing and reaching back for him as he gathered my hair.

"Ah-ah." Shadows slipped around my wrists and bound them before me.

Perhaps it was the long seconds of absence as I'd knelt and waited, but now I was hyper aware of every sensation, his skin upon mine and the way this pose pressed my tits together.

"What did I say?"

"I'm sorry," I breathed as he wrapped my hair around his hand, pulling my head back. "I forgot."

He angled me so he could meet my gaze. "It's all right. I know you *want* to be good. I'll help you." He kissed me then, deeper and more possessive than anything before.

I trembled in his hold, body throbbing with want despite the number of times he'd already pulled me apart. When he cupped my breast and squeezed, I couldn't help moaning, and he consumed every drop of sound like a man dying of thirst.

By the time he pulled away, his breaths heaved, fanning my lips, pressing his chest into my back, and I absorbed it all, skin scorching. The purple stain of my magic covered my fingers entirely now.

Watching, he pinched my nipple, and smiled at the way I arched and whimpered.

"See? You are good—*so good.*"

The words blazed through me, and he touched my cheek as though he could see how much I burned for him.

"Show me how good you can be, my sweet flame." He released my hair and took hold of my hips.

I gasped and arched as his cock slid between my legs.

With a low sound, he tightened his grip and held me exactly as he wanted. "Patience." He laughed softly against my shoulder. "I can see your pulse pounding in your throat. Your whole body is practically vibrating with it. And you're even wetter than before."

"Please, Bastian."

He made a low sound of pleasure. "*There it is.*" He nipped my throat and pressed a palm between my shoulder blades. "Bend over, and I'll give you what you want."

In that moment, I would've done anything. Months ago, I

might've been embarrassed to admit just how needy I was, but that was a different lifetime—a different me.

His shadows pulled my wrists apart and guided them down, snaking up my forearms so I was forced to rest my chest and cheek on the bed. Between his shadows on my arms and his hands on my hips, I could barely move as his cock slid along me and nudged my aching bundle of nerves.

"Lift your hips for me, love." Then, when I obeyed, "That's it."

Only once he had me exactly where he wanted me did he finally take me.

Moaning as the ridge of his piercing slid into my entrance, I managed to arch my back and chase more, but that was the only movement he allowed.

Control. That was his version of safety.

Just like he maintained control of himself and his work because otherwise he thought something bad would happen, he needed control here.

So I let go.

Of control. Of who I'd been taught to be. Of *everything*.

I trusted it all into his hands and shadows.

And, Stars above, was I rewarded.

As he filled me, his cock pressed against my front walls, the same spot he'd crooked his finger and touched before. I cried out, body taut, pulling on his grip as pleasure lanced through me.

Out the corner of my eye, I could see him tower over me, and the flash of his canines as he grinned wickedly. "I promised I'd show you one of those positions, didn't I?"

His piercing. That was what I could feel dragging over the spot as he pulled out.

I didn't know how much more I could take of it without breaking.

Like that wasn't enough, his shadows slid between my legs and throbbed over my clit, pushing me closer.

He stretched and filled me, focusing each thrust over that point inside me until I didn't just let go of control, I lost even the concept of it.

I screamed into the bed, sweat slicking my chest and back as I gripped the sheets with poison-stained hands.

I didn't come, I fractured. With his pounding rhythm, shards became splinters became dust until I was nothing, just motes of awareness as bright and drifting as fae lights.

The world was dark and light and fucking beautiful, but it had no form beyond that.

Time was meaningless.

I had no name.

There was only a relentless pounding and thunderous pleasure.

Dimly, slowly, I came back to what might've been reality, arching into Bastian as much as I could. His movements had shifted—harsher, faster, something feral in the bite of his fingers into my hips. Each breath tore from him on the edge of a moan.

A moment later, he let out a harsh cry and twitched inside me. That twitch and the sudden fullness threw me over the edge once more, and we sank into the mattress together.

I could barely catch my breath as he lay beside me and his shadows released my arms. Huffing, he kissed my shoulder and stroked the hair from my face.

"That... that was..."

How it always should have been.

I trembled as the truth crept over me—not thoughts or words, but something that rooted far deeper.

I *believed*.

Sex wasn't something for shame. It wasn't something horrible where one party used the other. It wasn't something to be done for duty.

It was beautiful. It was pleasure beyond reckoning—beyond containment in a single body.

It was something shared.

"Kat? Love?"

When I touched my face I found it wet. "Why am I crying? That was incredible. I'm sorry... I don't..." I shook my head, staring at the tears glistening on my fingertips.

"Don't you dare apologise," he said, a rawness in his voice as he gathered me close. He nuzzled away my tears. "It can be intense, especially after... everything."

After all I'd known before. I nodded.

This was overwhelm. Utter overwhelm. Of my senses, my body, and perhaps most of all, my heart.

"I'm not sad." I splayed my hand over his chest, fingertip edging his pierced nipple. "Not at all. I don't know if I've ever been so happy."

He kissed the edge of my smile. "Good. Because you did so well."

I exhaled, no energy left to laugh. "I didn't do anything."

"Oh, you did." He carried me from bed towards the bathroom. "You were exactly what I needed—more than I'd imagined, in fact. Now"—he kissed the tip of my nose—"no more arguing. Let me look after you."

Every part of me was heavy, so I sank into his hold as his shadows raced ahead and started the bath running. I must've nodded off, because the next thing I knew, we were lowering into the water together. Its heat and the lavender scent dragged me deeper into drowsiness and softened my aching muscles, turning me into something blissful and liquid while Bastian gently washed me.

Time became a distant concept and I had no idea how long passed with me lounging against his chest before he helped me out.

"Thank you," I managed to mutter as he wrapped towels around us both.

"There's no need to thank me." His face had gone soft, less cutting than usual, but his eyebrows scrunched together as he carried me back into our room.

"But there is." I blinked up at him, eyelids so heavy I could drift off at any moment. "You showed me. I asked and you did. And it was perfect, Bastian." I barely managed to lift my head and skim a kiss over his jaw. "*You* are perfect."

I more felt than heard the sound he made as he lifted his chin. Proud. Happy. I didn't even have the energy to doubt that they were the things I read in him.

He sat in one of the armchairs with me in his lap and called the fire higher as he held me close. The last thing I remembered was his smile lined with orange-pink light and perhaps the words "Sleep, my dear flame, and know how much I love you."

68

KAT

Waking with him was delicious. Slow and warm and safe. We kissed and he pulled me close, and for a while I forgot we were prisoners to a princess who was meant to be dead.

I'd certainly forgotten about that last night.

Nestled into the crook between his arm and body, I ran my fingertip over the steel spikes of his piercing and watched how his nipple hardened in response.

"You are fascinated with that, aren't you?"

I gave him a smirk and grazed his nipple. "I'm fascinated with what it does to you."

A low sound rumbled from his chest into me. "I'm sure I'd be fascinated with what it would do to you. You're already so sensitive. If you got pierced, I think you might explode if I so much as thought of touching you." One canine flashed in a lopsided grin as he traced the lightest line down my back, making me shiver.

I wriggled away, body too sensitised to cope with being

stroked like that. "How long does it take to heal?" I asked as I fished his shirt up from the floor.

Propped on his elbows, he watched me pull it on before pulling me back into his arms and nipping at the peaks of my breasts. "With the right salve and care, not long."

Could I, the terribly proper Lady Katherine as he'd once called me, get mine pierced?

Maybe. At least being in Elfhame had given me the space to be the kind of person who would consider it.

But there were other things in the fae realm less enjoyable. When he lay back, finished with my nipples, I nestled against him and broached the subject of Princess Nyx's death, giving Sura's version of the story. His body grew tight beneath me. "I need to do some research."

See? The princess was wrong about his loyalty to the Night Queen—it wasn't blind. He was going to find the truth.

"Was Sura wearing any unusual jewellery? Could be an artefact we've seen no record of. Or a potion, perhaps. Did you see her drink anything before telling you all that?"

When I looked up, I found him frowning at the canopy over the bed, and my heart sank. "You think she found a way to lie."

"She must've."

Hiding a frown, I padded over to the side table and poured us water from a jug that kept drinks cool and fresh.

When I carried our glasses over over and knelt on the bed to pass his, he tugged on the hem of the shirt. "I missed this."

I made a sound of query as I took a long draught of water.

"I didn't like the reason you were in my suite or how you felt while you were there, but I liked it when you wore my shirts." He gave a crooked smile, then raised his cup as if to hide it. "You always left your scent on them... and on my pillow."

I might've melted into my drink. Certainly, my heart overflowed.

Before I could say anything more, there was a knock at the door. The guards hadn't bothered to knock any other time they'd entered our room—maybe they'd heard enough last night to make them wary.

"Enter," Bastian called, and his wicked smirk should've warned me. But fae reactions were quicker than human ones, and the next thing I knew, he'd kicked off the blankets, revealing his very naked body, and snaked his arm around my waist. Somehow I was straddling him, and only the gods knew how I kept my drink from spilling.

The silver-haired guard entered. She didn't blush, but her gaze trailed over my bare thigh, and she cleared her throat before telling us the princess had requested my company for breakfast.

Bastian grumbled and tugged me against him. "*I* was planning to have you for breakfast."

I lit up at that promise, but reluctantly made myself presentable while the guard hovered in the doorway. Bastian didn't make the slightest bit of effort to cover himself up, and remained sprawled in the bed watching me.

When I ducked to give him a kiss, he grabbed my arm and murmured in my ear, "Be safe, Kat."

"That's grown increasingly hard since meeting you, but I'll try." I flashed him a grin more cocky than I felt and pressed a kiss to his lips before leaving with my escort and manacles.

Last night, I'd let everything free, and now the iron made it as if there was *nothing*. No magic tingling on my skin. Nothing to pull close and tight. No risk of killing anyone or making them suffer that awful pain. Just a sickly feeling in my stomach.

I arrived at the private dining room, finding the princess and the man with celestial tattoos already seated. Unease tickling my spine, I joined them at a setting that included a pair of gloves.

"Let's make a deal." She smiled, but it was as stiff as her back.

"I'm your prisoner." As the guard removed my manacles, I narrowed my eyes. "I'm sure I don't have anything you want."

"You have Bastian."

The tickle became a flood of goosebumps. I wanted to get up and walk out. I wanted to go home—to our rooms in the palace, I realised with a jolt. But these were impossible things right now. There was no escape, only a careful treading through this situation—whatever it was exactly. "You're the one who has him locked up. You don't need any bargain."

"He's pledged his magic to you," the tattooed man spoke up, voice hard and rough like granite, as though it hadn't been used in a long while.

"How did you...?" I huffed, embers lighting in my gut. "That heaviness in the air. You've been reading my thoughts."

Get out. I blasted those embers at him, making them flare His flinching was my reward.

Good. I hoped it hurt. Dipping into my private thoughts— how dare he? They were *mine.* I had been used as a pawn in men's games. My body had been touched and pulled around without my permission. My words had been moulded to serve and please others.

But my mind was my own.

Kaliban had touched it, but only when I'd been thinking so loudly it projected out or when I'd given him permission to remove troubling memories. I'd learned to keep my thoughts much quieter—this fae had gone digging to find them.

"That was a violation." My leather gloves creaked as I fisted my hands tighter and tighter. Now I knew, I pulled tight and made my thoughts spiky—a thorny plant impossible to swallow.

And stay out.

Wincing, he rubbed his forehead and shared a glance with Sura.

She leant forward, interlacing her fingers. "I needed to know if you were open to the truth about my mother or as closed as the Serpent."

"You could've asked," I gritted out.

"And you'd have told me, would you?" She laughed.

Never reveal your heart.

"Probably not. Why?"

"There is something he needs to know. Something he's not ready to hear, but he will be one day—he has to be. I need to plant that information close for when he's ready."

"You want to... tell me something so I can tell him?" It couldn't be that simple.

"It's vital this doesn't fall into the wrong hands. I need to tell you but then lock the memory." She exchanged a look with the tattooed man. "You won't have access to it until certain conditions are met."

I laughed. "You want me to let him poke around in my mind again?" This wasn't the same as Kaliban taking memories I didn't want. I'd helped him when he was at his most vulnerable. He'd worked with my memories to *my* benefit, only asking for errands in return. Over the past months, I'd grown to know him and even like him, despite his gruffness. He had never delved where he wasn't welcome.

Jaw tightening, I stood. "I want breakfast back in my room. We're done here."

She let me reach the door, no doubt feeling safe thanks to our bargain.

"It will save his life."

I stopped, about to turn the handle. "What do you mean?"

"You must know I can't tell you the specifics. But this knowledge... when he has it, it will save his life. And if the wrong people find out, it will end it. That's why I can't risk you revealing it to anyone until the right time... but I also can't risk him never finding out."

I tried to swallow down the thick feeling in my throat like someone's hand was around it. I turned and eyed her a long while. "You're saying he'll die if I don't accept?"

She spread her hands. "I can't know for sure, but it's highly likely."

Shit. She had to know I couldn't risk that.

"And I get to name my terms for this bargain?"

"Within reason."

Right now, there were three things I needed that she could help with. I raised one finger. "You let us go today, unharmed with all our belongings. Two, you give me some charm or object that contains iron."

She narrowed her eyes at me. "To block your... interesting power?" She nodded at my gloved hands. When I clenched my jaw and didn't reply, she rolled her eyes. "I need to know, because if that's your purpose, it needs to fit close to the skin, even if the iron doesn't touch you directly or else it won't work."

I couldn't always keep my cards close to my chest. I nodded.

"I can get something made, but it won't be ready until tomorrow."

"Fine. We leave then. And"—I raised a third finger—"you

give me the guard's insignia patch when she comes back in." I shot the tattooed man a glare. *Stay out. Stay out. Stay out.*

He winced and looked away, giving me space to think.

I'd found her surprise about the Solstice attack convincing —it felt true. If I could compare the patch to the one we'd taken from the dead prisoner, it might help me prove her people really weren't behind the attack. Giving her no warning meant she couldn't doctor one to ensure they wouldn't match.

"If that's what you really want." She cocked her head at me as though hoping for an explanation. When I remained quiet, she shrugged. "Anything else?"

"You have yourself a deal."

We sealed it with the words of power and a gloved handshake.

Then she sent the tattooed man away and sat me down. "Only three people know the hidden truth I'm about to tell you..."

69
BASTIAN

When Kat returned from her meeting with the princess, she looked as pale as I did when I wore the iron manacles and muttered something about a headache. She dropped into bed and slept the rest of the day, waking only when I had the guards bring willowbark tablets. She took them, ate a few mouthfuls of dinner, and went back to sleep.

I, on the other hand, lay in the dark that night, listening to her steady breaths, barely dozing. There was only one outcome of all this: execution. I'd observed the patrol patterns of the guards outside. I knew when ours were due to change. Not tonight, Kat had barely managed to stagger to the bed—she was in no fit state to flee. Tomorrow night.

If I suggested to the princess that there was more I could tell her, she would keep us alive at least that long.

She'd promised her archers would aim for Kat, but they'd have to find her first. My shadows would hide her, and I would shield her.

506

I'd probably have to leave my Shadowblade, but I could get another, albeit with difficulty. I couldn't get another life, and I couldn't get another Kat.

I wouldn't lose perspective on how much she mattered again. I would not be that fool.

When the silver-haired guard brought breakfast, Kat barely ate but insisted she was fine. My lovely liar.

I passed her the small tin of tablets. "You don't need to—"

A pounding knock broke our peace. The guard entered, and as soon as I saw two sets of manacles, my blood turned to ice.

If they were collecting both of us, that had to mean execution.

I swallowed and gave Kat a reassuring smile as I bent my fork's tines and slid it up one sleeve and my knife up the other. Our bargain was not to hurt Sura's people, but I could break the manacles all I liked.

Once they were off and my shadows free... well, *they* and *I* were two different things, weren't they?

The cold shock of iron never grew familiar, and it dragged on me as soon as the manacles closed around my wrists. I hunched over and kept one foot going in front of the other while I focused on getting the fork's tines into the keyhole.

I jostled into Kat like I could barely walk, using the sound to disguise what I was doing.

But iron dragged on my mind and fingers as much as my strength, and by the time we reached the grand double doors we'd visited on that first day, I only had one manacle unlocked. I'd have to do the other one in there and hope Sura didn't realise.

My pulse grew heavier as we entered. She stood before the long table together with the tattooed man who'd been present at some of our meetings. She'd never introduced him and etiquette meant I couldn't ask.

Sura's daughter sat behind the table, hands gripped—maybe she'd never seen an execution before.

Stars above, did she look like her mother, though. And there was something else familiar to her—the golden tone of her hair, a cocky thrust to her chin. It made me think of Dawn, but my mind was too sluggish to pick out an exact person. Sura must've had a lover in Dawn—unusual in itself—but to get pregnant by him...

As I eyed her, the guards brought us to a halt and retreated. Clutching my stomach allowed me to hide the fork and the loose manacle, but if she came too close, she'd spot what I was up to.

"I have made a decision about what to do with you two."

I bowed my head and twisted the fork, searching for the place I needed to catch the mechanism. Thank the gods iron items like this were simply made, since they couldn't be worked with our usual spells and charms to make their locks intricate and impossible to pick. Even at full strength, I'd have been royally screwed, then.

"I've decided to let you go."

I jolted, almost dropping the fork from my iron-clumsy fingers. "What?"

She smiled slowly. "With two conditions, of course."

Eyes narrowing, I stamped down my hope. We had no bargaining chips on our side—not when she held our lives in her hands. "*Of course.*" At my side, Kat was very still.

"You cannot tell the queen that I'm alive, and you allow us to remove your memories of this place." She indicated the tattooed man, who straightened.

The nausea knotting in my stomach doubled. Not telling

Braea, I could understand, but forget all this? Forget me and Kat? The feel of her in my arms, coming on me again and again, and most of all, the fullness—the *wholeness* I'd experienced making love to her.

I'd fucked a lot of people, a lot of times. But this? This had been something else entirely.

Dimly I became aware of Kat stepping forward. "No. That wasn't what we agreed."

I shot her a look. "What you—?"

Her tight jaw and frown silenced me. She'd done some deal. I didn't know whether to shrink with dread or grow with pride.

She lifted her chin, looking taller. "Just the location. That's all you can have."

The tattooed man leant forward and whispered in Sura's ear, and she nodded. "Very well. I'll let you keep the rest. Do you both agree?"

Without iron, I might've done a better job at hiding my relief, but exhausted by its embrace, I sagged. I didn't want to forget a single moment with Kat—not from that night and not from any instant before. Even the worst times—they had led us to this point.

I slid the fork back up my sleeve and nodded.

The guards removed our manacles, and the silver-haired one arched an eyebrow at me when she found one side already unlocked. I shrugged and gave her a half smile, the nausea already fading now the iron had been removed.

The tattooed man started on Kat. Thankfully, they let her sit before he set to work, because she slumped over the table as he did.

"Kat?" I started forward, but she raised a hand, face screwing up.

It was a torturous lifetime watching her endure that. I should've realised he was like my father when Sura brought him in to one of our meetings. She'd given up after that first time and I hadn't seen him again until today. You didn't grow up with a mind-reading parent without learning how to shield your thoughts while in hostile territory.

When it was my turn, I understood the look on Kat's face. The tattooed man's magic was nothing like *Athair's*. A wire brush scoured my mind, erasing the path we'd taken to get here as well as the Lady of the Lake's description of where to go to find our answers... and my salvation.

I clung to that word as he took away the rest. Sura hadn't brought me salvation but Kat... maybe she had. Maybe my love for her would be enough when weighed against all my wrongs.

After, my head didn't ache but *stung*. His work was clumsy and brutal—all raw ability as opposed to honed skill like my father. Sura had to only be using him because she had no choice. This kind of magic was a rarity.

"And the other part of our deal." Sura took a small box from the table, nose wrinkling as soon as she closed her hand around it.

Kat opened it, revealing a plain ring. She glanced to one side, not quite at me.

"It's as you asked," Sura went on. "Encased in silver."

"Iron," I breathed. From a foot away, I couldn't feel it, but it would explain the look of discomfort on the princess's face and the one of relief Kat wore as she slid it on her finger.

Seeing it, I couldn't even be angry. I'd heard her whimpering through nightmares since poisoning those people.

As Sura led us through the half-ruined palace, I gritted my teeth and told myself that this ring was only a temporary measure. For now, Kat needed the reassurance, but given time the fear would fade and she'd let me teach her how to use her magic safely.

With the iron gone, I could think straight, and a horrible realisation came to me. This was too easy. Sura could've driven a much harder bargain in exchange for our survival. "Why are you really letting us go?"

"I have my reasons."

"*What* reasons?"

She huffed and rolled her eyes. "You really can't just accept your good fortune, can you? Fine. The queen will come for us if we kill her Shadow, so it's in my best interests not to do so. My forces aren't ready to face hers. Not yet."

It still felt wrong, though. Unless she was using us. The tattooed man could've planted something as he'd wiped our memories.

I walked on as though I accepted her answer, but I felt around in my mind. Nothing *felt* off, just the missing space about this location.

Before they took us outside, they blindfolded us so we wouldn't be able to see any landmarks.

"Your stags are here," Sura told us. "We've healed them and fed them well. Your belongings are all packed too, including your *interesting* weapons."

I could practically feel her look. A Shadowblade that shouldn't be in this realm, and a bow made from the Great Yew. A bow that practically sang when it was in Kat's hand.

"My people won't bother you on your journey. But we will see each other again, Bastian. I hope when we do, you choose the right side."

"I already have," I ground out. Even now, she was trying to persuade me to turn against Braea. Had she succeeded with Kat? Had the tattooed man done something to her mind? She wasn't familiar with mind magic. She wouldn't realise, and there was nothing I could do. It wasn't as though my father would help check her over.

Close by, she scoffed and I heard the pat on my stag's shoulder. I squeezed the reins, jaw clenched so hard it hurt. To sit here powerless... it grated on my bones.

"Even if you don't choose me, remember what happened last time you took my head."

I grunted. "You grew another." Her daughter. No wonder she'd chosen the hydra as her sigil.

"Remember that. If you kill me next time, there will still be more."

Then there was a flurry of movement with hooves crunching over gravel.

"What did you agree with her?" I asked Kat as Sura's people led us ahead.

"To tell her what I knew about the Circle of Ash in exchange for letting us go free."

My brow furrowed against the blindfold. "*What?*"

"It's not like we know much, is it? I let her believe it was more so she'd think it was worth our lives."

I huffed through my nose. "That's... genius, actually. I should probably be scared by how well you've taken to fae intrigue."

Instead of laughing, she gave a soft grunt. The sound echoed in me, troubling as we rode away.

70
KAT

The journey back to Tenebris-Luminis felt like slowly waking from a dream. For the first day, my head was hazy and sore, and the world seemed distant. The lack of magic humming against my skin heightened the effect that I was someone else merely watching this woman called Kat.

When we stopped at an inn that night, I had a vague plan to lose myself in Bastian, but by the time I reached the bed, my headache had become so intense it was as though something was growing inside my skull, so big it threatened to burst out.

I caught him giving me sidelong looks as we rode the next day. He was worried about me, and mentioned something about the iron only being a temporary solution. But it took all my energy to stay on my stag and keep my eyes open. Perhaps my deal had been a bad idea. Perhaps the iron was, too. What information had they planted in my mind?

But the third day was better, and we managed to chat as

we rode, and that night I lost myself in him over and over until I couldn't even think about moving.

By the time Tenebris's walls came in sight, smoky and dark, I felt mostly normal, save for the iron. I had a faint worry that faced with so many people and the judgement of two courts, Bastian might regret what had happened between us. But wasn't worry standard?

As we entered the gates, nodding to Dusk's guards, he rode just as close to me as on the road, knee brushing mine. Maybe I had nothing to worry about.

We left our stags with the stable hands, and I ran to Vespera. Wearing the iron ring, I could finally enter the enclosure that had been set up for her. She bounded over, chuffing in greeting, and butted her great head into me.

I didn't have to push her away, and at last, I hugged her.

I buried my face in her neck and took in the deepest breath of the dry, musky scent of cat fur, while she rumbled in a purr so deep it thrummed through my entire body like the strongest magic.

When I finally pulled back, Bastian was right there. Smiling, he scratched Vespera under her chin and swept a stream of tears from my cheek with his other hand. "I think she needed that as much as you did." Then he dipped close and planted a kiss on my lips.

I pulled back, blinking. "People will see."

His smile became a wicked grin. "I'll fuck you in front of them all if I have to—if you'll let me."

The image of Caelus watching me ride Bastian's hand burned into my mind, making every inch of me flush as hot as any brand.

While I tried to regain control of my racing pulse, I fussed Vespera some more, then we headed to the grand hall.

"Or," he said, bending close, "I'll settle for having you in nothing but those boots tonight."

I bit back a laugh and lengthened my stride, suddenly keen to get back to our rooms. I really had nothing to worry about.

Oh, how the world must've laughed at that thought, because as we entered the grand hall, a pair of faces awaited me that I'd forgotten to look for.

The red hair caught my eye first. I followed it. Blinked.

My stomach fell through the floor, and the pulse in my ears became a close roar.

Uncle Rufus.

And at his side, bland, hateful face pinched, was Robin.

I must've stopped, because Bastian turned, a few steps ahead. "Kat? What's...?"

He followed my gaze.

I couldn't move, especially not as Robin's gaze landed on me and he nudged Rufus.

With both of them looking my way, an entire world hit me, as cold and solid as ice.

Sit straight.

Knees together—you're not a whore.

You need to learn.

Keep still.

Bastian's lips moved, but I couldn't hear what he was saying.

They started towards us, and it was like the rest of the pillared room drifted further away.

How? *How?*

I thought I'd left them in Albion. Last I'd heard, Robin had fucked off on more of his travels, and Bastian had warned Rufus off so thoroughly, I'd barely seen a strand of his red hair since the night he'd tried to force me to Caelus's rooms.

515

No. *No.* I clenched my hands into fists and pulled on that word. *No.*

I seized my anger and breathed life into its embers.

Because I was not the woman they and my father had squashed into a mould. I was not quiet and meek and mild.

I was fucking furious.

Maybe I didn't know everything about who Kat Ferrers was, but I knew that much.

With a pop, my hearing cleared.

"—here with you," Bastian said, voice low and vicious. "No matter what, they can't hurt you."

It was a triumph to see Robin's step falter as he met my glare. Uncle Rufus wasn't the slightest bit affected. I'd take one out of two.

With fire racing through my veins, I could take in the rest of the room, and I blinked when I saw Prince Cyrus at Uncle Rufus's side.

I bit my tongue against asking what the fuck they wanted —didn't seem wise with a prince right there.

Cyrus gave Bastian a wide, wide smile, the kind that I imagined the Big Bad Wolf giving Little Red Riding Hood right before he ate her. "Throne room. Now."

We were past sunset, so the summons had to be from the queen.

The queen who'd murdered her own daughter.

"Your Majesty, this is the fae who stole my wife."

"What?" I blinked from Robin to the Night Queen, then glanced back at the throne room's main doors, wishing I could escape through them back to Dusk. "Your Majesty, that is *not* what happened. I'm a person, not a fu—"

I clamped my teeth around my tongue and cleared my throat. "I'm a person, not an object." I shot Robin a sweet smile. "I can't be stolen."

Fingers biting into the Moon Throne's arm, the queen sat rigid, but it wasn't me she was looking at—it was Bastian.

And that look could've killed a mammoth at fifty paces.

Up on the dais, framed by the gilded and silvered doors only she and the king used, she looked every inch the ancient monarch she was. Dangerous and dazzling.

It cooled my anger, letting fear smother me.

"A woman can't be taken away from her husband, though, can she?" Uncle Rufus stepped forward, and I refused to look directly at him, even as I tugged the collar of my coat. "Or so His Highness led me to believe."

"His Highness is, of course, right." The queen gave him a rictus smile, and I could see all the ways in which she wanted to rip him or anyone else apart right now. "Do you have anything to say for yourself, Bastian? Any defence for breaking our laws and coming between husband and wife by bringing her across the border?"

"I brought her here." He slid his hands into his pockets, but I spotted them fisting on the way in. His shadows kept close, rippling like a pool full of eels, agitated and ready to break free.

"Approach," the queen barked, and her glare snapped to me. "*Both* of you."

We obeyed. Of course we obeyed—she was a fucking queen.

"What the hells were you thinking?" she hissed at Bastian. "How could you be so foolish to leave yourself open like this? You're lucky you got back after nightfall, but with Cyrus involved, you know I have to punish you." She sat back, waiting for his response.

He gave none.

"Do you understand, Bastian?" She bared her teeth. "The rumours about the two of you are one thing, but bringing her here without his permission?"

It took every scrap of control not to blurt that I shouldn't need my husband's permission—or anyone's—to come to another country. When had I ever given permission for his travels around the continent?

It wouldn't help. From my understanding of fae law, permission wasn't required because I was a woman and he a man, but because we were married.

I swallowed back my anger and fear, which had merged into something lukewarm and sickly, and tried to summon an ounce of reason. "He gave permission." I glanced at Bastian who stared straight ahead. "Bastian told me."

"Is that right?"

He took a long time working his jaw side to side, his nostrils flaring. "We made a bargain."

I shot him a look. He hadn't told me that part. So Robin viewed me surviving as a thing that helped him. He had some plan for me.

The queen cleared her throat and straightened. "I understand a bargain was made." She narrowed her eyes at Robin.

But it was Uncle Rufus who scoffed and stepped forward. "Under what terms? My nephew-in-law is no foolish girl to go making bargains with fae."

"We had no bargain." Robin folded his arms. "I spoke no words of power. I didn't shake his hand."

"Did you?" The queen raised an eyebrow at Bastian.

"No."

She blasted a sigh. "Then I have no choice but to decide your punishment."

"The rules are clear," Cyrus said with a lilt that told me he would enjoy Bastian's punishment.

"But if he hadn't brought me here, I'd be dead." I stared from the queen to Cyrus.

"Your Majesty," came a voice from the back of the room. "*Cousin.*" In the doorway that led to Dusk, Asher bowed before approaching. "Technically, there would still be a bargain if both parties received the agreed upon benefit." He raised his eyebrows at Bastian, prompting.

Bastian remained silent, giving the slightest shake of his head.

"That is true." The queen inclined her head, expression easing a touch. "What did you give her husband in return?"

I frowned up at him. He hadn't mentioned any exchange. Asher was clutching at straws and, from the look on Bastian's face, coming up empty handed.

Did this mean I'd be sent back to Albion? My antidote and cure—they couldn't send me back knowing it would kill me. Surely—*surely* that was worse than breaking the contract between me and that man.

As if he felt my hatred, Robin shuffled and scowled at the floor.

"*Bastian,*" Asher said from between gritted teeth, eyes widening.

Bastian lifted his chin, though his gaze remained downcast. "I wanted to bring her here, and I did."

A growl laced the queen's breath out, and Cyrus wore that awful smile again.

My pulse thundered like the stags' galloping hooves as we'd tried to escape the Ascendants. We'd survived them and finally got past every bastard thing that had kept us apart for so long, only to now be divided by this.

This.

I wanted to scream.

"Bastian paid him."

Every pair of eyes in the throne room turned to Asher.

I blinked. "Paid?"

"No," Bastian rasped. "Don't—"

"If you won't defend yourself, I will." Asher lifted one hand. "Bastian wanted to bring her here. The husband refused." He shot Robin a look as he raised his other hand in balance. "Then he demanded a large sum of money, which Bastian paid. Both sides of the bargain were fulfilled."

"*You...*" I stared at Robin, mouth hanging open. "You demanded payment before you'd let him bring me here *to save my life.*"

He didn't even have to good grace to look at me.

So much for ninety-five percent arsehole.

How had I ever believed anything else?

"I'm sorry," Bastian murmured, bending close despite the glares. "I didn't tell you because I didn't want you to feel like an object bought and sold."

Trying to protect me. Of course. "I know *you* don't think that."

Robin spluttered. "But we didn't shake hands. I didn't say the words." He stared from the queen to Cyrus. "You said it only counted if I made a bargain."

"As Asher says, you received your *payment*." Cyrus spread his hands, though his lip curled like even he found the idea distasteful. With a momentary wince, he turned to the queen. "Your Majesty, I am satisfied the human is here legally."

She exhaled. "Agreed."

"Although"—the edge of a smile curved the prince's mouth—"I'm sure you'll agree he should be allowed to see his wife at will."

A beat of calculating silence, then the queen countered, "And I'm sure you'll agree he should be accompanied by guards as he travels through our side of the palace."

He bowed his head. "Of course."

"Now, leave us." She beckoned Bastian closer. "I need a word with my Shadow."

I didn't know whether to be furious, relieved, or something else as we started towards the twinned main doors. My body settled on a heavy emptiness.

As Asher stepped through Dusk's door, a hand closed around my arm. Uncle Rufus stood over me.

I stilled, though my heart pounded.

He smiled, fingers biting in. "Have you forgotten about duty, my girl? He is your husband and you still owe him a child."

After everything, *I* owed *him*? I bit the inside of my cheek, afraid the words would snap out.

"Remember, family is the most important thing. There are many, *many* opportunities here for us. With you in Dusk and me in Dawn..." He raised his eyebrows as he squeezed so tight, I knew there would be marks when I removed my shirt. "You're a clever girl to get yourself involved with the man in charge."

Of course. He saw Bastian and the Night Queen yet only saw the man. The queen was nothing more than a figurehead to him.

And, *of course*, he expected his niece to do his bidding.

I tried to ease my arm from his grip. If Bastian saw...

"Let me go," I whispered, glancing back at Bastian who was in an intense conversation with the queen.

Uncle Rufus followed my gaze, then yanked me close. "I'm here as the prince's guest. Your friend can't touch me." He thrust me away.

I hated him for being right.

As I stumbled towards Dusk's door, he gave me an unpleasant smile. "Enjoy warming his bed; just remember where your loyalties lie."

Oh, I new exactly where my loyalties lay. Not with him.

71

KAT

I thought taking Bastian up on his offer with the boots would help me sleep.

I was wrong.

As much as I lost myself in the moment, afterwards I lay in the dark thinking about the fact Uncle Rufus was in this building, the other side of a thin, thin veil. He could even be in this same room on Dawn's side of the palace.

What had become a sanctuary, he and Robin had now made unsafe. I hated them for it. Hated the world for their existence. And hated myself for allowing them to break all I'd built up.

Come morning, Bastian pressed a familiar sphere into my hand. "I was meaning to give this back to you, permanently. Now seems like the right time." He slid my thumb along the chain. "Remember."

Gripping the orrery, I drew a shaky breath. "This is real."

He nodded and left me in his bed with a kiss and the promise that he'd dig into how Rufus and Robin had managed to weasel their way here. "Get some sleep," he ordered before leaving for work, ready to write a report on our trip for the queen.

For once, I didn't obey.

I couldn't. Not with the feel of Rufus's fingers biting into my arm and the stuttering images of *that night* coming to mind. When I thought I spotted Dia's skeleton in a dark corner of the room, I dragged myself from bed. Not even the rich red roses in my room could make me smile. Without bathing, I dressed and headed out. The guards went to fetch Rose to accompany me, but I told them I was going to visit Vespera.

Which I did. But then I went into the city. It was still wintry, the air crisp, but snowdrops bloomed in gardens and the sky was clear. The sun made me glad that I didn't have to bundle myself up so fully. I left off my gloves and kept my coat unbuttoned, enjoying the chill breathing through my shirt.

I picked up supplies on my way and stopped on Kaliban's doorstep with a basket laden with food.

"Where have you been?" was his only greeting.

"Oh, you know how it is." I shrugged as I entered. "Quests for the queen, getting captured by enemies. That sort of thing."

He shut the door behind me and narrowed his eyes. "You're not even joking."

I started putting the food away—by now I knew where everything went. "Is there any point in trying to keep things from you when you can dip into my thoughts?"

"You know I don't—"

"I know. But... my request today would've taken us in that direction, anyway." I took a long while arranging potatoes in their basket. "Can you erase *any* memory? Even old ones?" I'd planned to get rid of the sight of all those people in pain because of my poison, but if he could dig further back...

Being unable to remember that night had been uncomfortable, especially as shards pushed through into my thoughts at odd times, like at Lara's funeral.

But, really, remembering had been the worst part. Those shards and then the eventual crash of it all coming together as he'd held my throat in the corridor. That was what had almost destroyed me.

If Kaliban took that memory, wouldn't it be better? No shards could poke into my consciousness—he'd make sure they were erased rather than only buried.

And I wouldn't have that uncertainty—I'd *know* there was something bad I'd chosen to rid myself of.

It might leave me less afraid of Uncle Rufus.

So I held my breath and waited for Kaliban to answer.

"Older memories are harder. They tend to be more thoroughly integrated in thought patterns and behaviours, with more memory echoes—times you've thought about the memory. Essentially, they're integrated with who you are. But I can take a look."

I bit my lip as a flood of unshed tears blurred my vision. A life without that memory. Without the constant fucking fear.

Wouldn't I be stronger, then? I could face Uncle Rufus and tell him all the things I thought. I'd be free of his terrible lessons.

I'd be free to be myself.

"I have to warn you, though..." His hesitance filled the room, and I blinked away my tears. "I'd have to poke into your mind more thoroughly. I might see things you don't want me to."

I put away the bread and straightened. "Even if I really focus on it?"

"Hmm." He tilted his head side to side. "With the strength of your thoughts, perhaps."

Bastian had warned me about trusting people here, but Kaliban had become a friend. Any time he'd erased my memories of Elthea's treatments, he could've taken advantage and pushed further into my mind. Yet he hadn't.

He eyed the empty basket. "You brought a lot of food today. It's a heavy memory, isn't it?"

The way his expression softened as he turned his attention to me threatened to bring back the tears. I bit my lip and nodded.

"The choice is yours." He gestured to the chairs at the kitchen table where he did his work.

A life free of fear. Or at least, the fear of that night and my uncle.

I sat and eased the slightly tight ring off my finger, breathing a sigh as the sickly discomfort faded. My relief was short lived though, as I forced my thoughts to Dia and Fantôme's open grave and the night sky above.

As Kaliban stepped behind me, my heart sped, getting louder and louder.

Soil spilling on me. The cold dampness seeping through my nightgown. The desperate need to keep still.

My breaths tried to gasp in and in and in, but I caught myself, and, gripping the table's edge, I counted in for five and out for six, like Bastian had showed me.

In. Slowly. *You're not there. You're just thinking about it.*

Out. Fully. *You'll be rid of it soon. You'll be free soon.*

"Good gods." Eyes round, Kaliban flopped into the seat by mine. "What the hells happened? Who's been in there?"

"My uncle, he—"

"I don't mean the memory..." Eyelids fluttering, he shook

his head. "That's horrible, yes, but... I mean who's been fucking around in there?" He tapped his temple.

The tattooed fae. I seized the thought before it grew too loud and broke the bargain we'd made. "Our captor would only let us leave if they erased our memory of the location."

He grunted and rubbed his face as if weary. "Holes everywhere. And something with a trigger. A butcher would've left less mess. I can't do anything."

The memory with Uncle Rufus was too ingrained, and made worse by my deal with Sura. Shit. "Fine," I sighed. "Thank you for trying. I... I hurt—killed some people with my poison." I examined my fingers and the stain spreading over them now there was no iron blocking my magic. "Can you take away that memory instead?"

"Katherine." He leant forward, forcing eye contact. "I don't think you understand—I can't take anything. Not anymore."

A chill crept over me like the soil from that night. "What do you mean?"

"Whatever they did, it was brutal. A botch job. They've left so many holes—if I alter a single thing, your mind could collapse."

"You're speaking like my mind is a structure. But this isn't a broken bone in danger of crumbling apart. These are only my thoughts."

"Considering how strong your thoughts are, I didn't expect to hear you calling them 'only' anything." His brow tightened, and a knot tied in my stomach at his disapproval. "Your mind *is* a structure. Just because it isn't a physical one doesn't make it any less real. Your mind can be injured or sick, the same as your body. You've been getting headaches since this was done, haven't you?"

Bile licked the back of my throat. I swallowed it down and nodded in silence.

"Your mind is who you are. If it collapses, you will lose yourself. Your fear and courage. Your humour and kindness. Your loyalty and determination. Everything you love, and everything you hate. They are 'only' thoughts, and yet..."

And yet those things *were* me.

Even the fear.

Especially the fear.

Wasn't that the thing that had made me all the more determined to keep Ella safe from unCavendish? Wasn't that what had driven me to ride at night as the Wicked Lady? And weren't those the nights I'd felt most free?

I rubbed my chest. Maybe I did know Katherine Ferrers far better than I thought.

"I understand."

In truth, I'd never understood anything about myself so well until that moment.

72

KAT

Over the following days, the queen kept Bastian busy with work. He told me it was because of the coming wedding and the fact he'd been away, so she needed him all the more. After using Princess Nyx's death as a warning, I suspected it was because he'd been away *with me*.

Though he did find out how Rufus and Robin had secured permission to come to Elfhame. As Caelus had said, Uncle Rufus had told anyone who would listen that I, the woman who had saved Albion from war, was his niece. It was only a short step from there to worming his way into the good graces of Queen Elizabeth herself.

So when she had to choose people for her diplomatic mission to Elfhame, my devious uncle was an obvious choice. Then, cut off from credit, Robin had caught wind of opportunity.

What a pair of fucking vultures, feeding off anything I left.

It felt like they were feeding off *me*.

Other than taking Vespera for a ride with Rose, I kept to our rooms and tried to lose myself in research and, when that didn't work, in a bottle. With the iron ring, the magical effects of fae drink didn't affect me, but the regular alcohol Bastian kept in his rooms was intoxicating once more. I even managed to sleep without any nightmares about poisoning people, so the iron was doing the trick.

But one morning, Bastian made time to have breakfast with me. I should've known it wouldn't only be breakfast.

"Hold this." He passed me an apple as we ate.

"You... could just put it on the table or your plate, you know." I raised an eyebrow at the fruit's bright red skin.

"Indulge me." He narrowed his eyes, a hair's breadth from rolling them.

I huffed and held it up, waving it side to side to show my obedience.

"As tight as you can." He nodded at my plate. "You can continue eating—this is going to take a while."

I screwed up my face, trying to decipher what this was about, but he gave no further explanation, so I gripped as hard as I could and speared a mushroom with my fork.

"*Good.*" He gave me a half smile, knowing what that tone of voice did to me. "I promise this has a purpose."

"I'm dying to hear it."

"I said I'd help you with your magic, didn't I?"

I went still, clenching my jaw. This wasn't something I had to worry about anymore.

"When you weren't wearing that thing, you could feel it, right?"

Slowly, I nodded and glanced at the apple. "The Lady of the Lake said I held on too tight. I did hear her, and I tried letting

530

go. It got a lot of people killed." I frowned at him. "Why does this feel like a trap?"

"It isn't, Kat. I just... I want you to understand what you can do—how it works. And *why*." He peered at me over his coffee cup, a plea in his eyes.

When I said nothing, he took a sip and went on. "Magic is everywhere, but most people—fae and humans with gifts—they can only feel the magic that's inside them."

Like Rose had described when she'd tried to teach me. She'd spoken of reaching inside.

"But we can feel what's *around* us. Think of it as tethered and untethered. Enchanted objects and people—their magic is closely tethered. That's why Horrors have to go right up to them to feed."

I grimaced at the memory of Horrors feeding on people in the city streets.

"Remember the apple."

I sighed and re-focused my grip.

"On the other hand, animals and plants vary depending on their age and intelligence—their will."

"The Great Yew—I'm guessing that's tightly tethered."

"Exactly. While the magic of the land is untethered. It's the easiest thing for us to draw upon, just as it's easiest to Horrors to feed upon."

"So... unseelie draw on magic and Horrors feed upon it."

"Hmm." He nodded and something flickered over his expression before he took a long draught of his coffee.

I thought of the monsters' void black eyes and the void blade of his unseelie sword. "Have you ever thought about the similarity between them and unseelie powers before?"

He exhaled through his nose, tension twitching around his eyes. "I have. Often." He dragged his gaze up from the table to me. "I suspect Horrors came from the Underworld, the same as unseelie. Or that unseelie magic was used to create them. But it was so long ago and their creators or summoners were all executed after the war. There's no way to know."

And, through him, I had something in common with those monsters. Until I was cured, at least.

"I think that's long enough. You can put the apple down." He fetched a thick book off the shelf and brought it over. "Now, hold this, your hand at the top, the book beneath."

My forearm ached as I placed the apple on my plate and turned my chair from the table. When I tried to take the book, it only stayed there a moment before slipping from my grasp.

Crouching, he caught it. "The tighter the grip, the sooner it breaks."

I half groaned, flexing my stiff fingers. "And there's the lesson."

"I told you there was a purpose." He sank to his knees before me. "I think this is what the Lady of Lake was getting at. You hold on to the magic near you, even when you don't realise. But you need to let it flow through and around you, like you're directing water rather than trying to hold it."

"Look, I appreciate you trying to help me, but this isn't going to matter soon."

"Your cure," he murmured, gaze dropping to my lap.

Silence washed over us for long seconds.

"Well, just in case it doesn't work or you decide to take off that iron ring other than when you sleep..." He gave me a quick smile and squeezed the fingers of my other hand. "Letting go is an important part of holding on. It's something my father taught me when I was learning to control my magic."

"And when do *you* let go?"

He pulled away slightly, but I kept hold of him. "I've been doing this a long time."

"*When?*"

He took a long breath as though he needed to steel himself to go on. "In small pleasures... and recently, in greater ones." One corner of his mouth rose.

"You mean beauty and sex?" I frowned. "But you're so... in control."

"I create parameters that mean I can let go."

The way he'd slammed into me after I'd asked him to give me everything. He'd only allowed it once I was held down by his shadows. Hadn't I thought before that control was his form of safety?

"I'm glad it works for you. And I'm exceedingly glad that I can help with your magical control." I kissed him, pulling back when he tried to deepen it, though the heat in me wanted to answer in kind. "Ari's coming before she opens the shop."

He sighed and glanced at the orrery, thumbs tracing circles on my thighs. "And I should get to work." Yet he didn't make any move towards leaving.

I gathered his hands and pushed them away but couldn't resist planting a quick kiss on his brow. "You should."

WITH GREAT FORCE OF WILL, we got him out the door just as Ariadne arrived. She gasped when I grabbed her for a hug.

"But... your poison?"

"Iron." I held up my hand and showed her the ring, smiling despite the queasiness that came after I ate while wearing it. If it wasn't the iron making me feel faintly ill, it was the poison. At least this way, I didn't risk killing anyone by accident.

"Oh!" She pulled me into another hug, squeezing hard. "Need to make up for all the times we haven't been able to."

I laughed, and when we finally broke apart, I took her to the sitting room and showed her the insignia Sura had given me. "I was hoping you could tell me something about this."

She bent over, examining it.

As the silence wore on, I fidgeted. Ari had seen the one from the Solstice attack, but Bastian had it locked away with his evidence. "I can get hold of the other one I showed you before, if you want to compare them more—

"No need." She shook her head, flipping the patch over and checking the back. "The differences are stark. The style— they're by different hands, which isn't a surprise." She shrugged. "If you needed lots of these, they wouldn't all be sewn by the same person. Your fingers would drop off, even with a thimble." She flashed me a grin.

"So... they're different, but that's explainable?"

"Yes... and no." A crease pinched between her brows as she held it out and pointed to the hydra's golden eyes. "The gold-work on this one is only on the eyes, but the other one. I remember it clearly, because the thread is so unusual. I've never seen anything like it. Two-ply..." She glanced up. "Sorry, I'm not sure how much you know about sewing..."

"Only enough to make exceptionally mediocre repairs."

She snorted and went on, "Well, a two-ply thread is one made up of two yarns. In the case of the other insignia you showed me, one scarlet thread and one gold. Real gold, too— high content."

"Sounds expensive."

"It is. A length of that probably could've paid my rent for months back in Briarbridge."

It probably could've gone a good way towards clearing Robin's debts.

"Anyway, this..." She tilted the patch so the goldwork glinted in the light. "This is standard crimson thread for the hydra and gold for the eyes. To my mind, the stitch difference makes sense, but the colours..." The crease between her eyebrows deepened.

"What are you saying?"

"These weren't just sewn by different hands but... for different people. Do you think if Bastian asked for crimson like this, he'd be happy with that other insignia? It was almost vermillion, for goodness' sake." She snorted, shaking her head.

I sat back. I'd never seen Ari so animated.

Yet... I could understand. The black and charcoal serpents on Bastian's clothing were always perfect—the difference in their shades just enough to show the intricate embroidery. Dawn's guards wore pale, pale grey, while the Kingsguard wore pure white. Dusk's had that deep blue-black, differentiating them from the Queensguard's black.

Subtlety in colour mattered to fae.

"The scarlet and gold thread might as well be yellow—that's how different it is from this." I held up the insignia.

Ari gave a single nod. "Exactly."

I thanked her, and we drank tea and chatted before she had to go and open her atelier. I couldn't tell if I made good company, not when my thoughts snagged on the idea that we had two versions of Hydra Ascendant, a real one and a false one.

That evening I showed Bastian and explained what Ariadne had told me. He peered at the patch a long while, a deep frown furrowing his brow.

"I'll look into it," he muttered before tucking it into his pocket, though he sounded unconvinced.

It was better than nothing. Once he saw them side by side, he'd have to realise the truth. Sura was not behind the Solstice attack.

73

KAT

"And here you are undoing all my hard work." A few days after Ari's visit, Ella stood in the doorway, arms folded, one eyebrow arched at the (very full) glass of brandy.

I gave her a rueful smile as Urien carried in a chest I recognised—the one that contained all her beauty concoctions.

Once he'd left, I shrugged. "It's only a little bit."

"Yes, but the night is only young." She sighed and plopped onto the settee beside me. "And I know you intend to polish off at least half of that bottle."

I grumbled and tucked my notes into the research book I'd brought back from the library. I wasn't fae, but I didn't *like* lying to Ella.

She slid me a sidelong glance as she pulled bottles and jars from the chest together with a small paper-wrapped box. "At least you're not denying it, even if you are denying everything else."

"*Oof.*" I clutched my chest like she'd landed a wound there. "I wish you'd tell me what you *really* think, Ella."

She shot me a wicked grin and I knew I'd made a mistake. "Your wish is my command."

I groaned and opened my mouth to argue, but she seized the opportunity to pop in a chocolate truffle and silence me.

When silence tasted of chocolate, I didn't mind it as much.

"There. No denial while you're eating that." She dusted off her hands and passed me a bottle of hair oil. "Have you noticed your hair getting thicker and shinier since being here?" She ran her fingers through hers.

I nodded and made a noise around the rich mouthful of truffle. "Ari said it's the food," I managed once I'd swallowed. "So what am I denying?"

"Gods, where do I begin?" She flashed me a grin before taking a bite from one of the truffles. "Your magic, for one thing. Though I'll give you credit that you're no longer denying your feelings for the delectable Bastian Marwood."

I'd filled her in on all that had happened while we'd been away, and she'd taken it all in, open-mouthed. When I'd hinted about Bastian's piercing, she'd squealed.

"Thanks so much," I muttered, reaching for the bottle to top up my glass.

Ella's teasing grin faded as she moved it to the other end of the table. "And that's the other thing." She flicked her fingernail against the glass and it let out a dull chime. "In fact, I think they're all related."

"And I must be psychic, because I have a strong sense that you're about to explain your master theory." I scowled and downed what was left in my glass—I was going to need it to get through this.

"Ah, ah, ah." She tapped the spot between her eyebrows. "Wrinkles, remember."

I narrowed my eyes. "*Ella*."

She huffed a sigh and discarded the box of chocolates. "I wasn't going to bring this up until later, but if you insist." She shrugged, then curled her legs under herself so she was focused fully on me. "I know finding *them* here when you got back has shaken you. And I know you're trying to numb your fears and some horrible memories."

I had to look away. I didn't have to tell Ella my heart: she saw it. The fact brought a little flutter of panic to my chest.

"But you can't choose what you numb. If you're deadened, you lose the good and the bad. Numbness doesn't help. It's just a temporary escape."

What other kind was there? Despite all my attempts, I certainly hadn't found a permanent one.

I picked at my nails and tried to swallow down that fluttering feeling as it rose into my throat.

"You heard what the Lady of the Lake said." She covered my hands, stopping me from pulling my cuticles apart. Her warmth was like the first sip of brandy after a night riding through the cold. "You tried holding on to control all the time and that didn't work. And letting go entirely when you were attacked... Well, you said that frightened you because you couldn't stop."

I shivered, pushing away the image of the bodies—the pain on those people's faces.

"What if the middle is what's needed?" She widened her eyes at me. "I think that's what she meant: you need to give up control sometimes to be able to keep it at others. Time where your magic is free. Time being yourself. Sitting with your thoughts and feelings rather than regulating them for other people. Time fucking the brains out of Bastian Marwood."

"I let go." I frowned at her perfect fingers squeezing around mine. "That's exactly what the drink is for."

"No. Drink isn't for ceding control—it's for running away. Drink lets you pretend there's nothing to let go of."

A low sound escaped me. No playful clutch of the chest required this time. She'd landed a direct hit.

If I felt it so deeply, it had true. And I didn't want it to be.

Drink was an old friend—an older one than Ella. It had comforted me in the early days of my marriage when I'd discovered just how disappointing every aspect of married life truly was. It had kept me warm in the bitter winters. And it had pushed away the darkness that had threatened to sweep in as the estate's situation had grown more desperate.

Drink had got me through unCavendish and Robin's arrival in Lunden. Without it, I wouldn't have survived.

I pulled my hands away and shrugged. It was a moot point. "My magic is blocked right now, anyway, and I plan to keep it that way."

"But your mind is still there. You can't block that, however much you might wish to."

Kaliban's words came back to me, echoing Ella's. *Your mind is who you are.*

"Why do you—?"

"Katherine Ferrers, if you're about to ask me why I care, I'm going to be forced to murder you." Despite the dangers of wrinkles, I found Ella giving me the sharpest frown I'd ever seen. "I care about you, you massive idiot. And..." Her throat bobbed as she looked away, interlacing her fingers. "We all know the stereotype of someone who drinks too much. A man who gets loud and aggressive, who turns to violence and hurts others. Or who takes his carriage out and crashes it into someone... But my mother wasn't like that."

My breath caught. She'd told me of some happy childhood memories with her mother—there'd never been a hint of anything to turn the corners of her mouth down like this.

"She was a delight at parties, witty and beautiful. And outside parties, she was always kind and sweet to me, careful to make sure the nursery maid and, later, my governess were there to look after me in the evenings. She never harmed anyone... except herself." She frowned down at her wringing hands.

It was my turn to reach across and squeeze her fingers.

She looked up, eyes gleaming, making my heart ache. "She died in her sleep, far too young. I was fifteen."

No fights. No carriage accident. No tumble down the stairs. Simply there one day and gone the next.

She'd missed her chance to see Ella grow into the wonderful woman sitting before me.

My eyes burned as I pushed stray hair from her cheeks so it wouldn't get caught in the tears trickling down them. "I'm sorry. I'm so sorry."

"I'm not telling you this for my sake, Kat." She caught my wrist and leant closer, piercing me with the intensity of her stare. "I don't want to see that happen to you."

A chill rushed through me.

I'd always known she wasn't just worried about her "hard work" being undone. But this? That she was afraid for my very life? I'd never imagined that might be the price.

When I began drinking, I'd had a miserable, small existence. A couple of months ago, I'd told Bastian my life wasn't worth saving, but now...

"*There.*" Ella's voice cut through my racing thoughts. Her smile was like the dawn, a slow brightening. "You see it."

I opened my mouth but couldn't find the right words. There was too much in my head—Kaliban would've called my thoughts deafening.

Instead, swallowing, I shook my head. "I'm sorry, Ella. I didn't... I never thought..."

She laughed softly at my mangled attempts at sentences. "I know. I can see the cogs turning. I'm afraid I may have overloaded the machinery."

I rubbed my forehead as a fresh ache throbbed to life. "I feel like it's broken machinery at the moment."

"Well, I think I need to let this pretty little contraption process all this." She rose and planted a kiss on my brow, then nodded towards the book with my notes tucked inside. "You know, you could use some of that paper to write your thoughts —it might help."

"They won't make sense."

"Does that matter?" She spread her hands as she backed away. "It's just for you."

I was still giving her a bemused smile when she blew me a kiss from the doorway and disappeared.

The blank pages peeked out at me from the book. I did have plenty of paper—this wasn't like at the estate where I had to scrimp and save to afford just a handful of sheets. And the pens in Elfhame were incredible—instead of constantly dipping in a well of ink, they were filled with the stuff and could write for hours.

I grabbed the one I'd bought from the shop next door to Ariadne's—paid for with my wages from Bastian. Weighing it in my hand, I eyed the paper.

I could give it a try.

So I took a sheet and removed the lid from my pen.

Where was I supposed to start?

Ella had suggested my thoughts, but that didn't seem quite right—there had been a trigger for them. So I began with what she had told me and then all that had come to me after that, and the next thing I knew, I was turning the sheet over and writing on the back. Soon, I reached for the next page and another and another.

And then I found myself writing about how I'd once been a potbound plant, confined to a small existence by other people's rules. But now—*now*—I had space to grow.

Maybe I even kind of *liked* the person I was becoming.

Good gods. No wonder Ella was worried for me.

Yes, there were awful things, too, but did I really want to numb the rest just to escape those? There had to be a better way.

My eyes were full of tears—the good kind—when there was a knock at the door. I had no idea how long had passed, but a stack of pages sat on the low coffee table and my hand ached. Ella's chest of beauty alchemy still sat to one side.

I chuckled as I went out to the antechamber. "You were so excited you forgot your—"

But when I opened the door, it wasn't Ella.

Pasty-faced and glowering, in the doorway stood Robin.

I blinked at Robin. Not once had even a mention of him appeared in the stream of thoughts I'd inked on the page.

He stomped past me—I barely got out of his way in time.

Out in the corridor Urien guards caught my eye. His gaze skittered to the floor. "I'm sorry. He was escorted from Dawn's side, and as you're his wife, I couldn't stop him."

Before I could reply, he strode off down the hallway.

His wife.

His possession.

But I was mine. I belonged to myself and whoever else I said. I was Ella's friend. Bastian's lover. My own self.

I gritted my teeth and closed the door. Robin had already made his way to the sitting room, and I found him clinking through Ella's chest, nose wrinkled.

The sight of him in *our* space, encroaching on Ella's belongings bubbled in my blood. "Leave that—"

He shoved it across the floor and rounded on me. "What have you told them?"

I blinked as he advanced, his nostrils flaring. "Pardon?"

"None of the fae women here will so much as look at me."

A half-muffled guffaw came from me. "I can't imagine why."

Lip curling, he took another step closer. "You think you're so funny, don't you?"

"No, Robin, I just think *you're* ridiculous." I bit my tongue against calling him foolish and instead planted my hands on my hips. "The fact we're married counts both ways. I know you're not used to that, but just as much as I'm *your* wife, you're *my* husband."

He blinked like I was speaking gibberish.

"That fae law saying Bastian couldn't bring me here without your permission also means that no one can take you away from me without *my* permission. No fae will sleep with you because of our marriage contract."

He blasted a humourless laugh. "I've never heard such a load of nonsense. You belong to me—that's the only law that matters." With a shaking hand he pointed, coming closer until his finger was in my face. "No, you told them some lie about me. Scared them off somehow. What did you say?"

I swatted his hand away when it was an inch from my nose. "I haven't spoken a word about you. Your name hasn't passed my lips in months."

He flinched like I'd slapped him.

After everything he'd done to me, after all I'd endured, he had the gall to look affronted?

It felt like my veins were going to sear their way out of my body, and if not for the iron ring, I'd have been battling to contain the purple haze of my poison.

I blamed that for my tongue running away with me, as I went on. "In fact, until you appeared, I'd forgotten you existed. And you know what? It was fucking glorious. Now get out." I stepped to one side and gestured to the door.

It was only when I looked back at him that I realised my mistake.

As much as there was a fire burning in me, one ignited in him. Maybe it was because I'd laughed at him or because I'd forgotten him. Maybe it was that last part when I'd dismissed him.

Whatever the reason, a vein in his templed throbbed and his eyes bulged as he started forward.

He didn't go for the door.

Pulse racing, I darted to one side, but I was too slow, and his grip closed around my wrist.

My head snapped back as he yanked me close. The sickly sweet scent of sherry rolled off him. How hadn't I noticed it before?

"Get off me." I pushed at his chest, but he caught my other arm.

"No, Katherine. I won't *get off you*. You're my wife and it's about time you acted like one." He shoved and I stumbled back, my heel hitting something.

For a horrible instant there was nothing under me, just air and the world tilting, tilting, tilting.

Then the breath whooshed out of me as I crashed into the coffee table. Glasses and jars smashed, unleashing a cacophony of scent. I tried to inhale, but my lungs spasmed, and I could only manage little squeaking gasps.

Just winded. I'd get my breath back in a second.

"I had to turn back from my trip, because no one would give me credit." Robin closed in. "I bet that was you, wasn't it?

Whispering lies into people's ears like the poisonous little bitch you are."

Shaking my head, I clutched my stomach, not able to form any words.

"That's why I had to come here. I practically begged your uncle to help me." He bared his teeth as he towered over me, crowding my feet so I couldn't place them on the floor and stand. "Do you have any idea how humiliating it is for a Viscount to beg someone for help, Katherine? *Do you?*" Spit flecked his lips as he shouted that last part. "Almost as humiliating as being called to Lunden by your wife's uncle because she's whoring herself around."

He was humiliated? After I'd dirtied my hands in a dozen ways to pay off his debts? After I'd presented myself to a queen in rags? After I'd let unCavendish paw at me and set me to work to seduce a man I didn't know?

What version of reality did he live in?

I managed to drag in one breath and another. "I've spent a decade clearing up your mess." My voice came out hiccupy and fractured. "This one is entirely of your own making, and this time I'm not fixing it."

He took half a step back, and I scrambled to my feet in the small space he left.

"You're clutching your stomach." His gaze crawled down me.

"I'm winded." I edged to one side, trying to get from between him and the table.

"No." He caught my wrist, fingers digging in. "*No.* You're fatter too. That fae... you're pregnant, aren't you? You've been fucking him and now you're carrying his child! After all these years of denying me an heir."

"*What?*" I laughed.

It was the worst thing I could've done.

The backhanded strike sent me spinning. I almost caught myself on the table, but slipped off the side and landed hand-first on the floor.

Cold shock rolled through me. Something wrong.

My eyelids fluttered as I rolled to a sitting position, brain rattling, room spinning.

Then the pain erupted. A hot flush in my arm followed by an icy wave. I tried to move it and a fresh eruption rocked through me. When I looked down, bile lurched up my throat.

That angle wasn't right.

Not right at all. In fact... there wasn't meant to be an angle there in the middle of my forearm.

I blinked at it. "You've broken my arm."

His shadow fell over me. "You needed a reminder of who I am. I think you need something more permanent, though." He smiled.

He smiled.

And above that, his eyes glittered with pure malice.

That was when I knew.

He was going to kill me.

It wasn't a question or even a thought but a certainty, like the earth beneath my feet.

I grabbed the iron ring on my finger. If I could get it off and land a touch or let out my misting poison...

At the same instant, his foot slammed into my stomach.

Blinding pain burned through me. The next thing I knew, I was on my back, blinking at the ceiling.

Fight back. Fight.

I shook off the daze.

Go for the soft bits—that's what Faolán had told me.

I lashed out with one foot, aiming for his balls.

His roar was a reward, momentarily outshining the agony of my arm. He bent over, clutching himself.

Good. I hope it fucking hurt.

Joints—they were easy to break.

A kick to the knee felled him, and I huffed my relief as I dragged myself away.

Then he was on me, snarling with inhuman rage.

I tried again to wrench off the ring, but it was already a tight fit and my fingers must've swollen from the break. Pain bloomed in my face, pale against the sharp agony of my arm.

He was going to kill me.

One-handed, I managed to block some of his strikes, but my brain rattled and I couldn't remember anything else Faolán had taught me. Wasn't sure I remembered my own name.

"You always thought you were better than me," Robin spat as the blows stopped. "We'll see how great you are when I put you in the ground."

His fingers closed around my throat.

75

KAT

I froze.

Every moment of terror I'd ever known slammed into me with horrible clarity.

Papa shouting and smashing plates. Avice locked in a cupboard as I snuck her food.

Uncle Rufus snapping Fantôme's neck. Dangling above the grave she shared with Dia with his grip around my neck in a reenactment of her death.

My wedding night. The nights after.

The highwayman pointing a pistol at my head. Later, being the one with the pistol, heart hammering as the Wicked Lady stopped her first victim.

The moments stretched on and on, each one clamping me in ice.

But then as I wheezed, my mind reached for something else.

Riding Vespera. Her fur tickling my face as I hugged her.

Ella's laugh as she teased me about my name at our first

meeting. The brightness of her smile, and its fragility after unCavendish hurt her.

Dancing with Bastian. Being found by him in the maze and in the library, and all the many encounters after.

And now.

Sharing these rooms with him. Choosing him to share my body and my heart.

Grey hazed around the edges of my vision and the world grew dimmer, but it was like I'd woken up.

Because this was a life—or at least the early buds of one. *A life*—not just survival.

I wriggled and tried pushing him away, but it would've been a challenge with two hands. With only one, I stood no chance.

Black blotches crept in as Robin bent closer, this look of fascination on his face.

He was enjoying this. He *wanted* this.

My heart thundered against my ribs as the rest of the world faded further and further away.

No. This was not it. I had too much to lose.

My hand groped across the floor.

Robin squeezed.

Thicker and darker blackness closed in, pulsing with every laboured beat of my heart.

I wanted to live. My life *was* worth saving. And this arsehole wasn't about to take it from me.

My grip closed on something.

My tingling fingers barely registered how it felt. I had no idea what it was.

But only a pinprick of light remained in my vision. So I clung onto that, and I clung onto whatever I'd found.

When you have nothing left, even a scrap of something is important.

I struck.

Hot liquid spurted over me. I managed half a gasping breath.

I wanted to live.

I wanted to live.

There was only darkness and that pinpoint of light.

I reached for it. Death didn't get to come for me today.

Not today.

Spluttering. Gurgling. More red. The weight on me grew heavier. Robin's mouth gaped.

Someone was roaring. Not in terror or pain, but in ten years of hate and hurt and rage.

It took me long moments to register that I could breathe. My arm was still going, stabbing and stabbing and stabbing.

The roar was mine.

Robin slumped to one side, a shard of glass in his eye, his face and neck a bloody mess.

The soft bits.

I wheezed, sucking in as much air as I could, pulse hammering on my ears.

My broken wrist and sliced hand should've been in agony, but every part of my body was alight with terrible and glorious fire. It buzzed through me like potent magic.

Blood everywhere.

My hand, my face, slick with it.

From the state of him, he had to be dead. I didn't need to check his pulse.

I should be sorry, shouldn't I? Upset? Scared? *Something?*

But all I could do was blink at his blank eyes and slack face.

Then the shadows came.

GENTLE SHADOWS LIFTED Robin's body off me and cradled my broken arm. My head spun as I sat up, something warm helping me. I had to blink several times before I registered the blackest of black hair, the silver eyes surveying me, and beyond that, the door hanging off its hinges.

Bastian's lips moved, and he cupped my cheek, turning my face away from Robin. It was only as I took long breaths that the thunder in my ears abated enough to hear what he was saying.

"Don't look. You're safe. I've got you."

I blinked up at him, then smiled when I realised he was trying to protect me from the sight of what I'd done. "I'm... I'm all right." Dimly, pain broke through my daze, as if speaking had brought reality back.

I pulled away from Bastian's protection and I *looked*.

The shard of glass from one of Ella's bottles glittered.

Even a scrap of something is important.

Was it ghoulish to laugh at a time like this?

Robin's remaining eye was wide in shock. Maybe that was why he hadn't protected himself from my blows—he hadn't expected them.

Blood. Gore. Torn flesh.

The sight of him utterly destroyed didn't horrify me as the people I'd poisoned had.

"He earned this." My voice came from somewhere far away. "He... he tried to kill me. Not just now, but... all these years." I shook my head as Bastian's words from Lunden came back to me. "A slow death."

Bastian nodded, eyebrows tight together. "He did. He *did*."

He pressed a kiss to my brow and another to my mouth—warm and alive and *mine*.

It was only when he pulled away with red on his lips that I realised my face was covered in blood. I reached out to wipe it away, but it coated my hand too. My dress and cleavage. The floor around me.

My gaze snagged on the broken door, shockingly white compared to the crimson.

I frowned at Bastian, somehow, impossibly here. "How did you know?"

"Urien. He couldn't stop Robin entering, but he could come and tell me."

More ridiculousness. I could be left alone with that man, yet being with Bastian was wrong?

He gave a long exhale, shoulders sinking. "Thank fuck he did. Though..." He glanced at Robin's body. "It looks like you didn't need me."

I might've smiled. It was hard to say. Everything felt a bit fuzzy, except for the pain radiating from my wrist and palm.

He tore a strip from the hem of his shirt and bandaged my hand, staunching the bleeding. "I'll send for Asher to heal you, then we can get you cleaned up."

"No." The firmness of my voice shocked even me. "Help me up."

He frowned but obeyed, shadows holding my arm steady.

"You're going to take me to the Hall of Healing and we're going to walk the busiest corridors of the palace to get there."

Maybe I was losing my mind. Maybe I was still running on adrenaline. But after everything, I was standing, and Robin was not.

The corner of Bastian's mouth rose in a bemused smile as he cocked his head.

"I will not hide away in here." Head high, I took his arm, allowing for my sliced palm. "I'm not the one who should be ashamed. Let's show your fellow fae what blindly clinging to their laws caused."

76

BASTIAN

Urien's eyes widened when we left our suite. I wondered if Kat noticed, but she seemed focused on the end of the corridor like she'd seen a prize and wouldn't stop until she had it.

With a nod, I ordered him to guard the broken doors. We would have words later. I didn't know whether to kill him for letting that man in or kiss him for fetching me.

I'd smashed into that room, body and shadows coiled to strike. My hands clenched with the knowledge that under all the blood, bruises marked Kat's skin. I had failed to keep her safe.

And yet...

And yet she'd saved herself.

Somehow that trumped my guilt, because my ember had erupted into a flame and utterly destroyed the life that had threatened hers.

Maybe I was sick. Maybe it was my unseelie side bleeding through, but I had never felt more proud than I did in that

556

moment. Not when I earned my place in the Queensguard. Not when I was made Braea's Shadow.

Nothing—*nothing* matched walking through the palace corridors with this woman on my arm, broken but unbowed, wearing her dead husband's blood like it was a badge of fucking honour.

Just as she'd ordered, I chose a route through the busiest corridors. Mouths dropped open. Eyes bulged. Everyone who saw her forgot to hide their curiosity.

Whispers broke out in her wake, and Ella appeared at my elbow, pale and aghast.

By the time we reached the grand hall, she'd amassed quite a crowd, and more stopped in their tracks here, as folk from both courts returned from theatres. Even Cyrus paused as he swaggered in, eyebrows inching up. Their murmurs drifted with the lights, which clustered around us as though attracted to her.

Between the rumours and the fact she'd lived in my rooms for the past few months, we were beyond trying to hide what she meant to me. This appearance would seal that and, with a little luck, spell out that, not only was she under my protection, but she would deal with any threat ruthlessly and bloodily.

She nudged me, and I leant closer, alert to where she wished to steer. I followed the subtle pressure of her touch to the fountain and helped her step up onto its lip as an expectant quiet stole over the large space.

Inwardly I winced at the tightness around her eyes—any movement had to be agony, uncovering new injuries.

Stars above, was it tempting to just carry her to Asher or the Hall of Healing, but this was what she wanted and, I suspected, what she needed.

"People of Tenebris and Luminis." Her voice rang through the silence. "I hear the whispers beginning already. I'm sure there will be plenty of rumours to explain my state. In case there is any doubt about the truth your kind love so much, let me be clear." She flashed a smile, teeth shockingly pale against the blood covering her face.

"My husband, the man you all believed had a right to me, did this. And he did it because he thought that exact thing. He *thought* a contract drawn up by him and my father over a decade ago meant he had a right to me." Her chest heaved as she looked out over the crowd.

Ducking, she scooped a handful of water from the fountain and used it to clean her face. As she straightened, she pointed at the cut on her lip. "This is where he hit me." With a wince, she touched the back of her head. "This is where he slammed me into the floor." She splayed her fingers over her stomach. "I have bruises here where he kicked me because he thought I was carrying another man's child and couldn't stand the thought of someone else sullying *his property*."

Bile flooded my mouth, and my hands fisted so tightly my knuckles ached.

If that man wasn't already dead, I'd rip him apart. Maybe I still would. There wouldn't be enough of him left to bury.

My shadows curled around me, demanding it, and people nearby edged away.

After all she'd been through, she could so easily be a wreck curled up in a corner. I'd have cared for her if she was.

And yet she stood here, shoulders square, chin raised.

"He was going to kill me. I know that, because he told me while he had his hands around my neck."

Murmurs rippled out across the room. This kind of

violence wasn't tolerated in Elfhame—it certainly wasn't allowed under the law like in Albion.

"And yet this man?" Her voice rose as she gestured to me. "The one I *choose* to be with. The one who showed me I had a fucking choice. He's the man you call oathbreaker, while you let my husband enter my rooms and try to kill me."

There was no sound but the fountain and Kat's words ringing to every corner of the room. The folk around us frowned, and a few glanced at me, then looked aside when they met my eye.

"You and your laws forced my hand tonight. When I was lying there with my husband's hands around my throat, moments from death, I took his life and in doing so, I claimed *mine.*"

My chest filled with her ferocity, and if not for the crowd, I'd have knelt at her feet then and there.

She surveyed them, letting her words sink in. This close, I spotted the moment she gave a short gasp.

When I followed her line of sight, I spotted a head of red hair. Her uncle.

Good gods, I hoped she would release me from my promise not to kill him. Technically, he was a foreign dignitary, yet that wasn't enough to offset what he'd done to Kat *as a fucking child* or the fact he was responsible for Robin's arrival in Elfhame.

But instead of falling quiet, she drew a long breath and gave her audience a fierce frown. "Remember this next time you cling to a contract long after it should've been broken."

With a nod, she held out her hand, and I helped her down.

"You are fucking incredible," I murmured against her hair.

She grunted and leant more heavily on me than she had before. "It won't make any difference, not when your laws...

your central belief structure... they all need to change and see some nuance in contracts. But I couldn't not say it."

"I'm not so sure. These things begin with one voice."

I wasn't sure if she heard me as she swayed on her feet. I knew the tired look glazing her eyes—the aftermath of adrenaline.

"Come on, let's get you healed."

When we turned, Faolán blocked our path. "Kat." He started closer, and a growl rumbled from me, stopping him short.

I didn't intend to make a sound, but I'd readied myself for one fight tonight, and *my* adrenaline hadn't faded. Somehow, I held myself still and bit my tongue.

"Are you all right? Let me help—"

"Not now." At his flinch, she huffed. "You know me, Faolán, and yet you still placed that contract above my wishes."

He stood there, a giant fae who could turn into a massive wolf silenced by a five-foot-three human.

"Enough." Half holding her up, I steered around him and tried to ignore his hurt look, even though it pierced me.

All those years ago, I'd saved him from an angry mob who'd decided their village didn't allow shapechangers. I'd never for an instant regretted that decision—it had brought him into my life as my closest friend—but I wished he understood the parallels between that situation and this one. The foolishness of old beliefs.

He took a step after us. "But the law—"

Leaning into me, Kat turned. "Just because something is legal, doesn't make it right."

I slid an arm around Kat's waist and glanced back.

Faolán stood, head bowed, eyebrows knotted together, gaze skimming the floor like he might find answers there.

77

KAT

My trail through the city to the Hall of Healing left more ripples of shock. Whispers from the grand hall followed with news of my speech.

Elthea admonished me as she cut the iron ring off my swollen finger. "There's a reason I didn't give you iron." She said it with such fury, I almost thought she cared. The healing took energy, she explained, but that once I'd recovered, she had a cure ready for my poison. Dazed, I barely registered the comment as she healed all my injuries and catalogued them, including the bruises on my neck.

When the city guard arrived and saw her notes, they had to accept my story. Self-defence. No need to arrest me. No charges for murder. I could've collapsed with the mingled exhaustion and relief.

By the time we returned to our rooms, the door had been fixed, the floor cleaned, and there was no sign of Robin's body. It was like it had never happened, except for the blood staining my clothes, matting my hair, stuck under my nails. Bastian ran me a bath and washed my hair—all I could do was lie there and let him.

I slept long and deep that night, but the ripples kept spreading. News would reach Albion soon enough. So the next day, I wrote to the queen and Morag, hoping to get ahead of it and stake my claim on the estate. Bastian sent his own letter, corroborating my story and explaining that some misfortune had befallen Robin's body and it wasn't available for burial (I didn't ask, but I had suspicions.). He signed it as the Night Queen's Shadow, lending that weight to my innocence and my claim.

A couple of days and several visits from my friends later, I brushed my hair at Bastian's dressing table as I got ready to face the world once more. I still wasn't sure if that speech was the right decision. It had felt right at the time—righteous, even. But part of me had cringed small and tight when I'd spotted Uncle Rufus in the crowd.

I had been anything but silent and dutiful that night.

"You don't have to do this, you know." Bastian's hands cupped my shoulders and he nodded to me in the mirror. "I saw that little grimace."

I touched my cheek. I was getting too comfortable around him, forgetting to control my reactions as well as my magic.

My arm was mostly fine, just a little achey. Elthea had told me that would fade after a week or two. She'd found a couple of cracked ribs and some internal bleeding, but they too were healed.

Certainly no reason to miss this meeting.

I smiled at Bastian in the mirror and dipped a kiss to his hand. "The bride-to-be specifically requested me—I'm not about to turn down her offer."

Zita had claimed she wanted input on this meeting about

the wedding ceremony from a fellow human. Bastian suspected it was a goodwill gesture towards Dusk, but I noted she'd only asked after I'd killed Robin. From what I'd heard, she was... unusual. Maybe killing a man made me more interesting in her eyes.

Bastian's grip tightened, and I raised an eyebrow. "Wouldn't declining cause offence to Dawn?"

His shoulders sank. "You're right. You're getting too good at fae politics." But his smile belied his grumbling tone, and he pushed my hair back, bending close. "Far, far too good," he said against my skin, lighting up my nerves.

I tilted my head to one side, letting him kiss my neck, each touch somewhere between ticklish and exquisite. "What time is this meeting?"

"We have time." He nipped the point between shoulder and neck, making me jolt with pleasure. "Barely."

"Maybe we shouldn't, then." But I reached back, fingers threading through his thick hair. "We wouldn't want to be late."

"Mm-hmm." The sound rumbled into me as he removed the brush from my grasp and placed it on the dressing table.

He sucked on my pulse, and it was a struggle to get out my next words. "It would cause offence."

"Your clothing offends me." He slid the night-coloured dress off my shoulder. "Too much of it," he growled and bit my earlobe as he palmed my exposed breast.

I stared in the mirror, both watcher and watched, cheeks flushed, eyelids half closed as I let my head fall back on his shoulder.

"You like to see this almost as much as I do." He smirked, catching my reflected gaze.

With that smirk, I should've expected it, but when he pinched my nipple, it still made me cry out and arch.

Need flooded me, raw and hot.

"I do. It's like I'm really seeing myself." My voice came out on a husky breath, not quite my own... or maybe it was entirely my own, just freed from a weight I'd carried too long. "When you're touching me, no one else's rules exist."

"Good. Fuck their rules." He ran a canine down my throat, right above the vein. It could've been a threat—from anyone else it would've been. But here, now, him—it was a demonstration.

However vulnerable I made myself in his hands, I was safe.

And that mattered. Good gods, how it mattered.

Since Robin's attack, we'd kissed and cuddled in bed, but I'd been too exhausted and perhaps rattled for anything more. Now, though...

I slid the other side of my dress off my shoulder and held his gaze. "You'd better get on with it, Bastian. Tick-tock."

His eyes narrowed, and he huffed a laugh over my skin, making me shiver. "Whatever my lady wishes." He grabbed a handful of hair and angled me for a deep and dizzying kiss, while his other hand kneaded and teased my tits until I squirmed, thighs pressing together.

When he pulled away, his eyes were dark, only thin rings of silver irises visible. "On your feet."

I obeyed, letting my gown pool on the floor.

"Perfect." He pulled the chair back, and over my shoulder, I caught him grabbing the hem of his shirt. "Eyes forward, ember." There was a rustle of clothing, and I tried to see what he was doing in the mirror, but my body blocked the view.

I bit my lip, anticipation buzzing over my naked flesh. The

purple stains covered my fingers and hands, entirely. I had more control now, but I still didn't trust myself to touch anyone but him. Perhaps this was a good idea—letting go before the meeting.

"Now, come here." His gravelly tone, sudden in the silence, made my breath catch. Then, after long moments standing without anything but the cool air touching me, his hands wrapped around my hips and sent goosebumps chasing over my skin. He pulled me back a step. "Sit."

"But—"

I half fell into his lap, his shadows catching me, and landed with his hardness pressed against my entrance.

He held me at that teasing point, my back on his chest. With his shadows taking my weight, I couldn't even sink down onto him, and I gave a frustrated little huff at the fact.

His low chuckle reverberated into my back. "Haven't I told you before about patience?"

I managed to circle my hips over his tip, moaning at the pressure so close to entry and yet not quite. It raked through me, making my breaths come harder, faster. "We don't have time for patience."

"I don't care," he growled in my ear. "We're doing this properly this time. Me, not my shadows. *Look.*" His shadows tilted the mirror so I could see myself suspended over him, his shadows dimpling my thighs as they lifted and parted them. His length stood ready, my wetness coating its tip. The steel of his piercing glinted, coiling my anticipation tighter.

Just as we'd been at the inn, but his cock instead of one made of shadows. This was what he'd imagined that false night, and now we could make it real.

He'd thought of me, just as I'd thought of him. My heart kicked up in speed.

"Please, Bastian." I bit my lip, holding his gaze in the mirror.

Groaning, he reached between my legs. "You and that word."

His middle finger circled my clit, and as I let out a blissful "Oh," he pulled me onto his dick.

His teasing had me wet, but his thickness still stretched me in the most delicious way, and I arched into it, taking more and more.

Watching him disappear inside me, knowing we were joined in a way that meant more than simple fucking only drew me tighter. I whimpered when his piercing rubbed against my inner walls, lifting me closer to the bright joy we found together.

Once he was fully buried in me, he kissed my cheek. "Even better than I imagined. You're so perfect, love."

With his praise, I could only pant, gripping the edge of the chair as he played me. My pussy clenched around him, the fullness building my pleasure higher, faster—almost unbearably so.

"I... I can't..." I tried to lift off him a little to ease the rising pressure, but he clamped an arm around my waist and held my thighs with his shadows.

"Oh, I think you can. I can feel you're close." Dark tendrils spread over my breasts, teasing my nipples. He grazed his lips over my shoulder, and tremors ran through me. "Stop fighting it, love."

All at once, he bit my shoulder and his shadows tightened around my nipples, and he broke me apart.

He groaned as I cried out and arched in his hold. Every part of me tensed and shattered, bright and fractured into perfect shards of bliss.

Yet he didn't let up, and a second climax chased the first, their edges blurring as I broke around him, muscles contracting, while the rest of me burst into oblivion.

"There. Such a good flame, burning for me so brightly." His tongue lapped over the place he'd bitten, and his shadows soothed the tight peaks of my breasts.

He shifted his grip, bringing my thighs together and looping his arm under my knees so I was bundled against him. Somehow it brought me tighter around his dick. "*Now* you get a little reprieve." He lifted me up until his piercing slipped out, glinting with my wetness, and my eyelids fluttered at the intensity of it.

For a moment, without him filling me, I could breathe fully, and I let my head fall against his chest, nestling beneath his chin. "Bastian... I'm yours."

I'd said it before, but this time...

His eyebrows squeezed together, and his fingers tightened around my thigh, and I knew he understood.

This time, there was only us.

No Robin. No contract that said I belonged to anyone else.

In every possible sense I was my own woman and I could say what I gave, if anything, to anyone else.

And I was Bastian's.

I chose him.

And now no one could get in the way of that.

"Yes, you are." His canines flashed as he pulled me down his dick, wringing a strangled cry from me. "Mine, Katherine. *Mine.*" He said it with each thrust, gaze flicking between mine and the point where he disappeared into me.

The pleasure in me soared, no longer building—that was a mundane thing on the land—but flying higher and higher, untethered by anything so tedious as gravity, almost at the sun.

"And I'm yours." He said it savagely, like he dared the world to tear us apart again. "*Yours*," he bellowed as he filled me so thoroughly, I thought I might die from it.

I reached that bright and obliterating place, body burning up with pleasure, heart too full, mind fractured and unable to hold things like fear or thought.

All I knew was Bastian's body locked with mine in ferocious joy, and my fingers digging into his arms, like that would stop me spinning away into space entirely.

He went rigid as he gushed into me with a hoarse cry, joining me in the overwhelming oneness of us.

Slowly, like a feather, I drifted back to earth. Slick and sticky with sweat, we caught our breath. He smiled and kissed my shoulder as he lifted me off himself and watched as his come spilled from me.

I bit my lip, something fascinating about the sight. I felt at once completely powerful and utterly filthy, like maybe the second of those two things wasn't *bad* like I'd been told but actually a secret path to the first one.

"Katherine," he murmured against my skin, "I love you. Beyond all reason. Beyond all control. Beyond everything. I love you."

My heart didn't just skip—it tripped and fell. I broke away from the mirror and turned in his lap, meeting his gaze directly. "And I love you. There is no reason when I'm with you. I give up control. I give you everything, and I love that you give everything right back."

We kissed, slow and deep—deep enough to touch my weary, broken soul.

And perhaps Bastian's hobby wasn't only contained to his

workroom, because I felt a little less broken than I had before coming to Tenebris.

Eventually, he pulled away, cupping my cheek. "We should have a wash and get ready."

I scoffed and nudged my nose to his. "I *was* ready until *someone* had other ideas."

"I can't imagine what you're talking about." He grinned. "We have time for a shower... together."

The promise of it fluttered through me. Bastian had a shower in his bathroom and its warm rain was my new favourite thing. The water spilling over my body and my scalp was like a thousand touches, and the first time I'd used it, it had brought me to my knees.

I glanced at the orrery on the mantlepiece. Barely enough time. Though a glint in his eye told me that he was ready for more.

Eyes narrowed, I pressed a hand to his chest. "*Just* a shower."

78

KAT

It was *not* just a shower.

And we *were* late to the meeting.

But Prince Sepher and Zita didn't seem to mind. In fact, while pouring coffee, she invited me to their bed. I chuckled to myself about that the next day as I walked through the city to Kaliban's house, taking a break from research.

When he opened the door, he eyed me and the basket of food. "You do remember I can't take your memories, right? Or has your mind broken and you've forgotten?"

"I remember. Are you going to let me in?"

He made a low sound but let me pass. "Why are you here, then?"

"I don't know." I shrugged and placed the basket on the side as he watched me from the doorway. "Maybe I just can't get enough of your outstanding hospitality."

He grumbled in the way Morag did when I was hardest to love. "I suppose you're going to want tea, aren't you?"

"See? That's exactly what I mean. *So welcoming.*"

Filling the kettle, he muttered, "You're almost as sarcastic as..." As he put it on the stove, his words faded into silence and a tightness pulled around his features, making my heart clench in response.

The slippers. His partner must've been sarcastic too. Maybe his prickliness was understandable.

"I got you some cake." I held it up as I emptied the basket. "Lemon drizzle—one of the queens of cake, if you ask me."

He raised his eyebrows, peering at the wrapped loaf cake. "*One* of the queens? You have... some sort of ranking system for cakes?"

"It's more a hierarchy. But doesn't everyone?"

Eyes narrowing, he canted his head. "I'm sure I'm going to regret asking, but... what is your hierarchy of cakes?"

I gestured with the bunch of kale I was putting away. "So, the queens are top tier. Obviously, they're lemon drizzle, coffee cake (*without* walnuts), and lemon tarts."

"Oh, *obviously.*"

"And pastries are included. It would be ridiculous to have a whole separate system for those."

"Yes, *that* would be the ridiculous part."

I pointed a carrot at him. "Don't think I missed the way you eyed it. You *know* she's a queen. And I know you're dying to get your hands on a slice." I finished putting the food away and dusted off my hands. "It goes perfectly with a cup of tea."

"Ah, so I'm getting out plates and a knife as well as the cups, then." As he fetched them, he frowned.

"What's wrong?"

"Not wrong, just..." He ended on a brisk sigh and poured us tea. "There's something different about you."

I stiffened as he slid my cup across the table. "I thought you weren't going to read me."

"No, not like that." He stirred a dash of honey into his drink, eyeing me like he *was* seeing into my soul. "I heard what happened... that you're no longer married."

"I prefer 'happily widowed.'"

He chuckled. "It fits nicely. Though, I thought it would leave you afraid. Closed. But... your demeanour. You're embracing... well, everything, rather than trying to shut some things out."

I sat back, rubbing my chest. Was I so obvious? "I'm not sure how to take that."

He lifted one shoulder. "It's not an insult, and it's not dangerous, either. But I think you're starting to understand—you can't shut some things out and let others in. You shut the door and you lose it all."

You can't choose what you numb. If you're deadened, you lose the good and the bad. It was like he'd been speaking to Ella.

"Your magic seems more under control, too." His gaze dropped to my fingers. "No gloves. You must be feeling more confident."

I pushed my hands into my lap in case he decided to test out my control. Only the nails were purple, but I still didn't trust that to mean I was safe to touch anyone. That I hadn't hazed by accident for a while was a small matter of pride for me. I'd take my victories where I could. "It seems... a little easier to keep hold of."

The corner of his mouth rose. I couldn't decide if it was an amused smirk or a happy smile that he tried to smother. "And let me guess—it's because you've been letting go a little?"

It was my turn to grumble as I focused on stirring lemon and honey into my tea.

"It's all about balance, Kat." When I looked up, I found him placing the teaspoon on his finger, finding the balancing point.

I raised an eyebrow. "Rather a literal illustration, don't you think?"

He huffed and grabbed the spoon, using it to point at me. "Such a disrespectful child. Fine, let me give you a more metaphorical one. As a human, I doubt you've heard how the universe was created."

I blew across my tea. "I'm all ears."

"Blunt ones," he muttered. "In the time before, there was only the eternal nothingness of the heavens and the Celestial Serpent. He ventured through the darkness searching for something, *anything*, but there was only himself—as dark as the night itself."

"That sounds lonely." I ran my nail over the rim of my cup.

"Hence his search. After an age, he finally spotted something—a light in the distance. It took him aeons to reach it, but he kept his gaze fixed on that distant light, since it was the only thing he had. Little by little it became clearer, until he realised it was another serpent. The Tellurian Serpent, as bright as he was dark—his equal and opposite. She was as overjoyed as him, for she had a similar story of journeying and loneliness and a search for something amidst the void."

Although it was a myth—and a myth about two snakes no less—I found myself smiling. I'd never searched through endless space, but I had known the void of loneliness.

"In their joy, they shared themselves, all that they were, all that they'd thought in their journeys and had no one to speak of it to, and in the lifetimes their conversations stretched over, they fell in love. Because although they were opposites—him angry where she was joyful, him guarded where she was curious—they brought out the best in each other. Her curiosity drew him from behind the walls he'd built. His anger at the universe for leaving them to suffer alone gave her a drive.

Coming together changed them both. Glimmers of light began to twinkle in his scales. Points of darkness speckled hers."

The panel in Bastian's office. "A light serpent with dark stars, and a dark serpent with light ones."

Kaliban inclined his head. "Though there were no stars then. Only the two serpents... until they mated."

What was a fae story without sex? I hid my smirk by taking a sip of tea.

"The Tellurian Serpent grew thick, and the Celestial Serpent slowed his pace and helped her in their eternal flight. But when her time came, she didn't lay an egg." A hint of sadness marked his downcast gaze. "Her body heaved and broke apart, glimmering scales creating the sun and stars, one eye forming the earth, its black pupil the Underworld. While her other eye formed another world."

"She died to create everything?" I hugged my cup close. "And... there's another world out there?"

"There *was*. The Celestial Serpent did all he could, trying to gather the broken parts of his beloved, trying to stop her falling apart, but to no avail. She was gone, and although life sprung up on those worlds, he was alone in space once more. He blamed what they'd created for her death and in his rage set about destroying it. He ate the other world and then turned towards earth, but before he could eat that too, he was stopped."

An entire world destroyed, and ours close to the same fate. All those lives obliterated in an instant. "*How?*"

"Some versions of the story say a great fae hero fought him and forced him back. Others say the Tellurian Serpent's spirit visited him with a reminder that these were their children, that their love had created all this—that she loved it all as much as she loved him."

It was only a story. Objectively I knew that, and yet my eyes stung and my heart was sore. She had given everything. And he had lost everything.

"The Celestial Serpent agreed to only eat the sun each evening and return it come morning. So their children on earth wouldn't be left in darkness as the serpents once had, her spirit lit up the night, coiled in the form of the moon."

"They're always apart."

He gave me a wistful smile. "That's what makes the eclipse special. It's the only time they come back together again."

"A bit like the king and queen."

"Hmph. I suppose. But for vastly different reasons. The Sleep allows them and their people to share this land without killing each other.

"True." I kept my thoughts quiet, trying not to let them turn towards the fact the Sleep was under threat. Frowning at my cup, I cleared my throat. "The serpents' story is a sad one, though."

"That wasn't the point. People tend to see the Celestial Serpent as a traitor—a destroyer—but they forget he helped create the world, too."

Bastian. That was why they'd called him Serpent after he'd killed his father. A traitor to his own family. I swallowed, throat suddenly thick.

Kaliban held up the teaspoon once more. "The universe has balance because of his dark and her light. Destruction, creation. Order, chaos. The universe needs duality and balance."

"Control and letting go."

A smile dawned on his face, not sad or sardonic or even amused, but something warm and genuine. "Stars above, I think she's got it."

I turned my hands over, purple nails stark against my tan skin. "You think I'm making progress because I've found a middle ground. Venting at times, so I have control at others." Just like Ella had said.

"Exactly. Bring it to just one finger."

I took a deep breath and shifted my focus to the hum of magic on my skin. Instead of clawing at it all as I had when the Ascendants had attacked, I pulled on just a little, channeling it to the third finger of my right hand, where Bastian's ring sat. The purple stain spread down from my nail.

When it reached the base of my finger, I thought hard, like when I'd pushed Kaliban from my mind, *Enough*.

It stopped.

"I heard that." He winced. "A little clumsy, perhaps, but you controlled it. Try a different finger—just the first knuckle."

I let go of the magic I'd channeled, making the stain fade before cupping more magic at the tip of my left forefinger. I tried not to shout *Enough* in my head this time, and the stain bled a little further than the knuckle, but...

"Not bad." He nodded slowly. "Try somewhere else. What about a poisoned kiss? I'm sure that could be useful."

I scoffed and let the magic from my finger dissipate. "You'll have to tell me if it works." Another deep breath and I focused on my lips.

"The perfect blackberry lipstick." He chuckled. "I suspect as you gain experience, you might be able to do it without any colour giving you away, but I'm not sure. Everyone's gift is different and yours is unique."

I touched my tingling lips and grinned back at him before letting the magic fade. "It worked. Ella was right." For the first time since learning about my magic, I thought about it and my chest filled with something other than dread.

Now it was mine to use rather than something that used me.

"It really worked."

"It did." He rose, circled the table, and held out his hand. "You have control over your power."

Swallowing, I squared my shoulders. I could trust myself to do this. I wouldn't kill him.

Still, my heart hammered as I took his hand.

But no dark tendrils of poison spread over his skin.

He didn't gasp or twitch in pain. He just shook my hand. "I'm Kaliban, and I'm pleased to meet you, Kat."

A laugh burst from me, close to a sob, and my sight blurred with overflowing tears. "You're not dead."

Chuckling, he pulled me to my feet and into his arms. "Far from it." He slapped my back. "I'm so proud of you."

That was the thing that broke me, and I sobbed into my friend's chest as he told me over and over.

"I'm proud of you."

I RETURNED to the library still high on my success. Curled up in a comfortable armchair, I set to work reading the next book in my pile and practised controlling my poison. The huge space stretched on around corners and out of sight, but I hadn't seen anyone else here today and my chair was tucked into a corner, so it was safe to experiment.

Since the space was large, with massive windows reaching to the ceiling, I tried to haze while reading the introduction, but nothing happened. With a *hmm*, I tried again, pulling on the magic around me, trying to push poison out through my pores.

Nothing.

The other times I'd hazed, it was either because I was losing control entirely or because I focused completely. Or, in the case of the clearing, both.

My heart squeezed, and I frowned at the page. Reading about the Underworld, the realm of death, didn't exactly help distract me from the image of Bastian dying, his Shadowblade fading as the light in his eyes went out.

Not thinking about that.

I tightened my grip, the edges of the book digging into my fingers as I pulled a sudden flush of purple to my thumb before making it disappear just as quickly. That I could do with my attention divided.

This passage explained that the Underworld was ruled by the Kings of Death, which sounded very dark and dramatic. It said there were seven, but I'd seen another book mention nine. These accounts were written by fae of this realm who'd probably never set foot there, so no surprise their information wasn't accurate—or perhaps had been accurate at one time but wasn't anymore.

They might've split over time or some had united. Knowing what people said about the unseelie, conquering seemed more likely.

The next paragraph talked about how the Wild Hunt was loyal to one of those kings, which made me sit back and frown.

Loyal? The Wild Hunt?

In all the stories I'd heard, they were described as nothing more than wicked, ancient entities cursed to ride and hunt forever, single-minded and wild. Hence the name.

But this made it sound like they served a master.

I made a thoughtful sound before moving on to the next line.

And blinking.

And bolting upright in my chair.

I re-read the line.

"My gods," I breathed, heart pounding as I scribbled in my notes, starting towards the door.

I needed to show Bastian.

79

BASTIAN

My eyelids drifted and I had to force myself to re-read the line.

Supplies in from...

If I had to read another report about suppliers for the royal wedding, I was going to pluck out my own eyeballs.

I sat back and massaged the bridge of my nose.

There was a very real danger of Ascendants trying to sabotage the event, so I had spies on every supplier and guard, the city gates—anything and everything I could think of. So far there was no sign of Sura's people trying to infiltrate the city.

That didn't mean they weren't, though.

Kat was convinced they weren't behind the Horror attack but she didn't know our courts like I did. She didn't know Sura. She wasn't there for her coup attempt.

So many would've died—not just that night, but all the nights after in the war that would've followed the queen's assassination. Some would've stood by Sura as the heir, but others would've rejected her for killing her own mother.

A subject I knew plenty about. I grunted and scratched the rash on my wrist.

Damned hemlock. I'd been wearing gloves as I'd worked with it, but my sleeve had ridden up and the plant had brushed my skin. I thought I was fine, but when I caught the sun in the practice yard later, red welts had broken out.

They'd calmed over the past couple of days but still itched like mad. Poison wasn't an area of expertise for Asher's healing —he was better with injuries—and no way was I giving Elthea another chance to extract a favour from me. So, salve it was. I pulled out the jar from my desk and smoothed it over the pink marks.

How had Kat endured *consuming* poison when I could barely stand touching it?

The door flew open, and there she was, so breathless I was on my feet in an instant. She had an appointment with Elthea tomorrow, but had she brought it forward? Had Elthea hurt her again? "What's wrong?"

She shook her head, panting like she'd run all the way here, and held up a book. Gold lettering glinted against a deep forest green cover.

I let my muscles relax and chuckled. "Nothing wrong, but you forgot how to knock?"

"Look." She spread the book on my desk and pointed. "Look!"

I craned over the book. "Your research. You found a reference."

"Not just that." She fanned her face, cheeks pink. "We've been working from a coded version up until now, right? And potentially a coded version translated from the High Valens."

I nodded, reading over the passage. Only a brief mention of the Circle of Ash in relation to a King of Death. Not promising.

"And—and whoever wrote that note translated it as ring or circle of ash, yes?"

"*Yes.*"

She pointed again at the page, eyes wide. "'*Coronam cineris.*' Don't you see? This is one of the books from that special pile—you said they were from 'Granny's house.'"

"*Oh.*" I checked the cover. "They're old books." I still felt a step behind, but her excitement kindled in me along with the fact I'd never seen her so flustered.

"Old, *old* books. What if this is the original? Or at least closer to the original than the book in Riverton Palace?" She tripped over her words like she wasn't filtering them, like she was just speaking her mind for once.

"Which would mean? I'm not following your line of thought."

"*Coronam cineris.*" She said it again like it should explain everything. "I checked against your book of High Valens, and it's the same as Latium. *Coronam* could mean ring, wreath, diadem, garland. The writer of the note originally translated it as ring or circle. But *corona* also means *crown.*"

I straightened. "A crown that could end the king and queen's Sleep. That makes a lot of sense." My mind raced over the possibilities. Were there references we'd missed because we'd been looking for the wrong thing?

"That's not all. Whoever did the original translation from the book in Riverton's library did a bloody awful job—or maybe they were just trying to keep things vague in case the message was intercepted." She shrugged. "Either way, they wrote *ash.* We thought that meant the tree or its wood. But that would be *fraxinus* in High Valens."

"Whereas *cinis* means ash, as in left behind after a fire."

She grabbed my sleeve and shook me. "*Exactly. Coronam Cineris* means Crown of Ashes. We've been looking for the wrong thing this whole time."

I sat on the edge of the desk, staring ahead. "Fuck."

The room spun.

I had to tell Braea when she woke. This would ease her bad mood over Sepher and Zita's wedding.

We had an original reference, and a potential lead with the King of Death. "Kat. You're a genius." I pushed myself to my feet, chest full. "My beautiful fucking genius."

Her eyes widened and that pink tone on her cheeks deepened to the one I adored.

I couldn't help myself. I grabbed her, kissed her, worshipped her with my lips until she made a little moan of want that set me alight. She clutched my shirt and arched against me, tongue tangling with mine. My shadows burst around her, tugging at her gown, pulling her as close as possible.

With a sweep of my arm, the papers scattered from my desk, books thudded to the floor, and I replaced them with the thing that mattered most.

Katherine. *My* Katherine.

Biting her lip in a way that drove blood to my cock, she glanced at the door. Brynan had gone for a break, but beyond his office the door to the hallway stood open, and guards waited just outside. "Someone might see."

"Do you care?" I kissed the column of her throat and nipped at her pulse, drawing a gasp from her. "It's not like you're married anymore."

Her fingers threaded into my hair, scraping over my scalp deliciously. "I'm not sure I do."

"Good. *Good.*" I slid the gown off her shoulders and trailed kisses down to her chest. My cock twitched at the sight of her —the perfect, overflowing handfuls of her breasts, the brown nipples tight and pointed and begging for attention.

When I slid my arm around her waist and pulled her close, she arched back for me, and I could resist no longer. I sucked first one into my mouth, then the other, humming my approval when she moaned.

How had I waited so long to have this? As soon as she'd forgiven me and made it clear that she did in fact want me, that should've been the end of denial and the start of this.

She watched me, lower lip caught between her teeth, eyes dark with desire. She wanted me. She *loved* me.

I half laughed against her flesh and flicked my tongue over her nipple as she hooked her legs around me. "Come here," she said in a breathless murmur, reaching for my trousers.

"Love, you forget yourself." I caught her wrists with my shadows and pulled her hands back to the desk. I let more tendrils whisper over her thighs, pulling her gown up, but it was *my* fingers I used to grip them and drag her to the edge of the desk.

She let out a yelp, falling back, cheeks now a blazing pink that made me want to take her this instant.

"These thighs... fuck, Katherine, *these thighs.*" Not wanting to let them go for long, I used my shadows to unfasten my trousers, and peeled off my shirt as quickly as possible, before returning my grip.

Her gaze drifted over my bare chest, trailing over my scar in a way that lifted the hairs at the nape of my neck.

If her look could have that effect on me, what would happen if I gave her free rein to *touch*?

It was too much. Sharing space with her, my work, my

body, my secrets... it threatened to overwhelm me as it was, but to let her take my control too? I hovered on its edge enough when she was close by.

To hand it over, willingly...

Something bad would follow. It had to. That was how the world worked.

My heart pounded all the harder, making my dick throb as shadows slid my trousers down and freed it.

Without my instruction, shadows had already slid between her legs, working her pussy and back entrance at once, rippling over her clit, leaving her writhing and whimpering before me.

"Fuck. Aren't you a picture?" I lifted and spread her thighs, getting a better look at her slickness as my shadows disappeared inside. "I'm going to need a whole gallery of all the different ways I get to fuck you."

She arched under my gaze, teeth digging into her lip until it went pale. Part of her was trying to keep quiet because of the open doors. I'd thought her past that, but hadn't the world thrown those men at her? A recent reminder of every lesson she was trying to escape.

I ran my cock along her, and the sounds she tried to hold in grew louder. "Please," she gasped, before going right back to biting her lip.

"Are you asking for this, love?" I slid my dick over her again.

She nodded, every muscle in her growing taut as my shadows and I worked her.

"Ah, but my ember isn't quiet, remember?" With my thumb, I gently pulled her lower lip from between her teeth. "She has nothing to be ashamed of. She is a fucking queen and she deserves to be heard, doesn't she?"

"Yes." Out loud, but not loud enough.

"*Doesn't she?*" My shadows' thrusts grew deeper with those two words, and the ones in her pussy curled forward.

"Yes," she cried out, trembling. "Yes!" Her eyelids fluttered as she came apart in my hold, coating my length in her sweet wetness.

"That's it. Perfect." I pulled the shadows from her channel and set myself at her entrance. "Now my forest fire gets what she asked for."

Movement on the edge of my vision distracted me from the heave of her chest as she sank down from her peak, though I didn't let my shadows ease up, still inside and around her.

Out in the corridor, a guard passed.

"You might gather an audience, love."

Half dazed from her orgasm, halfway to the next one, Kat's gaze turned to the doorway.

I stood ready to have my shadows shut the door, if that was what she asked for.

For a long beat she watched as someone else passed, and I wasn't sure if she realised her back arched, displaying her curves even better. "Then we'd better give them a show."

The sight of her, the words, the feel of her trying to push onto me—they sent a jolt of heady, tight pleasure down my spine.

"Yes, we had," I rasped out, gathering myself. Setting one hand on her belly, I adjusted my grip on her thigh and brought my shadows around the other. "*We had.*" It came out firmer this time, and I trusted myself to drive into her.

She cried out, all attempts at quiet forgotten as she clenched around me. The feel of her parting, hot and wet and tight was maddening, soul-tearing, sublime. I set to a fast, deep pace, chasing her pleasure and my own, which rose far too quickly, snapping my hips into hers.

"You're so good, love," I told her as she rocked to meet me, and a dazed smile lit her face.

Stars above, I fucking loved her. More than I thought possible. I might've said it out loud—I wasn't sure.

A bone-breaking tension rose in me—a tingling that pulled every muscle more taut and made every thought more fleeting.

With every thrust she let out another cry, each one more breathless than the last, her tits bouncing. The sight of her stole the air from my lungs, the sanity from my mind, and my fingers dug into her as she screwed her eyes shut and lost herself in another writhing climax.

"Fuck. Fuck!" I followed her, balls tightening as electricity exploded inside me and the world disappeared, leaving just the image of her, the feel of her, the sound of her moans.

Just her.

There was only her.

I barely caught myself on the table instead of collapsing on her, my muscles melting into blissful ease. Shadows ebbed around us as if exhausted. Freed, she draped her arms over my shoulders and murmured my name. I kissed her throat, still inside her and yet needing more points of connection as I tried to gather myself.

As I caught my breath, I pressed my forehead to hers and met her sleepy gaze. Her green eyes were the colour of forests and grass and the leaves of the roses she adored so much. She was a thing of life—a goddess of it—and it felt like she'd finally started to live.

With a half smile, she touched my cheek, fingertips brushing my earlobe, sending a ripple of pleasure down my spine.

"Love," I managed to say, foolishly—not a complete sentence.

But she destroyed me. In the best possible way, she destroyed and re-created me.

Shaking my head, I nuzzled her nose. "I love you, my beautiful genius—I fucking love you."

80

KAT

Without the prospect of Kaliban to take my memories, I went to the Hall of Healing the next day with a sickly feeling in my stomach. My nerves hummed, the magic around me too, and if not for numerous chances to let go recently, my hands would've been covered in my purple stain. I might even have hazed.

"Are you sure you'll be all right?" Rose stood beside me at the bottom of the stairs. "I can come in with you."

"I..." I blinked up at the marble building. "I was about to say I'd started this journey alone, but... that isn't true. Bastian was here when I woke. And you've been with me almost every day since." I gave her a sidelong look. "Would you?"

"I offered, didn't I? And it wasn't out of politeness, but... if she really does have a cure for you, I want to be there to support you. I'm sure Ella would come, but..."

"But she isn't the best with blood." I scoffed, the tightness in my stomach easing to know I had Rose.

"Gods willing there is no blood, but…" She shrugged, then nodded towards the doors. "Shall we?"

I squared my shoulders and offered a silent prayer to the gods I'd told to fuck themselves more times than I cared to admit.

Please, please let this be the last time I have to do this.

ELTHEA GAVE ROSE AN EVALUATIVE GLANCE, but otherwise gave no reaction to her sitting at my side.

"Well." She clutched the notebook, fingers tapping an agitated rhythm on its cover, but said nothing more.

"You said you'd made progress with my cure?"

She drew a long breath, chin rising. "I think I have. In fact, I'm *sure* I have." A fleeting smile lit her face, and I had to bite back a laugh.

Elthea, the woman who remained calm and deadpan ninety-nine percent of the time, was *excited*.

"I realise my mistake now. I was attempting to cure all of your 'affliction,' but"—she shook her head and sighed—"magic is *not* an affliction or an illness or anything bad at all." She raised her hand. "It's not good, either, to be clear—it just *is*. Like fire—it can be used for good or ill, but in its own right it's a neutral state."

I blinked at her speeding sentences, barely keeping up.

"But your having magic isn't bad for your body. Only the poison attacking your system is. My work has shown me there are two separate things going on in you. Magic and poison. The poison lingering in your bloodstream is one element. But your ability to draw on magic—your gift, which manifests in a poisoned touch in your case—that is a separate matter entirely. And they're not as closely intertwined as I thought."

She gave a breathless little laugh. "It's so obvious. I should've realised sooner, but there's never been anything quite like this before. The poison you took is what's trying to kill you each day. All the attempts to save you are what gave you magic."

She opened the notebook and pointed, but she pulled it away again before I had a chance to read any of the spidery text. I only glimpsed a sketch of what might've been branching veins or a tree.

"All right. And what does this all mean? Separate cures for the two elements?" I bit my lip.

She waved her hand. "That's not the really *interesting* part. It's what he put in the poison." She went on, words tripping over each other like mine had when I'd explained to Bastian about the Crown of Ashes. "Not only aconite. I knew there was some magical element, but without a sample, I couldn't deduce what that was, exactly. The fact I couldn't heal you said it was powerful. But now I've taken a good look at you and gone over all my findings, I understand why."

Avoiding my question. Did that mean there was no way to get rid of my magic?

I exchanged a glance with Rose, who widened her eyes to say she understood as much of this as I did.

"Where is this all going?" She folded her arms, head canting to one side.

Elthea huffed. "Sun and Stars, I make the most exciting medical-magical discovery in centuries and the only people I get to explain it to are a pair of *humans*." She spread her arms and took a deep breath. "In order to strengthen the poison and make it incurable, thus ensuring the Serpent could not be saved by the antidote, he used a great power source." She spoke slowly and loudly, like we were particularly stupid humans. "He used part of the Great Yew."

I fell stock still. Rose gasped.

My eyelids fluttered. "Dusk Court's Great Yew?"

"Do you know of another one?" Elthea clicked her tongue. "Bark or leaves from it, perhaps. But if I was a gambling woman, I'd bet everything I own that he used a berry—after all, they're poisonous. At least now it makes sense why it resets each evening—the trees, the Great Bargain, the change between king and queen... they're all connected."

"What does this mean?" My thoughts raced, finally catching up. A bow made from the Great Yew's wood had chosen me. Had it felt the tree's power? *Like reaches for like*, or so I'd read in my research. "The Great Yew is... it's tied to the magic of Elfhame—that's what I was told." With the Oak, it was a marker of great power. If that had fuelled the poison I'd taken, it didn't sound like the sort of thing that could be stopped.

I swallowed my rising disappointment. "You said you had a cure. How could *anything* counter that level of magic?"

She straightened and smiled like I'd asked exactly what she'd hoped. "Only its equal and opposite—an acorn from the Great Oak." Gaze flitting to the door, she cleared her throat and pulled a small vial from her inside pocket.

Inside, something dark writhed against the glass. Shimmering gold danced through the viscous, moss green liquid as it worked *against* gravity.

"Officially, that isn't what's in here. No one's meant to gather anything from either tree, but..." She spread her hands. "Well, sometimes rules must be broken in the name of science."

I exhaled, not quite a laugh. In the name of science, she'd done things so terrible I'd entrusted my mind to a stranger to erase them. And now this—something that had to come with a much steeper punishment.

In that moment, I finally understood her.

She wasn't interested in hurting me. Nor was she interested in helping me. There was only science. Understanding. A puzzle to be solved.

I wasn't sure if that was better or worse than it being personal.

She held my gaze a long while, then lifted her eyebrows. "You realise this is a danger to me. I have to trust you not to reveal what I've done with the acorn, and you have to trust me to take this. It works both ways. Understood?"

I dipped my chin, and she held out the vial. Its contents lapped at the glass where my fingers touched. "How is this supposed to work?"

"It's an updated version of what we tried before. I've refined it, so it won't be so painful. Your magic fights the manticore venom—a distraction—while the antidote, powered by the acorn, deals with the aconite in your bloodstream."

I nodded like I understood what she was talking about. One of the appointments I'd erased. "So the venom won't harm me?"

Frowning, she cocked her head and gave me a long look. "I told you before—you're immune. Are you having memory problems? Perhaps I need to—"

"No, I just... I haven't been sleeping well—since the attack, you know?"

"Right." She was still giving me that odd look, though.

I cleared my throat and tilted the vial so the liquid shimmered. "And my magic?"

There was a long pause before she pulled another vial from her pocket. "You have a choice. Take that alone and the poison attacking you will be cured. Take this after, and the iron in it will nullify your magic."

"Iron?" I grimaced at the memory of how unpleasant it had felt to wear the ring for a long time. "You said I should steer clear of it."

"Because it's dangerous. It will *wrench* your gift away. This isn't a cure but... an injury. It's normally hard to get hold of, but I used your ring to make this. You must take it *immediately* after that—it's reliant on the acorn and antidote and venom all working together. If you drink it in a week's time, it won't work. This is a now or never deal."

I stared at the rusty-coloured liquid.

All I'd wanted for so long was a cure. It had meant going back to what and who I was before. Here she was offering me that.

And yet...

There was no going back. I didn't fit in that mould anymore. I may still be haunted by memories of the old Kat's lessons and rules, but I didn't live by them.

When I shot Rose a look, she gave me a reassuring smile.

Swallowing, I drew a deep breath. "I'll just take this one."

Elthea smiled at that, shoulder sinking.

Before I lost my nerve, I removed the cork and downed the fortified antidote.

It slithered over my tongue, making me gag as it wriggled against the back of my throat. I covered my mouth, afraid of coughing up a precious drop. It burned on the way down, and I braced for pain, but it faded a moment later as my gift fought back. Magic hummed over my skin, my body sucking it in on instinct.

Then, nothing.

In fact, I felt... *good*—better than I had in months.

"Kat?" Rose leant in.

I blinked, touching my belly. "It's... it's gone." A constant feeling of wrongness in the pit of my stomach—only now it was gone did I realise how much I'd forced myself to ignore it.

Elthea smiled wide enough to show her canines—I hadn't seen them before—and Rose leapt up with a crow, like my victory was hers. Tears stung my eyes as I laughed and let her grab me in a hug, secure in my ability to hold in my magic and not hurt her.

I was free. From Robin. From needing a daily antidote.

I wasn't bound to Bastian by an accident of magic. Every touch between us was our choice.

Everything that happened now was for us to decide.

81
BASTIAN

For the second time in as many days, Kat burst into my office. Anyone else, and I'd have destroyed them, but for her I preferred the kind of destruction I'd enacted on this desk yesterday.

I looked up from another dull report. A delivery of guard weapons missing... or perhaps not. It wasn't clear if this was a clerical error or if they'd really disappeared. Thankfully this was the last of the reports, since the wedding was tomorrow.

I arched an eyebrow as Kat shut the door. "Don't tell me—you've *found* the Crown of Ashes this time? I wouldn't put it past you."

She shook her head as she caught her breath and approached. "She did it."

With a gasp, I sprang to my feet. "Elthea. Your appointment."

Half laughing, half panting, she clutched my arms and gave them a little shake. "I'm cured."

My pulse tolled loud in my ears. She'd wanted to be rid of her magic and the poison, and she looked so happy...

I swallowed, searching her grip. Her nails dug into my shirt, still purple. "But you're still marked."

She nodded, smile widening. "The poison in my system is gone—it isn't killing me. But I chose to keep my gift."

As she made the stain spread over her fingers, she looked just as happy to have her magic as she was to no longer be poisoned.

I exhaled my relief and bent, kissing her fingertips. Her poison tingled on my skin, a pain I'd grown to enjoy. A shiver skittered through me. "And I'm still immune to it."

Eyes bright, she nodded. "Poisonous, but not poisoned. At last."

"And you don't need me anymore. You're free to go where you wish." I smiled as I said it, like I wasn't torn apart by the idea. I didn't want her bound to me, as she'd put it. I *wanted* her to be free.

But I also wanted her... maybe even needed her.

Her lashes fluttered, and she swallowed. "I... I am."

A long moment passed, and I tried my best to look entirely happy. Maybe she could read me—maybe despite my efforts she knew that I was crumbling as I held this smile.

"And..." She spoke very softly, gaze flicking away before edging back to me. "What if I wish to be right here?"

My breath hitched like I'd just found solid ground. I cleared my throat and managed a laugh. "Well, it would be a little inconvenient to have you in the middle of the floor, but I'm sure I could work around you."

"Bastian!" She swatted my arm. "I'm being serious."

Grinning so much my cheeks hurt, I pulled her close. "I know. I'm sorry, I just..." I bent close to her ear. "I was afraid."

She arched back and gave me a wide-eyed look. "That I'd leave?"

I nodded, cheeks warming.

"Idiot Shadow." She grinned and squeezed me. "I don't want to go anywhere... not for the foreseeable future, at least." She winced. "I might need to travel to Albion to settle things with the estate at some point. I haven't heard anything about whether he has any living relatives."

"I mean... if he does, we could always get rid of them."

"Bastian." Another swat. "We are not killing some random person because they're a little inconvenient."

"*Very* inconvenient," I muttered, catching her hand. I planted a kiss on her palm. "If they take that estate from you..." I let my glower complete the sentence.

"With a little luck, he has no relatives left, and the queen will decide I should have it. Service to the crown and all that." She shrugged, but I spotted her brief wince, like she wasn't at all convinced.

"You did stop unCavendish."

"As I recall, I was lying on the floor when you killed him."

"But I wouldn't have known to kill him if not for you. Your queen owes you. We should petition her to give you the estate on that basis. I could draft a letter and ask Braea to sign it."

This time her face scrunched up in more than a brief wince. "Perhaps."

"We'll fix this." I took my time kissing away her wince.

When I pulled back, she made a little sound of complaint, fingers digging into my back.

This was what I'd seen in the woman who'd held herself so tightly in Lunden. Passion. Pleasure. A thirst for beauty—for *life* in all its expressions that had been kept locked away.

And now here she was, coming in to all of that.

Heart full, I kissed the tip of her nose. "Since you're staying, I can show you this." I disentangled myself from her and locked the door leading to Brynan's office.

She watched, brow furrowed, as I went to the panels depicting the Celestial and Tellurian Serpents and opened the hidden door. "A secret passage? You really are a spymaster."

Wide-eyed, she followed me into the darkness, letting me guide her and whisper the directions in her ear so she'd know in future. When we reached the courtyard door, I took her hand and showed her how the ring I'd had made for her fit the indent and opened it.

As we stepped into the secret lodestone, she gave a soft gasp at the shift from one plane to another, and her mouth fell open when she saw the courtyard, which was no longer over-grown. I'd planted it with aconite, foxgloves, hemlock, and other poisonous plants—ones I was fairly sure she could touch, despite her magic. Ones that could hurt as well as kill, as my itching wrist reminded me. I'd even managed to get the fountain working, and lily pads crowded the edges of its pool.

"What is this?" she asked, bending over the purple bells of deadly nightshade.

I held my breath as she stroked its petals. The plant didn't so much as droop.

"Yours."

She snapped upright. "What?"

"It's a secret lodestone. I'm giving it to you. Only one other person has a key for Dawn's side." I nodded towards the other door. "But if you lock it with your ring, they can't come through and startle you while you're in here."

She looked at me as though I was speaking in tongues.

"I planted all this for you. Well"—I gestured at the foun-tain and the other side of the courtyard, which I'd cleared but awaited plants—"half of it. I thought you might like to do the rest. Now you can control your magic, I'm sure you can plant some roses."

She blinked at the empty flower beds. "I... I don't..." She touched her chest. "You did this *for me?*"

"Of course. I hesitated about telling you about it before you had a cure. I didn't want you to feel obligated to stay because of this. But now you've decided to stay for a while at least, I thought it would give you some pleasure."

Her chin trembled, and she frowned at the plants. "I don't know what to say."

"Say nothing. Just enjoy it."

I stood back as she walked a slow circuit, skimming her fingertips over plants, the fountain's stone edge, the bench I'd uncovered beneath the brambles.

"Bastian," she said at last. She clasped her hands before her. "This is so much—so perfect. Thank you."

"It's my pleasure—truly. I look forward to seeing what you do with it."

"Hmm." She nodded, glancing at the plants. "It's so warm in here, everything's flowering months early. The palace walls —their magic must create a microclimate." She went on, muttering to herself about soil type and rose varieties.

I shut my eyes, letting the passion in her voice flood over me as I had in Riverton Palace's gardens. Listening to her speak to the supposed gardener about roses had revealed the fire behind her guarded exterior. From that moment I'd been doomed.

"You know..." She said, suddenly close, and when I opened my eyes, I found her only a foot away. "I haven't properly shown you my gratitude for being my antidote all these months."

"You don't need to thank me for that."

"I wasn't going to thank you." She peered up at me from beneath her lashes. "You like the feel of my poison, don't you? When it's just a light dose."

My cock twitched at her tone, yet my chest grew tight. This felt dangerous, like it might be a trap to allow her to wrestle control from me. With hesitance, I nodded.

She blinked up at me, all innocent, but the way she slowly licked her lips was anything but. "Then tell me to get on my knees so I can show you exactly how grateful I am."

A groan so low it was just beyond hearing reverberated in my chest. Still... "You don't have to do—"

"I know." She placed her hand on my chest, touch hot through my shirt. "I choose to. Now *tell me*."

I slid my fingers into her hair, breaths suddenly a little too fast. "On your knees, love. Show me what that lying little mouth can do."

With a smirk to put the Wicked Lady to shame, she obeyed.

82

BASTIAN

I had every one of my spies stationed around the palace and key routes through the city. An army of entertainers, cooks, and guards filled the building with unfamiliar faces, but somehow we reached the start of the wedding ceremony and nothing had gone wrong.

As the queen's representative, I stood on the throne room's dais, with the royal entrances behind me, one in each corner. Ahead, the aisle led to two sets of double doors—the main entrances used by most folk from Dusk and Dawn. Snowdrops, narcissi, and golden suns decorated the space for Dawn's triumph—marrying off one of its heirs and the hope more would come from their union. The ceremony would be held in here, followed by a ball in Dawn, then we'd return here late this afternoon for the eclipse when Braea would appear and make a speech with the king.

I'd exchanged a few polite words with Lucius and his wife, who sat to one side. Questions about unCavendish and the

Crown of Ashes plagued me whenever I saw him, but they were questions that had to go unasked.

From the rows of seats, a steady murmur of conversation filled the room as guests waited. Towards the back, Faolán's bulky form stuck out, and I met his gaze. He went still, brow furrowing. Mine matched it.

This was only the second time I'd seen him since Kat had rid herself of her husband. The first had been a terse exchange, giving him orders as part of the security preparations, and Rose had given me an apologetic look after.

It felt like I was the one who should be apologising to her —she was the one caught between us, after all.

I pushed myself to give him a nod. He wasn't to blame— not solely. And hadn't I held on to old rules too long, myself? Childhood lessons were hard to escape.

As I continued surveying the crowd, I caught myself searching for rich red hair, even though I knew she wasn't here yet. Force of habit.

As an offering of friendship to Dusk, Zita had asked Kat to be one of her attendants. I struggled to believe their good intentions, but Sepher told me she'd taken a liking to Kat.

There was plenty to like.

I tugged on the collar of my formal shirt, stomach dipping at the memory of Kat on her knees for me yesterday. Holding my gaze as she took my cock down her throat, she'd responded to my directions exquisitely and gone on with her own explorations until I'd erupted over her tongue.

After, perhaps high on being cured or what she'd done to me, she'd begged me to take her to a piercer. I'd sat there as she'd bared her breasts and had them pierce her nipples. She'd barely flinched as they'd pushed the needle through, but last night I'd been gentle and thorough with my ministrations, cleaning her skin and applying a healing salve.

Just when I thought I knew her and all that she was becoming, she surprised me.

I'd left her getting ready in our rooms a few hours ago, and now I burned to see her.

"You look more excited about all this than I do." From his seat, Sepher arched an eyebrow at me. Ankle resting on his knee, he spread out, taking up the chairs either side of his.

"Aren't you eager to see your future wife?"

His lips curled. "Not as eager as you are to see yours."

I had to bite back a smile. Now *there* was an idea.

This new Sepher—the one who'd been exiled from the city for years—I almost liked him. If not for our shared past and divided courts, we might've been friends.

I let myself indulge in his suggestion. What would it be like to stand up here as the groom waiting to marry Kat? It felt warm and tight like one of her hugs—like I was safe.

The cello struck up at that moment, soon followed by harp and flute, breaking through my daydream.

I kept hold of a wisp of its disappearing form and tucked it in my heart.

Sepher flashed a wide grin and stood. "It's time." His hands clasped together, knuckles whitening, and for a moment I had a glimpse of the nervous excitement behind his easy façade.

I waited to one side, making space for the ceremony. I only had a small part to play in—

Every thought I'd ever had shattered.

I couldn't draw breath.

My heart might've stopped.

Because at the end of the aisle stood a goddess.

Loose red hair spilled against a gown that seemed to be

made of molten gold. The strapless bodice draped over her full breasts, clinging and cupping to highlight every curve, even the points of her nipples and the fresh piercings either side. It nipped in at her waist before the skirt flowed over her round hips like liquid metal.

She carried a simple bunch of white narcissi, signifying spring and growth—the potential of new beginnings. Each step revealed her thigh through the long slit, and on that glorious thigh sat a golden serpent.

This time it wasn't only *like* she was mine—she truly was.

For a moment, I thought someone had added a drum to the lilting music, but it was my pulse, heavy and so, so loud it could've shaken the earth.

Even from this distance, I could pick out the deep green of her eyes locked on me. A faint smile edged her lips—perhaps because I was staring.

I could bump Sepher out the way—fight him for the spot—and make this into our wedding instead.

As she arrived at the front and nodded to Sepher, I swallowed. *Get a grip.* This was a royal wedding. I was here for professional reasons.

You are the Night Queen's Shadow, not a lovestruck boy.

Though maybe I was both.

By the time she handed Sepher the white narcissi and went to one of the chairs in the front row, I'd pulled myself together enough to incline my head to her, though my eyes might've burned a hole through her dress in the meantime.

Fuck. I mean, *fuck.* She had no business looking that good —not when I could do nothing about it.

With a deep breath, I dragged my attention away from her, though it kept flicking back, especially as, now she was seated, the skirt fell open, showing off her legs even more.

A tall, willowy woman followed as the next attendant. It took me a moment to recognise her as one of Sepher's childhood friends.

When Zita arrived, I caught Sepher gulping as a lovestruck expression spread over his face. In deep cerulean blue, she looked beautiful, but she wasn't Katherine.

My Katherine.

Those two words went round and round in my head as the ceremony started, and it was only because my shadows nudged me that I stirred from my daze in time to give Dusk's blessing to the marriage. Kat's gaze seared into me as I spoke, and the need to get her to myself grew more intense.

The rest of the ceremony felt like it took at least a century to pass, and even once it was over, I had to wait for Sepher and Zita to leave, followed by the other attendant, and then Kat, her hips swaying as she walked away. I could only stare at her exposed back and her backside clad in the metallic fabric.

I rubbed my fingers together, wondering if it felt slippery.

Once she was out of the room and the guests started filing after her, I checked the mezzanine for two of my operatives, posing as guests. With a moment's eye contact, they confirmed all was well.

Ceremony done. Now for the ball.

83

BASTIAN

I t felt odd to pass through the door leading to Dawn's side of the palace, but they were our hosts. I tried to catch up to Kat, but a guard pulled me to one side with a question about weapons.

Guests had to surrender them in the grand hall before entering Dawn. I'd left my Shadowblade in my office. If anything happened, it wasn't far, and I didn't trust it with anyone else. It sat on my desk with Kat's bow and dagger—her ring would allow her to enter and pick them up if she needed to.

Gods willing, she wouldn't.

By the time I entered the party, music and chatter already filled the large entrance chamber as folk gathered drinks and stopped to talk or continued into the ballroom itself. I spotted Faolán towering above everyone else and the top of Rose's strawberry blond head next to him. She nodded enthusiastically to someone in their group, and as the crowd shifted, I caught a glimpse of deep red hair and molten gold. My legs were already moving before I consciously registered it was Kat.

On the far side of the group, King Lucius passed, acknowledging Kat with a nod as he did. It left a little twitch of unease in my gut. What had unCavendish told him about her? I would have to press my spy to get closer to him.

But that was a matter for another day.

I eased in beside her, hand sliding around her waist as I nodded at the rest of the group—Ella, Asher, and Perry. Fluffy, a bow tied around her neck, came and sat at my side. Ariadne and Lysander were already dancing.

Kat's chest rose and fell as she straightened and saw it was me. "Why, if it isn't the Night Queen's Shadow." Holding two drinks, she gave a mock bow, which gave me an excellent view of her cleavage. "To what do we owe the honour?"

"I heard there was a goddess here and wouldn't believe it until I saw for myself, but..." I let my gaze glide over her. "I see the reports were no exaggeration."

Ella chuckled over her wine glass. "Painted in gold, no less. How Ari made it, I have no idea."

Kat's cheeks went that pink shade I loved. "She's a genius. I'm just a canvas." A flicker at the corner of her mouth belied her pleasure at being admired.

I traced a small circle on Kat's back and ate up the shiver that worked through her. "Ari clearly has good taste in art supplies."

Asher smirked and looked away, shaking his head. He hovered at Perry's side, not quite touching her. As Rose squeezed Faolán's arm, he met my gaze with an apologetic smile. We needed to talk, but now was not the time.

As the others started chatting about the ceremony, Kat

held out one of her glasses of wine—the kind that could get her drunk despite her magic. "I got you a drink."

"Don't you want it?" The other was almost empty.

She glanced away, shaking her head. "I decided to only have one today."

A tightness I'd been carrying in my chest since she'd woken in Elfhame eased. I took the glass and passed it to Asher. "I'll save it for after we dance." I held out my hand. "If this goddess will bless me with one, that is?"

"There are a lot of people here."

I shrugged. "Well, you're no longer married, and I'd say the cat's somewhat out of the bag when it comes to the fact you're important to me. *Please*, divine one. Or will you make me beg?"

The corner of her mouth twitched. "How could I possibly say no to such a pious devotee?" She passed her drink to Ella, then took my hand.

I escorted her to the ballroom as the next song began—a waltz, just like our first dance. The less formal dancing would start later, after Braea's appearance at the eclipse. At the far end of the room, Lucius joined Sepher and Zita on the dais. He gave a stiff smile, but I caught his lip curling as Sepher's smooth tail flicked from side to side.

But I had much more important business to attend to. Lashes lowered, Kat held my gaze as I took her hand and waist and pulled her as close as possible. The fabric was slippery, like skin oiled for a massage, and I added that to my list of things for us to try, especially with how sensitive she was.

As we set off across the floor, I bent and murmured in her ear, "You look incredible. I want to do all kinds of delicious things to you."

Her breath caught, making her breasts heave at the dress.

How the thing stayed on, I had no idea, but since Ariadne had made it, I suspected it involved magic. Interesting. Perhaps there was a word to make it fall off.

"Like what?" Kat asked, voice husky as her thigh slid along mine.

"Like splitting in two and fucking you with both parts of me at once."

Just as I'd expected, her step faltered like it had in Lunden. And just as I had then, I caught and lifted her seamlessly.

But instead of scandalised as she would've been last year, she looked eager. Her wide eyes skimmed between mine as though she was calculating how that would work, how it would look—how it might feel.

As I lowered her, I grinned wickedly and crushed her against me, enjoying her softness. "I was going to ask if you thought you were ready for that, but the look on your face already answered." I dipped to her ear, fingertips tracing up her spine, making her arch against me. "Would my ember like that?"

Her throat bobbed. "You just turned the next few hours into torture."

I chuckled as I led her across the dance floor again. "I prefer to think of it as foreplay. Now, every time you catch my eye, you'll be thinking about having two cocks buried in you."

As her pupils blew wide, her grip on my shoulder tightened. "Where?"

"Hmm, my ember is greedy for details, isn't she? You need to answer one of my questions first. Are you wearing anything under that pretty dress, Katherine? A scrap of lace, perhaps?"

"Not a thing."

I groaned as I spun her away. When I pulled her back

against me, my arms around her waist, her backside upon my twitching cock. "So good, love. You've more than earned your answer." I swiped my lips over her neck and murmured onto her skin, "In your pussy and your naughty little mouth, first, I think. Then perhaps we'll try front and back at once, like my shadows do to you. But we might need to work up to that. I wouldn't want to break you."

She made a soft wanting sound that shot straight to my dick like I was already buried inside her. "Can't we go now?"

Goosebumps flooded her skin, and I watched the pulse leaping in her throat as we manoeuvred across the floor. "Later," I breathed in her ear, making her shiver. "I promise."

I had to lead her more strongly than usual for the rest of the dance, as she had a glazed look in her eye like she couldn't focus on anything other than our plans. That suited me. She would be more than ready by the time we got to our rooms, and I would take my time making her come undone deep into the night.

Truth be told, by the time I escorted her from the dance floor, I was a little dazed myself, calculating whether we could leave and return in time for the eclipse. But no—for this I didn't want to be rushed. If she was going to take both of me, I needed her completely relaxed.

It was only when she sucked in a little gasp, staring ahead, that I remembered anyone else existed.

My daze evaporated as I followed her line of sight. Her uncle. I needed to ask her to release me from that promise not to kill him. The sooner, the better.

But she didn't miss a step, and with nothing more than a slight frown she turned with me.

"Are you all right, divine one?" I squeezed her hand.

She threw me a stiff smile and nodded. "I am, but I going to go to the ladies' room and catch my breath."

I nodded and kissed her brow, then watched her saunter away. Understandably, she wanted to regroup, but this was not the same woman who'd fled him back in Albion.

84

KAT

Orrery in one hand, I splashed water on my throat, cold enough to make me gasp. The shock rooted me in the marble bathroom and Uncle Rufus's disapproving stare faded.

From above, daylight filtered and refracted through a series of crystals set into the roof. I counted the colours like Kaliban would've told me to. Azure and indigo. Violet and scarlet. Orange, gold, and true, verdant green.

My pulse slowed as calm rolled over me.

I wasn't as afraid of Uncle Rufus as I'd once been, but when I ran the cold tap over my wrists it was a relief to see only my nails were purple. As my heart had lurched at the sight of him, I'd feared my magic breaking free, despite all my progress.

Calmed, I replaced the orrery in my bodice. This dress had no pockets, but a generous cleavage could double up as storage.

I gave myself a tight smile in the mirror. The rainbow light coming through the crystals glimmered over my gown and painted my skin. I turned this way and that, taking in my reflection and the way the fabric made it look like gold paint had spilled over my body.

Perhaps Bastian's staring was understandable.

My smile eased into something more confident. A smile the Wicked Lady had been too desperate to give. A smile Lady Katherine of Riverton Palace had been too crushed beneath rules to allow herself.

It, like this body clad in gold, was all mine.

Perhaps that was what Bastian had always seen.

I wouldn't want to break you.

Stars above, in that moment, I'd wanted to be broken. By him, on him, with him. I'd have slipped my gown off then and there if he'd offered to pull me apart with both sides of him.

Later could not come soon enough.

Fuck Uncle Rufus.

As I left the bathroom, I let my mind linger on the thought of being sandwiched between two Bastians, like some sort of fucking delicious cake. Or should that be "delicious fucking cake?"

I was biting back a laugh as I rounded a corner and stopped short. At the end of the corridor walked a fae with fox-red hair bound in a braid.

The fae from Lunden.

They disappeared around the corner, and I hurried after. "Excuse me," I called out. "Hey!"

I had to hike up my dress to run, but it was worth it, as I finally caught up. "Hello?"

They turned, lips pursed, brow furrowed. Brown eyes bored into me.

"You... You were in Lunden, weren't you?"

Arms folding, they nodded once and went to turn away.

"Wait, no. I'm not done." I tried to grab their sleeve but caught the hem of their coat instead.

They stopped stock still.

But that wasn't why my breath caught. Beneath their coat sat a sword with a bronze fox head pommel and a matching dagger.

No weapons were allowed on the palace corridors today. Guests had been made to surrender theirs at the grand hall. Even Bastian had left ours in his office. I'd tried slipping his old dagger into a leather garter on my thigh, but it was impossible to hide anything under this clingy fabric. I suspected Bastian had something stashed in a boot, but, officially, no weapons.

As they turned, I dropped their jacket and pushed a friendly, foolish smile on my face like I hadn't seen.

"What do you want?" they ground out.

"At the race. You helped me, didn't you? When that tree fell..."

Their eyes narrowed, but they didn't deny it.

Why did they have the blades? They didn't look dressed for a wedding, so perhaps they had other business in the palace. Perhaps.

I blinked, realising how long I'd left the silence between us. Too long for someone who wasn't suspicious. Cocking my head, I shrugged. "I just want to know why."

They huffed a long breath out through their nose and rolled their eyes. I could almost hear the way they wanted to mutter *humans*.

"You saved me from the snare. I owed you."

So they *were* the fox.

"Then I saved you from the waterfall."

A transaction. Said like a true fae.

They took a step closer, towering over me. Their arms

dropped to their sides, putting their hand close to the hidden weapons. "Now, I owe you nothing."

My heart stuttered as I took a step back. It was a job to keep my smile empty-headed and bright—thank the gods for long years of practice. "Thank you. I don't know what I'd have done without your help." I glanced down the corridor. "Well, I'd better get back to the celebrations."

"You should." Their jaw tightened as I turned away. I could feel that stare follow me—an itch between my shoulder blades.

It was only once I was out of sight that I allowed myself to frown. It might be nothing—it probably was, but I needed to let Bastian know they were armed and in the palace. For all I knew, they might be one of Dawn's guards. That would make sense.

It took another couple of turns before I realised I was lost. Dawn's layout was similar to Dusk's, but not quite. In running after the fox-haired fae (and trying to ensure my breasts didn't bounce out of my dress entirely), I hadn't paid enough attention.

Still, I hadn't come far. I just needed to find my way back to the bathroom, then I'd find the ballroom from there.

Left at a familiar hallway, then right. Yes, the bathroom was round the corner from here, I was sure of it.

Just as I reached the end of the corridor, a figure in grey stepped out, continuing straight at the T-junction I was about to turn onto.

Black hair, slate grey leather armour, a cleft chin, he glanced this way, then did a double take and slowed. His hand rested on the hilt of a sword at his belt. A dagger sat beside it.

I sucked in a breath, gaze flicking back to his face, but the skin around his eyes tightened. He'd seen me spot his weapons.

Palace guards didn't wear grey. Not that shade of it, anyway. And people who lived in the palace didn't tend to wander around in armour. What were the chances of *two* armed fae walking the halls for benign reasons?

"Hello, pretty one." He gave a slow smile as he stalked this way, but his eyes pierced me, intent and calculating. "What are you doing here?"

"Bathroom. But I think I'm a bit lost." I touched my chest and managed a chuckle that said "silly me" but my heart beat grew heavier and heavier with each step he took.

"Very lost. No one's supposed to be here." He cocked his head, gaze skimming over me. It rested on my cleavage.

My fingers tingled, and I curled them into loose fists at my sides, away from his focus on my tits.

"What say I show you back to your friends? You never know what kind of trouble you might get into in the wrong place at the wrong time." His smile eased, brightening, and I almost believed it.

Almost.

Because he angled his shoulders in that way Bastian did before he drew his blade.

As soon as he reached me, he would attack.

85
BASTIAN

It felt like Kat was gone for a very long time, but I fully accepted that was down to my infatuation—one minute felt like forever. Between fetching more drinks and deciding to dance, the rest of the group filtered off until Faolán, Rose, and I remained at the back of the ballroom.

She stared off to one side, nursing her drink. Faolán examined his, brow furrowed. I couldn't stop scanning the room for Kat's return.

"Oh, hmm. Yes." Rose craned over the crowd towards the entrance chamber. "I think Perry needs my help over there." She pointed, but I saw no sign of the woman. "Back shortly." She flashed me a bright smile before lifting Faolán's chin and forcing him to meet her gaze. "I'm sure you two have plenty to talk about." She nudged his chest before slipping away into the crowd.

Once she was gone, I sidled closer to him. "Look, I'm sorry."

"I'm sorry," he said at the same time.

We laughed, and it was almost like we hadn't argued.

"No, I'm sorry." His scowl deepened. "The marriage laws were the only thing that kept Rose safe when she came here— the reason we *got* married in the first place. It terrified me to think what might've happened if..." He shuddered, hand scraping over his chin, which was already stubbled even though he'd been clean shaven at the start of the ceremony. "Suppose it made me cling to those traditions too hard."

"Well, I'm sorry too. Part of my couldn't let go of them until I almost lost her entirely. And... I was taking my own guilt out on you... especially with her hurt like that."

He rubbed his chest. "She looked awful. Must've been in a lot of pain."

"Not that she'd let anyone else know about it." I scoffed, even though my heart tightened at the memory of her injuries.

"She was right though. Her speech, I mean. Some of our rules and beliefs are outdated." He frowned at his glass before emptying it in one go. "It was unfair of me to hold her *or you* to a contract she never chose to go into." He met my eye, fingers tightening around his glass. "And for that I'm sorry. After everything we've been through, I should've trusted your judgement."

Muscles easing, I clapped him on the shoulder. "I'm not sure *I* trust my judgement when it comes to Kat." I gave a rueful grin. "I think I'm starting to understand why you lost your mind when Rose was in danger."

The corner of his mouth twitched, then he was hugging me. He slapped my back, making the air burst from my lungs. "Never thought I'd see the day." He pulled back and gave a wolfish grin. "The Serpent of Tenebris is regretting his comments about 'human brides.'"

Scowling, I muttered into my glass.

"Don't look so grumpy—Rose says that's my job." He squeezed my shoulder. "Honestly, I'm happy for you. Kat is... I like her a lot, and so does Rose. And I like you. It's a good match."

"Considering you dislike most people, that's high praise indeed."

He made a sound halfway between a growl and a laugh, and we stood there for a while, watching the dancers in companionable silence. It was a weight unloaded to no longer have this tension between us.

"Hmm." He eyed me sidelong. "Do you think you'll make her your 'human bride?'"

I rolled my eyes. "You're not going to let that go, are you?"

"Not for the next couple of centuries."

"You know she gets a say in the matter, don't you?"

"And I'm pretty sure I know what she'd say, if you asked."

I wasn't so sure. Not after her experience of marriage so far. "You're married for a couple of years and suddenly you're the expert on relationships?"

Chin lifting, he straightened to his full height. "Actually, yes. Rose and I are very happy. In fact, we're—"

The high whistle of something moving at speed cut through the music. Adrenaline surged through me as two arrows streaked overhead and pinged off the king's throne.

Fuck.

"Shit," Faolán growled.

We thrust our drinks at the nearest people, starting for the dais.

Kat. A shudder chased through me. There was an attack, and I didn't know where she was. I glanced back at the ballroom doors as alarm rippled through the crowd.

This had to be what Sura meant about uniting the throne. A coup against both sides.

We shoved past folk fighting to get out and ordered them to remain calm. The last thing we needed was a panic like at the Solstice.

At our gritted instructions, they clutched each other, eyes wide. Some stared up at the mezzanine overlooking the ballroom where the shots had come from.

As word spread, chaos broke out.

The music stopped and screams and shouts took over. Dark clad figures dropped from the mezzanine, blades glinting, and more burst from a side room as archers covered their advance.

How the fuck had they got in?

I gritted my teeth and drew the dagger from my boot as Faolán produced a blade. Of course he'd had the same idea. It was why we were friends. Always ready. Always armed.

Side-by-side, we worked our way towards the dais, though my heart dragged me back.

I didn't give a fuck about the king currently hiding behind the throne. I wanted to find Kat.

But if he died...

And if this was Hydra Ascendant...

The chaos wouldn't be contained to this room—it would break out across the realm.

A pair of the armoured attackers reached us, clearly aiming for the dais and the royal family there.

My muscles thrummed with energy, glad to have somewhere to direct it.

I dodged, shoving a civilian out the way with my shadows as a blade cut through the air. The next strike rang on my dagger and up my arm, and my attacker grinned as if pleased I only had a small blade.

Idiot.

My shadows swarmed around his feet, only meeting a little resistance from his magic. More powerful fae made it more of a struggle. But not him.

He jolted as they tugged on his ankle, and I took my opening.

Gripping his sword arm, I pulled him close and drove my dagger into his throat.

His eyes went wide. He gurgled, blood bubbling at his neck and from his mouth. Then he slumped to the floor.

A second later, Faolán had his attacker taken care of, and they fell at his feet, a wicked gash across their shoulder, neck twisted at an unnatural angle.

"All right?"

He answered with a grim nod, and we took the attackers' weapons before continuing forward.

I craned to check the situation on the dais. Cyrus shielded himself with a chair, and bent over his father, ushering him through a side door with guards following. Before the throne a huge sabrecat roared, baring its teeth at anyone who came close. Russet stripes ran through its golden coat.

Not it—*him*. Sepher.

Cyrus had the king's escape in hand, and Sepher covered it. I even spotted Zita pressed against the throne, dagger in hand, wearing a look that dared anyone to sneak up on her new husband.

We weren't the only ones who'd broken the rules about weapons.

I grabbed Faolán's arm. "They don't need us."

He nodded. "Look." He held still, forcing the crowd to

break around us, and from across the room, I made out Asher's black hair and the purple gleam of Lysander's. He whistled and they turned towards us, arriving as the crowd's flow became a trickle.

"Have you seen Perry?" Pale, Asher scanned the guests pressing at the exit as guards pushed in.

"No," I muttered, signalling to the guards to hold a line around the double doors. If they entered on one side, they could help civilians out the other. "Nor any of the others." The words were bitter on my tongue.

Lysander held out his hand for Faolán's spare blade before shadowstepping out of sight, leaving flecks of darkness behind. An instant later, he materialised behind an attacker on the other side of the room who had hold of a pregnant woman by the arm. With a single thrust, he drove the knife into their spine.

While he helped the woman, I gave Asher my dagger. "Focus." I said it as much to myself as him.

Blood bathed the ballroom floor by the time the first group of guards reached us, and most of the guests had escaped. But a few guards still fought the attackers, and screams echoed from the corridors. This wasn't over.

"The king and Prince Cyrus went that way." I pointed out the side door. "Go after them and protect their backs."

One started in that direction, but another caught her shoulder—Amandine, who'd stopped Kat at the bridge. The others exchanged glances. "But Dawn's Ascendant," someone muttered.

Amandine scowled. "And as far as we know, this is an attack by Dusk. You could be sending us into a trap."

I bit back a groan. Fucking daytime.

Faolán bristled, and Asher's shoulders squared. I could feel his "I'm the queen's cousin" card coming this way, but it would make no difference. These guards were all clad in Dawn's pale grey.

I straightened and lifted my chin, fixing Amandine with a look that could wither trees. "Dusk has nothing to do with this. I knew nothing about it until the arrows started flying. Now, *go and protect your king.*"

Her nostrils flared.

"For once Dusk is talking sense. Stop being damn fools and do as the man says." At my side appeared Sepher, in his fae form, naked and bloodied. Back on the dais half a dozen attackers lay dead... or at least parts of them did.

Beside him, Zita stared daggers at the guards, her actual blade stained red.

Amandine sucked in a breath and bowed her head. "At once, Your Highness." The guards trooped off after the king and Cyrus.

I nodded my thanks to Sepher and gestured to the bodies and pooled blood. "Sorry your wedding turned into... this."

As he slid an arm around Zita's waist, he flashed me a feline grin, not the slightest bit concerned by his lack of clothes. "Like they say, the couple who slays together stays together."

"I'm sure that isn't a saying," Asher muttered, gaze skimming over the dead guests.

"It is now." Sepher smirked. "What're you doing now?"

It took me a beat to register that the fighting in here had stopped, and above, the mezzanine was empty except for a handful of guards.

"We need to get proper weapons, secure the queen's apartments, find Kat and the others, and ensure the king is safe."

Inwardly I winced at how long the list was. "Not necessarily in that order."

With a snort, he shook his head. "I'd say definitely *not* in that order." He stroked Zita's hair and they started towards the door. "We have some friends to save." He turned to me and raised his eyebrows, backing away. "I'd suggest you examine your priorities, Marwood. Choose the ones who'd choose you. Fuck everyone else."

He wasn't going after the king—he was choosing his friends over the father who'd banished him from the city for so long.

"Good luck." He nodded before turning and shifting midstep, feet becoming paws, striped skin becoming a furry coat, his tail growing thick fur as it swished from side to side.

Faolán watched him leave, a thoughtful frown etched between his eyebrows. "Well? Where to?"

Good question.

86

KAT

My heart slammed against my rib cage, harder with each step the armoured fae took.

I fixed a smile on my face even though I wanted to vomit.

The corridor was empty, but if I unleashed my poison, it would linger in this closed space and kill anyone who came wandering along—innocents included.

If I let him get too close, he would draw his weapon and run me through before I managed to touch him.

Two shitty choices, and a fae who only stood eight feet away.

"You know," I purred, tilting my head back to bare my throat, even though every part of me screamed against that vulnerability, "I came out here hoping to find a strong man like you." Shoving down my instincts, I sauntered towards him.

He blinked, stride faltering, gaze skipping to my lower lip caught between my teeth.

"Maybe you can help me with something else before you

take me back to the party." I gave a slow smile, despite my pulse throbbing as I entered the range of his sword.

Keep going. Keep going.

I didn't need him to believe me, I just needed him distracted for long enough.

Shifting my focus, I felt the vibration of magic around me.

Not yet. I didn't want him to spot the telltale purple spreading over my skin.

Soon.

Fingertips trailing over my collarbone, I pushed my hair back and let him see that my hands were empty.

Nothing more than a harmless human. Not even a fae mark to say she had magic.

There was a creak of leather from near the hilt of his sword —his gauntlets perhaps as his grip shifted to the dagger. Much better for close work.

I didn't dare lower my gaze to check.

His eyes narrowed as I took another step, but they flicked down to my tits as I arched my back so hard it felt like it was about to break.

They said fae enjoyed human women's curves. Well, I was staking my life on it.

His eyebrows squeezed together in something that looked like regret. "I don't think we have time for—"

"But I'm sure we do." Closing in, I placed a hand on his chest and let him stare at that as I called magic to my other hand and rose on tiptoes.

"I'm sorry, darling." He shook his head, and the unmistakable sound of a blade being drawn dried out my mouth.

I cupped his cheek, palm stained purple. "Me too."

His eyes bulged as he must've felt the first sting. Breath held, I concentrated the poison as much as I could, drawing power from all around me. I didn't want him to suffer, but I needed him dead.

Him or me? I chose me.

He flinched, breaking contact.

Too late.

Darkness outlined the shape of my hand on his cheek, already spreading. He went rigid, a strangled sound coming from his mouth, spittle flecking his lips.

His dagger clanged on the marble floor a moment before he slumped.

Only then did I let myself breathe—great gasps that shook through me as I checked up and down the corridor. Still empty.

Was this Hydra Ascendant? Sura had mentioned she wasn't ready *yet*. And the wedding brought together all of Dawn's royal family in one place at once time, while the Night Queen slumbered. Sending people after the king and princes would allow her to go and kill her mother while she was in Sleep, leaving just her for this "united" throne.

I grabbed his dagger and the sword. I didn't know how to use one, but when I reached Bastian, I could give it to him.

Bending over, I was about to check him for any identifying marks—a hydra insignia under his armour, perhaps—when soft voices drifted around the corner.

Hushed and urgent—these weren't the voices of guests at a party. More attackers.

I needed to get to Bastian and our friends and warn them. I hurried towards the ballroom.

Screams bounced off the walls.

"An attack!"

"Help!"

I stopped in my tracks as fae charged around the corner. Eyes round, mouths agape—just as they'd been at the Solstice.

A panicked crowd of strong fae in an enclosed space like this? My weak human body would be crushed.

I turned tail and ran. Thank the gods, I hadn't hazed in the corridor. But if they reached me...

I darted down the next turning and the next, gambling on blind panic carrying the fleeing fae in a straight line—the quickest, clearest escape.

Their cries and screams rolled over me as sweat slicked my palms, but after a few turns, they grew quieter. Eventually, I had no idea where I was, but I could hear nothing of the crowd.

I slowed and caught my breath, rubbing my chest where my heart thundered with a potent cocktail of adrenaline and fear. It made me shaky, breaths threatening to gasp in too fast.

Swallowing, I slid the dagger into my garter and pulled Bastian's orrery from my cleavage. Not exactly befitting a grand palace. I chuckled to myself, a desperate sound much too close to a sob for my tastes, and ran my thumb over the chain.

Rather than cool, its metal had been warmed by my skin. But the familiar texture of its links allowed me to breathe more easily and take in my surroundings.

Fine embroideries showed the sun rising over heroic fae with gold thread woven through hair of caramel and green, straw blond and chestnut brown. Lost in Dawn's side of the palace. Great.

I'd taken down one armoured fae who shouldn't be here, but judging by the frightened crowd, there were more. Many more.

Bastian had to know already. They must've attacked the ballroom. Was he all right?

Was the fox-haired fae involved? They were armed, but

they hadn't attacked me, despite saying they owed me nothing. It *might* be a coincidence.

If they were involved, that meant whoever this was attacking had links to Dawn Court. Sura had mentioned spies. The fox-haired fae could be one. Perhaps?

I shook the thoughts away—that was a puzzle for later.

Right now, I walked alone through the wrong side of the palace with a sword I didn't know how to use, a dagger I barely did, and a dress that threatened to spill my tits every time I did anything other than saunter.

Things were going swimmingly.

As I was about to turn a corner, a sound reached me—so fleeting I couldn't work out what it was.

I froze, breath held, ears straining.

Nothing more.

Then a voice, too quiet for me to catch the words.

More attackers. Had to be.

Stashing the orrery back in my cleavage, I searched left and right. The nearest door was locked when I tried it. I hurried to the next. Also locked.

Distrustful lot, these Dawn fae.

Lungs begging me to gasp for air, even though it would be noisy and undoubtedly heard by keen fae ears, I tried another door and another. No fucking luck.

Shit.

"Kat?"

I blinked.

"Kat?"

Wait, I knew—

Around the corner bounded a white hound, ears, eyes and paws wreathed in red flame.

"Fluffy." Followed a moment later by Rose, peering around

the corner. I sagged as Fluffy circled me, rubbing against my legs, her tail wagging.

Soon Rose, Ari, Ella, and Perry surrounded me. With brief hugs, I assured them I was all right and they reassured me of the same. That was a start.

"And is Bastian?" I glanced at Perry and Ari. "And the others?"

Their gazes dropped.

Ella pursed her lips, a smear of blood on her cheek, which I hastily wiped away for her. "We haven't seen them."

"We were separated when the attack started." Rose frowned back the way they'd come. "But I know Faolán snuck a knife in, so they're in a better position than we were." She had no weapon, but had shifted her fingers to make them long and clawed. "Looks like you're doing all right though." She nodded at the sword.

"Not that I know how to use it. But I think a former pirate might." I offered it to Perry. "Think Bastian snuck a blade in, too."

"And last time I saw them, they were together." Perry nodded as she took the sword. "Plus I think Asher and Lysander were talking."

"Fingers crossed, that means no one's alone." Rose smiled and reached for my shoulder. She hesitated.

"It's all right—I'm safe to touch."

She huffed and squeezed my shoulder. "Now we've found you, no one's alone. So, what now?"

Ari glanced back the way they'd come. "Do we go back to the ballroom?"

"There may still be fighting back there." Perry shook her head. "If the attackers get bedded in, the guards could take hours to get past their lines. We're better off steering clear."

I ran my thumb over the unfamiliar leather-wrapped hilt. "Do we know if there's fighting in Dusk's side, too?"

Ella shook her head. "We haven't got much sense out of anyone since it all broke out. The crowd went a bit..." She shuddered, and I understood.

"All the more reason to steer clear." I gave her a reassuring smile. "In that case, let's try to find a lodestone and get back to Dusk. Once we're there, we'll be safer—or with our own people, at least. And maybe there'll be word of the others."

Four pairs of eyes turned to me, and one by one, my friends nodded as though relieved to have a plan.

Action was always better.

And my plan might not be the most intricate or even the best, but with the information and resources we had, it seemed the right choice.

Perry checked out a window, confirming the sun's position, and made her best guess of which way was south—the south-ernmost part of the palace was the grand hall, and it would give us a route back to Dusk.

We set off, watchful and tense, Fluffy at my side. It was long minutes before we hit another major corridor and she whined softly, ears pricking.

Rose cocked her head and raised her hand, calling us to a halt. "There's someone ahead," she breathed.

I swallowed and nodded back the way we'd come, but as we turned, her hand flew up again. "And that way."

Cornered.

Shit.

87

BASTIAN

I should go to the queen. I should ensure her rooms were secure. I should check whether they'd also attacked our side of the palace.

Should. Should. Should.

But I *wanted* to find Kat. I *needed* to know she was safe.

"Grab weapons, if you need them." I nodded as Lysander returned to us. "I'll be back in a second."

I slipped into a side room and ensured I was out of sight. Only Kat, Faolán, my fathers, and a few lovers had knew about my ability, and I planned to keep it that way. Thank the Stars, it was a couple of weeks since one half of me had died fighting Sura's, and I'd regained my strength enough to split in two.

We nodded at each other in perfect unison. Unlike my Shadowblade, which was linked to me, these mundane weapons didn't double when I split in two. We'd need to find another weapon once we left this room.

One of us stayed in the side room, while the other returned to the ballroom and rejoined the others. As Asher and Lysander buckled on belts with scabbards, I noted where a sword remained so my other self could pick it up when he emerged.

"Hmm." Faolán scowled, turning over a long knife he took from one of the fallen attackers. "Guard issue."

Eyes narrowing, I scrutinised my sword. The same leather wrapped hilt. The same stamp on the blade. I clenched my jaw and nodded. "Like those the Ascendants took in their raids."

"And..." Asher pulled the damaged leather cuirass from one of the attackers, revealing an insignia on the shirt beneath.

A three headed hydra.

Both in the ballroom and in the side room, my blood boiled. I should've killed Sura. I'd spent the past fifteen years dealing with that guilt—I might as well feel it for something I'd actually done.

Then she wouldn't have been able to do this. A dozen wedding guests wouldn't be lying on a blood-soaked dance floor.

She had to be behind the Solstice attack too.

But there wasn't time for blame—of her *or* myself. We had work to do.

I jerked my chin towards the doors, keen to give myself a chance to creep out of the side room without two Bastians being spotted at the same time. "Come on. Let's find the others."

From a crack in the door, I could see through my own eyes as I crossed the floor.

With a deep breath, I pushed that side of my awareness away, making it as dim as my peripheral vision. Two awarenesses, we both saw and felt equally, but one of us focused here.

AND ONE OF us focused here.

I watched myself leave before removing my black jacket and replacing it with a blue one I found on the back of a chair. I pulled my hair into my face. Not a great disguise, but it would have to do—it should be enough to make anyone who caught a glimpse of me leaving assume that I wasn't Bastian but some other Dusk guest.

As soon as the guard who'd watched me leave turned away, I slipped into the ballroom and hurried out to the corridor.

With one side of me searching for Kat, the other could go after the queen.

Alone, I moved quickly along the corridors, aiming for the nearest lodestone—the shared dining room. Rarely used now, it had once been a space for feasts, back when Dusk and Dawn had been more closely allied.

I passed guards who nodded when they recognised me and came across several skirmishes. Each fight broke up once I joined in and the palace guards got the upper hand, sending Ascendants scattering.

It felt like a distraction.

A distraction to allow Sura to reach the queen? I scowled and increased my pace.

When I reached the lodestone's corridor, I sucked in a breath and ducked back around the corner. Ascendants guarded the entrance.

"More on their way, ser," one panted as though he'd run here.

"Good. We'll be able to hold this position as instructed."

He scoffed, eyeing the messenger. "You do look ridiculous. But, I suppose, needs must." He raked a hand through his hair, and several of them glanced at each other, chuckling.

What could that mean? I waited but they said nothing more, and I didn't have time to waste.

I couldn't fight all of them, especially not in such a wide corridor. If I had Kat or someone else with a bow to cover me, then perhaps.

But she might be lying dead somewhere.

She isn't. A flash of a corridor from my other side. *We haven't found her yet, but we will. Focus on our task.*

I took a deep breath and pushed away my other side's view and thoughts. We would find Kat safe and well. We *would*. She had her poison: she could look after herself.

Dagger in one hand, sword in the other, I stretched my neck side to side.

I didn't need to fight them all—I just needed to get past them.

I sent my shadows creeping ahead—down by their feet where they wouldn't notice. Then, at the door leading to the lodestone, I let them coalesce into a figure.

One cried out in wordless shock as my shadow form loomed over them. As the alarm spread through their group, they turned.

Steel flashed as they sliced at my shadows, which split apart and reformed. My shadow-self dissolved and slithered between one man's legs before rising behind him.

Round eyes stared this way and that, unsure where the shadows would appear next.

"What is it?"

"*Who* is it?"

"An unseelie demon."

While they tried to fight darkness itself, their backs to me, I sprinted down the corridor.

One huffed as my dagger drove into her back. The next one was similarly unaware until my sword bit into their side, spilling blood and guts. They managed an agonised groan as they slumped to the floor.

Their companions turned.

I ducked one blade, dodged the next. One man stood gaping between the shadow figure and me. I shouldered into him, blocking another strike with my dagger, filling the corridor with the ring of steel upon steel.

Two left between me and the door. Eight more behind.

I sent slender tendrils of shadow backwards. I couldn't spare a glance over my shoulder, but I could make the floor treacherous with dark tripwires.

The main bulk of my shadows took form behind one of the attackers ahead.

The other pointed, eyes wide. "Behind you!"

Before he could turn, shadows circled his neck.

Pain seared my shoulder blade, but, grunting, I twisted away from the worst of the strike. At least, I hoped I did.

"Reinforcements are here!"

No time to assess damage. My sword opened up the remaining attacker's guard as she raised her weapon to catch it, and I lunged, shoulder crying out as I stabbed her in the armpit.

She slumped, and I barrelled into the door as the reinforcements' arrows struck it.

The world pitched, jolting my injured shoulder as I tumbled into the lodestone. Chest heaving, I lay on the floor and found myself facing a dozen bristling spears.

88

BASTIAN

"Marwood?" Evin's eyes widened, and he pulled his spear away. "It's all right. It's the queen's Shadow. Stand down."

I nodded, catching my breath.

"No time for lying down on the job, Serpent." He narrowed his eyes at me but held out a hand.

"Well, it looked like you had it all under control." I smirked like I wasn't bothered by his tone, and truth be told, I'd grown used to it. Evin had known my father well before the Wars of Succession, and he'd taken his death personally. Perhaps even more so because he'd helped train me.

I let him help me to my feet. As I checked my shoulder—just a shallow cut that hurt like hells—the groans and sobs hit me.

Another makeshift infirmary. But where Hydra Ascendant's had contained orderly rows of beds, this one was chaos incarnate. Folk lay on the long dining table as folk tried to stem their bleeding or splint broken bones. Uninjured guests stood or sat together in tight knots, heads bowed in urgent conversation. Some just huddled together and cried, their finery soaking up tears and blood in equal measure.

"We're trying to manage them, but..." Evin shook his head. "They're a gnat's ballsack away from panic."

"That's a delightful image."

"These are delightful times. Dusk guards are holding our door from the other side. Looks like the attackers are trying to get in here." He jerked his chin towards the far end of the room.

I'd known it was likely, but the confirmation made my stomach clench. "Any word on the fighting on our side? On the queen?"

"It's not as bad there as it in Dawn. The Queensguard has secured Her Majesty's apartments."

"Good." And not just because Braea was safe in her Sleep, but because it meant both parts of me could search for Kat.

Still nothing, my other self confirmed when I shifted my focus towards him. His sword was bloody, his muscles warm. No pain, though.

"Go and get yourself bandaged up, Marwood. We don't have any full healers, but he'll be able to take care of your injury." He jerked his chin to one side.

"It's only a scratch."

His mouth went flat. "On your shoulder. Perfect for making you flinch. We taught you better than that."

My father had always said it was the small cuts that made you hesitate, and it was that hesitation that got you killed. With fighting in the palace and Evin's echo of his lessons, a sudden heaviness pulled on my chest.

I inclined my head and followed his gesture, finding myself face to face with Caelus.

We stilled, holding each other's gaze. His gleaming,

sunlight hair was stuck to his sweaty forehead, and a smear of blood covered his cheek. Not his usual perfect self.

I made a soft sound of acknowledgement and shrugged off my jacket, wincing. "You all right?"

He nodded. "You're not, though." He beckoned me closer. "Show me. And while I take care of it, you can tell me where Katherine is."

Gritting my teeth, I turned my shoulder towards him and unbuttoned my shirt. "Why would I tell you that?"

"Because I don't see her here and I'm worried that means she's—"

"She's not." She couldn't be. We'd been through too much for that to happen.

He huffed. "I forgot how much you believe your will really can change the world."

"Just get on with it." The tingle of his magic flowed into me, golden and warm. "Didn't know you were a healer."

"Not much of one. Fixing bodies isn't my primary gift." Instead of a rueful smile, he gave a meaningful smirk.

"And what is?" I edged the bounds of politeness, asking about his magic, but he'd bridged part of that gap by hinting there was something else.

"I can do all kinds of things with bodies, Bastian." He glanced at my hand and a tingling sensation crept over my skin, not wholly unpleasant. "It's a pity Kat didn't get a chance to discover that sooner. I think she might've chosen differently. But I can take care of minor injuries, and stop bleeding from the major ones while we wait for a true healer to get here... or for this to all be over." He frowned at Dawn's entrance.

Perhaps he and I weren't so different.

The warmth of his magic shifted, stinging now. It was always the way with healing—the sensation of flesh or bone knitting together was not a pleasant one. And the worse the injury, the worse the pain.

"... a run for it." A voice drifted from a nearby couple.

"We should get out of the palace." A gold-haired woman clasped her hands at her chest as a few more guards sidled over.

"Not just the palace—the fucking city." The man with her, tall and slender, shook her by the shoulders and cast his gaze over the rest of the group forming around them. "First the Horrors, now this?"

Sighing as Caelus's magic withdrew, I rolled my shoulder. No pull of sliced flesh. No hesitation. Evin and my father were right.

"Don't be idiots," I called to the group. "Stay here."

The man scowled. "Why should we, Serpent?"

"Or don't." I buttoned up my shirt. "It's all the same to me. But if you want to live, you're better off here. There are only two entrances for enemies to attack through, so it's easier for the guards to defend. If you go that way"—I pointed to Dawn's door—"well, last time I saw, there were almost a dozen guards and more arriving. And that way"—I indicated Dusk's door—"is more fighting."

Caelus folded his arms as I pulled on the blue jacket. "You're no safer over there."

The tall man's shoulders slumped.

Patting his back, the blond woman gave us a tremulous smile. "We'll stay." She pressed her lips together before dipping her chin. "Thank you for the warning."

The group around them dispersed.

"Thanks for that." Caelus huffed. "He's been stirring since he got here, and I've been trying to calm him down, but..." He gestured at the injured folk around us.

"And thanks for this." I raised my shoulder. "Here." I handed him my borrowed sword. If everything went according to plan, I would soon replace it with my Shadowblade. "Just in case."

With a tight smile, he inclined his head. "Good luck, Marwood."

As I turned, Dusk's door opened and a falcon shot through, grey wings tight to its body. Slowing, it enlarged, legs growing longer, feathers retreating. A second later, a fae landed, accepting a cloak from one of the other guards.

I sidled over as Evin ordered the panting shapechanger to give her report.

"We tried to get to the throne room, but the way was blocked." Her voice rasped. Someone pressed a drink into her hand and she took a gulp. "The king and the Kingsguard were spotted fighting their way through, but more Ascendants closed in on their position."

"Shit." Evin echoed my thoughts.

Whatever Hydra Ascendant's bigger plan, they were after the king for now—perhaps also the rest of Dawn's royal family.

Knowing the queen was safe, I could return to Dawn's side of the palace and look for Kat... or aim for the throne room and protect the king.

His two heirs meant his death wouldn't be as catastrophic as Braea's, but with Hydra Ascendant clearly made up of Dusk Court fae—every one I'd seen had midnight hair—if one of them killed Lucius, it would become more than a diplomatic incident. I wouldn't put it past Cyrus to argue he'd been assassinated by Dusk—technically true, but not the full picture.

I shared a glance with Evin before asking, "Have reinforcements been sent to His Majesty?"

The messenger's eyes widened when they landed on me. "We tried, ser." Her voice shook. "But the attackers have secured all entrances to Dawn. They're on their own."

Evin swore again. "Every lodestone's cut off? You're sure?"

"Every one, ser."

Not *every* lodestone.

89

KAT

As Fluffy bared her teeth at the sounds of attackers approaching, Rose backed off from a door and braced, ready to shoulder it open.

"Wait, no," Ella hissed. "We won't be able to lock it if you break it. Give me a second." She knelt and held out her hand. "Any hairpins, ladies?"

Ari pulled half a dozen out of her hair and dropped them into Ella's palm.

Ella blinked at the pile. "I only needed two, but... thanks?" She set to work, feeling her way with the lock.

Fists clenching and unclenching, Rose glanced between the two corridors we were cornered between. "Hurry up," she muttered.

In contrast, Perry stood still, sword raised, breaths even like she was utterly calm and completely ready. This was the Perry who'd served in my sister's crew. Seeing her at court in pretty gowns, I'd almost forgotten she'd seen more battles than the rest of us combined.

The approaching voices grew louder, as did my pulse. If I used my haze, it would kill my friends. I had the control to call poison to different parts of my body, but I hadn't managed to manipulate the haze once it escaped. I could run at the attackers, perhaps, but that would still leave the other set, and my—

"There." Ella threw open the door and we rushed inside.

As Rose eased it shut, we found ourselves in a small parlour decorated in buttery yellow the colour of dawn clouds. Ella bent to the door again, working on getting it locked, while Rose leant against it.

"Are they out there?" I whispered.

Rose cocked her head. "In the corridor," she mouthed.

Everyone suddenly breathed very quietly. Even Fluffy crouched in silence, baring her teeth at the door as if daring anyone to try to get through.

The click of the lock turning into place was deafening.

Ella winced, and I swallowed but managed to give her a reassuring smile. They were always going to find us in here—a shapechanger could follow our scent or any fae concentrating would be able to pick up some sound we made.

Ari plonked herself on the elegant settee, rummaging around in her pocket. "Get over here—each of you in turn."

The door leapt on its hinges.

My heart leapt to my throat.

"Quickly," Ari clipped out, and when I turned, I found her holding up a threaded needle. "I'll add enchantments to our clothes. It's too late to hide ourselves, and I don't have time for anything complicated, but I can make us harder to hit."

The attackers thudded into the door again.

I flinched, grabbing my necklace and rubbing my thumb over the smooth potion bottle.

Focus. They're breaking in whether you like it or not. This is unsafe whether you like it or not. You need a plan.

I'd planned out vegetable planting to keep us alive. I'd planned the best routes on nights when balls would bring out the Wicked Lady's prey nice and late.

I couldn't fight, but this? This I could do.

"Perry, help Rose." She was second strongest out of us. "Ella, let Ari work on your dress."

I blinked when they obeyed. No question, just action.

Perry and Rose grunted when another assault hit the door.

I tried the windows, but they only opened a crack, and the ground was several storeys below. Not an option.

"Right." I turned, finding Ari stitching away in the hems of Ella's gown. "They're going to get through that door soon—it isn't made to survive an attack. But we can control how and when. Ari, can you make Fluffy bark, please?"

She frowned at her sewing, muttering magic into her stitches. "Uh, yes... Speak. Fluffy, speak!"

The hound barked and under the cover of that noise, I circled to my friends, whispering instructions in their ears.

"We're going to get in there," someone shouted through the door, "and then we're going to string up your little lapdog."

Stars above, were they in for a surprise.

Ari only had time to stitch into three of our outfits before the door started to splinter. Rose shrugged, gritting her teeth. "I'll be fine." Ari's gown already had protection in it. I fingered the hem where she'd stitched the tiny mountains in the seam allowance. Ella and Perry's dresses carried similar designs.

My heart pounded as I took my position to one side of the door. It thudded again, and I held my breath, counting in my head. Their strikes had taken on a steady rhythm now the door had begun to break.

This had to happen at the exact moment.

Ella already had the door unlocked, and Rose and Perry stood against it—the only things holding it shut. Ari and Ella kept back, one holding a poker from the fire, the other a heavy candlestick, Fluffy guarding them.

One second more.

"Now."

Perry leapt back, and Rose turned the handle, pulling the door open as fur sprouted from her body.

Three men in grey armour fell through, as the door they tried to shoulder open *wasn't there*.

I dived for the nearest bit of skin I could find, drawing magic from the palace's stone. Warm flesh, then a gagging gasp and twitching body.

Steel flashed as Perry lunged, piercing the throat of the second man, while Rose, somewhere between woman and wolf, leapt over the bodies.

A scream shattered the air, then a spray of blood coated the corridor's carpet.

Perry darted out to help Rose, and I reached for the third man's exposed throat—his gloves narrowed down my targets.

But with a grunt, the bastard twisted away.

And instead of grabbing him, I found only thin air. The floor slammed onto my hands and knees, jolting through every bone. Blood filled my mouth as I bit my tongue.

Steel filled my narrowing vision, coming this way, hard, fast, followed by his sneering face. "You poisonous little whore."

I tried to scramble away, but bodies made the floor treacherous and I fell.

Fuck.

Fuck.

Rolling onto my back, I kicked and made contact with something hard, but his charge didn't falter.

Then there was a flash of gold and a shriek, and his mouth dropped open.

The sword slid from his grip.

He fell.

And over him, bent Ella, smashing her candlestick into the back of his head. "Whore is she? *A whore?*"

He twitched and went still as she turned his skull into a bloody pulp.

Dimly, I became aware of the quiet surrounding Ella and her relentless assault—the fight was over.

Ari watched, eyes wide, jaw slack. Perry leant on the doorframe, eyebrows almost at her hairline. Even as a beast-woman, Rose looked shocked, panting as she stared.

"Ella?" Magic contained, I caught her wrist. "You got him."

Aside from the breaths heaving through her, she went still and blinked at the gory candlestick. Slowly, she nodded and swallowed, her creamy skin and caramel hair spattered in blood. "I did, didn't I?"

"You did." I patted her arm and pulled the makeshift weapon from her grip.

Her eyes narrowed and she gave me a firm nod. "*Good.* If we were all poisonous, they'd watch their fucking tongues."

I huffed a laugh. "They would."

Rose bared her teeth. "They really fucking would."

The fading rage left Ella trembling and pale, so I urged her onto the settee and wiped the blood off her as best I could.

Perry and Rose checked the attackers. They looked pretty dead. It might've been useful for questioning, but our survival was more important.

Eight in total—three in the parlour and five more in the corridor. Considering only two of us were trained fighters, we hadn't done too badly.

"Nope. Dead as a doornail." Perry winced as she checked on the last of the fallen fae, and I caught her clutching her thigh. Blood seeped between her fingers. Hers, not her enemy's.

"Shit, Perry." I rushed in at the same time Rose did, and we caught her between us.

"I'm fine." She waved us off, and we let go just long enough to prove that she couldn't stand on her own.

"You're not. The question is *how* not fine are you?" My heart clenched as Rose pulled up Perry's skirts to get a closer look, shifting back to fully human.

"It's a clean cut, but deep." Her eyebrows drew together. "No major blood vessels, but you're not going anywhere—that will only make you bleed more. Ari, can you embroider some makeshift bandages to help staunch it?"

Ari—mild-mannered, shy Ari—knelt by the man Ella had killed, pulling off his leather cuirass and peering at the bloody clothes beneath.

"Uh, Ari? I didn't realise you were into dead bodies, but... we could use your help."

Face flushed, Ari turned to me. "You're going to want to see this."

90

BASTIAN

As soon as I set foot in Dusk, I exhaled.

Granted, archers meant I had to huddle behind upturned tables acting as makeshift barricades, but this was still the right side of the palace—as close to home as any place got. And the reports said there was less fighting on this side, which would allow me to move freely and get back to Dawn to find the king, while my other half searched for Kat.

Dusk guards acknowledged me as we waited for the barrage of enemy arrows to abate from when I'd opened the door.

"You holding up all right?" I asked the violet-haired woman sharing the table with me, as thud after thud struck the surface.

"Just another day at work." She flashed a grin. "We're expecting reinforcements soon. That's what the messenger just said, anyway." She nodded towards the lodestone.

"Good. Just hold on until then and you'll flank them nicely.

Plus, this is your home, not theirs. They're in unknown territory."

As she nodded, the arrows fell silent—no sense in wasting all their ammunition.

I waited to the count of ten, then sent out my shadows as I had at Dawn's door.

This time, just as I charged, there was an answering cry from the opposite side of the gathered attackers. Our reinforcements.

"On me," I shouted to the guards at the door and smirked as the attackers turned.

With their attention split, they fell under our wave.

I slashed and stabbed with my dagger and slid beneath a swinging blade, scooping up a sword from a fallen attacker.

Ascendants had stolen our blades—it seemed only right to take them right back.

Righteous rage burned through me, keeping me going as strike after strike aimed and missed or landed on my weapons.

My shadows tripped and jerked enemies off balance— imprecise actions that didn't require much strength were easy while I focused on parrying and attacking.

By the time the last attacker fell, the breaths sawed through me. But I had no time for exhaustion.

I caught up with the highest ranking guard, a broad-shouldered woman with a scar on her cheek. "What's our status?"

"Her Majesty's safe. There have been a few attacks from the lodestones, but they appear to be testing our defences rather than actually trying to break through."

As I thought. Sura wanted to secure Dawn and assassinate King Lucius. Question was whether they'd come for the queen next or wait until another day. If I had my way, they wouldn't succeed with the king. And if she was here...

Well, no bargain bound me not to hurt her, did it?

"Good work." I inclined my head to the guard. "We've got injured in the dining room and attackers just inside Dawn's door. Get everyone evacuated."

Before she could answer, I set off again. Still too winded for a sprint, I jogged through the familiar corridors until I reached my offices.

The wards on the entrance were intact. Either Sura's people hadn't reached here yet or they weren't after my secrets. With her interest in the Crown of Ashes, I suspected the former.

I locked the doors behind me, grabbed my Shadowblade and Kat's weapons from the desk, strapped them on, and strode into the secret passage.

Since I didn't need to show her through the darkness, I could run to the courtyard.

A trowel and a trug sat on the bench, together with Kat's gardening gloves.

The simple domesticity of it smacked into my chest. She had to be safe. *Had to be.* She couldn't be in here gardening one day and then gone the next.

I wouldn't allow it.

Squaring my shoulders, I listened at the other door. Aside from my spy, no one from Dawn should know about this place but just in case, I edged it open.

Another dark passageway led away. No sign of life.

Good.

I crept ahead, ears straining to catch the sound of anyone ahead. Occasionally the shouts and metallic clang of battle reached through the walls. Other times, as I passed the peep-holes, I caught the whispered conversations of folk in hiding.

Nothing of use.

At last I reached a door that led into a small office and eased out. No one here. When I closed the door behind me, it looked like part of a bookcase.

I snuck through corridors, getting my bearings. Although I'd spent little time in Dawn's side of the palace, I'd pieced together plans based on my informant's sketches and partial designs from various refurbishment projects over the years. It was amazing what you could find in architect's sketches. Soon, I understood where I was and how to reach the throne room.

A couple of times, I came across Hydra Ascent's troops, usually in pairs. Seemed they were more focused on holding the lodestones and keeping the corridors clear so they could move freely.

That made my job easier.

Hide around the corner, send my shadows to knock a vase over, then while they were distracted, sneak out and cut the first one's throat. That left just the second, and in a one on one fight, with shadows on my side, they stood no chance.

Arrogant, perhaps, but I'd spent years of my childhood training with a former general until I was ready to drop. Some days I had dropped. Even then, he'd shown little mercy.

That had only come when he'd cut me from chin to gut.

He'd let me land a blow after that.

Let me. Like he'd had a taste of hurting me and realised he didn't want more.

I swallowed and squashed the memory. This might be another attempted coup by Sura, but it wasn't the time to dwell on my father's death.

Years separated us now. Just like guilt and hate separated me from my *athair*.

I scowled down at the second guard's body and the slash across his chest. My Shadowblade had cut clean through his leather armour, consuming the little power remaining from when it had been a living thing. The cut edges crumbled like ash, revealing the hydra embroidered on his shirt.

I blinked at it, something off now I took a moment to look more closely.

Gold glinted amongst the red stitches and blood, the same as the patch from the prisoner captured at the Solstice.

With a flick of my dagger, I cut away the embroidery. Thread made of gold and red entwined, whereas all the insignias and banners I'd seen at Sura's palace depicted red hydras with gold eyes.

If she was telling the truth about the Solstice attack...

I scraped my thumbnail over the smooth, even stitches. Good quality, like Ari had said.

Ascendants had stolen swords on their raids... but there was potentially a "missing" order of guard weapons, too.

Was all this *meant* to look like Hydra Ascendant when actually someone else was behind it?

I didn't have enough pieces of the puzzle to tell.

Whoever it was, they were still here, and I still needed to reach the king.

No matter who killed him—the result would be the same. They'd blame Dusk.

91
KAT

Ari held the insignia up. "It's the same as the one you brought me after the Solstice attack. Are these the same people?"

I blinked at the glittering hydra. Based on the information most people had, that seemed a safe assumption. There weren't likely to be two separate threats, after all.

But most people didn't have all the information, Ari included.

Sura had told me she hadn't attacked the city, and I believed her, even if Bastian couldn't bring himself to. Someone else was taking advantage of her rebel group to cover up their own identity and motives.

And if that wasn't her, it meant this wasn't either. "Thank you," I muttered as Ari pressed the patch into my hand.

She went to help Ella tearing up curtains for Perry's bandages. Meanwhile, Fluffy stood guard as Rose examined the door, planning out loud how we could barricade ourselves in, since Perry couldn't be moved.

I checked the other bodies and cut out their insignias. If this attack wasn't by Hydra Ascendant, who could it be?

Queen Braea? My mind skipped there a little too quickly, perhaps because of what Sura had told me about her sister's death. How might this benefit her? Was I just being uncharitable?

Who else?

King Lucius? A way to frighten people into giving him more power? A way to persecute Dusk folk, like he had with those executions?

But Perry had said the archers in the ballroom were aiming at him. Though, they had missed. And fae were good shots... It could be a ploy to make him look like a victim.

Prince Cyrus had shielded his escape—could he be behind it? Making him look like a hero? That was the kind of self-aggrandising thing I could see him doing.

But, no, Lucius seemed more likely. He was behind unCavendish. He wanted the Crown of Ashes. This could all be a distraction to help him get it or information on its where-abouts. Or maybe even assassinate the queen.

My head buzzed with the possibilities, aching behind my eyes.

"I think the king's behind this." When Ella shot me a wide-eyed look, I added, "Maybe. But if he is, then Bastian's in danger."

Ari used her emergency sewing kit to stitch into the makeshift bandages, whispering her magic. Not missing a beat in her chant, she tilted her head in question.

Ella passed her another strip of torn fabric. "I think Ari's wondering what makes you think that."

"If Bastian believes it is Hydra Ascendant, he'll ensure the queen and king are safe. Since the attack seems to have broken out here, the king seems the more likely target, so Bastian will go to him." Though most likely he'd split in two so he could check on both, but I couldn't reveal his secret. "And if the king is behind this..." I swallowed and clenched my hands as a chill slithered down my spine. "Well, he had unCavendish try to take Bastian off the board once before. What better way to get rid of the queen's greatest asset than in a 'rebel attack?'"

"Doesn't that mean Asher's in danger?" Perry pushed herself up from lying on the settee. "And the others too, I mean."

Ari pressed her back down, but shot me a fearful glance. Those "others" included her husband.

"Perhaps. But I think they'll be looking for you rather than the king." Bastian would choose his duty, but he wouldn't stop the others coming after the people they cared for.

Ella arched an eyebrow. "What's your plan? I assume you have one."

"Find the nearest lodestone and get to Dusk's side of the palace. Either he'll be at the queen's apartments or someone there will know where he is."

Or I'd find one side of him guarding the queen—at least then if the king managed to kill his other half, it wouldn't matter. Explaining his apparently death without revealing his secret might be a challenge, but changelings made an excellent excuse.

"Good plan." Rose planted her hands on her hips. "Let's help barricade Perry in, then get going."

"I'll stay." Ari looked up from wrapping bandages around Perry's leg, while Perry squeezed Ella's hand. "I'm no fighter— I'll only slow you down. I'll be safe here."

"Me too." Ella winced as Perry let out a pained grunt. "I think I've had my fill of fighting for one day." She gave a tight little smile, gaze flicking over to the blood stained carpet. We'd piled the bodies in the corner.

That settled it. We moved Perry into the next room along the hall, since the door to the yellow parlour was damaged. Ella would lock it after us, then she and Ari only needed to slide some furniture against it and wait out the rest of the attack with Fluffy to protect them.

Not ideal, but we had no ideal options.

As I readied to leave, Rose held out her palm. We fell silent as the clink of metal passed outside. She lifted her nose and sniffed as the sound faded.

"That was a large group." Her brow creased. "Ten at least —maybe a dozen."

Shit.

Too many for me and Rose to take if we encountered them while we were out there.

But if I hazed...

My heart tolled, heavy in my chest. "Why don't you bring over that cabinet so Ari and Ella don't have to move it far? That'll give that group a minute to get clear away before we head out."

"Good thinking."

Rose headed over to the heavy item of furniture, and the instant her back was turned, I slipped out.

"Wait," she called as I shut the door. "Kat?"

I slid my stolen dagger into the lock and hammered my fist on the hilt. The tip pinged off the dagger, so I shoved it further in and hammered again. The lock clunked. Jammed or broken.

Someone rattled the handle as Rose called, "Kat? What the hells are you doing?"

"Katherine Ferrers." Ella's voice snaked up from the mangled keyhole. "You let us out *this instant*."

"I'm sorry." I glanced along the corridor, but there was no sign of the troops returning. "If I'm on my own, I can unleash my poison without fear of hurting you."

"Fuck," Rose huffed, followed by a scraping sound like she slid down the door. "Fuck!"

"I'm sorry. But I need to do this."

I pressed my hand to the door, as a frustrated sob filtered through.

"You'd better stay safe," Ella hissed, voice cracking.

"Don't I always?"

"No! You fucking don't."

"Well... maybe this time will be different."

With that, I squared my shoulders and started down the corridor. By Perry's reckoning, we were on the western side of the palace, roughly towards the middle. The throne room had to be east from here, so I aimed for a turning that would take me that way.

This time *was* different.

I was different.

I had thought my identity erased the moment I'd taken that poison and given up on survival.

But I knew who I was.

I knew *exactly* who I was.

I'd killed Horrors. I'd faced one of the Ladies of the Lake, a princess thought dead, and a changeling who'd fooled and abused me.

I'd killed a husband who'd wronged me more times than I could remember.

I'd endured Elthea's treatments, even when they crossed the line into torture.

I'd learned how to turn power that had been thrust upon me to *my* ends. I'd turned poison into a gift.

And today I'd used that poison to protect my friends.

My gift might be death. But I used death.

I was not the powerless woman who'd woken in the Hall of Healing.

I was Katherine Fucking Ferrers, and I was going to go and save the man I loved.

92

BASTIAN

F aolán's nostrils flared as he lifted his head.

"A scent?" I murmured as we passed through the wide corridor.

"It's them. They're all together." He shot ahead, and we followed. Each turning he took without hesitation made my heart beat faster.

We have them, I told my other self. A few times, I'd felt the slight dizziness as our awareness came together and he checked in to see whether we'd found Kat. *I'll show you when we find her. You focus on the king.*

I felt his grumble but also that it was edged with relief.

She would be fine. She had to be. And if she or any of the others were injured, we had Asher.

The trail led us to a bloodstained carpet and a busted door. My stomach dropped.

Faolán scented the air. "Not theirs." Blade ready, he crept into the room.

More blood and something pulpy mashed into the carpet. Lysander wrinkled his nose.

Faolán shook his head. "Still not..." He stilled, then hurried over to the bloody settee. "Hmm."

That *hmm* made my veins freeze. "Faolán?"

Exhaling, he strode out to the hallway, while Lysander and Asher gave me questioning looks. I shrugged and followed him. They didn't understand his different *hmm*s, and I wasn't going to dangle bad news in front of them until we knew more.

I found him sniffing at the next door. Its keyhole had been mangled beyond recognition.

Frowning, I touched the damaged metal. "Someone's jammed the lock."

"Rose," he shouted, pounding on the door.

"Faolán?"

A ragged exhale came from him as his head bowed, and for a second I saw how close he'd been to breaking through all this. Then he straightened. "Stand back."

A second later, he smashed the door hung off its hinges, and we rushed in.

Faolán grabbed Rose, burying his face in her strawberry blond hair.

Lysander pulled Ariadne into his arms, swinging her around. "Thank the gods you're all right."

Asher rushed to Perry, who sat on an armchair with her leg up, bloody bandages around her thigh. They kissed long and deep, all attempts at hiding their relationship forgotten.

Ella stood in the middle of it all, wearing an awkward smile.

Laughing with relief, I turned, looking for *her*. As I turned full circle, my heart grew tighter, heavier. "Where's Kat?"

She locked us in and headed for the throne room. She went after you.

Ella's words to my other self reached through my mind as I crept through a glazed garden room full of plants and cosy seating. The sound of low voices drifted from a stone corridor ahead.

Gods damn it. If she'd just stayed there we'd be with her now. I'd know she was safe.

Instead, I had all the more reason to reach the throne room to find both Kat *and* the king.

Could this all be Lucius's doing? He was behind unCavendish, so maybe it wasn't such a huge leap.

If it was, he could cross over into Dusk and beg for sanctuary from this attack. Then he and his people could use that as an opportunity to gain access to the queen.

Muscles thrumming with tension, I entered the corridor lined with busts on plinths and peered around the corner. A dozen fake Ascendants.

Shit. I was a few minutes from the throne room, and this was the only way there without looping back on myself to take a long detour.

On the plus side, this narrow corridor meant only a couple of them would be able to reach me at once, and my shadows...

I adjusted the grip on my Shadowblade and sent wisps of shadow ahead. In their incorporeal state, they could take up more space than the concentrated form, which could touch objects and people. Although these formless shadows couldn't trip anyone up or choke the life from them, I could feel where they were.

When they reached the attackers, I let them spread, and gave a vicious grin as troops swatted at the rising darkness.

"What's—?"

"I can't see. Am I blind?"

Sword and dagger ready, I closed in.

"No, I can't eith—"

I cut his throat.

Although I couldn't see, I could feel the shape of the corridor, the plinths, and every place my shadows weren't. I aimed for those fae-shaped pockets of emptiness, a slash here, a stab there.

"The shadows are attacking!"

A grunt. A gurgle. Two more dropped at my feet.

One swung wildly. I barely dropped in time, the blade whistling past my head.

"Ow! Fuck! Was that—?"

Spinning on one knee, I drove my dagger into her thigh. Blood sprayed through my shadows as I rose.

"Fuck. Fuck! My leg." As she fell, bleeding out, her panicked voice stirred whimpers from the others and more flailed into the darkness.

A wild slash caught my arm. I bit back my pain.

"Backs to the walls," a firm voice cut through the rising fear as I crouched and cut the injured woman's throat. "Anyone in the centre is an enemy."

"You'd better hope they can't hear you." A chuckle edged my voice as I straightened. "Oh, wait, I *can*."

But before I could reach the wall, someone swiped for me. On instinct I darted to one side, but my foot caught on the dead woman, and I stumbled below another slash.

White flashed over my vision and pain burst through my skull as I hit a plinth.

Darkness. Vague, spinning shapes. Shadows subsiding.

I blinked.

Incoming, something in me whispered.

I rolled to one side as sparks rained from the plinth, right where my shoulder had been an instant earlier.

"I see him! It's the Serpent!"

Shadows. Get them up. My other side hissed in my head.

My pulse surged, the world suddenly clear. In my daze, I'd let my shadows sink and lost my only advantage.

A strike jolted up my arm as I caught it on my sword. More flew at me from two attackers, and it was all I could do to dodge and parry, retreating. Sweat snaked down my spine.

If they forced me into the garden room, they'd be able to surround me, and I'd be fucked. My other side would survive, but I needed to get to the throne room before Kat. If she went there alone...

Teeth gritted, I made a neat riposte, slapping my enemy's blade away before diving in with a lunge. The resistance of flesh told me I'd hit, but the other pressed in, stealing my attention as their sword slid along my dagger.

As the first one fell, another took his place.

Parry. Dodge. Swipe. Duck. On and on and on without a moment to focus on bringing my shadows back.

Pain lit up across my stomach, blinding for a second, followed by the warm spill of blood.

Fuck. Bad.

My lungs heaved and sweat bathed my skin as I fought on, strength sapping. Really bad. I thought I caught a sweet-sharp scent, perfume perhaps or something from the plants in the garden room. Didn't they say senses grew heightened when you were about to die?

I didn't have time to die.

I blocked and hacked and slashed, muscles burning, head swimming.

Then the Ascendant I was fighting frowned. One glanced down. I took the opening from her momentary distraction and ran her through.

Her companion's eyes widened. "What's...?" He sucked in a strangled gasp and fell.

One by one, they all fell, disappearing in a purple mist that mingled with my shadows.

"Thought you could use a little help."

That voice.

I spun on my heel.

My goddess. Mere feet away. Saving *me*.

My weapons clanged to the floor as I closed that distance and pulled her into my arms. "Katherine." Warm and soft and sweetly poisonous. I breathed her in—narcissus and the freshness of spring, plus the sweet-sharp tang of her magic. "It *was* you. Are you all right?"

"I was about to ask you the same thing. Sorry, I had to stay out of sight. I can't focus on anything else when I haze." She squeezed me, gasping when I couldn't hold in the grunt of pain. "You're bleeding."

"I had noticed." I tried to smile, but the last of my strength faded, and she had to help lower me to the floor.

"Bastian!" She pulled back my shirt, eyes going wide. "What do I do? How do I—?"

"You can't." I caught her fingers and gave a reassuring squeeze. "Take your bow. My other side will be here soon."

Her chin trembled. "But you're..."

"Not really." My fingers tingled and the edges of my vision dimmed.

Eyes gleaming, she shook her head. "It feels real. My

heart... it hurts just the same." She dragged in a long breath and smoothed the hair from my face.

Her skin was so warm, I could've soaked it up for the rest of time. "You don't need to do that... to comfort me."

"What part of *it feels real* don't you understand?" Tears tracked through the blood on her cheeks as she planted a kiss to my lips.

"It isn't real. It isn't..."

93

BASTIAN

I found her sitting with my dead self's head in her lap. Her cheeks were soaked, but she had her bow drawn, an arrow trained on me. "Bastian." She sagged.

"Not the best day to turn on me, love." I flashed a smile as she lowered her bow. "But if I'm going to die at anyone's hands, I'd pick yours. Though, for the record, I'd prefer your thighs."

She made a sound that wasn't quite a laugh or a sob as I stroked her hair and helped her up. "You may have mentioned that before." Her gaze lingered on the body. "It doesn't feel right to leave him."

"Look away." I hefted a marble bust from its plinth.

"What are you—?"

I smashed my other self's head in. "No one can know. This will stop them recognising me." I stood, shielding her from the sight. "I'll have to make sure I get hold of the body during the clean-up, though. Here..." I pulled moth-hilted dagger from his hip and pressed it into her hand. "Had a feeling you might

668

need your weapons. The Wicked Lady doesn't hide away, even during an attempted coup."

She strapped the dagger in place. "It's just Katherine." She nodded, a crease between her eyebrows. "The Wicked Lady. The ember. It's all me. It always was. Only... before I couldn't bring all those parts together. I think now, I'm nearly there."

My chest filled. Stars above. She really was a goddess, standing before me in blood and gold, ready to march into a fight without saying she wasn't brave, only desperate. Without needing to wear a mask or a false name in order to break someone else's rules.

I lifted her chin and kissed her. I wanted to make it long—I wanted to kiss her to within an inch of her life. But time wasn't on our side.

She blinked up at me. "What was that for?"

"To show you."

"Show me what?"

"How much I'm constantly awed by you."

She looked away, but I caught her smile first. "Flatterer. We still need to get to the king, though." She pulled a wad of fabric from her cleavage. "Look. It isn't Sura. These all have that mixed thread. One being different, I could understand."

I blinked at the collection of bloodied insignias. "But all of them? It would be a mighty coincidence."

"Exactly." She gave me a beseeching look.

"You're right. I don't think Sura is behind this. Could be Lucius or someone trying to assassinate him."

"If he caught you unawares, he could use it as a chance to kill you and blame Hydra Ascendant."

I retrieved my Shadowblade, smiling at her concern for me. "Well, thanks to you, I'm not unawares. He was last seen heading to the throne room. Come on."

She frowned at her hands, clenching and unclenching them as the purple stains faded. Tension thrummed through her shoulders as her gaze flicked to the bodies. No shadows or purple haze hid them anymore.

I held her shoulders. "This is what your power is for—for you to use. Not to be denied. Not to keep you isolated, but for you to exert your will upon the world at last." I squeezed until she looked me in the eye. "You are the one in control."

She lifted her chin, back straight, jaw set, something regal in her determination. "I am."

94

KAT

I didn't know whether to be relieved or horrified by how easy it had been to kill so many attackers with my magic. But tired from hazing, I didn't have the energy to pick that tangle apart.

As we approached the corridor leading to the throne room, the sounds of battle reached us: metal and cries, the groans of the dying.

"Kingsguard and Cyrus's personal guard," Bastian muttered as he peered around the corner. "No sign of Cyrus or Lucius—they must already be inside."

If these false Ascendants worked for the king, why were they fighting his guard and Prince Cyrus's? Commitment to the deception? Had they turned on him?

Focus. What did this mean in practical terms?

"No haze, then." That would make it harder to keep him safe, which was all the more important now his other self was dead. I unhooked my bow from the strap crossing my body.

He touched my back, palm warm on my bare skin, tethering me here rather than to the possibilities of what might be about to happen to him in that fight. "I'll go in, you stay here. Duck around the corner if they fire back."

Just as he went to turn away, I grabbed his hand. "I need you not to die, Bastian. Do you understand? When I saw you..."

He gripped my fingers. "I know exactly how you felt." His gaze flicked to my chest where there should've been a scar. "I'm not dying today and neither are you." With a nod, he stepped out into the corridor.

As he charged, blades ready, shadows racing ahead, I fired.

My arrow cut through grey leather armour, and when my first kill fell, the teal-haired woman who'd been fighting him looked up. Her eyes widened, first on Bastian, then me. With a fierce smile, she inclined her head and turned to her next foe.

As warmth filled me, I already had another arrow nocked, but it took painful seconds to pick out my target. Bodies jostled left and right, in constant movement, so where one instant I had a clear shot at the enemy's throat, the next, one of Cyrus's guards stood in the way.

Bastian drove into the enemy as silent and dark as his shadows. He cut one down, then another—surprise on his side. And that opened up a shot for me.

I took it, and another fake Ascendant fell.

In the chaos, with shadows ghosting left and right and dozens of bodies packed into the open space before the throne room doors, I could half watch Bastian.

His fighting wasn't like a dance—dances had too many pretty flourishes.

Here, every movement served a purpose.

He dropped to one knee, dodging a spear point, then pivoted on that knee inside the wielder's guard. As he rose, he drove his dagger up beneath their ribs. The whole thing flowed with such precision, it seemed like just one movement.

But as the spear wielder fell, another fake Ascendant took their place.

So many. I fired and fired, taking out my fair share, but there was always another. Thankfully, his shadows kept skittering across the floor, bringing arrows back to me.

Steel flashing, Bastian blocked another strike as I nocked my next arrow. Behind him an Ascendant grabbed the fallen spear and readied it while another approached with daggers.

Fuck.

I pulled the bowstring taut, heart in my throat with the knowledge that if both parts of him were killed, he would die —*really die.*

Not while I still drew breath.

Jaw ratcheting tight, I squeezed my bow, which tingled in my grip.

Exhale. Release.

I was already nocking my next arrow before this one burst through the spear-woman's hand. Her agonised cry rose over the battle clamour as the spear clattered to the floor.

I got the dagger wielder in the eye, and as the spear-woman turned and saw me, I readied my next arrow and aimed for her heart.

Shot after shot. It was like I couldn't miss.

The air around me hummed, and I had to check poison wasn't seeping from my pores.

No poison. Just my will to keep Bastian alive.

Breathless and buzzing, I fired and fired.

And then there were no more targets.

My shoulders slumped as the full burn of all that work hit

my muscles. Despite Bastian's shadows, only one arrow remained in my quiver.

I hurried over and clutched his arm to reassure myself he was alive.

He stroked my back like he needed that same reassurance. "Impressive shooting."

"*Very* impressive." The head of the Kingsguard, a fae with deep bronze hair and skin, surveyed me. "Do you need a job, by any chance? I'm sure the Serpent won't mind you switching courts, and my numbers are suddenly diminished." They pursed their lips at the bodies littering the floor.

"What happened?"

Their lips pressed together even tighter, and for a second I thought they wouldn't reply. "Ascendants managed to separate us. His Majesty made it inside with the other half of the Kingsguard, followed by Prince Cyrus. Someone else slipped in before they closed the door—someone with red hair. I didn't recognise them."

"Fae or human?" I asked, a thin edge of dread cutting into me.

"Fae."

Cut deepening, I gave a brief description of the fox-haired fae.

"That's the one. Do you know them?"

I exchanged a look with Bastian. "Not exactly."

One of the Kingsguard approached. "We're ready, ser."

"Right. Thanks for the help. We're going to—"

"We'll go." Bastian circled them, guiding me to the throne room's double doors.

"You and..." They glanced up the corridor. "Just you two?"

I gave a reassuring smile. "His shadows can kill big groups more easily if they're not worried about friendly fire."

Bastian nodded, hand slipping to the small of my back. "We'll come back for you once it's clear."

"Very well." Their eyes narrowed. "Wouldn't want to lose more of my people—especially not to friendly fire. We'll await your signal."

We approached the huge doors. No sound came from the other side, but lodestones were like that—no sight or sound escaped them.

"Ready?"

Shoulders squared, magic humming on my skin, contained for now, I nodded.

95

KAT

I entered with bow drawn, poison ready to spread across the room, and found a scene of carnage. Near the royal doors behind the dais came a flicker of movement, but when I lifted my head, I found only more of the same.

Blood and bodies.

Kingsguard with their beautiful armour. The prince's guards with their cerulean blue cloaks. Fake Ascendants in grey leather. Servants in nothing but cloth—no armour, no weapons. The nearest lay in crimson pools, their throats slit.

Eighty, maybe a hundred people in total, all still and silent.

My eyes burned at the sheer scale of the massacre. Because that's what this was—the servants. They'd stood no chance. "What happened here?"

Bastian's brow set low, shadowing his eyes. "We need to check them. If anyone's alive, they can tell us."

I glanced back. "Should we call the others in?"

Jaw twitching as he surveyed the room, he shook his head.

"Not until we know we don't need to use your magic. False Ascendants could be hiding among the dead."

I swallowed and nodded, then started picking my way through the bodies. The chairs from the ceremony had been cleared ready for more folk to file in for their chance to see the king and queen together for the eclipse. That couldn't be far off now.

As for the people—their glassy stares told me enough.

It looked like the fighting had been thickest by the main door that led to Dusk—the one most people entered through, whereas the queen and her officials used the one behind the dais. Bodies piled upon bodies, almost blocking the door. Blood completely hid the marble floor, making it slick and treacherous.

"Anything?" I called to Bastian as he worked on the other side of the room.

"No."

The word echoed off the high ceiling, making the hairs rise on the back of my neck.

Hours ago, I'd walked through here worried about nothing more than the fire in Bastian's eyes as he saw me in a pretty dress.

And now...

I locked eyes with a man I recognised. He'd held the door open for me as I'd arrived and given me an encouraging smile before whispering, "You look beautiful, Lady of Dusk. A star in your court."

Now, gold green hair sat in his eyes and the fact he didn't blink it away twisted in my gut.

"Are you all right?"

I bent and closed the kind man's eyes. "Yes."

"You don't have to—"

677

"I do." Whoever was behind this, these people had been murdered as part of the game of courts, and they deserved to be witnessed.

Tears blurred my vision by the time we reached the wide dais. Bright blond hair glimmered on the next body. A dagger's hilt gleamed bronze, still buried in his stomach.

Eyes shut, face slack, he almost looked peaceful, and it took me a moment to recognise Prince Cyrus.

"Shit," I whispered, bending over.

"Kat," Bastian called from behind the dais. "The king. He's alive."

Stomach lurching, I ran over.

Bastian had him on his back, cradling his head. Alive. Just.

Blood oozed from his throat like someone had done a bad job of cutting it. His lashes fluttered, but his eyes were glassy— almost as glazed as those of the bodies I'd checked.

A wheezing, bubbling sound came from his lips as they moved.

"What is it?" I squeezed his hand, hoping that might bring him back to himself enough to make him speak louder.

The wheezes rose, and I bent my ear to his lips.

"Fox."

At least, that was what it sounded like. Did that mean...? The fox-haired fae had done this.

Then, with a horrible groan, the king fell still.

His empty eyes stared at the door leading to Dusk.

96

BASTIAN

S hit.

"Cyrus is dead too," Kat whispered, staring at Lucius's body.

Shit.

We were fucked.

The fact Dawn had a second heir was a small, *small* comfort. Sepher had to survive today—he was too arrogant to die. Was he behind this?

I shook away the racing thoughts and lowered the king to the floor. "Did you find Sura?"

Kat slid Lucius's eyes closed. "No. Not a sign of her or the fox-haired fae. I'm sure Sura didn't do this."

"Maybe you're—"

A groan broke the quiet.

We followed the sound and found Cyrus on the dais, clutching his stomach. Despite the dagger buried in it, he was still very much alive.

"I thought..." Kat stared, a tightness in her face that made my bones ache. "Sorry, I was about to check him when you called, and—"

"It's all right." I touched her cheek in reassurance before crouching by Cyrus, who was well enough to scowl at us. I tore off a piece of cloak from one of his guards and bundled it up before applying pressure around the wound. I wasn't removing it without a healer ready to stop the bleeding—I'd seen a woman die after a recruit made that mistake in a practice yard accident. "Not looking too good, Your Highness."

"I'm sure the blood's quite ruined my outfit." The sardonic twist of his lip faded as his eyes widened. "My father. Where is he?" He let out a grunt as he tried to sit up, and Kat caught him as he fell back.

"Don't move." She pushed the hair off his face.

Everything in me went tight, and I put more pressure on the wound than strictly necessary. I tried not to smile as he cried out.

She meant nothing by the gesture, but Cyrus didn't deserve her comfort. Not when he was such a prize prick.

I dragged in a deep breath. "He's dead." I couldn't bring myself to soften it, not with his head in Kat's lap.

"No." He grunted again but managed to sit with Kat's support. "It can't... He was right behind me when... when..." He touched the dagger's hilt. His eyelids fluttered as his gaze shifted to the space behind the dais where his father's body lay.

The great Day King cramped in that little space behind the dais, reaching for Dusk's door. No matter how I felt about him, something about that was obscene.

Tears gleamed in Cyrus's eyes. "Father. My... my father." His hand shook as he covered his mouth. "Is Krae here?" He scanned the space nearby. "They stabbed me. They were working with these people." He gestured at the body of a nearby Ascendant. "Helped them all get in. I trusted them and..." He shook his head.

I shared a look with Kat.

Was this what the attackers wanted? Lucius dead? Did they pretend to form an alliance, then betray him? *Were* they working with Sepher? Cyrus was lucky to be alive—if we hadn't arrived when we did, he wouldn't have lasted much longer.

I nodded to Kat. "Take over while I get help."

Blade drawn, muscles coiled, I slipped through Dusk's door.

I could've collapsed with relief when I found ranks of Dusk guards readying themselves to enter.

"Bastian!" Faolán pushed through, followed by Asher.

"I'm fine. And the throne room's clear." I grabbed Asher's arm as soon as he was in reach. "Just who I need. Explanations after."

I dragged them both into the throne room and Faolán bounded over to Kat. "You're alive!" It was just as well I had Asher to heal Cyrus, because Faolán plucked her away from staunching the bleeding and swept her into a hug.

I set Asher to healing Cyrus. There was nothing he could do for the king.

The guards filed through, and I sent one to fetch the rest of the Kingsguard on Dawn's side, while Kat disentangled herself from Faolán.

"Report," I ordered.

"It's over on our side. Minimal casualties. The last of them have fled, but we're doing a sweep of the palace to be sure." Faolán shrugged. "Whatever it is they wanted, they got it."

"The king is dead."

His eyes widened. "Oh." Slowly, he nodded and stroked his chin—beard back in full force. "Hmm. I see."

More reports filtered through from both sides of the palace—the fighting was over in Dawn as well. Their casualties were far from minimal, though.

News of the king's death rippled through the room as more guards arrived. They offered Cyrus condolences, and I caught a snatch of conversation where one referred to him as a hero for trying to shield his father.

"Are you all right?" Kat murmured as I massaged my temples.

"I've been worse." I gave her a tired smile. "But no rest for the wicked. It's almost time for the eclipse. And I'm going to have one hell of a report for Her Majesty when she wakes."

97

BASTIAN

A couple of hours later, I stood back in that throne room, Asher at my side. With the bodies cleared and the floor cleaned, it almost looked normal.

Except Prince—no, *King* Cyrus occupied the Sun Throne. Beside him, the silver Moon Throne sat empty.

On his other side stood Sepher and Zita—proof that Dawn's royal family had survived the attack. Queen Meredine sat near the edge of the dais, face ashen, expression blank. Soon, Braea would join us, proving she was also alive and well. That should be enough to quash the rumours that both royal families were dead.

The last thing we needed was anyone getting ideas about forming factions and leaping into a power vacuum.

For reassurance, I sought out Kat in the crowd. Still in her gold gown, with the blood hastily washed off her skin, she gave me a quick nod.

The gathered courtiers hadn't changed from their wedding finery, but more Dusk folk swelled their number. They hadn't been invited to the wedding, but they needed to be here for this show of unity.

The crowd shifted uneasily, and guards from both courts stood at alert. I glanced at the huge, arching windows that stood behind the dais. Their glass was stained golden yellow for Dawn, and the sun sparkled through it, but soon the moon would cut across its disc and bring darkness and the Night Queen.

The past couple of hours had been at once tense and yet somehow a chance to let out my exhaustion from the fighting and all the fear I'd felt while searching for Kat.

I'd spent it checking the secret passages, since the guards couldn't sweep hallways they knew nothing about. I took Kat with me, telling myself it was because her poison would be useful if I came across a group of Ascendants holed up.

And it would.

But also, I was a weak fool and couldn't stand to be parted from her after all the day's uncertainty.

We found no sign of anyone, Krae included. And the guards hadn't taken any Ascendants alive to question. Some had been spotted fleeing through the city, but their trails disappeared into the river and not even Fluffy had been able to pick them up again.

After the search, we had the joy of meeting with the Convocation, Cyrus, and the newly married couple, who'd got through the attack with nothing more than cuts and bruises.

I narrowed my eyes at that but kept my suspicions to myself. There was no love lost between Sepher and his father. I still found it surprising that Lucius had tolerated his return to the city, tail and all. Two living heirs and the promise of grand-children must've been enough to tickle his desire to get one over on Dusk.

There'd been no time or excuse to go to Dawn's side and retrieve my other self's body. I would need to find out where they were being taken and find a way to extract him before he was identified as *me*.

Messy. Very messy.

I didn't even know whether Dusk or Dawn were to blame. Not for sure. The attackers looked like they were from Dusk, but I struggled to believe it.

I met Kat's gaze in the crowd. She put a lot of stock in these insignias, but standing here now, my doubts crept in. It could be they were newer and shinier, ready to celebrate Sura's ascension to a unified throne when everything went to plan.

For all we knew, she'd offered King Lucius an alliance, promising to get Braea out of the way, and had turned on him. Was Krae one of the spies she'd mentioned? It wouldn't be the first time folk from the two courts had worked together. I had my own spy in Dawn, after all.

More questions than answers.

Head aching, I gathered my scattered thoughts.

The long and short of the Convocation meeting was this: Dawn blamed Dusk. Dusk thought it was a Dawn trick.

And Cyrus was "such a hero" for getting stabbed.

Between me, Cyrus, and Sepher, we managed to broker an uneasy peace between the Convocation members. Not two people I ever thought I'd be allied with, but whatever it took. As long as we weren't immediately trying to kill each other, that gave us time to investigate.

My head throbbed harder at the idea.

Brynan appeared at my side. "Her Majesty is here. She'll be awake any minute."

I glanced at the moon passing across the sky—once it touched the sun, her Sleep would be over for the seven minutes or so it took to complete the eclipse. "Thank you." I patted his shoulder. "Go and join Gael. I know it's been a difficult day."

With a grateful smile, he slipped into the crowd and hugged Gael close.

I spared a smile for Kat before passing through Dusk's door. In a small preparation room opposite, I found Braea posed in an opulent chair. Her attendants had dressed her and carried her here in a litter so not a precious moment of the eclipse would be wasted in the corridors.

As though she knew something was wrong, even in Sleep, her eyebrows were knotted together.

Over the past hour, I'd thought of a hundred ways to explain everything that had happened, but when she stirred and blinked at the blood making my black clothes even blacker, I settled for straightforward.

"People wearing Hydra Ascendant insignias attacked. Lucius is dead and over a hundred more with him—guards and civilians. Cyrus sits on the Sun Throne, and we need to show everyone that you're still alive too. We're at peace, but it's an uneasy one."

Her eyebrows rose slowly and she sat in silence for long seconds.

"The moon has barely touched the sun, but we don't have long."

She swallowed and slowly nodded. "Very well. Have the new king come to me. Just a minute will do, but I'm sure we can make this uneasy peace a better one."

Wasting no time, I hurried to Cyrus. I'd expected him to toss his head and huff at being ordered around now he was king, but he agreed at once. An ashen pallor clung to his tanned skin—perhaps he was too exhausted from blood loss to throw his weight around.

"Wait for me in the throne room." With a tight smile, Braea gestured to the door. "This is work for a king and queen alone."

I bit my tongue against reminding her to be quick before clicking the door shut behind me.

When I stepped out onto the dais, the crowd muttered, glancing at the moon halfway across the sun. We were quarter of the way through the eclipse.

Kat tilted her head at me in silent question.

With a shrug, I mouthed, "I'll explain later."

We had perhaps five minutes left by the time Braea and Cyrus emerged.

The room gave a collective exhale.

The Night Queen lived, and we had a Day King. Stability was assured as long as we could get to the bottom of the attack.

"Good people of Tenebris," Braea said, spreading her hands as she took her place before the Moon Throne.

"And good people of Luminis," Cyrus added with a similar gesture.

"I gather today has been a tragic one for both Dusk and Dawn, and I extend my condolences and sorrows at the death of His Majesty, King Lucius. A thousand years ago we allied to push the usurpers from these very thrones, and I knew him well."

Cyrus smiled at her. "Dawn, in turn, extends its gratitude for your support at this difficult time."

It seemed they'd put this meeting to use and agreed a unified approach. My shoulders eased. As soon as this was over, I'd collapse in bed and sleep for a million years.

"Many of these attackers may have been from Dusk's families originally, but rest assured that we reject their actions whole-heartedly—they are no reflection of our high esteem for Dawn."

The Dusk Court fae in the crowd nodded, but some from Dawn still frowned and threw suspicious glances at them.

"As a marker of good will on both sides," Cyrus picked up, "Her Majesty and I have agreed to exchange guests."

I bit back a snort, though exhaustion gnawed on my self control and I twitched at the announcement. "Guests" meant "hostages." An unusual solution, but not unprecedented. If that was what was required to keep the peace, then so be it.

"From Dawn you shall have..." Cyrus listed half a dozen names. Mostly low-ranking courtiers—folk who wouldn't be missed—but among them was one of his close friends. Perhaps he intended to use him as a spy. I'd have Orpha tail him.

One by one, they approached Braea and kissed the back of her hand to show their fealty upon entering her court.

The totality of the eclipse hit at that moment, sending us into darkness.

"And from Dusk," Braea said, "Katherine Ferrers..."

I didn't hear the rest of the names.

My heart burst. That was the only explanation for the jolt in my chest.

Katherine... *My* Katherine. Sent to Dawn as a hostage.

No. *No.*

Every part of me ached, sluggish and slow like I'd been plunged into freezing water. Asher gripped my shoulder, waking me enough to turn as the crowd parted to let Kat through.

Pale, she stared back at me, clasping her hands. Even from here, I could see her knuckles were white.

I threw Braea a glance, hoping I'd misheard or that she'd said the wrong name by accident.

She raised her chin, profile regal and strong.

She meant this. She'd chosen Kat or let Cyrus choose her. She'd agreed to this.

This.

I'd killed for her. Worked to the bone for her. I'd taken my father's life to save hers.

And in return, she did this.

98

KAT

"And from Dusk, Katherine Ferrers."

The world pitched. The queen's voice distorted in my ears turning the other names into nonsense.

My body felt like a puppet held on a long, long string. From miles away, I told the puppet to fold its hands and mind its magic and control its expression like a good little girl, while the crowd parted.

Up the path leading to the dais, Bastian stared at me. To someone else, he might've looked calm and collected, but not to me.

His face was... empty.

The queen hadn't told him she was going to do this.

That made the little puppet's little puppet heart hammer —a silly little drum in her chest.

It wasn't part of some plan they'd concocted together to... I don't know... send me to Dawn to spy on them, then marry me in secret to Bastian before revealing our marriage, so they were forced to let me go home to him.

690

Home.

My eyes burned.

Home.

He was home.

"Approach." A commanding voice broke through my fractured thoughts, and King Cyrus smiled at me, holding out his hand.

Someone prodded me in the back. One foot, weight forward, then the other. It was like I'd never walked before—I had to tell my body to do every part of the motion.

"Kat, don't." Ella grabbed my arm, but someone hissed at her to stop and Perry pulled her hands away.

Near the front, I spotted a hateful head of red hair, and Uncle Rufus gave me a wide, wide smile.

But I glided past him, strings pulling me onto the dais.

I spared Bastian only the briefest glance. If I looked at him a moment longer, I would throw myself into his arms and refuse to go.

Pathetic, but all I wanted.

Jaw clenched, I dug my fingernails into my palm.

I needed to do this. I could help assure the peace. And there would be some way to get back. Eventually.

One step up the dais. Two.

The queen's mouth curled.

She'd done this deliberately. What better way to get rid of me than sending me to Dawn? Hadn't Bastian always warned me about setting foot in that side of the palace? Hadn't he feared what his enemies might do once they knew I was important to him? Now everyone knew, and the queen had placed me in their hands.

The world throbbed in time with the pounding in my head. I yanked in my magic as I realised it wasn't my pulse but that of the power around me. The last thing we needed today was for another king to get killed.

I clung to that thought—beautifully practical—as I approached the new Day King.

Eyes soft on me, his smile was almost kind, like he understood my shock and horror. His hand moved an inch higher and I blinked at it dumbly for a second before taking it.

His skin was warm and smooth, and a faint masculine scent wafted up my nose as I bent closer, closer.

Some instinct shrieked at me, but I didn't understand the words. Alarm. Danger. That much I knew. Hadn't I always understood those things?

The moon's darkness slid off the sun as we entered the last phase of the eclipse. Light hit the king's cuff, twinkling on the intricate stitches of Dawn Court's rising sun.

As I brushed my lips over his knuckles, my breath caught.

In the embroidered insignia glittered thread made of scarlet entwined with gold.

The king's smile widened, showing his sharp teeth. "Welcome to Dawn, Katherine. It's going to be a pleasure to have you."

*Kat and Bastian's story continues in **A Promise of Lies**.*
Pre-order and send your proof of purchase to claresagerauto@ gmail.com to get the opening chapters ahead of release and be in with a chance of winning a hardback copy.

Read on for a note from the author...

AUTHOR NOTE

Last time I started my author note with "Welcome to Tenebris-Luminis!" I suppose this time I'll say: *Welcome to Dawn Court*!

Yeeeeah. Sorry about that. But I swear I have a plan. (For starters, I can now tell you why this was always conceived of as a trilogy—three courts, three books, see?)

Dropping Kat in Dawn aside, I hope you enjoyed reading this second part of Kat and Bastian's story.

It has been a real journey for me as well as them.

I was so nervous releasing *A Kiss of Iron*. I put so much into it—of myself, of aspects of the world that troubled me, of dark things that have happened to others... and I was afraid others wouldn't like it.

It isn't for everyone, of course—no story is.

But wow, was that book for a lot of you. The reception has been overwhelming in the best possible way. So I really need to start this author note by thanking you for joining me on this journey and for all the love you've given Kat and Bastian.

Many of you have messaged or emailed me to say how

694

much you resonated with Kat, and I've said this before, but I'll say it again...

I'm both touched and saddened.

Saddened because I wish no one could relate to her trauma and to its aftermath. In an ideal world (which I truly wish this was), her experience would be pure fiction.

Unfortunately too many can relate to that.

But since we live in this very much *not* ideal world where some people do some awful things to others, I'm touched that many people could see themselves in Kat.

She's not a warrior heroine like Xena. She's not kicking arse and taking names.

But she is strong.

And I wrote her for all the real women and NB folk out there who aren't like *those* "strong female characters" but who have gone through SHIT and yet are still able to go on and be kind to others and loyal to their friends and *fight* without any blade.

That is its own kind of strength and I am in awe and love with every single one of you.

Many of you have also told me how much you've loved seeing a heroine like Kat—a woman with thighs for daaays!

And I hope you enjoyed getting to see Bastian giving those thighs their appropriate worshipping after the... well... frankly, edging of *A Kiss of Iron* (Sorryyy!!!). (Someone may have called me the Queen of Edging. As titles go, I'll take it!)

I hope you can all forgive me now.

And, as a reminder, I always promise my main couples an HEA... eventually. So although I've left Kat and Bastian split between two courts, you know they'll find their way back to each other.

I'm so excited for the last instalment of their story, and I can't wait to share it with you in 2024.

In the meantime, please consider leaving a review of A Touch of Poison (and KOI, if you haven't yet) on Amazon and/or Goodreads. Reviews are so important for helping to spread the word. They help other readers to find books they'll love, which gives you new people to chat with about them! <3

I always love hearing from you—feel free to drop me a line (clare@claresager.com) about your favourite scenes or tag me in social media (I'm on Instagram the most @claresager). I do try to reply to all messages, but I apologise if it takes a while or if I somehow miss you.

Another way to keep in touch is by joining my newsletter (https://claresager.com/freebook/) where I share sneak peeks, behind the scenes news, and giveaways, as well as some free stories that are only available to subscribers. It's where you'll find out launch info about *A Promise of Lies*.

Finally, if you really, really want to be the absolute first to find out all the info, see new artwork, get your hands on NSFW art, and read deleted scenes and bonuses, you may want to support me on Ream. It's like Patreon, but it's made specifically for authors and readers and is spice friendly.

Thank you again for joining me, Kat, and Bastian on this adventure—I am thrilled to have you along and look forward to venturing forth with you on our sabrecats! <3

All the very best,

Clare, September 2023

   x

PS – You can find bonuses, like playlists and a downloadable map, over at: https://claresager.com/koibonuses/

ACKNOWLEDGEMENTS

Huge thanks to everyone who has helped with this book. There are lots of you, because although writing a book can be solitary at times, it isn't something we do alone.

Carissa, Lasairiona, and Tracie—my wonderful author wives. Thank you so, so much for listening, advising, and helping kick me up the arse when it's needed.

Alyssa—my right hand woman, assistant, and friend, who has had to listen to WAY too much of my thinking out loud stream of consciousness decision making on Asana, and who picks up all the things I forget. My gods, how did I manage without you?!

Alyssa (again) and Andrew, Andra, Clare, Karolina, Laura, Mariëlle, Marie-Lyne, and Noah—the beta reading/editorial dream team! Thank you so much for your time and attention, plus the real-time reactions—you know I live for them!

Bibi—my agent and all round delightful person. Thank you for your love of KOI and for getting it into the hands of more readers in more languages.

ACKNOWLEDGEMENTS

My author friends—you make walking this path much easier and far, far less lonely.

The awesome Nate Medeiros—thank you for the beautiful artwork for the naked hardback cover. ADORE those sneks!

Maria Spada—for the stunning cover for this book. I'm SO excited to share the final cover for the series soon!

BookishAveril and Wictoria Nordgård—for the beautiful character art included in the print version of this book. Your artwork is inspiring and it's been an absolute privilege to work with you! <3

My friends and family—for your love and support always... even when you can't pin me down to actually meet because I'm hanging out here in the Sabreverse with imaginary people.

Deedee and Dash—my own little sabrecats and feline overlords for keeping me company... even when I don't want it. (Seriously, lying over my arms while I'm trying to write isn't helpful!)

All you readers—for so many squeeing posts and OMG WHAT DID I JUST READ messages, emails, fan art, reviews, and for being all round awesome people. Thank you so much for allowing me to keep doing this. I cannot overstate how much of a difference you make.

I'm totally honoured and humbled to have Ream supporters. The fact you like what I do this much blows me away. Love and hugs to you all, and special thanks to Bastian's SILFs: Tracy, Brenna, and Laura. <3 <3 <3

I always save the best for last, so, finally, thank you to Russ. My number one person worldwide (universe wide... *multiverse* wide, in fact). The one who wrestles me from the keyboard and reminds me what it is to live. THANK YOU. <3

ALSO BY CLARE SAGER –
SET IN THE SABREVERSE

SHADOWS OF THE TENEBRIS COURT

Gut-wrenching romance full of deceit, desire, and dark secrets.

Book 1 – *A Kiss of Iron – Now in Audio*

Book 2 – *A Touch of Poison*

Book 3 – *A Promise of Lies*

BOUND BY A FAE BARGAIN

Steamy fantasy romances featuring unwitting humans who make bargains with clever fae. Each book features a different couple, though the characters are linked.

Stolen Threadwitch Bride (Ariadne & Lysander)

These Gentle Wolves (Rose & Faolán)

MORTAL ENEMIES TO MONSTER LOVERS

Five fantasy romances each by different authors, set in their own worlds. These enemies to lovers stories are united in their promise to deliver "I came to kill you" angst, scorching romances with inhuman, morally grey heroes, and happily ever afters.

Slaying the Shifter Prince, by Clare Sager (Featuring Zita and Sepher)

Discover the full series here:

www.mortalenemiestomonsterlovers.com

BENEATH BLACK SAILS

An enemies-to-lovers tale of piracy, magic, and betrayal. Featuring Kat's sister Vice. Complete series.

Book 0 – *Across Dark Seas* – *Free Book*

Book 1 – *Beneath Black Sails*

Book 2 – *Against Dark Tides*

Book 3 – *Under Black Skies*

Book 4 – *Through Dark Storms*